MW01036505

The Resistance Painter

A Novel

Kath Jonathan

PUBLISHED BY SIMON & SCHUSTER
New York Amsterdam/Antwerp London Toronto Sydney New Delhi

A Division of Simon & Schuster, LLC
166 King Street East, Suite 300
Toronto, Ontario M5A 1J3

This book is a work of fiction. Any references to historical events, real people, or real places are used fictitiously. Other names, characters, places, and events are products of the author's imagination, and any resemblance to actual events or places or persons, living or dead, is entirely coincidental.

This Simon & Schuster Canada edition March 2025

SIMON & SCHUSTER CANADA and colophon are trademarks of Simon & Schuster, LLC

For information about special discounts for bulk purchases, please contact Simon & Schuster Special Sales at 1-800-268-3216 or CustomerService@simonandschuster.ca.

Interior design by Wendy Blum

Manufactured in the United States of America

1 3 5 7 9 10 8 6 4 2

Library and Archives Canada Cataloguing in Publication

Title: The resistance painter / Kath Jonathan.
Names: Jonathan, Kath, author.
Description: Simon & Schuster Canada edition.
Identifiers: Canadiana (print) 20240408683 | Canadiana (ebook) 20240408810 | ISBN 9781668013618 (softcover) | ISBN 9781668013625 (EPUB)
Subjects: LCGFT: Novels.
Classification: LCC PS8619.O5225 R47 2025 | DDC C813/.6—dc23

ISBN 978-1-6680-1361-8
ISBN 978-1-6680-1362-5 (ebook)

To my parents
Thelma and Stanley

And for Janina Zaborowska
Ala Giżycki
Irma Zaleski
and
Bianka Kraszewski

. . . there is not a single thing on earth that oblivion does not erase nor memory change . . . no one knows into what images he himself will be transmuted by the future.

Jorge Luis Borges, *Dreamtigers*

Warsaw under German Occupation 1939–1945

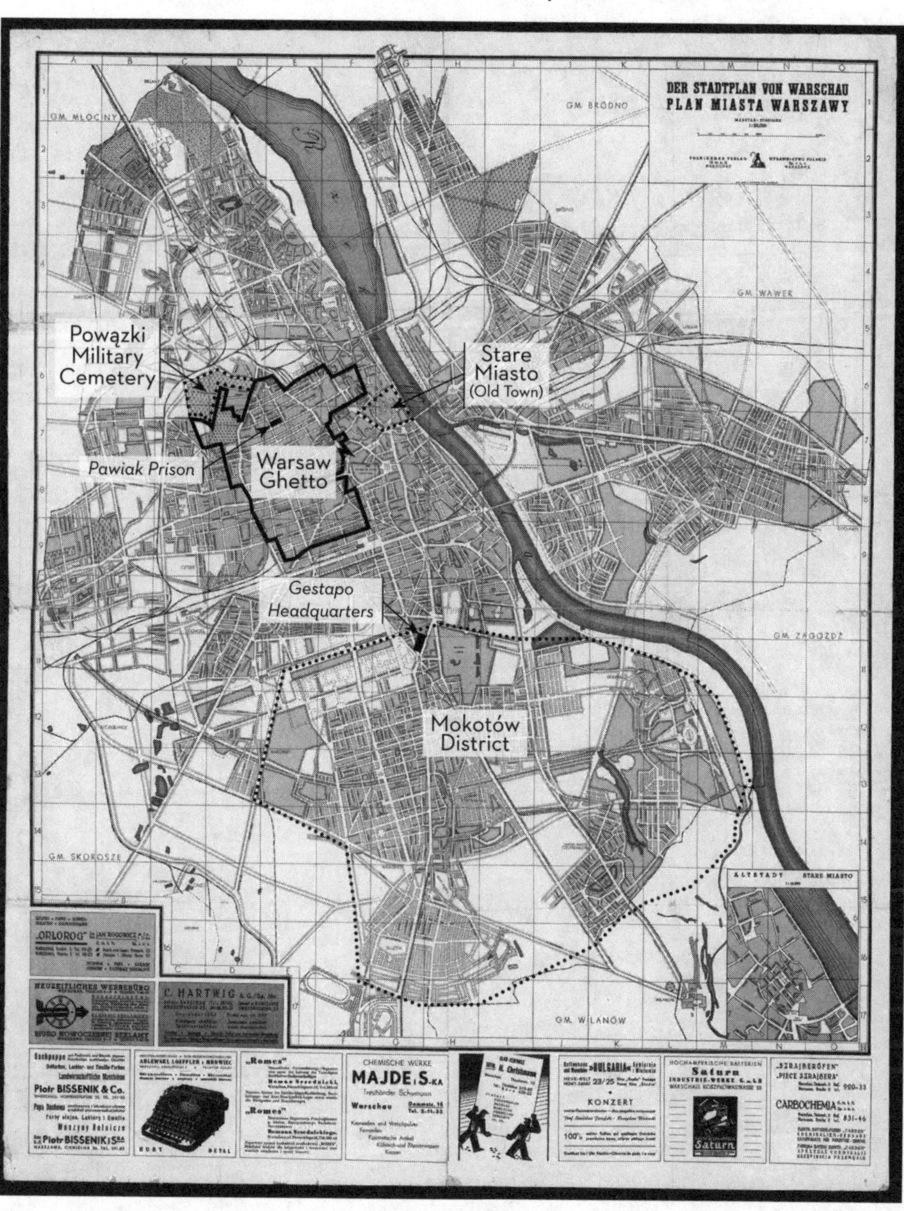

Part One

One

Warsaw, September 1, 1939

Night—yet there's movement in the flat across from ours. With my nose pressed between the blackout curtains, I follow the erratic pattern of a torch being carried about—in another flat, a candle blinking as though someone might be signaling. I push on the window to see if it's real, and it doesn't give. Far off to the west of Warsaw, the sky erupts in bursts of light.

My toes feel a path to my bedside, and I fumble for Papa's pocket watch crowning the hill of sketchbooks beside my bed. I peer into its flat white face: five minutes before three.

Hurry, Irena! My mind crashes through drowsiness, yanks open a door to bark at me—*They're here!*

I wheel to face my sister, still breathing softly in her bed—"Szarlota!"—shaking her until she rolls onto her back. "The Germans are here, Lotka."

Bolting upright, she crosses herself before scrambling out of bed.

I open our bedroom door to find Mama in the doorway, eyes wide with terror, her hand clutching her neck as though her head might fall off. My heart softens, but she brushes past me sobbing, her arms reaching for Lotka's ready embrace.

"There's no time for crying." Hardening my voice doesn't stop my own tears welling. *Not now.* "Everybody, get dressed. Gather your bags and be quick."

Lotka ushers Mama back to her bedroom, cooing comfort while our mother whimpers. Ever since my father's death, our mother's suffered from nerves. Months riddled with rumors of war made things worse for her, and while I struggle with impatience, my sister's only been kind.

I tug the gray skirt of my Girl Guide uniform over my nightdress, throw on the blouse, not bothering with the lower buttons. I think of our Guide leader, Marysia, who's been reminding us that Poland's Scouts and Guides have a long military heritage and hinting at what's ahead.

"Young women," she said, in a tone much softer than her usual commands, "if the Germans attack, we Guides will have the serious work of helping Polish citizens. Some of you may be called on to do even more for our country."

Fired by her words, I memorized her speech, sometimes reciting it to myself as I lay in bed. Now I take a deep breath and reach for Papa's woolen scarf, which I've put aside for this occasion. If I'm going to face death, I want to be in uniform, with something of Papa's close to me for courage.

Morning shadows lay themselves across our beds as light filters through the window. There's little point swearing at the sun, rising beautifully even as the Luftwaffe wings toward us. But what a horrible thing it is to be waiting for the devil to arrive. I grab a sketchbook from the pile and wedge it into my rucksack. Not for the first time, I wish I were a man. Men are welcome soldiers in Poland's fighting army—flying planes and firing artillery guns, while sixteen-year-old girls like me must scurry into cellars without even a rifle.

With my rucksack poking my back, I march into the kitchen, sidestepping the sand pails and the water pails Marysia instructed us to have ready. At the table, my sister's fastening the straps on her first-aid bag, her jaw set in concentration.

"Got everything?"

She nods, adding a bundle to an already bulging pillowcase. "I made everyone's favorite sandwiches."

That means chopped egg with wild chives for me, plum jam for Mama, cheese for herself, and extras for our old neighbor, Mr. Godlewski. I can't help beaming at my sister.

Glancing down the empty hallway, my smile turns to impatience. "Where's Mama?"

"In the bathroom."

The air-raid siren begins its rising, ebbing wail. Lotka clutches my arm, and we rush to the bathroom, where I rap on the door. "The bombing will start any second, Madame Iwanowska. There's a bucket in the cellar for your convenience. Please come out now!"

"Don't shout at her, Irena." Lotka switches to a caressing tone. "Mama, Mr. Godlewski will be waiting for us. He'll be so worried."

When my mother comes out, her hat's angled, lipstick perfect, her one remaining silk scarf tucked into her Sunday blouse.

Where does she think we're going? But there's no time for petty frustrations. My hand flies to my hammering heart, my whole body in thrall to the sound of planes drilling close by.

Instinctively, we all dive for the tight space under the kitchen table.

Mama prays in a breathless voice: "Our Father, who art in heaven."

Lotka slips an arm round her shoulders: "Thy kingdom come, thy will be done."

A scream like a child in pain drowns out their prayer. It's followed by a piercing whine. I screw my eyes shut, dig my nails into my palms. For the space of two heartbeats, our lives hang in deathly silence before the ground shudders from the impact of a bomb.

Mother Mary, protect us.

Explosions from shattering glass echo in my Mokotów neighborhood. Another bomb, and a moment later, another just north of us.

To dampen my panic, I crowd my mind with questions: How many German planes are blocking out the sky? If a bomb falls on us, will our coal cellars become tombs? Does it ever make sense to shelter under a kitchen table?

The Sobieski Residences, where we live, are four peeling buildings reluctantly facing a treed courtyard, each with two flats enfolding combinations of mother, father, sisters, brothers, grandparents. While my mind rattles with useless questions, my ears pick up the splattering debris on the roof, the jangling kitchen light swinging slowly to a stop as the roar above us recedes.

Mama's praying, coming in gasps now, suddenly mobilizes me. I struggle to a crouch, my rucksack scraping the underside of the table. "They're heading west. Come on."

Lotka and I grab Mama's arms and pull her up. We scan each other for blood, then scan the kitchen: no shards of glass, no splintered, smoking ceiling, no need for the pails just yet. We run our mother down the hallway, hat askew, lipstick smudged, out the front door, down the stairs to the courtyard.

Everyone's heading for the cellars—women carrying crying babies, older children hopping foot to foot, pointing excitedly at the sky—the women's sharp voices mustering them in, and all the while the chorus of the air-raid siren underscoring our efforts. My gaze travels to the orange flames dancing on the rooftops a few streets away. Like the picture of hell in my old Catholic catechism, black smoke billows across the sky, erasing the steeple of St. Anthony's.

Inside the main gate to our building, two women are struggling to carry a man toward their cellar door. Blood darkens his trousers. His leg must be broken, yet he's trying to lift his body to make himself lighter. I could help. Lotka with her nursing skills could stop the bleeding, but the planes are returning, and as we hurry to save ourselves, I feel helpless, hopeless. Seeing our neighbors' terrified faces, I wonder if there's anything more absurd than the idea that we can prepare for war. All that running, climbing, bandaging my friend Leah and I have been doing in Guide meetings, smothering fires with pillows, making a meal out of weeds. Have she and her family made it safely into their cellar?

"Good morning, Mr. Godlewski." Lotka waves at the old man hurrying toward us, cradling a bottle of what I hope is water. Like the children, his eyes shine with excitement.

"Dzień dobry, Pani."

Mama perks up as he gives her a courtly bow and I worry that a series of formal Polish greetings will prevent us from getting to the cellar before the Luftwaffe returns. He winks at me, and, charging ahead, says, "Come on, Irena. What are you waiting for, a special invitation from Hitler?"

I can't help but smile as we follow him down the short staircase.

For weeks we've known that the German chancellor would send his army to attack us. Stefan Starzyński, the president of our city, has been on the radio constantly—warning Warsaw's citizens to prepare for a likely invasion. Mr. Godlewski himself, a former journalist and veteran of the Great War, has half-jokingly offered me lessons in strangling a man, with a bonus lesson of how to fire a revolver. Mama and Lotka wouldn't hear of it. I'd settle for sitting in his kitchen while he listens to his shortwave radio, but I haven't been invited. The BBC has been keeping him abreast of the Führer's route to war against us, and, in exchange for a cup of tea and a slice of Mama's apple cake, we get the latest news from abroad.

I shut the wooden door, sliding the recently installed bolt across, and we plunge into dank darkness, coal dust wafting into our noses and eyes. I sneeze; Mama sneezes; Lotka has a coughing fit. While our neighbor navigates his way past the coal chute with the dwindling pile of coal, the three of us huddle close for comfort, letting our eyes slowly adjust to this familiar yet foreign space.

After the frantic faces in the courtyard, I'm suddenly afraid. Not of dying, exactly. I'm afraid we'll be in this cellar for days, that Warsaw will crumble and I'll never see Leah or any of my dearest places again. For a brief moment after waking, I imagined I was Major Irena Iwanowska, caught up in a daring mission. Not anymore. I find my torch in my pocket, and when my sister's eyes meet mine, we bolster each other with little shrugs: *What can we do?*

"Here we are," I say brightly, following Mr. Godlewski to the small space where we've arranged two dining room chairs, a cot, and a thick living room rug from his flat, which he had Lotka and me drag down here after insisting they were useless to him upstairs.

"Look, Mama," Lotka smiles, "how sweet and cozy our little hideout is."

Our mother converts her disagreement into energy, taking off her hat, straightening the cot, the chairs, before producing a blanket from a pillowcase, shaking it out, and laying it across the dusty rug. I cover a sigh. Most often these days, it's disgruntlement, even anger, that brings her to life.

Our plucky mood shatters when the planes return screeching overhead, the strange whine of the bomb as it falls, then that pregnant stillness followed by a massive blast. *Heaven help us!* Our building shudders. Heads together, Mama and Lotka clutch each other. Mr. Godlewski grasps the back of a chair, while I pull myself into a crouch, arms hugging my body. From the floor above us, sand filters onto our heads. I touch the grit on my scalp, roll it between my fingers.

"That was close." Mr. Godlewski pulls up a chair, caking Mama's blanket with dirt from his boots. When he removes a tin cup from his jacket pocket and pours a drink from his bottle, he doesn't offer us any, confirming my suspicions that the water is, in fact, vodka.

"Are they gone?" Lotka sounds like a frightened child.

"For now," Mr. Godlewski says, his cup halfway to his mouth. "But they'll be back."

My sister's grimace becomes a tight smile when she sees Mama's panicked face. "Are you all right, Mama?"

"How can you ask me that?" Our mother quivers with indignation.

Good point.

Despite her trembling, my sister manages to light a candle she's inserted in an empty bottle. The glow spreads a warm circle around our group. Mama's eyes narrow when she sees my yellow nightgown protruding from my Girl Guide skirt, and she turns despairingly to Lotka. I make a show of tossing Papa's scarf smartly over my shoulder, but the ache in my heart mocks any claim to indifference.

Lotka and I settle awkwardly on the bouncy cot. We don't need to be quiet with all that ruckus going on in the sky above us, but I can't help whispering. "I hope Hitler isn't marching through Piłsudski Square right now."

"Do you think they bombed the hospitals?" Lotka sinks her head into her hands.

"No, they wouldn't. They probably bombed Okęcie Airport." I pat her knee. "Don't worry, Poland's never giving in to these filthy dragons."

"They call it a *blitzkrieg*," Mr. Godlewski says, and Lotka, who's been studying German, nods.

"A lightning war."

He smiles grimly. "First, they start a big lie to convince us that the invasion's all our own fault, since apparently, we attacked a few German radio stations." He snorts. "Of course, the German people expect their army to retaliate, so what could be more natural than invading our peaceful country?" Raising his arm, he dives sharply for my right leg. "First come the bombers destroying our barracks, railroads, and airfields; then they have a little fun, paralyzing ordinary citizens by bombing us in our beds. You'll see, they'll even bomb our churches and schools."

Mama makes the sign of the cross.

He wags his finger. "If you really want to avoid a headache, Agata, don't even think about their pact with the Russians. All this will make it nice and easy for the tanks and troops to march in and conquer Poland for the German Reich." He pauses for another sip.

How I hate hearing this matter-of-fact news. "We'll fight back," I say calmly, as though he hasn't thought of that. "We'll shoot down their planes with our own planes."

"Dear Irena, our old P7s are no match for their Stukas. They have the newest weapons and thousands more soldiers than we have."

His certainty galls me. How can he be so willing to give up? "That doesn't matter," I say, trying not to shout, but catching the dismay on Mama's face. "Warsaw will fight to the death."

"Of course we will," he says, holding my gaze. "We'll have to. They're moving across the countryside now, marching at great speed toward us. They'll be here in days." He sighs. "Thank God my Katya's not here to see this."

I shift uneasily and feel Lotka's hand on my shoulder. "Don't be so eager to fight, Renka. I wouldn't want to see you on a stretcher at the hospital."

I lay my hand over hers. Rising from the precarious cot, I shuffle into the darkness at the back of the cellar, my heart cleaving. I don't want to die, yet, most certainly, I want to fight.

Unballing my fists, I search the dusty shelves that once held jars of Mama's *ogórki kiszone* pickles and Mrs. Godlewski's jam. With Mama working at the Education Ministry, Lotka at nursing school, and me in my last year of high school, we've had little time for pickling or preserving. Since Papa's untimely death, we eat whatever Mama's salary buys.

Returning to the yellow glow, I raise a pickle jar triumphantly. "Look what I found!"

Mama briefly glances up; then she turns to Lotka. "You sure you brought the jewelry bag?"

"Of course. Don't worry, the ring's safe." My sister reaches into her pillowcase and removes the sandwiches and a flask. "Is anyone hungry?"

I move to the blanket, and while Lotka pours us sweet, hot, heavenly tea, Mama performs a miracle, lifting an apple cake from her pillowcase. I'm resolving to be more patient with her when she graciously offers Mr. Godlewski my egg sandwiches.

"You're very kind, Pani," he says bowing, and I'm afraid he's going to fall over. It's a good thing we're eating because his bottle's half-empty. I slap the bottom of the pickle jar and twist it open. *Smells all right.* The carefully packed items in my rucksack are hardly edible: extra torch batteries, Swiss Army knife, nails tied to a length of rope that I plan to hang things on, extra toilet paper, a book on modern painting, my sketchbook, a box of pencils and charcoal.

After we've eaten, Lotka and I help Mr. Godlewski lower himself onto the cot like a piece of folding furniture. My cellar mates find ways to distract themselves from the Nazis' autumn tour of our country. Lotka studies her German textbook by the light of my torch, Mama's hands play piano on her knees while she absently hums the tune, and Mr. Godlewski—out cold—colors Mama's waltz with his percussive snoring.

As for me, my ears grow ears straining for the steady sound of the all-clear siren. But as often happens, my mind strays to Leah and her messy, laughing family—her father's terrible puns as he drives us to our Saturday classes at the Art Academy; her trouser-wearing mother dangling baby Joel on one hip while demonstrating how to feather a brush line on my watercolor. I smother my fears by conjuring a wistful scene in which Leah, her mother, and I are painting together beneath palm trees in the South of France.

Thoughts of painting send me reaching for my sketchbook. I begin drawing Mama's rigid back, Mr. Godlewski's head, snoring, Lotka tying her hair in a ponytail. Can I draw without seeing clearly? I let my hands move over the pages as if they were my eyes.

As I work, a low humming strums my throat, and I start to sing, *Poland has not yet perished.* Lotka adds her pure soprano—*So long as we still live.* Mama smiles woefully, while a wakened Mr. Godlewski struggles to salute our national anthem. I mute any crying sounds yearning to escape, but I can't control the tears dribbling down my neck. I need to be strong like my mountain-climbing father, but he's not here to show me how. I send a hopeful glance toward my mother. It's her hand I want to clutch, her fingers I need to feel stroking my hair, but she's too busy brushing crumbs from her blanket.

Lotka pulls me close. "It's okay. I promise nothing bad will happen to us."

Exhausted from trying to forge myself into steel, I let my head fall onto her shoulder.

The minutes pass, and we're all safe in our private shells when we hear the planes returning, seemingly from all directions now. A shelf rattles with the impact of a close hit. I clutch my chest and notice that Mr. Godlewski's right hand has performed the same involuntary action. For the next hour, we're maddened by the shrieking of planes, which begins like a hundred out-of-tune violins, accelerates quickly to high-pitched screaming that makes my heart race and my ears ache. Mr. Godlewski says that the German Stuka bombers have wind sirens under the wings and even on the bombs, fiendishly designed to terrorize our ears and minds.

We wait out the raid, each breath held like a tightrope until we make it to the next breath and the next. In the dark, our eyes seek each other, less for comfort, which we have no strength to give, more for confirmation that we're ready for the next round when it comes. When it all passes, my heart's left hammering and I'm soaked in cold sweat.

So. This is what survival feels like.

Two

Warsaw, September 1939

Five days into the invasion, and Tuesday is another disappointingly dry, warm day. At church last Sunday, Father Joseph led the congregation in a prayer for rain, so that our less than perfect roads could swamp the German tanks rattling toward Warsaw. When I told Mr. Godlewski, he shook his head.

"How desperate we are," he said and advised me to listen instead to General Czuma's radio messages begging Polish citizens to help his army defend Warsaw. If only my mother had as much sense as Mr. Godlewski.

After a hasty breakfast, I try again. "Mama, I can't sit here any longer doing nothing. Everyone's digging trenches near Opaczewska Street."

"Absolutely not. Are you forgetting? You promised to keep studying after your school closed."

I exhale as loudly as possible. "It didn't exactly close, Mama. It was destroyed by a bomb."

She turns back to the sink, clattering dishes to drown me out, but I move right up beside her, crossing my arms to harden my heart.

"So, should I simply ignore General Czuma's appeals? All the messages

President Starzyński's been sending on the radio? We have only a short time before the Germans start shelling again. He made that very clear."

She tightens the tap and turns to face me. "Well, of course, if you think you can do more than the British army."

"They're not here yet!" I take a deep breath. "Everyone in our Guide troop will be there. Marysia will be angry if I'm absent. Ask Szarlota."

My mother's expression becomes earnest. "It's just not fitting, Irena."

Not fitting! This well-worn phrase, familiar since early adolescence, really means *No suitable man is going to marry a girl who digs trenches and you'll end up without a husband to take care of you and our whole family will be shamed.* I'm working my way toward rage when Lotka comes out of the bathroom with a basin of washing.

"I'll go with her," she says.

I'm surprised and grateful. My beautiful sister doesn't like getting mud on her boots—in a city, it's a sure sign that you're from the peasant class. Lotka's upper-class friends stopped inviting her to parties after Papa died and we drifted into poverty, but we still see them at church. Suzannah, her once best friend, gave her a box of clothes she no longer wore because they're out of fashion. Lotka dumped them in the charity box at St. Anthony's.

I send my sister a smile before aiming a conquering look at our mother. "Thank you, Lolo. It's our duty to fight in whatever way we can."

Mama hesitates before turning away, her shoulders hunched in defeat.

"Don't worry," Lotka says, hurrying to rub her back. "We'll be back before lunch."

I help my sister hang the washing on the line I've strung in front of the window, not feeling the least bit guilty about my subterfuge. I'm hoping to find Leah at one of the trench posts, and knowing how Mama and Lotka feel about our friendship, this is a chance to spend time with my friend while defending my city.

I'm lacing up my boots at the front door when Mama sticks her head into the hall and volleys one last round at me. "Don't come back here shedding dirt all over my clean floors."

My aggravation vanishes when we step through the iron gate securing our group of flats. We walk straight into a mad landscape, still shocking only days after the first bombing. Across from us, the entire front of a building has been ripped away as if by a giant hand. Slabs of plaster flatten the shrubs growing at the entrance; soot blackens the outer walls; girders hang like horns from ceilings. People's lives are completely exposed.

Lotka and I stand gaping at the violation: beds unmade, a jug magically untouched on a table in one flat, and right next door everything upended in a heap of shattered glass, twisted wood, charred sofa cushions, shoes, dishes, chairs, all clownishly topped by a kettle. I close my eyes and the scene remains like a stain on my eyelids. Yet the building is still inhabited. In a third-floor flat, a family has hung cardboard, curtains, and sheets for privacy, risking an unsafe building to continue a shadow of their lives.

"We've been lucky so far," I say.

"Shh! Don't bring bad luck. Spit over your left shoulder, quick."

Which I do, even though I'm not at all superstitious.

ON OUR WAY to the barricades at Opaczewska and Grójecka streets, we come upon a scene of hope and horror. Outside St. Alexandria Church, all round us, ordinary people are doing their part—heaving up fallen rubble, finding bodies, digging graves. Mr. Godlewski told me there aren't many Polish soldiers left in Warsaw, but here they are, laid out in neat rows.

Afraid of recognizing a classmate or the father of a friend, Lotka and I skirt the filed bodies like careful dancers and come upon the very-much-alive person of our high school history teacher. Pani Olshefski, much older than Mama, is piling chunks of mortar and brick from the bombed-out rectory against the walls of the church. She kisses us both soundly.

"These are sad days, girls." Inclining her head toward the graveyard behind the church, she says, "There's no more room there. They're burying them in

Three Crosses Square." When she complains of the ache in her back, Lotka shows her how to bend her knees and advises a hot-water bottle when she gets home. Pani's sorrowful eyes find mine.

"I was over the moon to hear about your Art Academy scholarship. I'm so sorry you can't go."

I shrug, scuffing the ground with my boot. "Paris will have to wait. Who knows what will happen now with France declaring war?"

"You must keep painting," she says, and I wonder how she's read my mind. I look about me. The tilting buildings, the bodies lying in the heat—women, children, and old men left to bury them. Part of me wants to crumple to the ground. Another part wants to learn. Some might think it ghoulish, but if I had my pencils and drawing pad here, I'd be sketching. I give myself a shake. "I'm sorry, Pani, we have to go. We're going to dig trenches to stop the Panzer tanks."

Our old teacher smiles her encouraging smile. "Professor Iwanowski would be so proud of his girls."

Lotka tugs my arm, and I wave goodbye, thinking that if Papa were alive, he'd be an officer in the Polish army. In which case, he might either be fighting at the front, a prisoner of war, or lying in Three Crosses Square, waiting for his daughters to bury him. Better to die falling into an icy mountain crevasse on a crisp winter day doing something you love.

We hurry away, passing the Chopin Music Academy slanting like a caved-in cake, stately banks with boarded-up windows fronted by tall columns, many plastered with posters declaring *United We'll Defeat the Enemy.* My heart cheers the message, and I turn to share my pride with Lotka, but she's a few steps behind me. I pause in my tracks.

"Are you all right?"

"Just thinking about Papa." Her focus on me sharpens. "Renka, promise me you'll be kinder to Mama."

"What?"

"You don't know how hard it's been for her since Father died."

"I've been there all along, remember?"

My mind pictures that horrible day we had to leave our home, and before that, the whole horrible year Mama took in boarders—awful louts, every one of them. "Remember Professor Pawlowski's hairy hands?"

"Don't remind me. Remember Mr. Krupa banging his bread on the table when Mama baked her own bread?"

We laugh at these not-so-funny incidents, but how could I forget? After Mama made dinner and we did the dishes, they still expected her to play piano for them. And sing. I keep quiet about the incident that brought an end to the hateful boarders: Mama's realization, one evening at dinner, that Professor Pawlowski's butterfingers with his cutlery allowed him to crawl under the table and look up our skirts.

Lotka sighs. "We're all she has left."

My heart springs to the argument that I might be kinder to Mama if she were kinder to me, but my mind takes a nobler course. "You're right," I say, pressing Lotka's hand.

The one good thing that came from our social descent is that my sister and I grew closer, leaning on each other in the face of Mama's sad attempts at keeping up appearances.

On Opaczewska Street, a wagon toppling with a family's entire household creaks toward the Vistula River, hoping to escape the German army. Other wagons are drawn by donkeys, but this one's drawn by a middle-aged couple, their three children walking solemnly at their sides. The eldest cradles a ginger cat in a sling, and the youngest dangles a rag doll by the leg. *No one's left behind.* Lotka and I speed up to pass them.

Thinking of Papa reminds me that one single day in the universe can change your whole life. Soon after his death, my weekday art classes at the academy shrank to Saturday mornings with Professor Rank. When we moved to our small flat in an unfashionable neighborhood, Lotka was ashamed to invite her friends for tea after Sunday mass. In our huddles after school, they teased her about choosing a nursing career—such menial work.

"If you worked at La Parisienne we could visit you when we get our hair done," one of them giggled.

Lotka only blinked, but I felt her humiliation.

Four years after Papa's accident, I still remember his words: *Go your own way. Make your own friends.* That was his confident advice when he learned my classmates were bullying me for sitting in the Jewish section with Leah.

Now my life has changed again.

I'm bursting with excitement by the time we get to the intersection where bombed-out trams lie on their sides, positioned to block the German tanks from advancing into the city. This is what gives me hope: my fellow citizens, without weapons, thinking up clever ways to fight for our country.

We get directions to the digging, and when we arrive, I notice along the length of the trench, the road bricks have been torn up, leaving only a narrow section for pedestrians to pass by. I stare in open-mouthed wonder: the trench is much wider than I imagined it would be, and all the people up to their knees in dirt are women—young, old, ancient.

We wave hello to Marysia, who's handing out cups of water to the workers. I scan the trench for Leah and light on Elzbieta Zahorska's fair head rivaling the shiny buttons on her military-looking jacket. Lotka and I exchange raised eyebrows.

Several years older than us, Elzbieta's a university student and already a fiery legend. Rumored to have manned a heavy machine gun in the first days of the invasion, she's a hero to young people and an irritant to older ones who think she takes too much upon herself. During last Sunday's mass, Lotka and I conspired to sit behind her family so we could admire her straight back and her thick braids, which she wears crossed over her head.

Leah's red head emerges over the lip of the trench, and my heart leaps with joy.

"Ren! Get a shovel from one of the soldiers; I've got room for you here."

I look over my shoulder for Lotka's disapproving glare, but she's already tramping down the embankment toward Elzbieta. A soldier, much younger looking even than we are, hands me a shovel, while two others stand guard with rifles.

Leah helps me down into the ditch and we embrace with our usual greeting: *mwah, mwah, mwah, mwah*, one kiss more than the usual Polish requirement.

"You're wearing a dress?" Her blue eyes incredulous.

"You're wearing trousers!"

"My mother's. We decided they'd be better than my Guide skirt."

The sleeves of her shirt are rolled above her elbows. I eye her critically. "You look like Jean Gabin in *Pépé le Moko*."

She leans in for a furtive whisper. "I'd much rather be kissing Gabin than dressing like him."

Muffling our laughter, we dig each other in the ribs before bending to the work.

"How's your family?" I ask.

She shrugs. "As usual my parents are pretending things are okay. But I hear them whispering while my brothers are asleep. They're really worried." She tucks a stray lock beneath her Alice band and jams her shovel into the ground. "I'll tell you more when we're alone."

I stare at her face, all concentrated effort. My instinct is to protect her, to attack her attackers—the same instinct that moved me to keep sitting beside her in class as several classmates, and occasionally even our teacher, tormented us for it. I follow her lead and pick up my shovel. My gut does a little somersault, though. If Mr. Godlewski's reports are accurate, what's happening in Germany—the destruction of Jewish businesses, outrageous rules banning Jews from public transport, from teaching, attending their old schools, driving their own cars—all could happen in Poland if the British don't get here soon.

Eventually, the effort of heaving shovelfuls of soil onto the hill before me leaves little room for other worries. How weak my arms are!

Along the trench, the mood is surprisingly festive, and for a while, working beside Leah, I don't think about the dragons chomping at the edges of my beloved city. Finally, I'm doing something useful. Watching Marysia jump into the trench beside a toothless old *baba*, I know this is where I belong.

When a man with a camera walks along the lip of the trench, filming us smiling and digging, I wonder if my face mirrors Leah's sweaty, dirt-streaked cheeks. Marysia tries shooing the photographer away, and when he doesn't budge, she calls a soldier over, who orders him to move on. Instinctively, I look down the line to where Lotka's been digging beside Elzbieta. My sister's climbing up the wall of the ditch to check on me. I wave and give her a thumbs-up, but her arm summons me over in one commanding gesture. I smile and pretend I don't understand. The jolly mood's been broken by this odd incident with the photographer, and a somber tone sets in. Any second now, I'm expecting to find my sister standing above me, hands on hips, just a curt nod for Leah. But she doesn't arrive.

The ditch grows wider and deeper, the embankment more firmly packed with rocks unearthed in the digging. When I pause to look up, clouds are assembling thickly across the sky.

An uneasy feeling creeps about the edges of my body like an invisible hunter. I take a few steps up the hill, checking on Lotka—it looks as though she's engaged in a heated conversation with Elzbieta. Leah and I are resting on our shovels when we hear our national anthem being sung by a soft voice. *Poland has not yet perished, so long as we still live.* Others join in, including Leah and me, but we all follow the singer's lead and don't make a fuss about it. *What the foreign force has taken from us, we shall with saber retrieve.* Our anthem, dating from a distant, Napoleonic war, feels less ancient now.

Looking up, my gaze is caught by Marysia, using her shovel as an aid to clamber up the embankment. Our Guide leader confers with Elsa, one of the older members of our troop, and the two of them walk away from the trench in close discussion. Men and women pass by, children, too, pausing near our ditch. I'm imagining this strange scene from their perspective when Elzbieta marches to the top of the embankment and waves her arms for attention. Her clear voice rings out.

"Brothers and sisters, we know the enemy is nearing our capital. Their leaders are already declaring that Warsaw has been taken. But I tell you, fellow citizens, they are mistaken." She raises her fist. "Varsovians are still fighting! And we'll keep fighting as long as we yet live."

Silence and bewilderment greet this slight figure of a girl atop the hill. Then a smattering of applause. Leah and I clap as hard as we can. When Elzbieta tramps back down into the ditch, I spot Lotka climbing up and hurrying toward me.

"It's time to go," she says. "Now, Renka!"

"But our shift's not over." After Elzbieta's speech, I know I could dig for days. Yet I sense the same words have deeply troubled my sister.

"Mama will be worried. We have to leave now."

I say goodbye to Leah, confident in our arrangement to meet tomorrow at another dig. I shake hands with the old *baba* and the other women around me and thank Elzbieta for her speech. When I climb up out of the trench, Marysia's waiting with her tall jug of water. "Good work, girls." She jerks her head toward a nearby tree and I troop after her, Lotka reluctantly following.

When the couple lurking under the tree has left, Marysia raises an inquiring eyebrow at Lotka. "I'm glad to see you here."

My sister points her chin at me. "It's all her doing." Then she removes the headscarf she's had the foresight to bring and cleans her hands with it.

Marysia hands us each a mug, and I squint up at her tall frame. "Who was that man with the camera?"

Her face falls, and she speaks quietly with her back to the trench. "Be careful, both of you. Not every Polish-speaking person is against the invasion. He could be taking pictures of us to show the Gestapo, the German secret police."

Lotka and I share a look of shock. How could any Pole support these devils destroying our country? We thank Marysia for the warning. Then she's up and moving quickly with her water jug toward another woman climbing from the trench.

Walking back to our flat, Lotka and I go down a list of people we know and can't come up with anyone who'd welcome the German invaders. Then we try spotting traitors on the street and we're more successful, especially with the ones staring in dismay at our mud-caked shoes and dresses.

"I need a pair of trousers," I say. "It's stupid wearing a dress to dig a ditch."

She laughs and links elbows with me. "I saw a picture of Greta Garbo in trousers once. She looked quite glamorous."

I can't wait to get home to practice a sweeter, kinder tone with Mama, but my ears are picking up a faint drone. I jerk Lotka to a halt. We stare into blossoming white clouds, and then we see them—a flock of planes like giant hunting birds hanging in the air above us, their characteristic screech as they tip their wings, signaling their deadly intent.

I grab Lotka's hand. "Run! Run!"

We tear down the emptying street with no idea where to hide until I see a small group climbing into a hole in the ground. A man gestures for us to hurry, and we scramble down a rope ladder into a crowded tunnel. He pulls the cover closed and we're in total darkness, the whine and scream of the falling bombs high above us, a quiet pause and then the sounds of exploding glass.

"Where are we?" I ask the dark.

"Can't you tell by the smell?" A woman's sneer. "We're in the sewers, darling."

"Safest place during a bombing raid," another voice says.

"*Tak.* Unless you're already dead," the woman says. "Then you're really safe."

Three

Toronto, October 2010

The wind's at my back as I pedal up Mount Pleasant Road. As for timing, I've found a sweet lull in Toronto traffic that lessens my chances of getting smacked by a northbound truck. This day's been easy so far. The kind of blue-sky day I put my trust in.

Along the broad road, silver maples are performing their autumn leaf drop. Bring on the change! I'm eager to drop the misery of the last four months, have it wash away in a hard rain. Then I'll grow a new leafy canopy. Except, as my mother would have reminded me, there's this thing called winter to get through. Yet winter's never been a problem for me. A new sculpting commission means long hours of work, and months of frigid cold open me to the patient task of waiting for whatever ideas come.

"Hey!" A bike courier races past me on my left. I curb my impulse to swear at them, take a moment instead to admire their layering of leggings, shorts, and skirt.

Looming like an office tower, the Bennett Health Center has nothing in its bland brown exterior that marks it as a home, not even a home for the very old and chronically ill. I wheel into the parking lot and lock my bike to a No Parking sign, glancing up at the windows reflecting a long jet trail.

What's he going to be like, this Stefan Cegielski? This first interview might set the tone for what's to come. I gulp a lungful of confidence from the blue sky. An old man has summoned me to his home to tell me the story of his life. From that, and other alchemy, I'll make him a grave sculpture.

Inside, I sign in at the reception desk. *Reason for visit*: An interview before dying? I scribble, *Art Business*.

In the mirrored walls of the elevator, I examine myself: face browner, body rounder, hair redder after the long summer. I twist a springy curl behind my ear.

As I walk down the wide hall, Spanish guitar music drifts from one room and rending cries from another. I knock on the open door, surprised by the size of the room, its distinctly un-hospital furniture. By the window, an aged man reclines in a wingback chair, one arm languorously draped over the side.

"Mr. Cegielski? Hi. It's Josephine Blum."

"So nice of you to have come."

A charming, authoritative, surprisingly high-pitched voice for a man with such bushy eyebrows and a faintly Russian accent—like he's welcoming me to his dacha for a weekend in the country. When I bend to shake his hand, I'm tempted to curtsy, but something in his gaze makes me skip my little joke.

His palm is warm in mine, the skin spotted and smooth. "Thank you for inviting me."

We pause, each gazing into the other's face. White hair sweeps off his high forehead, violet-blue eyes dazzle below black brows. I smile widely to stop what's feeling like an investigation on both sides. With a courtly wave, he offers the reclining leather chair.

I do a little head bow and leave my bike helmet beside the vase of freesias on the window ledge, bend to take my notebook and recorder from my backpack.

When he called, I briefly described my interviewing process, but recording and note-taking can be intimidating. I remind myself now that my first three grave sculptures were for people I knew and loved—first my grandfather; and then Rudi, my wood-carving professor at Emily Carr. That was followed by my mother, and her own long dying, four years ago.

This winter, during the nightmare of Frank's affair and our final breakup, I finished work on a sculpture for a California mega-farmer kept alive by transplants, the care of three ex-wives, and his many children. The work keeps me going. Enmeshed in stories of other people's lives, I can store my own strife in a drawer for later. Stefan's my fifth grave sculpture.

I'm holding up my notebook, my digital recorder, checking if he's okay with them, when a tall man rounds the door and strides into the room. His long black coat tells me that he's not a doctor.

"Roland Cegielski," he says. No handshake.

"Jo Blum."

He sizes me up. "You're the gravestone carver?"

"The grave sculptor."

He twists a smile, takes a few awkward steps toward Stefan. "Hi, Dad."

Stefan smiles vaguely.

Roland remains standing despite a third chair against the wall, his coat still zipped up like a Prada cassock. He settles his gaze somewhere over my left shoulder.

"My father's insisting that you be the one to make his gravestone. I'm here to get a few things straight from a legal, financial standpoint."

I glance at Stefan, who seems not to be following this conversation, and turn back to Roland. "It's a sculpture, not a gravestone." Reaching for my backpack beside the chair, I decide I might as well sit.

"I was saving these for after my interview with your dad." I pull out the large manila envelope and hand it to him. "You'll find two copies of my contract in there, along with my fee and a description of all the stages in the sculpting process."

His long arms allow him to reach for the envelope without moving his feet. Scanning the papers, he says, "Privacy is important to us. Do you have to do these interviews?"

"Yes, she does." Stefan leans forward.

Well now. This is awkwardly interesting.

Frowning at his son, he jerks his chin at the door. "You can go now." The blanket around his knees slips to the floor.

Roland brushes back his graying maestro hair. "I'll have our lawyer look these over." He's about to say more, when his phone dings in the pocket of his coat. He puts it to his ear. "I'm just leaving. Thirty minutes, tops." He sends his father a furtive glance, but Stefan's tracking a plane through his window. Before he turns to leave, Roland hands me a card.

"We'll be in touch. Hold off on a second interview until we get back to you." No hug or kiss for his dad. The pristine white card has weight, a clean sans serif font: *Cegielski & Son*. And below that—*Prestige Landscaping*.

When he's gone, I feel a thick fatigue as though he's been grilling me for hours.

"I can ring for tea or coffee, Miss Blum." Stefan's charm surfaces like a palate cleanser.

Like we're in a suite at the Royal York.

"Or something stronger?"

Ha. "Please call me Jo. I've brought my own coffee, but can I get you something?" I pick up the soft blanket, lay it across his knees, pull my chair closer to his. All these intimate gestures for this man I've just met, a vulnerable man whose story I've come here to probe.

When we're settled, me with black coffee from my thermos, he with apple juice from his room fridge, I try to pick up where we left off. I'm eager now to get past the pleasantries, but conscious also that Stefan, in his pleated flannel pants, white shirt, and V-neck sweater, reminds me of my grandfather, whose deep attention to me required a similar presence on my part.

"May I call you Stefan?"

He makes a regal bow of his head. "Jo." In his mouth, my commonplace name takes on European flavor. "That's a beautiful blouse."

I'm angry at myself for blushing, but also pleased that this soft paisley blouse I inherited from my mother goes with my baggy jeans. Somehow, he's hit on the right thing to say.

"Are you going to record me today?"

"I'd like to." I place the recorder on the table close to him.

He nods.

"I'm curious how you found me, Stefan, and why you want one of my sculptures."

"It was that *Toronto Star* article about you. I read what you said, and thought, 'I have to meet this girl.' You said, 'The stories you tell can change your life for better or worse.'"

Shereen Patel's article from a few years back. Touched, I move in closer. "I think that's true."

"I have to believe that." His gaze edges toward the window. "Changing my life has been important to me. Very important."

I nod, intensely curious now.

"I built my landscaping business from scratch. One truck, a wheelbarrow, some tools. Later, I hired people of all races. Blacks, Indians." He angles an eyebrow at me. "My head designer was a Jew."

I wince. I was just starting to like him. Sophie always said prejudice reveals itself through charitable acts. My body steels itself, but my mind does some quick compartmentalizing. I steady my gaze. "Doing good is important to you?"

"Being decent is important. Treating these people with respect."

I look away, look back. "Tell me about your family."

Now he's the one to cringe. Or have I imagined that? He smooths the blanket around his legs, begins to tell me about his wife, Mary, and their two sons. In the once-upon-a-time start to his story there's lots of detail—Mary's Scottish frugality, the eldest son's hockey trophies, his first big landscaping contract with a rich Eaton family member—all of it a kind of recipe for immigrant assimilation into Canadian life. But as the decades motor on, he glides over details, dismissiveness swamping his tone. Infected by his mood, I press pause on the recorder.

"Stefan, where do you want your story to start?"

"With the war. The war started everything."

"Okay. We're talking World War Two, right?"

He shrugs. "Of course."

"Where were you when it started? Who were you with?"

"Poland. That's where I lived, in the capital of Warsaw."

I feel my eyes widen. I should have known from the last name, the accent, even though it's slightly different from my grandparents'.

His eyes focus inward, his breath becoming shallower, and I think that's all he's going to say. Then he continues. "My dear Ola was with me in the sewers. We were both in the resistance, guiding people through the tunnels to safety."

That startles me, but I'm careful not to let my surprise at this coincidence shift his attention. "What was it like in the sewers?"

"Horrible. The smell. The tunnels were four feet high in places. Sometimes we walked through sewage up to our waists." He takes a deep breath, as though he's run out of air.

"But you and Ola were saving people."

He gives me a curt nod. "Of course. We escorted many families through the tunnels when they were in danger."

"You mean the Nazis were hunting them."

With a shaky hand, he reaches for his juice. I lift the Styrofoam cup for him, bend the straw. He takes a few sips and sinks back against the chair.

When he says, "Miss Blum, that blouse is beautiful with your hair," smiling as though he's greeting me for the first time today, it completely disorients me. Do I play along with this backward jump in time? Or do I jerk him back into the present conversation about his first wife, Ola?

"Thanks, Stefan. I like the blue of *your* sweater." *Shit.* Am I really flirting with this old man? That earlier remark about Jews, aimed at me, hurtles from its compartment in my brain. I steer the interview back to Ola. "What did your Ola look like?"

"She had dark hair and big, dark, shining eyes."

"She sounds lovely." I look around the room for a photo. On the wall behind me is a fading picture of Stefan, his wife, Mary, and their two dorky teenage sons. Of course there wouldn't be a photo of his first wife. I turn back to meet Stefan's gaze. "What happened to her?"

His eyes lock onto mine. "The war killed her. The war destroyed millions of lives." A gurgling sound sputters from his mouth, and I stand to pat him on the back.

"Tired now. I want to sleep." He closes his eyes, his head rocking back against the chair.

I've pushed him too hard this first day. And his son's intervention sapped us both. "I'll wait for Roland to contact me about a second visit."

"Roland?"

A woman in purple scrubs hurries in with a banana, pill cup, and cup of water.

"Hello, Mr. C. Time for your pill."

I grab the recorder, my backpack, bike helmet, step out of her way.

"So nice you have a new visitor." She smiles at me, clips a bib around his neck, peels the banana. Stefan seems to shrink into his clothes.

Confused by the sudden disappearance of this man I was getting to know, I'm dragging my chair back into the corner when my eye's caught by the whiteboard hanging beside the family photo. *Stefan Cegielski*; *Non-ambulatory*; *Two person assist*, in blue marker. A language I understand from Sophie's hospital stays before her illness chased her home to die.

I wave at Stefan. "Thank you for today. I'll call you soon." The attendant slides the curtain around him, obscuring his response.

On the way out, I stop at the floor desk to say goodbye, strike it lucky with a chatty practical nurse who's charmed that I've come to interview Stefan.

What I learn: He's ninety-two, he's been here almost a year, he has frequent memory lapses where he thinks he's in the past, or where he doesn't recognize Roland. It's the daughter-in-law who mostly visits. Diagnosis: Alzheimer's. Prognosis: the nurse draws the line at that last question.

I take the stairs down to clear my head. I'm not feeling good about this first interview. I could get over the Roland incident if I don't have to deal with him again. It's Stefan whose grave sculpture I'm making, his openness I need. Yet his queasy comment about the people he hired put me off. Something so nice-sounding feeling so offensive. At the stairwell window, I pause to watch the wind lofting the branches of a white pine. Could be a rough ride south. The thing is—the thing is I'm excited by Stefan's story.

Thousands of people with Polish heritage make their homes in this city. It's an odd coincidence that he and Ola were in the resistance, in Warsaw, fighting in the sewers—just like Irena and Mati.

Four

Warsaw, September 1939

Even the weather's turned against us. It's cold, with a mean wind adding to our misery.

My sister's gone to her volunteer work at Infant Jesus Hospital, but Leah and I are huddled under the portico of the National Bank along with other members of our Guide troop. Under the direction of Marysia, striding about in a bomber pilot's leather jacket over her uniform, we're ladling out soup to a long line of shivering people in Castle Square.

Leah glances at me, then frowns into her soup pot. "Let's hope we're not poisoning anyone."

I can't believe she's still angry with me. Our troop was up early this morning collecting edible wild plants in Arkadia Park. I picked what looked like sorrel leaves near some ferns and threw them into my pail. A small bite of a leaf confirmed the familiar sour tang I love in sorrel soup, and when I showed my almost-full pail to Leah, she started picking some, too. Soon her palms began to itch, and when she showed Marysia the rash, she hurried over to examine my pail.

"Wood sorrel," she said. "Some people are allergic to the acid. Too much and you'll get bad cramps. Did you eat any?"

"No, thank goodness." Leah tossed her hair and looked away.

"Just one tiny bite," I said.

Marysia examined my face and hands. "You'll be all right. Both of you, follow me to the pond. Irena, first empty that pail in the hole by the fence."

After a good hand-scrubbing in the pond, interrupted only by Marysia trying to catch a swimming goose, Leah's itchy palms began to quiet. Our troop took the plants back to our new headquarters in the Art Academy, where we boiled them in the kitchen. Made from wild leek, lamb's quarters, garlic mustard, and grass, with fermented fish as a base, the soup tastes surprisingly good.

Next in my soup line is a thin girl with a plump baby on her hip. I give her double rations, and I'm pleased when she walks away smiling. "Have you tried some?" I ask Leah.

"No! I can't go home with cramps. My father has enough troubles."

"Oh?"

"Not here. And remember what Marysia said. 'A double ration for one person can mean no ration for the next person.'"

She's been like this all day. Not like the Leah who teases me about my love for film star Witold Zacharewicz, not even like the solemn Leah who sings a Kaddish prayer when we uncover a limb as we're sifting through the rubble of a bombed building. My friend's troubles make her distant from me.

Wending our way home afterward, with scarcely a word between us, she pauses outside the ruin of St. John's Church, then we scramble over concrete, brick, and charred pews to a clear space inside.

"You absolutely cannot tell anyone!" Her eyes are pools of seriousness, her voice quiet.

"Of course." My stomach's in knots.

"My father's planning to get us out before they . . ." Her face crumples.

"I know." The dragons are close. I give her hand a squeeze. She's crying freely now, and I see that she's been holding it all in, being stoic in the face of every torment, as she often is. She looks down at her boots covered in plaster dust. "Someone high up promised to get us documents." When she tries to blow her nose quietly, I grin. "Just let it honk like that goose Marysia almost caught."

Her smile lightens my heart. "How's your mother?" I ask.

"I'm helping her pack. We can't take much." Her mouth forms a grim line. "But Joel's in a bad way. He's been so sick, Ren. My father says it's because Mama's milk has gone bad."

My heart gets heavier with each sentence. Behind Leah, a massive wooden crucifix dangles from the vaulted ceiling by a coiled wire. All that remains of the plaster Christ figure is the upper chest and the head with its crown of thorns. "I pray to every one of the gods that your plan works," I say.

She gives me a wry smile. "Praying? Is this the same Irena I know and love?" Rooting in her rucksack, she comes up with a long package wrapped in brown paper, neatly tied with green ribbon. "My mother wanted me to give you this." I bounce the package in my hand. Heavy. Leah nudges my elbow and holds out a book of Colette's stories. "Page eighty-six, darling," she says in her Garbo voice. But there are tears in her eyes.

It takes me a moment to understand that these are goodbye gifts. The present slows, and I find myself off to the side watching the two of us together. *I have nothing to give her.* Quickly untying my rucksack, I remove my sketchbook and tear out a pencil drawing of Leah smiling in the trenches, her shovel over her shoulder. "For your mother." Then I find one of just our hands, drawing side by side at our desks in art class.

"Girls!" I jump in my skin. At the door, a priest and a woman, both wearing helmets. "You shouldn't be in here!"

We hurdle over the pews. Out on the street, Leah slips the drawings into the front pocket of her bag. We walk with our arms circling each other's waists until our paths diverge. In the sooty doorway of the burned violin shop, we hug quickly, then turn away in opposite directions. When I look back after a few steps, I see her marching steadily ahead. She raises her hand in a wave.

ꝒꝐ

A WEEK AGO, the Russians invaded Praga, a Warsaw suburb just east of the Vistula River. My heart breaks thinking about it. Trapped between two terrors, we're fighting on two fronts, while Britain and France do nothing. We live now with a desperate pragmatism, like a fish in that fatal moment when it knows it's caught, gasping for breath.

Helping Lotka with supper, I hack through the loaf I bought with two charcoal drawings of our baker's dimpled grandson.

"What day is it today?" Mr. Godlewski sits shivering in his coat.

"Wednesday, the twentieth of September," I say.

He makes a quick calculation. "That makes nineteen and a half days we've kept the bastards out of Warsaw." He looks terrible, no better than Mama, but while her face is red from crying, his has a ruddy vodka flush. "Who knew the Germans and Russians would fall in love and we'd be crushed in their embrace? Maybe our Warsaw miracle's about to end."

A week ago, I would have argued with his defeatist stance, but today I don't have the strength. To bring us to our knees, the Germans are starving us to death. No food gets into the city, and they bomb all the markets. People live with their chickens indoors. When Lotka saw a queue of people on Nowy Świat, waiting to carve up a dead horse killed in the bombings, we ran back with our newspaper, knife, and bowl. By the time we got there, nothing was left but a few bones teeming with flies. To make our journey worthwhile, I broke one of the giant ribs by kicking at it with my boot; we carried a piece home for soup. Thank God fish are still swimming in the Vistula River. Mr. Godlewski managed to get us a whole pike, which Mama cut up and pickled in oil, salt, and wild chives from the cloister garden at St. Anthony's.

The greedy Irena Iwanowska of last summer would have found it crazy to believe that anything could be worse than starvation. At the end of this bloody September, I can testify that a bombed-out Warsaw waterworks ranks much higher on the scale of disasters. They've cut off our supply of drinking water, and catastrophically, water for quenching fires. Our city burns while Guides and Scouts ferry water from a string of troughs dotting the squares, starting far off in the Old Town by the river.

While Lotka prepares what little food we've scavenged, picked, and bartered, we hang on every word of Mr. Godlewski's foreign news reports. As of today, the dragons haven't jammed the BBC shortwave radio signals, and Radio Free Warsaw is still broadcasting. I'm so tired of waiting—not just for the Germans, but for our overdue allies who've sworn to come to our aid.

I scrape my hair back from my face. "Were the British joking when they declared war against the Germans?"

Mr. Godlewski stretches a mirthless smile. "Any day now, Renka. According to Mr. Churchill, they're just putting the screws in the British planes, then they'll be right over."

"And the French?" Lotka asks, not hearing the mockery in his tone.

"Don't hold your breath," he says. "The Russians just arrived on the other side of the river. I'm sure the British are waiting for them to settle in before they rescue us."

My sister pauses to shake her head at him on her way to Mama's room. When I thank Mr. Godlewski for this latest war news, I mean to be as ironic as he was, but I catch a streak of fear in his brown eyes. By the time I soften my tone, he's turned his head to the window, his back hunched.

"My father was always disappointed in me."

I'm not following his train of thought, but the anguish in his voice halts any clever retort.

"He wanted me to be an engineer like he was, but I paid him back by becoming a journalist." He straightens. "Still, there are some things he taught me I'll never forget: how to build a shortwave radio from scratch, for instance." He swivels to face me and puts a finger on his lips.

"Check the pot, Renka!" My sister blasts frustration from Mama's room, but my eyes are locked on Mr. Godlewski's.

His loud sigh puffs the moment away. "Go check the pot."

I rush into the living room, where the pot is simmering on a grate over the fireplace. With the electricity out for weeks, only stumps of trees remain in the courtyard of our building. After its bountiful, juicy summer, even Mrs. Godlewski's plum tree became fuel.

Stirring the pot, my mind wanders to Marysia and my Guide troop. Mama and Mr. Godlewski are fish just waiting for the knife, but Marysia gives me hope. At our last soup station in St. Helen's Square, Elsa, Marysia, and I stood for hours ladling out soup. Leah wasn't there.

When my sister passes by with our shaky mother on her arm, I get up to serve the soup Lotka's made from cabbage and two flattish potatoes I discovered in the cellar.

"Is this cabbage?" I ask my sister. "It looks like pieces of grass."

"So what if it's grass, Irena? If you're not hungry, we'll eat it." In her face, I see my own self mirrored: hollowed cheeks, sunken eyes, filthy hair—her beautiful face made dull by fear and a pain so deep it threatens to displace her kind, peace-loving self.

We eat the tepid soup in silence, except for Mr. Godlewski's heroic slurping. I wonder idly if it's his way of making the soup seem more delicious than it is. The way cutting my slice of bread into quarters makes it seem like there's more bread.

Our old neighbor pauses his slurping to consult his pocket watch. "Turn on the radio, Renka. It's almost time for the president's report."

Mama rises abruptly. She cannot bear hearing the war reports.

"Dear Agata," Mr. Godlewski says, reaching for her hand. "Thank you for the hospitality of your home. It's been such a comfort to me these many weeks." He pulls a glass jar from his jacket pocket. "I brought something for you. The last of Katya's plum jam. I hoped we could all have a spoonful tonight. Will you join us?"

Mama can't bring herself to refuse. Lotka gets us each a teaspoon.

The bristle and hum on the radio turns to beeps, and then Stefan

Starzyński's voice comes through, hoarse as usual. I draw my chair closer, my hands pressed between my knees.

"My fellow Varsovians, tonight I bring you terrible news. Warsaw is forced to surrender to the Germans."

I breathe in sharply. Lotka and Mama are clutching each other, while Mr. Godlewski tightens his fists. Searching for something to hold on to, I settle for clasping my own face.

Starzyński's voice gains strength. "To save lives, to save what's left of our glorious, historical city, we must capitulate. Some of you will say that Warsaw should have surrendered much earlier, that we should have stopped defending our city, that I should have fled with the other government leaders. But I could not. How could I leave when so many of you were putting out fires, building barricades, manning soup stations to serve our beleaguered citizens? In Warsaw alone, many thousands of us have been killed, thousands more injured or rendered homeless, and yet hundreds of thousands of us have survived every barbaric effort the Huns have made to murder us. We are still here, and here I will remain. This is the last radio broadcast I will make, but it is not the last time you will hear from me. Be brave! Continue serving Poland and each other. May God be with you."

The sound goes dead, as though he's been sucked into a ghostly realm.

We sit in silence, too stunned to move or speak. I'm overcome with longing for Papa to be here and look to Lotka for a sign that she might be feeling the same. The creases in her brow unfurrow; a strange calm absorbs her features.

"Well, that's that," Mr. Godlewski says and gathers his pipe and tobacco. Then he looks at me. "And now the real fun begins. I'd wish you all a good night, but . . ." And he trails off to his flat where his vodka is likely waiting with open arms. On the table, the jam remains unopened.

Mama stirs in her chair. "We have the intaglio," she says, raising her chin.

Lotka nods agreement, but I can't meet my mother's gaze. I don't joke about the ring anymore the way Father used to. A gold intaglio with a swan and laurel leaves that belonged to Mama's great-grandfather, the ring is supposed to be proof that he was part of the Prussian nobility. Papa liked to tease Mama about this infamous count who squandered all his money gambling, but for Mama the ring has always meant she has noble blood. Since the German threat to our country, the ring has become a solemn insurance for her and Lotka. "If we're threatened," Lotka argued, "we can use it to prove we have German blood."

I made the mistake of asking, "Do we want to have German blood?"

"Don't be stupid, Renka," Mama growled. "Your sister makes a sensible point."

This line of thinking makes me itch all over. In the Warthegau, the part of Poland closest to Germany, those Poles considered ethnically German are serving the Nazi cause. And Hitler, Mr. Godlewski told me, considers the rest of us Slavs no better than cellar vermin. I'm not sure that a ring, even a gold intaglio, will convince the Germans otherwise.

Needing to feel my blood moving, I walk to the blackout curtains, reach behind them to open the window, and let in a blast of cold air. Our president's news was hardly surprising. I take a deep breath. I'm still young. If an old man like Starzyński refuses to run away, then I must find a way to keep fighting.

"Close the window, Renka!" Pulling her shawl around her, Mama hurries back to her bedroom.

"It may be the last free breath I take," I say, shutting the window quickly.

"Very dramatic and not at all helpful," Lotka says, clearing the table.

"Aren't you sad, Lolo?"

"What good does it do to be sad?" She looks up at me. "I hope this means the fighting and bombing are over now. Then we can start rebuilding our lives."

That startles me. "Do you really think they'll let us?"

"I don't know. But I heard that when our army destroyed a bridge to stop the Germans crossing, the Germans rebuilt it in one day. They won't want to live in a demolished city with no food."

I consider the possibility that the markets will reopen, that water pipes will be repaired, that cafés and taverns will once more fill with people. This way of viewing our defeat has not occurred to me, and I don't know what to make of it. I have an alarming thought.

"Does this mean that all along, you've been against our defense of the city?"

"You heard the radio, Renka. How many people dead, how many suffering still." She leans back against the sink, smooths her hands over her face as though she's cleansing it. "At the hospital, I closed the eyes of a small boy killed in the bombing. I don't want to do that again."

Dear, kind Lotka. In two steps, I'm at her side, my arm around her shoulders.

"It's your turn to clean up, Renka." My sister's tone turns gentle. "Don't stay up late. Who knows what tomorrow will bring."

Nazi soldiers occupying every corner of my beautiful city? Imagining that poor boy turns my thoughts to Leah and her young brothers. Has Dr. Freeman got his family out of Warsaw? Was that why she wasn't at the soup line? I wipe the dishes with a damp cloth, tie two cushions around the warm pot, rake the cold ash in the living room grate, all the while feeling myself drawn outdoors.

My chores done, I step into the cold night, and, closing the front door, make my way to the gate of our building and onto the street beyond. When I get there, I'm not alone. On this night of all nights, men and women, young and old, are milling about, determined to stretch these last hours into forever. We lift our faces to the stars, all dazzlingly blind to our fate. I set myself to marking this night with memories—seeing myself strolling down our main street all the way to Dreszer Park, delighting in shopwindows, crowded cafés, and art galleries, old statues, new sculptures, venerable steeples, all telling stories of my beloved Warsaw. My breath catches.

The fact is, it's almost impossible to recognize my city. The air is black. Small fires burn everywhere, and in the midst of it all, hundreds of tall, narrow brick columns rise from the smoking ground like goblin castles. It took me a while to understand they were chimneys—all that remains of the burned buildings.

I don't know what tomorrow will bring, but I have a diary of this bloody month. Back safe inside, I leaf through the drawings in my sketchbook. A charcoal of the ghostly chimneys is the best one. There's one of Leah hoisting a shovel, another of her posing like a fashion model with her hands on her hips. Along with those, a sketch of dead soldiers forming imperfect rows in Three Crosses Square. I flip the pages to the many cellar drawings in pencil and charcoal—Mama brushing Lotka's hair, Mr. Godlewski polishing his glasses, Lotka poring over her German grammar book, and aboveground, flames and smoke seen through our kitchen window, which I've drawn in bright reds, blues, purples, and orange.

I carefully tear out the drawings. In the bedroom I share with my sister, I hide them between the pages of our *Pan Tadeusz* poetry book. Because even if the Nazis rebuild our bridges and restore our water, I never want to forget how much they hate us.

MORNING ARRIVES ON this bright October day as though nothing significant has changed. Did the radio broadcast happen in another universe? I've been expecting hundreds of boots to come marching through Mokotów, but so far this week, no Germans have goose-stepped past our building. My city seems as quiet as a burned-out house.

"Don't be fooled," Mr. Godlewski says when I meet him in the courtyard. He follows me to the garden, where I spread the fireplace ash onto bare soil, the last of the winter kale eaten to the roots weeks ago.

"You're really going out?" Our neighbor has his carpetbag slung over his shoulder.

"Of course. To find supplies before things get more exciting."

I tip the remaining ash from my pail around the stump of the plum tree. "Is it safe?"

He leans toward me. "When's the last time you felt safe in Warsaw, Renka?"

I nod glumly.

"We can't sit here waiting for the trap to chew down," Mr. Godlewski says. "If you need something, you can come with me."

Lulled by the quiet, Mama and Lotka raise no objections and give me a list of things to find: bread, stamps, bacon fat, and garlic. I pack three jars of Mama's pickled pike into my rucksack to trade.

On the streets, everything seems painted with worry and fear: the jangling bells of the bicycle rickshaws, a car erratically mounting a curb, even the honking geese flying south out of Warsaw. A few shops are open and long queues wind around corners. Everyone has the same idea: stock up before they get here. We stop at the post office, where I mail Mama's letter to her cousin in Kraków; then we line up at the tobacconist for Mr. Godlewski's pipe tobacco. Everywhere we go, there are people who know him. As the day progresses, the city gains urgency, and by the time we get to Pani Nowak's private bakery, the queue on the staircase is a seething bazaar.

"What've you got?" a thin woman asks me. I show her a jar of pickled pike. She has a bottle of curdling milk, which I turn down. Mr. Godlewski, meanwhile, has shoved his way up the stairs to the front of the queue, feigning deafness and senility. I watch him disappear through Pani's door and hope that he doesn't forget the bread. Step by step up the chattering staircase, I manage to trade my jars for a whole garlic bulb and a packet of sugar. When Mr. Godlewski finally reappears, sprightlier and apologetic, I tuck in my arms and squeeze my way back down. Near the bottom, I'm shoved by a woman with long red braids. "Up or down, make up your mind," she says, pushing rudely past me. Catapulted out of the queue, I stagger onto the street to wait for my neighbor.

"Got what you want?" Mr. Godlewski touches my elbow. His carpetbag loaded with clinking bottles, we head back in the direction of Marszałkowska.

"Did you remember the bread?" I ask.

"Of course, Renka. I wouldn't want to incur the wrath of Agata."

He's a canny guide, and we take the side streets and alleyways until we turn a corner onto the main road and hear shots ringing out. *Cholera jasna!* For a heartbeat, we freeze while the air around us bristles with bullets.

"*Psiakrew!*" Mr. Godlewski ducks and pulls me behind a motorcycle with a sidecar. His bag of bottles clanks onto the pavement as bullets ram into the wall beside my ear. I throw myself onto my stomach and cover my head with my hands. Beside me, Mr. Godlewski does the same. Something wet seeps past my cheek, and I shudder, touching my fingertips to my face: vodka. A lull in the shooting, and I raise my head.

"Don't look," he says.

I do, and in front of the motorcycle, a pair of black boots lies splayed, then legs, then oozing blood where a stomach should be. I squeeze my eyes shut. My first sight of a German soldier and he's dead. So there are still Polish forces fighting in Warsaw. This thought should thrill me, but it doesn't. The soldier moans.

"Let's get out of here." Mr. Godlewski's breathing hard, and I briefly wonder if he can drive the motorcycle; instead, he turns the corner on hands and knees. I duckwalk after him. From the sounds of fire, the fighting has moved across the road. Risking a backward glance, I'm shocked to see two tanks stalled at the top of Marszałkowska. The trenches are working!

"Run," says Mr. Godlewski, struggling to gain his feet. The *vroom* of motorcycles escalates to a roar. *Mother Mary!* Desperate for a hiding place, we're whirring about when my eyes fall on the sewer cover just ahead of us. I motion climbing down, but Mr. Godlewski shakes his head. I nod insistently. The two of us kneel and, with great difficulty, heave the top up just enough to push it to the side. I squeeze in easily and climb partway down the rope ladder. He hands down his bag, manages to push the cover farther aside, gets his foot on the first rung and the next, until, puffing, he scrapes the cover over our heads. With a clang, it falls into place.

We stand at the foot of the ladder, pinpoints of light puncturing the holes in the manhole cover. Behind us the gloom of the sewer tunnel; above us the rat-a-tat of machine guns and the grinding of engines. I fish for my flashlight in my rucksack, and we discover the downhill slope behind us with a low shelf along one wall. Straddling the rill running down the middle, we make our way to the little shelf and lean back against the damp tunnel wall. I finally exhale, amazed that we've accomplished this little escape trick.

"Want some?" Mr. Godlewski hands me a small bottle.

"I already had some." I point to the wet front of my jacket. But I take a nip of the clean, smooth drink while he removes the cracked bottle, setting it on the shelf beside him.

"Don't tell your mother. Or your sister." He examines the scrapes on his hands. "Our boys are still fighting," he says proudly.

"Is there any point?" I hear the anger in my voice.

He stares at me in awkward silence. Then he narrows his eyes. "Well, you can be a chicken that plucks out its own feathers in preparation for the pot. Or you can peck the bastards' ankles and take a chance at saving some lives. Which would you rather do—pluck or peck?"

"Peck," I say immediately, and look away, annoyed that he's forced me into a decision I've been mulling for weeks.

He leans forward to peer at me. "Your first time under fire?"

My face turns to jelly.

He searches my eyes for impending crying. "Get used to it," he says, recorking the bottle.

I press my hands on my chest to contain the commotion. We sit in silence for a while, and I imagine that he, too, is traveling the short distance backward to our close encounter with flying bullets.

"They're using the Zündapp," he mutters to himself, sounding impressed.

"Was that the motorcycle?"

My voice seems to surprise him. "Yes. For the advance guard." He peers at me again. "Did you notice if it had a rear gun?"

"No rear gun. Just one mounted on the side."

"See any tanks?"

"Yes, two, but they were stopped behind the trenches."

He smiles, patting his breast pocket where he keeps his tobacco, but it must have fallen out while he was crawling. He sighs. "So, how did you know about this hiding place?"

I explain how Lotka and I joined a group hiding in the sewers during a bombing raid.

"It's important to have good hiding places," he says, hopefully searching his trouser pockets. "You know, it doesn't smell too bad down here."

"And we're safe from the dragons."

"That's what you call the *Hitlerow*?"

I nod. "I know everyone calls them rats, but rats are just looking for a meal, like us. Dragons grab all the gold and power for themselves."

His belly jiggles, but he smothers his laugh. "Mind if I steal your word?"

I weigh the possibility of bargaining with him: *I'll give you my word if you teach me how to fire a revolver*, but it doesn't seem a fair exchange.

When we don't hear the guns anymore, he climbs up the ladder and listens. Satisfied, he lifts the cover with his shoulder and looks about. "All clear."

Aboveground, the air smells metallic. I'm surprised by the number of civilians on the street who are unsurprised by our emergence from the sewer, and realize we're not the only ones who've been caught in the sudden skirmish.

His precious bag across his shoulder, Mr. Godlewski renews his zigzagging way home. I follow closely, determined to memorize his route. Outside our gate, he pauses with a hand on my shoulder.

"I won't say anything about our little adventure. I leave it up to you how much to tell." He squeezes my shoulder. "You've got the gift of cold blood, Irena. I would be glad to have you beside me in any battle."

Cold blood. I smile, unsure if I should be flattered by this compliment.

Unlocking the gate, he pauses once more to stare at me. "By the way, where did you learn to dive for the ground and cover your head like that?"

"Guides," I say, shrugging.

He nods. "Marysia has balls."

Five

Toronto, October 2010

Waiting for the green light, I'm balancing delicately on my pedals when my phone rings in my jacket pocket. I step to the curb—Tahira, my grandmother's neighbor.

"Josephine, Irena fell down. Can you come?"

My brain stumbles through a cascade of questions. "How is she?"

"I don't know. I see no blood. She's talking, but in pain, I think."

"Call 911. I'll be there as fast as I can. Can you please stay with her?"

It's a short, hard ride south to Irena's house, pedaling against the wind and the pounding of my heart. *She's conscious, there's no blood, she's talking.* All good, but it's her second fall in two months. The last one landed her unharmed on the soft living room carpet, but she couldn't get up, and, without her phone, she was stuck there for hours. It was pure luck that I dropped by.

The ambulance declares itself in the driveway as I wheel my bike into the backyard, the wall-to-wall window giving me a view straight into Irena's studio. Facing away, she's lying on her right side close to her easels. *Shit.* That friggin' wheeled piano stool, that concrete floor. Bending over her is a bulky ambulance attendant. Tahira looks up, raises a hand as I walk by.

I hang up my helmet and backpack on the hooks inside the back doorway, recognize the familiar slowness in my body that accompanies any crisis, giving the completely false impression that I'm calm and in control.

"Hi, I'm Jo, Irena's granddaughter. Can I talk to her?"

"Sure, just a sec."

Quickly, gently, they turn her on her back. She grimaces, clutching her right arm. Not her painting arm, thank God. Her eyes find me and she exhales. I kneel beside her. "I'm so sorry you fell, *Babcia*."

"Jo." Her gaze beckons me closer, her hair brushing my ear. "No hospital. You give me one brandy, I'll be very fine."

Great! Her breath's already boozy enough to set the house on fire. I smooth her hair from her forehead. "They'll just check you out. Make sure nothing's broken." I put my hand on her cheek. "I'll come with you."

ON THE TRIP to Sunnybrook Hospital, I hold Irena's left hand, feel the veins like blue bubbles beneath her skin, notice the paint—chalky blue, lemony yellow—caked beneath her unkempt nails. I stroke her hand with my thumb. *How many brandies did you have today?*

It's been seven years since my grandfather died. My mother was still living in the big house she shared with her parents, and in her fastidious way, Sophie took care of Irena, managing the household by hiring people to clean, garden, shovel, deliver expensive prepared foods. Ignoring Irena's objections, she managed her mother in the same way: regular hair appointments, manicures, pedicures, doctor and dentist visits, the occasional jazz concert, vodka martinis once a month with the Polish old guard—the ones still left from the early days. In fact, my mother managed me as well: scheduled invitations to dinners at fine restaurants where the maître d' knew her wine preferences.

The driver expertly negotiates the potholes and beeping construction machines of the city's mushrooming building projects. When the ambulance finally slows to a stop, I arm myself with a deep breath, look down at Irena, who's waking to pain, stroke her worried forehead. For the time being, we don't have to worry about money. Sophie had enough. Not just what Mati left her and Irena, but as a tenured professor, with her own chair in social work, she had a good salary, a pension, carefully managed investments. When she died, a few years after Mati, she left most of that to me, her only child. There's just Irena and me left—my parents having divorced when I was three; my husband, Frank, fucking off with Marta this June. An embarrassment of losses.

IN EMERGE, THERE'S a geriatric nurse specialist who bosses other staff until Irena gets her own curtained cubicle. She does a quick assessment while another nurse hooks Irena up to a monitor. I'm grateful, until the specialist starts questioning my grandmother.

"What's your name?"

Answer: "You find it in my purse."

"What day is it?"

Answer: Polish swear word.

"Can you tell me how you fell?"

Answer: "Down, like this"—pointing to the ground.

The nurse frowns professionally. "I'll make sure you get some pain medication. A doctor will see you soon." She steers me to an unoccupied wedge outside the cubicle. "How much English does she speak?"

"A lot." I give her the details she needs until the questions get harder. "How many times has she fallen in the last six months?" "What medications is she on?"

I'm saved by a doctor, whose last name Irena recognizes.

"You Ukrainian?"

The young woman nods, gently examines her, dropping in some Polish words here and there. She orders tests, pain medication, and when she leaves,

I feel a bit calmer, although dreading the return of the nurse with the hard questions. When she doesn't come back, I take out my sketchbook and show my grandmother some of my recent doodles, add a few more tiny, grotesque faces, which make her smile. Once her IV is attached, she drifts into sleep. Every part of me feels jumpy. I try some mindfulness breathing and let my mind wander to Stefan and his wartime resistance work. Would he know about Irena and Mati?

I always pledge confidentiality to my clients. Let the person speak openly and the sculpture will reveal the complex truth of the life. In Stefan's case, I'll try not to show by a nod or interjection my sketchy familiarity with the Nazi occupation of Poland. This is Stefan's story, not my grandparents'. He'll be free to wander in the warrens of his memory, free to return again and again to his cherished haunting by his beloved Ola. Unless the son finds fault with the contract.

I pluck my Staedtler pencil from behind my ear, start drawing my sleeping grandmother's face—the prominent cheekbones, large ears, high, curved nostrils, soft silver tendrils coming loose from her bun. Such a fighter she still is. My heart kinks around a new ache: How much longer do I have with her? I can't let anything worse happen. And I can't be a total orphan at thirty-two with not one living relative to love. To love me.

When the orderly comes to take her for X-rays, I walk alongside the stretcher, holding Irena's hand. The technician is quick and efficient and we're back in the cubicle thinking about tea for two when a new face appears. A smiling social worker. Just a few questions—all clearly focused on Irena's home life. But my grandmother's in a frazzle of nicotine withdrawal and won't cooperate. I try to answer most of her questions, fudging the answers when I don't know.

"Does she have someone checking on her regularly?"

"Sort of."

"Is she eating regular, healthy meals?"

"Kind of."

"Anyone making sure she drinks enough water?"

"No."

"Administering medications?"

"No."

"Has she considered an assisted living residence?"

Not bloody likely.

There were more. I feel my face reddening at the memory.

IT'S SEVEN IN the morning when we get booted out of Emerge. Irena's fractured arm is in a cast, her hip miraculously unbroken, painkillers flowing quietly through her veins. I'd hoped they'd keep her for a few days, but no such luck.

Waiting for a taxi with my grandmother soon morphs into a hair-raising experience. First, she insists on getting out of the wheelchair in the lobby.

"Just my arm is broken; not my legs."

She leans so heavily on me, I think, *If she falls now, there'll be two of us back in the broken-arm department*. I thought the painkillers might make her sleepy, but they've given her stamina. Beside me on a lobby seat, she's restless, agitated.

"You buy me some cigarettes. I pay you later."

"*Babcia*, they don't sell cigarettes in a hospital. It's bad for your health."

I have to turn away from the look she gives me to avoid bursting into flames. I'd like to get a coffee, some tea for her, but I can't risk leaving her alone. I offer her a drink from my water bottle, but she turns up her nose. Searching my backpack for something, anything, I find a lemon cough drop, which contents her until she sees a man popping a smoke between his lips on his way out the revolving doors. Her eyes light up.

"Go quick, ask him!"

Mercifully, a taxi driver enters the lobby, calling my name. Outside, he helps get her into the front seat because it's easier than the back. Once inside, she jumps on his pack of cigarettes, and for the duration of the trip home, the two of them happily blow smoke out their windows as if that makes the least bit of difference to anyone sitting in the back. Especially anyone who quit two years ago. *Shit galore*. How did Mati and Sophie cope?

Effortlessly polite, the young driver turns up the volume when she asks, "What is this music?"

"Bhangra." He smiles. "Punjabi music."

It's infectiously danceable, but I'm not in the mood. Irena was seriously dehydrated and malnourished according to the blood tests. The nurse specialist actually used the words "suffering from malnutrition." And then there was the elevated alcohol level. Drowning in guilt, I stick my face out the window, trusting the fresh wind to keep my head above water.

Even as she planned for her imminent death, Sophie was thinking of Irena, arranging for live-in help for her mother. When Irena refused a flotilla of able women, my mother made sure the weekly services would continue. She and I agreed I'd visit once a week and check in regularly by phone—unless I had a baby, in which case my Irena visits might be less frequent. It all seemed to work for the first few years, but one by one, my grandmother canceled every service except the gardening and snow shoveling. She didn't want anyone coming into the house; didn't trust anyone except me and Frank, and gradually even that changed.

Sunlight slants across leggy maples rushing by in a blur. My heart digs its own deep well. Of course it was Marta who had a baby, not me.

Back at the house, after a cigarette and a mug of sweet black tea, which I steady while she sips, I get her tucked into bed, her plastered arm on its own pillow throne beside her. I'm planning a light meal, but she's out like a light before I can close the curtains. *My poor babcia*. Leaning in to kiss her forehead, I spot the crucifix end of a rosary peeking out from under the stack of pillows beside her. Mati's side of the bed. Curious. They've never been religious. Polish Catholics, they raised their daughter to be an atheist, and that's how Sophie raised me. I switch off the lamp, keep the door open. Martin, my father, was

Jewish, but Sophie said he wasn't religious at all until he discovered Buddhism. What's driving my grandmother to sleep with a rosary?

On my way to the kitchen, I pause in the foyer to look up at her magnificent *River Dream* painting hanging on the brick chimney rising through the roof: a black sky dented with lilies of yellow light reflected on a dark green river. When I was little, leaning back to look up at it made me feel like I was levitating.

At the long kitchen table, I have the conversation with myself I've been avoiding all night: Is it time to move back into my childhood home—this beautiful house that Mati designed, with all its memories of life and loss?

Sophie was still working on her PhD when she became a single mom with a three-year-old. With Mati a consulting engineer and Irena working in her home studio, it made sense for us to move into their big house. Until I was ten, I lived on this little midtown island made idyllic by my grandfather's playful kindness. We baked, danced, dug weeds, listened to Sharon, Lois & Bram, laughed and talked with an easy grace. Irena was a different matter.

I had my own corner in her studio where my brush could wander off my small canvas onto the floor, across the baseboards, up and down my own body.

"Show me what you made today," she'd say. I'd roll up my sleeves and show her my painted arms. *"Śliczny!"* She'd smile and offer her bag of licorice allsorts. I basked in her praise.

Once I started school, and Mati picked me up from kindergarten, we'd all have an aperitif together—milk for me—and *kanapki*, little ham or cheese sandwiches with pickle. Then I was allowed to watch my grandmother roll from one end of her canvas to another on her piano stool, wielding a paintbrush or sharp scraper. I remember thinking, *This looks like so much fun.*

My drawing lessons with Irena began when I was six, and though I was disappointed that I didn't have my own rolling stool, I loved "fooling" Sophie and Mati with a simple line that created depth and perspective.

With Irena, I felt the urge to jump from ever-increasing heights with no guarantee she'd even notice. In my bones, I knew if I fell, Mati would always catch me.

Later, in my teens, I understood that I was in awe of my grandmother, but I've never understood the feeling that I'm entwined with her in a way that feels different from loving Sophie or Mati.

Pulling my Staedtler from my hair, I shake my smoky curls about my shoulders. Mati died in a hospital, but Sophie died here, just across the hall, amid a constant stream of friends, lovers, colleagues. They brought irises and peonies all through the winter of her dying. They took me aside for grief counseling. And Sophie had drugs that Mati didn't have—like weed.

I look around the kitchen. So much has changed since those days: nests of dirty dishes on the counter, the stink of unwashed oatmeal pots thick in the air. *Irena needs me.* With Frank gone, maybe I need her. I get up to empty the overflowing ashtray, bag the garbage, notice the half-full Hennessy bottle behind the row of cookbooks on the counter. Was it as bad as this when I visited a month ago? Before that I can't even remember when I was here. Shamefully, I've relied on Tahira popping in from time to time. Irena's never asked me for help. Much good that would have done her. The past four months I've been dealing with the epic shit of Frank and Marta.

I get up to check on Irena, who's snoring fitfully. I whisk the bottle of prescribed painkillers off her bedside table, just in case. In the foyer, as I'm zipping the bottle into my knapsack, my fingers find my recorder. That's when it comes to me: Stefan's eyes remind me of Irena's—blue, shot with an opalescent violet. In my head, I replay the story of his resistance work with Ola in the sewers of Warsaw, his discomforting attempts to be a decent man. Carrying my bag to my old bedroom, I stop at Irena's *River Dream* and remember Mati's warm voice telling me it was a painting of the Vistula in Warsaw, that the yellow lilies were blasts of artillery fire in the night sky.

Back in the kitchen, I fill the sink with hot water, search the cupboards for dish soap, and, when I can't find any, fill the empty bottle with water, shake it, crack a nostalgic smile. It was Mati who taught me to say *Sophie.* Proud that I could call my mother by the name everyone else did, no amount of cajoling could persuade me to call her *Mom.* I think that amused her.

Shit! I stick my cut finger in my mouth, scrabble in the soapy water with my other hand, find the handle of the offending knife. Outside the window, yellow birch leaves fly off the tree like startled goldfinches. *It's just you left, Josephine Blum.* And I've been a completely worthless granddaughter.

I scan Mati's neglected garden, imagining it as it was when I sat at the kitchen table and my toes couldn't quite touch the floor. Back then, when I asked why *Babcia* was absent from dinner, as my grandmother sometimes was, he'd share a conspiratorial smile. "She's a woman of mystery, isn't she?"

How likely is it that Irena, such a sticky guardian of her privacy, would want me living with her again? Yet, neither of us has much choice. Both the nurse and the social worker made that clear: if, in two weeks, nothing's changed for the better in Irena's living situation, they have the right to declare her a danger to herself.

Six

Warsaw, October 1939

A sad parade marches up Marszałkowska Street. Our soldiers make ragged prisoners and seeing them straggling out of the city, weaponless, so many bandaged or on crutches, adds a finality to the long defense of my city.

I left the safety of my home today to join my fellow Varsovians bidding goodbye to their sons and husbands. I want to call out *Dziękuję*, thanking our men and wishing them well, but the dragons are everywhere, ghastly in their perfect uniforms, menacing in their oily black boots that boast of polished cruelty.

Last week when I got home, after being caught in the skirmish, Mama and Lotka demanded to know if I'd been anywhere near the gunfire. I said no, but days after my brush with death, I finally told Lotka. She gasped and crossed herself. Then she gripped my shoulders.

"Why didn't you tell me? I'm so angry with Mr. Godlewski. He's completely irresponsible." She gave me a good shake. "Please, Renka! You must be more careful." I apologized for almost getting shot, feeling the absurdity of my apology, yet also feeling guilty for being the cause of my sister's tears.

At night, as we lay in our beds, her anger returned, aimed at a different target. "If you're going to be like Papa, doing dangerous things and never thinking of your family, how can we ever live in peace? Think how terrible it would be for me and Mama if you got hurt."

I didn't respond, but I lay there thinking, *Maybe I should have kept this to myself.*

I did not ask permission today to wave goodbye to our defeated soldiers. It's time to make my own decisions. Cowering behind that motorcycle was my first time at the center of close fighting. But it wasn't my first time seeing a soldier who'd given his life to his country. My drawings of Three Crosses Square are testaments to that. Yet my feeling of horror at those first Nazi bombings shrank in the knowledge I was doing all I could to help my city. Being caught in a skirmish was different. It was terrifying, and it was exhilarating—until I heard the dying soldier moaning. The dragons' black boots always provoke rage in me, but the splayed feet of the German soldier looked like a boy asleep. Just picturing them lames my heart, and I don't know what to make of this feeling.

Weaving now through the crowd, I stop short before I get to the front. The dragons push us back with their rifles, with their rough voices that seem trained for contempt, as though they're speaking to unruly cattle instead of humans. What is worse is their arrogant certainty that shouting will make us understand them. *Halt! Halt!* Then a sound like *Zurookggg.*

But the language gap works both ways. Beside me, two teenage boys mutter *fools, scum, dogs* in Polish, and when I snigger, one of them catches my eye.

"They're clearing the stage for Herr Horrible's visit," he says, winking at me. He's about to put his finger on his upper lip in the common parody of Hitler, when his friend smacks his arm down. Leery now, I move away from them toward the back of the crowd, pushing through sobbing women and somber men. But a stage is not a bad metaphor, and like it or not, I'm a side player. At intervals along the parade, men in long coats are filming the departure of our soldiers and filming us as well. Do I need ways to disguise myself?

Lotka was right about the Germans' zeal for refurbishing our city, but not in the way she anticipated. A week into October, Warsaw has been Nazified with red, black, and white banners hanging everywhere from lampposts, offices, and palaces. Crimson flags vibrate above the scorched gray buildings, taking proud responsibility for their destruction. *This is what the Wehrmacht can do to your country.* The sun shows its face between two teapot clouds as the last of the parade passes by. I tighten the straps on my rucksack and head for Pani Nowak's bakery to see about a loaf of bread.

WHEN I GET to her flat, there's the usual queue on the stairs, but the mood is strangely hushed. No one talks about the presence of the Germans, the brash motorcycles circling our squares, the rifles resting across shoulders ready for killing, the gray uniforms pacing in pairs at every intersection, the furious cleanup of certain streets that oddly does not take into account the bodies uncovered from the rubble or killed by artillery fire. These, I suppose, are to be left on display while the Führer's cavalcade drives around them.

The queue is moving faster now, and ahead of me is the same woman with red braids, her husky voice in my ear: "I hear the chancellor's coming to celebrate his glorious victory." I can't decide if she's being ironic or excited, so I avert my eyes, and in the process, catch the eye of a girl who subtly nods at me. I blink. Slowly seeping into my brain is the idea that Pani Nowak might be doing more than selling bread and vodka from her private bakery.

When it's my turn, I knock on the door at the top of the stairs and she appears. "Wait," she says, shutting the door, then opening it just enough to show me a photo of a young man in uniform. She slips the photo into a paper packet and says, "Make me a big picture to remember."

"Oh! I'm sorry, Pani." My face crumples in sympathy, but my mind conjures the unwelcome image of the dying German soldier. I shake it off and slide the packet into my coat pocket. She passes me a loaf of bread and waves away my proffered jar. Poor Pani. Mama's lucky she has no sons to mourn.

Outside in the sunshine, I unbutton my woolen coat. Everything's changing so quickly. I can't wait to tell Mr. Godlewski about our departing army. But do I tell him my suspicions about Pani Nowak? *Psiakrew!* I shouldn't be swearing like Mr. Godlewski, but dog's blood, for the first time in this godforsaken war, I don't know who to trust.

Where is Marysia? It would be nice if she were here to explain things, but I haven't seen her since the surrender. When I asked how he knew her, all Mr. Godlewski would say was "I knew her father." I ponder the triangle of Pani Nowak knowing Mr. Godlewski knowing Marysia.

Walking home, I pay scant attention to the posters on the columns of the vacant National Bank—until I get to a scowling caricature of President Starzyński. Gone is the *Citizens! Help Poland* poster. Replacing it is a drawing of a ragged woman cradling her emaciated baby, her arm pointing at Starzyński's face: *YOU did this to our city.* I feel my teeth grinding and spin around, searching for a sympathetic face to share my anger. But people are scurrying by, looking down. Turning my back on the portico, which once sheltered me from sun and rain, I tramp home wondering how I'll survive in a city teeming with dragons.

Do I follow Lotka and try to move forward, appreciating the fact that the bombing has stopped, that water and electricity have been restored? It seems so sensible, yet every atom in my body rebels at this idea. How do I appreciate someone giving me a hand up after they've kicked me to the ground? No, not when Leah and her whole family have had to flee.

At home, Mama is pleased with the bread, but even more pleased with the feast she's preparing for supper.

I hang my jacket on a hallway hook, careful to remove the photo Pani Nowak gave me. In our bedroom, I scan the short note on the back written from son to mother; then I replace the photo in the packet and shove it under my pillow, ready to study later.

Dinner is a joyous affair, at least for Mama. She and Lotka went to Powązki Cemetery this afternoon to mark the anniversary of her father's death, and there, they were surprised by a wild crop of morel under a fallen tree.

"We filled our pockets with them," Mama says, breaking her cardinal rule of not speaking with a mouth full of food.

"But we left some for others," Lotka adds. Our eyes meet, and we grin at Mama's greedy pleasure. I cut the fried mushrooms into tinier pieces and spear them with my fork.

"Our soldiers left the city today," I say. "I saw them marching out. Hundreds of them." I leave unsaid the thought that we are alone now with the enemy. Except for the vilified Starzyński and his cluster of government staff.

Lotka rests her elbows on the table. "Let's not talk of sad things now, Renka. Mama's already been crying at Grandpapa's grave."

I look at my mother, whose mouth is in heaven, and decide to drop the discussion. What's more important, after all? Morels, or news of the German occupation?

When Mr. Godlewski arrives late for supper with a thick slice of bacon that needs only a good rinsing to remove the green spots, our feast is complete.

"Agata," he says, handing Mama a sheet of paper. "This was stuck in your letter box." She recoils from the swastikas emblazoned at the top, and shoves the sheet at Lotka.

My sister frowns as she scans the page.

"Well?" I say.

"It says, 'Tomorrow, every people of Warsaw even small people are forbidden leave of their homes until Thursday or they will be rifled.'"

I burst out laughing.

Mr. Godlewski tucks into his meal. "I got the notice, too; it's funnier the second time around."

Mama scowls at me. "Why are you laughing? It's horrible news."

My unfortunate smile grows wider.

"So we can't leave the house until Thursday?" Lotka pauses her slicing.

Mr. Godlewski shakes his head. "And keep away from the windows. They'll have machine guns on the roofs all along the victory route." He looks down, surprised at his empty plate. "After the long Siege, they know what we're capable of. Right now, they're holding Starzyński and eleven of his council hostage. That way our new Lord and Master can make a tour of Warsaw without every Pole taking aim at him."

"Are they going to kill Starzyński?" I whisper.

He rubs his hand over his shiny head. When he looks up, his gaze is sharp. "This new General Government is starting to register everyone. You'll get a race card, ID, and ration card. Make sure you have your baptismal certificates ready when they call you up. All over Poland, people are disappearing. Professors, teachers, priests."

Our mother makes the sign of the cross.

"The Russians are doing even more," he says, aggravating Mama's distress. "My friends tell me journalists, writers, artists are next." He marches two fingers down the table. "They invite you for a nice long walk in the forest, and you never come back." He circles his grim smile around the table. "This may be the last time you see me."

"Antonin!" Mama lays her hand near his.

"No, no," he says, patting her fingers. "I mean, I have to get away. Very soon."

"Where will you go?" As soon as I ask, I know it's a stupid question. He smirks, but my worried face softens him, and he says, "I'll miss you."

"Will they take me, too?" Mama asks, her hand at her throat.

"No, don't worry about your music, Agata. But make sure you show them your husband's death certificate. They'll come looking for him otherwise, and don't expect—" he says, wagging his finger, and then he freezes. We all freeze. Someone's leaning on the doorbell. By agreement, none of our friends rings the doorbell unless there's danger nearby; to visit, they have their own coded knocks.

"Aufmachen!" The voice comes from deep in the belly. It's followed by more impatient bell ringing.

Mr. Godlewski looks wildly about him. "I'm sorry, Agata." Moving more agilely than I thought possible, he hurries from the kitchen.

Hammering threatens to split the door. *"Aufmachen!"* The sound jerks us to our feet like marionettes. I hear Mr. Godlewski diving in and out of rooms, slamming cupboards.

"Get the ring," Mama shouts at Lotka.

The door handle rattles violently as though someone's trying to wrench it off.

"We have to let them in," I say, looking at Lotka.

My sister and I walk quickly down the hallway clasping hands. I unlock the door, and opening it, come face-to-face with two Gestapo officers, one of them pointing a pistol at Lotka's chest. They step forward, shoving us until we turn around, hands raised, forcing us down the hallway and into the kitchen, where Mama and Mr. Godlewski stand petrified. At the sight of them, Mama gives a little yip and makes the sign of the cross, attracting the attention of the pinched-faced one, who screams *"Hände hoch!"* at her until Lotka tells her to raise her hands. But their real interest is Mr. Godlewski.

The shorter, pinched one motions with his rifle for him to raise his hands higher, while the taller one pats the length of his old body. Removing a flask from one jacket pocket, a spectacles case from the other, he inspects both before laying them on the table. There's a curt exchange in German between him and our neighbor, prompting the pinched one to hit Mr. Godlewski across the face with the back of his hand. A cracking sound, and Mr. Godlewski stumbles back.

I try not to whimper.

We're next. From the corner of his mouth, the tall one says something to the other one, who shakes his head. *"Nein."* The tall one's hands probe our bodies, squeezing, reaching under our skirts, throwing things from our pockets onto the table: hair ribbon, pillbox, pencil stub, acorn. Instinctively, I know that a cringe or cry will invite more elaborate abuse. We keep as quiet and still as our courage allows, while tears mix with blood on Mr. Godlewski's face.

They herd us round the table, where we stand facing each other, hands in the air, while they start a methodical search of the kitchen. Pots, dishes, cutlery, all grabbed from shelves and drawers, vinegar, bacon fat, dried chicory leaves, all flung to the ground, and after, the vacant drawers checked with a sweep of a hand or foot. The tall one keeps his pistol trained on us, while the pinched one takes his time searching the bathroom. Glass breaks against the sink or bath. Then they switch places and the tall one searches the bedrooms and living room.

What are they looking for?

So far, a strange numbness has kept me insulated, but with the sounds of bedroom drawers yanked open, objects thrown about, my heart leaps to my mouth. My drawings! The photo! What if Lotka has something hidden? And Mama's ring. I look at Mr. Godlewski's bloodied nose, and our eyes meet across the table. He wrinkles his brows, adds a slight tip of his head. An apology? My gaze darts to the guard, whose pale eyes are staring intently at Lotka. When I look back, Lotka's made eye contact with Mama, who's jerking her chin at the guard. My sister opens her mouth to speak.

"Offizier—"

"Sei still!"

We all shrink into ourselves.

The search continues in the living room while my eyes travel over the death's head skull on the short one's cap, the trim, belted gray-green tunic, and on the black collar, the lightning runes that signal the SS. Trying to decipher his rank from the little squares and stripes on the collar, I'm startled when the tall one marches back into the kitchen empty-handed. There's a quick exchange before the pinched one growls at Mr. Godlewski. When he lowers his arms, they drag him stumbling down the hallway and out the door. My heart runs after him. *Please don't shoot him!*

Mama collapses onto a chair. Lotka and I remain glued to the ground as though a pistol's still pointed at our heads—until the night wind rushes up the stairs, down the hall and wafts a yellow leaf into the kitchen. Afraid that they'll see me if I close the front door, I run down the hallway to the living room. Crouching below the windowsill, I lift a corner of the curtain and immediately drop it. Across the road, Mr. Godlewski has his back against a car while the short one punches him. I sink to the floor in a boneless heap. When the car roars away, I take a breath and lift the curtain again: no one in sight. The front door creaks in the wind, and I rush to shut it.

Goodbye, Mr. Godlewski. Goodbye.

In the kitchen, I'm shocked to find Mama guzzling the contents of Mr. Godlewski's flask. Numbness clouds me and I can't think of any way to comfort her. "Where's Lotka?"

"Getting the ring."

My sister's sitting on the bed in Mama's room, staring into the mirror of the dresser.

"You didn't find it."

She looks up at me with teary eyes, and shows me the empty jewelry box.

"Want me to tell Mama?"

"No, I'll do it. But not now."

We step into our own bedroom as though the floor is thick with land mines. The first thing I notice is the poster of Witold, our handsome film star, torn from the wall between our beds. The second thing I see is my drawing of the goblin chimneys, laid out with my other sketches like a deck of cards across the desk my sister and I share. I gather them into a pile and hold them to my chest. My pillow's on the bed, but when I lift it, the packet's gone. We stare at our nightgowns and underclothes flung across the floor, some with boot prints on them. A surge of anger reddens my vision, and I dig my nails into my palms until that pain hurts more than any other.

My sister falls to her knees in a fierce fit of weeping that starts my own chest heaving. I take a breath and, leaning down, cradle Lotka's head in my arms.

After a while, she gets to her feet, and we start gathering our clothes from the floor. Beneath a pile of jerseys, I find shredded pieces of the photo Pani gave me. *What do I tell her?*

Lotka pulls our washing basket from the wardrobe and throws everything into it. "They got what they wanted," she cries. "They didn't have to destroy our home."

It seems unlikely that the Gestapo came looking for our mother's family heirloom, and this was not a random raid to abuse us.

"They were hunting for something," I say, "but that something had to do with Mr. Godlewski." As Lotka leaves to check on Mama, I call after her: "Tell her he's alive; they took him away in a car."

Starting the cleanup in our mother's bedroom, I lift an empty hatbox and drop it on the bed. Will they take Mr. Godlewski to Pawiak or bury him in the woods? I can't forestall an image of Leah, hands raised before a Gestapo officer, eyes filled with terror. This is one fear I can't share with Lotka.

I remember my sister sitting me down at the kitchen table when I returned from a visit to the Freemans' home. "It's dangerous to be her friend, Renka. You heard what they did in Eryk's biology lecture? Some students turned against the Jewish ones and beat them up. The professor couldn't stop them."

"And the other students didn't try. Leah will always be my friend, and Mrs. Freeman's promised to—"

Mama plunked a plate of food in front of me. "You're not going back to that house. Last time, you came back with some strange cold and we all got sick."

"Everyone at school had a cold."

"You don't know what kind of germs those people have," and she took my plate away before I could take a bite.

LOTKA JOINS ME on the floor as I match up Mama's many pairs of old-fashioned shoes and gloves.

"He shouldn't have come here," she says vehemently. I can't disagree with her. They could have taken all of us to Pawiak Prison, where we'd be awaiting death or torture. They must have followed Mr. Godlewski and forced open the gate. They knew that he was in our apartment.

When Lotka and I drag ourselves to the grimy task of cleaning the kitchen, we're surprised to find Mama on her knees, scrubbing the floor. *Our mother's stronger than we think.* The thought comes to me in a flash, and the sight of her brings tears to my eyes. My sister grabs some rags, and I half fill a pail from our store of drinking water. Facing each other like cows in a storm, the three of us scrub and wipe, scrub and wipe.

DAYS LATER, NOTHING in the flat looks the same as it did before. Too many broken things. And nothing feels the same. Two SS officers forced their way into my home, into my cupboards and clothes, into my vilest imaginings. They robbed me of my dear neighbor.

Now I go to sleep in my clothes, eyes trained on the bedroom door until I can't keep them open any longer. In brooding visions, I close in on events of that night—the officer leering at Lotka, the flirty gaze my sister sends him. Have I imagined all that? Mr. Godlewski's mysterious signaling with his eyebrows. I replay Mama's silent scream when the officer starts searching her body, and my own anger boiling to burst my skin as I watch him.

Mostly what I feel is a red-black chaos, like a silently raging firestorm. My old loves, my old haunts, don't make sense anymore. I can't bring myself to draw. I start with my favorite charcoal pencils between my fingers, but it's as though my hands have forgotten what to do. Like Mama, I'm afraid to leave the flat. I'm angry at myself. Lotka is the only one who keeps venturing out every day to the hospital. With just a few Polish doctors allowed to practice, nurses are in high demand, especially in the maternity and surgical wards. My sister's training continues; her colleagues and her voluntary work give her great comfort. I have nothing to sustain me. I run my fingers over the three paintbrushes Mrs. Freeman gave me. If I only had some paint.

IN THE CATHOLIC calendar, November is the month of remembering our dead. The Germans have made it easy for us to spend every hour of this month in remembrance. I'm not sure if he's alive or dead, but on our way to Friday mass at St. Anthony's, I'm remembering Mr. Godlewski. He's disappeared, as have several people we know: Mama's doctor and the mother of Lotka's friend Danuta, who was Lotka's old chemistry teacher. Even Starzyński, our dear Warsaw president, is missing, rumored to be in Pawiak Prison, or in one of the German work camps, or already dead.

In the pale morning light, Mama, Lotka, and I walk three abreast for safety. If one of us is attacked, the other two can do something—we are not sure what, but that is our unspoken plan. Our legs are covered in thick winter stockings, Papa's heavy coat hangs loosely on Mama, my sister has her navy pea jacket over her jersey, and I'm swaddled in my old duffel coat and a pair of Papa's trousers, which I've cut short and tied with a belt. Our mother insists that it's harder to attack a woman in a coat and woolen stockings.

Our German occupiers have been grabbing young women off the streets for their brothels. Even mothers are torn from their children's hands and thrown into the back of trucks. On Pani Nowak's staircase, I've heard stories of soldiers pulling girls into doorways to do things that I'm afraid to imagine, yet to my horror, my mind does imagine in more detail than I'm able to control. I hear that it's worse in the countryside and even worse in the Russian-held sections of Warsaw. This is why women need guns. I regret now that I never took up Mr. Godlewski's offer to teach me how to fire one. By now, the dragons must have combed every inch of his flat.

As we walk past the grounds of Fort Mokotów, a relic from other ancient wars, we're jerked about by people running toward the redbrick building. Caught in the growing mob, and drawn ever closer to the fort, which our invaders have made into a prison, the three of us grip each other's hands. Lotka and Mama are twisting around, trying to resist the surge, but curiosity makes me hesitate. Our hands are wrenched apart, and I'm swept forward.

"*Irena!*" Lotka's voice spirals from far away.

Struggling to hold my position, I hunt for Lotka's blue beret, but all I see are pale faces above dark coats, rising and falling like a multiheaded beast. "Lotkaaa!" Are we being herded into the prison? Yet voices near me are excited, eager.

"What's going on?" I yell at the man beside me.

"Execution!" He grins toothlessly as he's carried away in the tide. "Elzbieta and Eugenia!"

Elzbieta! A fire flares in my chest, and I rampage through the crowd, butting and shoving my way forward. *Executed!*

Ahead of me, the bodies are more thickly packed, and I come to a halt. *What could she and Eugenia have done?* I crane my neck, jump as high as I can, and wish I could climb onto the wide shoulders of the man in front of me, but all I see are coats and hats, the smell of damp wool overwhelming everything.

"*Irena!*" From the corner of my eye, I catch a flash of blue struggling toward me. Lotka! Arms extended, she's pressing through when a man grabs her hands and holds tight.

Cholera jasna, I'll kill him.

She pulls back, but he keeps hold, pretending to draw her into a dance.

"Hey!" My voice booms menacingly. "Let her go!"

When I'm close enough, I kick him hard in the back of his knees. Tearing away from him, Lotka grabs my hand and we barrel our way to Mama waving at the edge of the crowd—a string of curses hurtling after us.

When I catch my breath, I find myself with a distant, yet clear view of a raised platform. Mama is transfixed by the soldiers pushing two women onto some chairs, the women's hands tied behind their backs.

"Dear God! Isn't that pretty Elzbieta from church?" She squints. "Her mother's the only one from the old days who still greets me politely."

Lotka regards me anxiously. I hold her gaze and nod. Her hand flies to her mouth.

Soldiers with rifles are swarming onto the grounds in front of the fort. On the stagelike platform, a row of officers in glittering black boots stands at attention. The thin one in the center holds up a megaphone and begins addressing the crowd. We don't understand any of it, but we're paralyzed by the rage in his voice, the gesticulating arm pointing at the two women.

"We have to leave," Mama says, straining to get away before the killing. But it's too late.

Blindfolded, Eugenia's marched to the wall below the platform. Shots ring out, and her body slumps, smearing the wall as it falls. The crowd shivers and groans. Numbness keeps me riveted, and I barely feel it when someone steps on my toes.

A few feet in front of us, a tall young man turns to the group behind him. "Elzbieta's refusing the blindfold," he tells them. The teenagers clutch each other tightly.

"Tell me," I say urgently, catching his attention. "What happened?"

"Elzbieta was caught tearing down a German poster. You know, the one that says 'England, This Is Your Fault!'"

"I hate that poster!"

"Shhh!" Mother glares at me.

He gives her a sympathetic glance before turning back to the platform.

A girl with eyes as liquid as a doe's lays a hand on my arm: "Eugenia tried to stop the arrest. They say she slapped one of the soldiers."

The crowd is heaving like a large animal bucking a tight net. Some people are crying, others are cheering. Here and there, fights are breaking out, and it's harder to see what's happening.

Elzbieta's thin voice rises in our national anthem and is silenced by a round of fire. The crowd recoils, and I have a glimpse of her head above her brass-buttoned uniform, upright for an impossibly long time before it tilts to the ground. Barely aware of Lotka's forehead kneading my shoulder, of Mama's sharp intake of breath on my other side, I follow a swoop of starlings racing across the sky, and for a moment I'm lifted from this place. In front of us, the doe-eyed girl begins to sing, *Poland is not yet perished.* The tall young man clamps a hand over her mouth.

"Come on," Mama says, pulling us away from the loosening crowd. My sister weeps quietly and so do I. *Elzbieta.* Seated behind her family in church, I studied her profile, aiming for that beatific look. Like so many young people, I wanted to be her.

"What a waste," Mama says, wiping tears with her gloved hand. We're marching down the street at a brisk pace. "To die for such a stupid thing."

I swallow my retort. I was just thinking that these two are my first women heroes of the war.

"A disgrace to her family," Mama continues, her hat slipping over her forehead from all her head shaking.

"May she rest in peace," Lotka says, ending Mama's tirade.

"Eugenia, too," I add, thinking, *Who will be next?*

Seven

Warsaw, November 1939

Lying to my mother, I take an early-morning tram to Leah's flat. I'll sleep better knowing that they've fled to a safer place. Next door to us, Mr. Godlewski's flat has already been taken over by a family of Volksdeutsche—Polish people who can prove they have German blood, and who, like our new neighbors' pimply-faced son, now have the right to call the rest of us Slavic scum.

On the tram, I stand swaying at the back—the front seats being reserved for Germans and Volk—shopping baskets overflowing with vegetables, fruit, even flowers in the middle of winter. The women prattle amiably as though nothing is amiss in the world. Hearing this German chorus starts an irritating buzz in my ears that quickly swells to a current burning through my bloodstream. It drives me toward the pit of red-black chaos that I dread. I take some deep breaths, and when that doesn't work, I press hard with the heel of my boot onto the toes of my other foot. Whatever awaits me in that pit is something so terrible I never want to reach it.

When the loudest women have left the tram, I go back to staring out the window, passing beloved old places along the route: Manicelli's pastry shop, the mint-green arch with its art nouveau lettering so broken now it reads *Ma cel.* When Papa was alive, he took us there as a treat. My sister always chose a cream bun, and I chose something different every time: walnut spirals, poppy seed twirls, raspberry *pączki.* Completely untouched is the new Kino Napoleon Film Theatre, which I could never afford to attend until Mrs. Freeman paid for me. Just this May, Leah and I went with her mother to see Loda Halama in *Krystyna's Lie*, and for weeks after, we were dancing and singing "*Lim Pam Pom*" along with everyone else in Warsaw. *Just six months ago.* That silly song can inhabit my head for hours, and I'm sorry now that I've thought of happier times—so recent, yet so painfully remote. Every few blocks, dragons with their rifles crowd the corners and squares of my city.

Arriving at Leah's flat, I stand in front of the solid black door with its brass lion's head knocker now blackened and dull. Few people are out on this once-leafy side street, its elegant townhomes fronted by trim gardens fenced in black wrought iron. Curtains are drawn at both top and bottom windows. Leah and I never established a coded knock. Perhaps we should have. I lift the knocker and let it fall. *Quiet.* I drop the knocker again, and this time, I hear footsteps. A moment while someone peers through the peephole. The door opens.

"Irena! You shouldn't be here."

Mother Mary! They haven't left.

Dr. Freeman pokes his head out the doorway, looks right and left. "Come in. Quickly."

I follow him down the wide hallway, notice the bald spot at the back of his graying head, the trousers hanging from his hips. "Everyone, it's Irena!"

"Ren!" Leah skids round the corner, flies around her father to embrace me. *Mwah, mwah, mwah, mwah.* I find the hollows in her cheeks, the hard curve of her ribs. She holds me at arm's length to get a good look, shakes her head as the corners of her mouth droop sympathetically.

Tears well in my eyes, and for a moment she's a complete blur.

"Come have some tea," Mrs. Freeman calls.

Leah pulls me down the hallway. Its walls were once thick with paintings hung frame to frame all the way to the ceiling—many of them by Mrs. Freeman, and all of them daring, modern splashes of color. Today I notice the gaps, ruby-red rectangles in the intervals between frames.

In the living room, Leah's mother is sitting on the sofa breastfeeding baby Joel. "Irena," she says, smiling and arching a black winged eyebrow. Even now, she's stylish in a way Mama could never be—dangling earrings and black hair cut short almost like a boy's. When I bend to greet her, I'm saddened by the purplish hollows at her temples, her tired eyes. Davey, Leah's younger brother, peeks out from under the sofa.

"See, it's only Irena," his mother says.

"I'll get tea." Leah disappears into the kitchen before I can offer to help.

Toys, books, magazines are scattered everywhere as usual. But the piano's gone. And so is the rich Persian carpet. And so is the Braque painting that held pride of place above the mantelpiece.

Mrs. Freeman's eyes follow mine. She pats the seat beside her, and I sit while she lays the baby in his rocker. "So, tell me, how's your family?"

I tell her about Lotka's work at Infant Jesus, say nothing of our visit by the Gestapo or the bullets that just missed my head. Instead, I find myself voicing my fears about Mama's nervousness, her odd piano playing, her constant disappointment in me that cuts me to my core.

Mrs. Freeman glances sadly at her husband, who pauses his book packing to shake his head. She puts her palm on my cheek and smiles at me as though she can see everything in my brain.

Ashamed of my complaints, I fix them both with a bright smile: "How are things with you?"

"As you see," Dr. Freeman says, and returns to packing his books. Mrs. Freeman picks up the baby, who's started to fuss, and covers him in kisses. Leah returns with a tray and lays it on the leather ottoman.

"Thank you, darling," Mrs. Freeman says. "You two can take your tea in your room if you like."

We leave the pot for Leah's parents and carry the tray up a short flight of stairs to her bedroom. At first glance, the room looks the same as it always has: a large world map on the wall pinned with places Leah plans to tour, a poster of Jean Gabin in a sailor cap above the bed. But the bookshelf's almost empty and the blue and white patchwork quilt stitched with the Star of David has disappeared. She lays the tray on her desk and starts to tremble.

"Oh, Leah."

"Close the door, please," she sniffs. "I don't want them to hear."

I reach for her shoulder, but pause my hand in midair. Suddenly, anything I could say or do seems hopelessly inadequate and intrusive. She stands staring out the window. I move beside her, looking out onto a little park with stone benches and a redbrick fountain, tall evergreens screening the lawns from the street.

"Obviously we didn't leave," she says, tossing her hair over her shoulder. *How long it's grown.*

"Something happened to Papa's connection. So, no documents."

"That's terrible."

"After all our preparations." She tugs a slim gold chain from the neck of her jersey, shows me the crucifix. "I was going to be Krystyna."

I rake my hair back. Could I find them a safe hiding place?

"Things are bad," she says, staring straight ahead. I force myself to be still and just listen: Joel, the baby, has infected lungs, and Dr. Freeman no longer has access to his own surgery, which has been given over to a Volksdeutsche doctor. Leah's father had the foresight to hide some medicines in their home, like penicillin and aspirin, but they've run out. The Polish chemist he's long dealt with was taken in the first swoop on educated Poles, and now her father's risking everything, begging from hospitals he once worked at, doctors and chemists he went to school with. He gets only refusals and threats. She turns from the window and plunks herself on the bed.

"Leah, maybe . . ."

"Please, don't say anything to your sister." She turns to face me. "I know you want to help, but the more people who know about us, the more danger we're in. And, Renka, you may be endangering yourself and your family, too. Promise you won't come back." She sighs. "The Gestapo destroyed my uncle's printing press. My mother's brother was the editor of a Jewish newsletter—it's been exposing the real intentions of the Nazis. They're still searching for him."

I blanch. "Have they been here?"

"Of course, several times. They barge through the door in the middle of the night, shock us out of bed, scream questions at us, even at Davey." Her hands cover her face for a moment. "One of them threatens to put us all in Pawiak Prison or send us to one of the work camps. The other one threatens to shoot Papa in front of us. Then they turn everything upside down and steal whatever they want."

I scrunch my eyes and nod vigorously.

"What? Don't tell me!" I open my mouth, but she says, "No! I mean really don't tell me. I may be forced to name names and . . . And now I've told you too much."

I take a deep breath and puff it out in a gust. A more thorough scan of her room reveals the mending tape on her map and poster, rips in the back of her desk chair, the empty spots where her cherished plaster busts of da Vinci and Michelangelo once stood.

"What happened to your Bohdanowicz?"

She opens the bottom drawer of her dresser, motions for me to look. Inside, the little landscape canvas is slashed in several places. "I guess they don't like women painters."

I examine the damage. "I loved this painting." My hand goes to my mouth as I begin to understand the Freemans' situation. *Mother Mary!* I know nothing about Mr. Godlewski's activities before his arrest. What if the dragons followed me here? I blurt out my worry:

"Do they watch your house? Do they follow you?"

"I can't tell you any more, Irena. Except that they confiscated our car."

The putrid dragons! I stare at my untouched tea. "I couldn't bear to lose you."

She reaches for my hand. "I feel the same."

I give her hand a squeeze. "I miss our Guide adventures." It sputters out like a breath of nostalgia.

"Guides was my second home," she says wistfully.

Our Guide meeting place in the St. Agnes School for Girls is mostly rubble now—destroyed in the last bombings of the Siege, but Marysia, being Marysia, had planned for this event, and we had two soup-making gatherings in our new meeting place at the Art Academy—until the dragons boarded up the entire building.

"I have a crazy idea." Leah spins toward me, hair flying.

I hear her out, sensing that, at best, this cloak-and-dagger scheme will never work, and, at worst, will get us both into deeper trouble. But her eyes are lit up and Marysia taught us to hide in plain sight. It's worth a try.

"Have you heard from Marysia?" I ask.

"Not a word. I hope she's all right."

I wonder again if our intrepid Guide leader might be in trouble. "She said she'd send us a message, but I never got one. Did you?"

Leah shakes her head. "These days it's far too dangerous to meet, anyway."

DOWNSTAIRS, DR. FREEMAN'S walking the sleeping baby back and forth. Mrs. Freeman's resting on the sofa with a magazine in her lap. She waves us over when she sees us.

"Come, you must see this."

We huddle close on either side as she opens the magazine to its center. "Picasso's *Guernica.*" She lifts her raven eyebrow. "The town of Guernica, bombed by Italian fascists and German Nazis during the Spanish Civil War."

Leah and I look at each other. *Guernica* could be a painting of the Siege we've just lived through right here—not just the killing and the dying, but the feeling of hopelessness and terror. Will I ever be able to make a painting like that?

"I hope you're still painting, Irena." Mrs. Freeman smiles as though she's read my mind.

I shake my head. "Thank you for the brushes. They're beautiful, but I have no paint."

"I never thought. Leah, go into my studio and bring my paint box."

I always carry a sketchbook in my knapsack, and *Guernica*'s chilling images give me license to show Mrs. Freeman my last drawing: three women scrubbing a floor in a mangled church with half its crucifix missing, and dangling from the torn ceiling myriad grotesque ears and eyes. She studies it a moment; then she kisses my forehead.

It doesn't matter that the lid of the paint box is crushed, that several of the tubes are dry, others squeezed clear to the cap; there's enough left to send my imagination flying. I spend a glorious hour choosing tubes of oil paint, pouring turps and linseed oil into jars for cleaning and mixing, while Leah and Mrs. Freeman discuss my drawings.

"See the lines on top of lines? The images seem to be traveling through time."

Hearing them talk about my work fills me with such gratitude, I burst out crying and wake the baby. Mrs. Freeman reaches for him and rubs his back.

It's time for me to leave this place. Sad and plagued as it is, it feels more like home than my own home. Leah leads me to the back door, and on the way, I notice a basket of white armbands on a table, the blue Star of David embroidered on them.

"The new fashion for Jews," she says, sounding eerily like Mr. Godlewski. "If we're caught without them . . ." But she can't keep up the pretense. Her eyes tear, and we grip each other's arms, sorrow flowing between us.

"Upstairs with you," I say before she turns and locks the door behind me.

It's still sunny when I step out onto a small paved courtyard—big damp circles where potted plants once stood, black wrought-iron furniture thrown haphazardly about. I open the iron gate and follow a path through tall fir trees into the quaint little park. Pivoting, I look up to see Leah at her bedroom window. I don't wave.

On a bench, a young mother sits absently rolling a pram back and forth, a white armband on her forearm. She jumps when she sees me. I smile apologetically and continue to the horseshoe-shaped wall with its lion's head tap shut off for the winter. When I'm behind the brick wall, I look up again. I can't see Leah anymore, and, behind me, the dense firs screen me from pedestrians on the other side. *So far so good.*

As Leah predicted, a brick—low down and close to the trees—is loose where Davey picked away at the mortar. Poking and digging with my pencil, I slowly wriggle it out. Inside is a tin soldier in a tall helmet. I place the note Leah and I wrote together in the hole, jam the little soldier into my pocket, and maneuver the brick back in place. "*Lim Pam Pom*" pops into my head, but I stop myself from whistling. This is no time for celebration—careening around the corner, a German truck pulls up beside the park. My mouth goes dry. Slowly, I back into the grove of trees.

On the side of the truck is a line drawing of a hand shaking another hand in greeting. Two soldiers jump out. One of them opens the rear and hauls out a lumpy brown sack. The other one calls me over. *Mother Mary!*

I step out from the trees, willing myself not to look up at Leah's window. When I'm a few steps away, one of them reaches into his bag and, smiling cheerfully, throws me a loaf of bread. I catch it. The truck begins to draw people, who run toward it. The young mother on the park bench wheels her pram hurriedly across the grass and reaches out to catch a flying loaf. A man shoves her out of the way.

"This is not for Jews," he hisses in Polish. Stunned, she bursts into tears, which catches the attention of the cheerful soldier, who wags his finger at her. "*Nicht für Juden!*"

My feet move in her direction, but when I'm close, I stop. Will they hurt her if I give her the bread? Or hurt both of us? Stricken, I inadvertently glance up and see Leah. She turns sharply away.

IT'S ONLY WHEN I'm close to home that I remember I told Mama I was going to bring some bread home. I've given the loaf to a boy sitting on a pile of rubble with his head in his hands. Empty-handed at our front door, I give our coded knock before turning the key.

"Hello, it's me."

Mama and Lotka are chatting contentedly in the kitchen. Lotka's eyes rove over my attire. "I'll sew that jersey so it fits you better. You can't go about looking like a ragamuffin."

"You look as beautiful as ever. Sorry, I didn't find any bread today."

Mama gives me her disappointed look. "Thank goodness your sister brought us a delicious dinner."

Lotka slides me a plate laden with half a bulging bun. "One of the doctors invited me and Danuta to join him for lunch."

"At the hospital?"

"The hospital can barely feed the patients. No, at a café."

"Szarlota! Not one of the German ones."

Her earrings jiggle as she shakes her head. "A Polish-German café. I could hardly refuse, Renka. He's my boss."

I look at the pickle sticking from the yellow bun like a green tongue, and my stomach growls in anticipation.

"And here, I saved this for you." She carefully unwraps a wedge of cream bun.

Something perverse in me wants to tell them about my visit to Leah, but, of course, I don't.

"Thank you, Lolo." I throw my arm around my sister's neck, whisper in her ear. "I'm going to save these for later. I have terrible stomach cramps. I need to run to the toilet."

When I exit the bathroom, my sister pulls me aside, feels my forehead. "How long have you had these cramps? Do you have diarrhea?"

"No. Maybe I'm starting my monthly."

"But you just had your monthly."

Cholera. How do you hide anything from a nurse? Deflecting further questions, I take the unusual step of replacing my dishwashing mother at the sink. She jumps at the opportunity to dry while pointing out the many spots I've missed.

Later that evening, I carry my sketchbook and pencils into the kitchen. Placing myself directly in Mama's line of fire is a good way to distract myself from worrying about Leah. We've kept up Mr. Godlewski's custom of listening to the radio after dinner, but now instead of General Czuma's appeals or President Starzyński news, we have Austrian waltzes and German songs, interspersed with Nazi propaganda in Polish: report any suspicious activities and you'll be rewarded; stay clear of germ-carrying Jews; apply for well-paying jobs with German factories at the Deutsche Frank building on Bahnhofstrasse—a street I fondly remember as Jerusalem Avenue, and the building as the National Bank of Poland.

All of it gives me a pounding headache.

Lotka goes to bed early; she has a double shift at the hospital tomorrow. Her gift of food sits uneaten in the icebox, while my warmish tea does nothing to fill my empty stomach. I remember the torment I went through when I found a ration card belonging to Frau Hüber's son lying in the courtyard dust. If I changed the name on it, our calorie ration would jump to over two thousand calories from the starvation diet of one hundred and eighty we're presently allotted. But how could I eat food that comes from the Warthegau or maybe all the way from Berlin? No. Not when Leah and other families struggle to get any food at all.

Moping at the kitchen table, I draw aimless curves and lines.

Mama looks up from her newsletter. "Isn't this wonderful? They're handing out free bread in Arkadia Park tomorrow. Irena, you won't have to go to Pani Nowak's anymore. Her bread always has a bad smell."

How I hate this Nazi pastime of starving us, then feeding us like animals in a zoo. Mama goes back to reading *Prawdziwe*, a propaganda newsletter carefully designed to look like a Polish publication. Following Mr. Godlewski's example, I stick to the underground *Information Bulletin*.

"Pani Nowak's son died fighting in this war," I say, determined to defend her honor. "He was a brave fighter pilot."

"Her son?" My mother frowns at me. "She had only one daughter."

I think back to the photo of the young blond man in a leather bomber jacket. "His name was Marian. She gave me his photo to draw, but the bastards tore it up."

Her reprimand is swift: "Irena!" Sniffing, she flips the page of her newsletter. "It wouldn't surprise me if that woman had a bastard son."

SLEEPING THROUGH THE night is a trick I can't manage anymore. Tonight, I toss and turn, thump my pillow, throw off my eiderdown, pull it up over my head. Is the Gestapo threatening Leah's family right now? Will they come back here? Have they gotten what they wanted out of Mr. Godlewski? I wonder how Lotka can sleep so soundly.

I give up and let my mind wander its own dark alleyways.

Often, I play out terrible scenes of me torturing the Gestapo soldiers who tore our home apart. The one who touched us. Or I drop bombs on the soldiers who shot Elzbieta and Eugenia. I've admitted to myself that if I'd had a gun, I would have shot that man who grabbed Lotka's hands at the execution.

With Mr. Godlewski gone, and Marysia completely silent, there's no one to teach me how to live in this new dragon-infested Warsaw. I need my own psychopomp to guide me through this underworld. It makes sense to return to Pani Nowak's tomorrow. She may know what happened to Mr. Godlewski; she might even know where Marysia lives, and it shouldn't be too hard to make up a story about her missing photo.

I'm getting far too good at making up lies.

I WAKE UP late and drag myself out of bed.

In the kitchen, Mama regards me reproachfully. "Look what the cat dragged in." In front of her on the table sits a hill of potatoes.

I put the kettle on the stove, and frowning, turn back to my mother, peeling potatoes at lightning speed.

"Mama, where did all these come from?"

"Pani Hüber."

"In Mr. Godlewski's flat?"

"Yes. I'm making a pot of leek and potato soup for us." She cocks her head. "She's an elevated person, Pani Hüber. Not like some of these ruffians moving into our neighborhood."

I'm speechless for a moment. "Mama, Frau Hüber is using you. As a Volksdeutsche, she believes she's your superior. Look, now you're her cook!"

Mama's knife clatters to the table. "Must you ruin everything? At least I'm doing something to keep this family alive. Your sister's healing sick children. You are doing nothing!" She smacks the table, her face red with tears.

What have I done? My mother was happy believing that she'd made a friend.

"I'm sorry, Mama. I'll find work, I promise."

FIFTEEN MINUTES LATER, bulked up in my trousers, boots, jacket, Papa's scarf wound around my neck, his tweed cap on my head, I set out for Pani Nowak's. With Lotka bringing home delicacies from her café invitations, and Mama befriending Pani Hüber, we may no longer need Pani Nowak's bread. But that's not the reason I need to see her. I pull my cap down and walk faster, pleased that my disguise not only shields me from unwanted stares, it also causes people to step hurriedly out of my way.

At Pani's flat, I mount the eerily empty staircase, passing through ghostly echoes of bantering, bartering voices. *Is she in mourning for her son?* At the top, I pause at the door and give the coded knock. A long silence. I take a breath, ready to try again, but before I can exhale, the door is wrenched open and Marysia stands glaring at me.

"Where have you been? I've been waiting for you!"

Confused, but pretending not to be, I follow Marysia into the front room—a rumble-tumble mix of dark wood furniture, dusty cushions, and even dustier velvet curtains trailing tassels on the floor.

"Sit," she says, indicating a tapestry armchair. The chair dramatically reclines, sending my legs into the air.

She speaks rapidly, impatiently. "First, nothing you hear or see in this flat can be told to anyone, not Leah or your mother or anyone else. Swear with your Guide salute."

I hold the three-finger salute to my heart. "I swear."

"This Guide meeting is by invitation only. Come on."

"Marysia," I whisper, dismounting over the arm of the chair. "About Mr. Godlewski . . ."

"Not now. The others are waiting."

I follow her down a passage to the kitchen with its tall oven against one wall, and, on the other, a vodka still attached to the sink by a hose. She puts her hands on the paneled wall to the right of the oven and slides that section aside. We enter a little vestibule as spare and clean as the front room is cluttered and dirty.

"Take off your boots, hang your coat up there."

I place my boots in line with the others on a mat, grimacing at my big toes poking through my socks. I hear an excited murmur before I see the girls sitting cross-legged on the floor of the long room beyond. Smiling, I take a place between sisters Małgorzata and Edyta, who laugh and shake their heads at my baggy trousers and stretched jersey. I mime Charlie Chaplin straightening his tie, but our focus quickly narrows as Marysia moves to the blackboard hanging on the far wall.

"We have one more girl to come, but I'm going to begin so you can all get home before anyone gets suspicious." She rolls up the sleeves of her Guide blouse.

"Once again, congratulations for solving the clues in the invitation. Every single one of you passed the test with flying colors, confirming my faith in your ability."

I feel my face reddening and cast a sidelong glance at Małgorzata, whose cheek is dimpling as though she knows I'm an impostor.

"Because you've all taken the oath of secrecy," Marysia continues, "I will make two announcements tonight, after which you'll have an important decision to make."

Anticipation streams round our circle like an electric current.

"Despite the Nazis' occupation of our country, the Polish state continues functioning in all capacities underground." Marysia points her ruler at a chart on the board. "At the top, we have our national government and military rulers in exile in Britain, then we have our local government and military here in the capital, and then—and this is the magnificent part—our schools and universities are continuing in secret, our presses still running, church masses, courts and theaters, art galleries, everything run by civilians. One thing you—"

Edyta has her hand up.

"Yes, what is it?"

"Does that mean I can continue my legal studies?"

"Of course."

"And what about me? I was going to be a social worker," Jadwiga says.

"Of course. If we have professors or senior students in your field, we will organize a class. Before you leave today, I'll make a list of every girl who wants to continue her studies. You'll be contacted by the professors."

"But who is this 'we'?" Heads spin toward a girl I don't know, bouncing her nervous knees.

"Good question." Animated by her own rhetoric, our Guide leader waves her arms about. "'We' is Guides and Scouts, yes, but also mothers and war veterans and—"

Loud knocking interrupts her speech.

"Wait here. In silence." She turns off the light and hurries out, sliding the heavy door behind her. A few moments later, we hear mumblings in the front room and then footsteps. The door slides open again, and she enters, followed by—Lotka! I hear my sister's gentle voice: ". . . snowing heavily. Boots?"

Tentative in the doorway, Lotka looks about before settling in the space Małgorzata and I have made for her.

"Excuse my lateness," she says softly to the group. "I just finished work."

I nudge her shoulder, and she gives me a little smile.

Marysia resumes her speech, but I'm not following her. My heart is jousting with shameful feelings: resentment, possessiveness. So Lotka also got a secret invitation. She said nothing about it. Or did she look closely at the photo under my pillow and understand it was Marysia? Did she read the writing on the back? Just a simple note, I thought at the time, from son to mother. I paid little attention to the date and numbers above the message.

Pushing aside my thoughts, I hear Marysia's voice blazing with passion. ". . . fishermen, farmers, engineers, poets." She nods at Małgorzata and Lotka. "Doctors, nurses—every patriot who's keeping our country running under the noses of Hans Frank and his General Government hooligans."

My heart soars. Ecstatic voices spark the air, and I know I'm not the only girl who's been longing to hear words like this. It's Edyta who asks the question at the back of our minds: "What if they find out? Won't they execute us like they did Elzbieta and Eugenia?"

Marysia doesn't blink. "It is a risk."

When she calls us up to her desk, I sign up for art classes. Lotka doesn't sign up for anything. When I take my place beside her, she and Małgorzata are deep in conversation.

"Don't you want to finish your diploma?"

Lotka shakes her head. "They're letting me do advanced training at the hospital. I can get my diploma that way."

With the study list completed, Marysia invites us to help ourselves to a mug of black tea from a tall canteen. While Lotka and I are pouring, our Guide leader sidles up to ask my sister, "Who are you studying with at Infant Jesus?"

"We have a team. A nursing sister and two doctors."

Marysia nods, clearly waiting for their names, but Lotka doesn't provide them.

The break over, our Guide leader joins us on the floor, hands clasped before her. She begins the second part of our meeting on a more urgent note.

"Many months ago, I said that you may be called upon to do more for your country. That time has come. I've said that our military leaders are in exile in Britain. Now they're asking Poland's Guides and Scouts for help. I've been given the task of forming a Guide troop that will receive special training. I can't give you more detail other than to say it will be difficult and dangerous. In a moment, I'll ask you to raise your hand if you want to join."

A thrill runs through me.

"Excuse me." Lotka's voice rings clear over the din. "Will it involve any sanitation or social work—for instance, delousing women at the baths, checking on babies?"

Marysia narrows her eyes. "I can't say more at this stage."

My sister nods.

Rising, Marysia claps her hands. "Now, stand, walk about, take a minute to think."

Springing up, I give Lotka a hand. "This is what I've been waiting for, Lolo. A call to action!"

Her body slackens. "Irena . . ."

I spin about, unwilling to hear any objections, longing to be part of the group hugging each other. When I turn back to my sister, she's slowly scanning the room.

"You're just tired after your double shift." I stroke her arm.

Her sad eyes find mine, and I say, "The things you see at that hospital, I can't imagine."

I have to lean in close to hear what she says. "Everyone here could be killed."

Marysia calls us to order, and we all hush. The moment feels charged—as though this short slice of time holds all the future.

When our leader poses the question, my hand shoots up. Only two of our ten decline to join: Edyta and Lotka. Marysia reminds them that, whether they join or not, they're still bound to secrecy by our Guide oath. We hug them goodbye, and they hurriedly tug on their coats and boots. While she walks them to the front door, I stand interrogating my socked feet: *Have I made the right choice?*

When Marysia returns, she draws us into a tight circle. Her words leave no room for doubt: "Welcome. You're now part of the Armia Krajowa, the AK—Poland's Home Army." Brow furrowed, her eyes search our faces. "I hope each of you understands what's at stake in our country. We are not giving up. We are occupied, but we're not beaten. Our job as Guides is to help our army win."

My mind reels. No one talks about beating the Hitlerow anymore. No one dares imagine we could drive them from our country.

I look around—the new girl is fervently saying the rosary. Małgorzata's batting her eyelids at the ceiling. Perhaps, like me, she's already mourning the divide that's opened between her sister and herself. My yes was a yes for Elzbieta and Eugenia, for Mr. Godlewski, for the Freemans. Yet I'll never be able to share this joy with the two people I love most in the world—my friend Leah, and my sister, Szarlota.

Part Two

Eight

Toronto, November 2010

Cheriblare announces her presence with a *prrrrt*, weaving her furry gray self between my feet before settling under Irena's chair. I worried that she wouldn't adjust to this rambling house, but she's left her trademark tufts of fur on every surface. I was ready for my grandmother's irritation with Cheri's catalogue—lap diving, ear licking, belly palpitating, needle claws in your knees—but three weeks in, she and Cheriblare are seriously sweet on each other. I'm shocked at how jealous I feel.

After a dinner of breaded pork cutlets that I improvised from a recipe in an ancient Polish cookbook, complemented by boiled potatoes and coleslaw from the Bulgarian deli, we're seated in Irena's sitting room. During Sophie's day, it was the only room where Irena was allowed to smoke, and, testament to Sophie's continuing power over us, so it remains.

"There, that's better." I've taken the precaution of cracking a window in each room adjacent to the windowless sitting room, letting in the chill fresh air. Ensconced in my usual wicker armchair, I struggle to make room for my wineglass on the round, glass-topped table between us, crowded with dog-eared mystery books—Louise Penny and Giles Blunt. Adding to the clutter are a primeval landline phone and the largest ceramic ashtray I've ever seen.

My grandmother makes an elegant over-the-shoulder sweep of her shawl. The fingers on her casted arm are still swollen, so I light her cigarette with her old Dunhill—engraved *To My Brave Girl. Love, M. 1972*—still working after almost forty years. Then we settle in for our post-dinner cigarettes and silence.

I'm used to noise—stone and wood carving are loud. When I'm working, I often have Patti Smith or Radiohead in my ears. My first week here, I thought these long silences would give me time to stew over Stefan's interview while I waited for Roland to send me his decision; maybe I'd even get stung by the spark of an idea for his grave sculpture. But, no. All I do is follow my grandmother's breathing, her minute gestures that I interpret as conversation.

I refill my glass, upend the bottle into Irena's glass. She does a little dip of her black cigarette holder, which I translate as *Thank you, Jo. And thanks also for that delicious dinner you made tonight, and all the shopping you did today.*

"How long you staying?" A puff of smoke, in fact, a smoke ring.

I return her politely inquiring look. "Not sure. Maybe until your arm's better."

"They said four weeks."

"Six to eight weeks."

It's not the first time we've had this discussion. I've been a complete coward, never finding the courage to tell her about the social worker's warnings, or the awesome help she's been these first demanding weeks. My grandmother now has a dosette for her daily medications. So far, I've managed to curb her brandy intake on doctor's orders—no painkillers with alcohol, and a limit of two glasses of wine a week, a rule we have broken every single day. Irena drinks two sips of water with each pill, far less than the optimum four liters a day. I had a cleaning company come in one Wednesday when my grandmother and I paid a visit to Mati's and Sophie's graves. They promised not to set foot in Irena's studio and charged extra for the heavier-than-expected work in the kitchen and bathrooms. I've been struggling to maintain the sparkle.

"What do you think about getting a cleaner in every two weeks on Wednesday while we visit Mati and Sophie?"

"I hate this idea. These people touch my things, and I can't find where I put them." She butts out her cigarette, plugs a new one in the holder. "You clean the kitchen, I clean my room and bathroom. It's enough. And I see Mati every week. Wednesday is good."

Lighting her cigarette, I smile the wide smile I learned from my grandfather, try some yoga breathing through the smoke haze. It calms the urgent need to run out the front door screaming. By now I'd hoped we'd be sharing chummy family stories or tales of our work woes and triumphs. Disappointment's clouding my reasoning. The fact is, I had no problem tidying our little flat in High Park. Frank cooked, I cleaned. Maybe Irena's right. As for visiting Sophie and Mati—

"I like to see them, too. We'll go to the cemetery this Wednesday." Pleased with my reasonableness, I take it a step further.

"Did you like the dinner tonight?"

She shifts in her chair, adjusts her cast on her lap cushion. "*Nie*. This meat is too hard. Only Mati made good cutlets."

I tamp down my disappointment. "He did—with mountains of mushrooms."

My grandfather's mushroom obsession sends us both into smiles.

The ringing phone wipes my pleasant memory and lifts Irena off her chair. I expect her to answer, but she doesn't. After several rings, I make a grab for the receiver, but it's too late. Not the first time I've noticed this phenomenon.

"You don't answer your phone?" It sounds like an accusation when I'm sure I meant it as a question.

Her silence builds a kind of pressure inside my chest—like a fast-growing storm. "I'll finish up in the kitchen."

"I prefer curry." It's thrown out fast, but I detect a conciliatory tone and my heart does a little leap.

"I love Indian food. We'll finish the cutlets tomorrow; then we can order curry."

"You put the *kotlety* away; we have curry tomorrow."

"Done!" I pick up the full ashtray, pause on my way out. Centered low on one wall is a print of *Mokotów Angel*, probably Irena's most famous painting, and one I used to run past with my eyes closed when I was little.

I turn to ask: "The original's still in Paris?"

She shrugs.

I guess I could google it. I choose my words carefully. "Such a powerful, enigmatic painting."

She doesn't bite.

Shit. Meaningless words, Jo. I step back from the canvas. There's the shimmery blue effect she gets in a lot of her paintings. A detached, almost journalistic perspective, eye level with a body lying half out of a manhole on the street. The upper body rests in a pool of blood—arms thrown forward, face turned from the viewer. Walking away, his back toward us, is a uniformed figure, gun hanging from one hand. I take a deep breath, an involuntary moan escaping the back of my throat. The work's in Irena's characteristic style—modern, primitive. The painting draws me closer, at the same time repelling me. The most troubling aspect is the huge wings on the back of the soldier—muddy green. I turn around and catch her staring at me. Her eyes are huge with fear.

In a few strides I'm beside Irena, my hand on her retreating shoulder.

She shrugs my hand off.

"I'll make a pot of tea," I say. "It's almost time for your pills. And there's cake. You need anything else?"

"I need the ashtray."

IN THE KITCHEN, I fill the kettle, drop three bags of black tea into one of Sophie's snazzy teapots—this one with a pink ceramic tulip for a lid—relegate the leftover cutlets to the freezer. Clearly, pain's plaguing my grandmother. But there's something else. If the kettle whistles—she jumps; twigs from the birch brush the kitchen window—she clutches her chest. On one hand, these seem like her normal trauma fears—as normal as trauma can be. Years ago, Sophie explained that since Irena was caught in the middle of a war, sudden movements, harsh sounds were going to alarm her, and I needed to temper my Keith Moon table drumming. More recently, Tahira told me that her Afghan parents hide behind the furniture whenever the screen door slams. But the look my grandmother just gave me was haunted in a way I haven't seen before. It felt like a plea for mercy. I cut a large slice of *szarlotka*, the Polish apple cake Irena likes—part of my master plan to fatten her up. I tilt my chin at the ceiling, take a deep breath. I'm reading far too much into that one piercing gaze.

Cheriblare greets me with her namesake *bleear* as I carry the tea tray into the sitting room. My grandmother's leaning awkwardly against the side of her armchair, asleep, a cigarette burning in the ashtray. I put down the tray, butt out the cigarette, notice she still hasn't opened the letter she received yesterday. I'd like to stroke her cheek, but I don't. Weeks ago, I touched her spontaneously. Ever since I came to stay, she's marked a border around herself that can't be breached without me asking permission.

In the kitchen, I wash the pans and pots. I've got to get back to my own work. Stefan's contract came through. I suppose the father overruled the son. A familiar excitement flutters my stomach: I've got work to do!

I pull my hair back, lance it with my Staedtler. I'll be seeing Stefan again tomorrow. As for Roland, I'm hoping our curt email exchange is the last I'll hear from him—until I finish the drawing for his father's grave sculpture. I've promised to show him what I've done. So far, I'm coming up blank. Not one twinge.

Cheri pads in and I scoop her up, rub her soft belly. "Is it my turn for a visit? Or you just reminding me of your nightmare snack?" *Oops!* Freudian slip. She gives me a slow green love blink. Down the hall in her sitting room, I hear Irena stirring. I help her to her room, where I get her nightgown ready, backing off when she says, "I can do this myself." Once she's in bed, I'm thinking she'll roll over, go back to sleep, but she puts on her reading glasses, takes out her Giles Blunt mystery.

I raise my eyebrows. "Nothing like a good murder before sleep."

"You should try."

She lets me peck her cheek.

LATER, IN MY childhood bedroom, I stare at the decal of Mother Goose parading across the wall and marvel at her everlasting ability to cheer me up. Still, it's two a.m. and I can't sleep. I'm not scared anymore that Irena's health team might force her out of her home. It's all the other stuff that makes my insides wobbly: entering Sophie's suite, smelling her perfume mixed with the ammonia smells of her last days. Walking into the living room, Irena glued to the hockey game, my eyes latch on to photos of her and Mati on the mantel—heads together, smiling on a bridge in Paris; heads together, smiling by the rebuilt Royal Palace in Warsaw; the four of us under the frothy flowers of the cherry tree in the front garden. That first day Irena and I got back from Sunnybrook Hospital, I removed the photo of Frank and me on our wedding day.

I'm fidgeting these memories away, plumping up my triple-decker pillows, when I hear a sharp cry. I run to Irena's doorway, and, in the glow of the nightlight, see her fast asleep at the foot of the bed, her face washed in tears. I rush back out, grab the big pillows from Sophie's suite, line them on the floor below Irena's bed in case she rolls off. Then I lie on the carpet with my head on one pillow—listening, trying to slow my own fast breathing.

This isn't the first time I've been woken by my grandmother's nightmares. When I was a child, it was Mati who came to rub my back while Sophie talked Irena down. I wonder, did Sophie give her some sort of tranquilizer that allowed us all to sleep?

My first night back in this house, I heard Irena shout out something like a name. I turned on the light and found her lying in a fetal position on Mati's side of the bed, eyes wide open.

"What are you doing here? Turn it off!"

I let her be, let her grieve.

Nine

Warsaw, June 1941

They are a pair of rascals, Mateusz and Zofia. I'm slowly getting to know them now that the three of us make up this unique cell. The way it came about is still a shock to me. At our last liaison meeting in the Vault, Major Marysia approached me with a new idea. We were standing in the bunker beneath the Art Academy, a hideout the Gestapo has yet to discover, when she steered me to an area where large paintings leaned in crates against the wall.

"The colonel and I have been talking about you, and we don't think you should be training recruits anymore. Stay back tonight so I can explain."

Her whispered sentence sent me flying—the head of the sabotage unit knows who I am!—then crashing—they're removing me from this work I love! The rest of the meeting was a blur.

If Guides was once my second home, my resistance troop has become my family—not just Marysia, but the other women in my cell, like Małgorzata and Pani Nowak, whose bakery was our classroom for the months of liaison training before Marysia began moving us from place to place. With them, I can talk about anything. Inside my frosty Mokotów flat, I endure a sort of half-life with my mother's constant disapproval and Lotka's certainty that I'm a misguided miscreant. I can never tell them about my achievements—not even the marvelous fact that within the Armia Krajowa, they call me Lieutenant Irena Iwanowska.

Mr. Godlewski was the first to tell me I had a natural talent for cold blood. In my first weeks of training, I found out what that means. I took to the teachings by Marysia and other senior members like a dedicated scholar—the first time outside of art classes that I've excelled at so many things: writing and interpreting coded messages, identifying warning signs, tracking people and losing followers; memorizing addresses, faces, phone numbers, places, situations; camouflage, signaling, using watchwords and message drop boxes, finding safe hiding places, evading pursuit by vehicle. I now have direct experience in all these skills except the final five: how to handle yourself if denounced, arrested, interrogated, tortured, and faced with execution.

Last November, Marysia invited me to join her liaison training team. As a trainer, I learned that I could lead, that I was good at teaching. So, that night in the Vault, when Marysia said they were taking that away from me, I was devastated.

When she saw the dejected look on my face, she put her arm around my shoulders. "Oh, cheer up, Ala," she said, using my code name, "it's not as bad as you think. We want you to start your own cell."

"My own cell?" Even now, I feel the shock of it. "Why?"

"You're always telling me how safe it is to hide in the sewers. You've taken your trainees into the field, and—"

"Yes, but—"

"We want you to explore the tunnels for the AK—not just for hiding in, but for traveling through."

I finally understood. "Once in the Old Town, there was a raid going on—screaming everywhere. I thought of crawling through the sewer to get away. But I'm almost as tall as you, Marysia. Only a kid could get through those low tunnels."

"They are low. But we didn't choose you for your height. We chose you because you don't give up, you don't faint under pressure, and, unlike most people, you enjoy not knowing what's up ahead. You won't be alone, Ala. You'll have two liaisons under your command."

I raised an eyebrow. "Both short and strong?"

"Well, one of them is. The other is taller than you. Come, let me introduce you."

Before I could protest, she led me toward two people laughing under a lamp. One was someone I knew—the fidgety girl from that first meeting in Pani Nowak's flat. She burst into a big man's laugh and threw an arm around me. "Marysia told us about your sewer plans. I'm Zofia. I've been so impatient to join you."

My sewer plans? Her large eyes held mischief, but I decided it was a mistake to think she wasn't serious.

"And this is Mateusz," Marysia said.

He's tall, stoop shouldered, with thick black hair straggling over his forehead. Meeting those two up close, I remembered where I'd first seen them together: the two young people I'd talked to in the mob at Elzbieta's execution.

In the Vault, Mateusz extended his hand and then pulled it back before I could touch his fingers. "Have you washed your hands recently?"

I couldn't tell if he was joking or serious, but I caught Zofia waiting to see what my reaction would be.

"I like to build up a good layer of germs," I said, keeping a straight face while extending my hand. "If you're the squeamish kind, I wouldn't join this cell."

He has a wide mouth, and his smile stretched so outlandishly, I had to smile back. *I'll have to be extra careful*, I thought, *if he can make me smile like that.*

Marysia stood beaming at us. "I have something special for you." From her satchel, she handed me a large waxed envelope. "The map of Warsaw's sewer system." Her eyes took in our amazement. "We had it cut it into sections and then duplicated by mimeo."

Zofia clapped, but meeting Mateusz's gaze, I saw he understood the great risk involved in stealing and copying the map. Someone in Warsaw's town hall likes us.

THIS MORNING IN Arkadia Park, the sun is fully risen. Behind me, a duck waddles out from the shrubbery toward the pond, trailed by her four ducklings. I smile wistfully at them, and not because I'm imagining a tasty roast. I have that familiar worry: it's an honor training other people, but war is a terrible classroom in which to learn.

I've come close to losing a trainee who spoke brashly to a pair of patrolling soldiers. When they grabbed him by the arms, I calmly led the other two away as though we didn't know him. We could only watch from a distance as they beat him, leaving him bleeding in the square, and challenging anyone who tried to help him. Later, when the soldiers had tired of their little game, I returned with an experienced team. We carried him on a stretcher through the alleys to a safe house, where a doctor was waiting. It took him months to recover.

When I met with Mateusz and Zofia to go over preparations for today, their questions impressed me, and they showed a good level of fear. Today, I'll find out if I can trust them.

Peeling my rucksack off my shoulders, I take a seat on the bench facing the Leda and swan statue, check my watch—coming up to six. When I hear Zofia's husky voice as she rounds the path, I break into a grin: it's easy to tell how much they've learned by how they're dressed today. Zofia has her gloves dangling from a string around her waist, her trousers rolled up to the knee, her long dark hair in a tight braid, and a black beret covering her head. Across her shoulders is her bulging water pouch. The only thing that worries me are the little slippers she's wearing.

Mateusz will have to roll those baggy trousers up when we enter the sewers. Work gloves tucked into the pocket of his trousers, boots on his feet, and tied around his neck the red scarf that sometimes covers his head like a pirate and sometimes covers his nose and mouth like a thief, cigarette stuck in the corner of his mouth.

I stand to greet them. "Clear."

"Clear," they both say.

Good. No one followed them, and I've checked that no one's close enough to hear us except the ducks.

Mateusz takes a seat to my right. "*Dzień dobry*, fearless leader."

Zofia giggles and covers her mouth with her hand. *Did I ever laugh as much at sixteen?*

I find my mood lifting, my nervousness settling, as it used to at the start of a training session. Bending to open my rucksack, I glance up at Mateusz. "Fear can be a good thing," I say, trying to sound stern. "Let's check our kit. Mateusz, you go first."

His hands in his rucksack, he calls out, "Torch, string, rope, wire, extra gloves, folding knife, delicious mushroom and bacon sandwiches, water, and . . ." He pulls out a burlap sack. "I brought presents," he says, winking at Zofia, who bounces on the bench.

He brandishes a thin iron rod about two and a half feet long. "One for you and one for Zofia. This might solve the problem of the tight spots."

The rod is heavier than it looks. I quickly push it into my rucksack, where it sticks out the top. Mateusz explains that if we jam it against the walls in the tunnel ahead of ourselves, we can more easily pull ourselves through.

"Fantastic." I shake my head in wonder. For our first scouting mission, I've chosen a tunnel under Malczewskiego Street that starts off narrow and low before it widens. We discussed ways of squeezing through the tight parts, and this is what Mateusz scavenged from a bombed office building.

A whistling man pauses in front of us to gaze at Leda and her vicious swan. Zofia and I leave first, arms linked. We meet up with a suspicious Mateusz near our designated park gate.

"Did you see that?" he says. "He's throwing perfectly good bread to the ducks." We all shake our heads. What Pole has enough bread to share with ducks?

"Have you packed everything on the list?" I ask Zofia.

She nods. "Yes, and I made these." She removes two green pouches from her bag. "Cut from my raincoat; then I just tie the rubber bands over them."

We stare at her uncomprehendingly. She demonstrates by pulling a waterproof pouch over her slipper and tying it on with a circle that seems cut from a rubber tire.

"Brilliant, Zofia!" Mateusz slaps her on the back. "And you, Ala, have you brought anything special?"

"You'll find out when we're underground. Ready?" I take the lead, and they follow at a sensible distance, managing to keep sight of my father's checked cap on my head even through the crowds on Malczewskiego.

When I reach the sewer cover in front of the fish shop, I pause. The corner's packed—men rushing by with wheelbarrows or sacks on their backs, a woman carrying a dead pigeon by the legs, children chasing each other—but no sign of dragon patrols or slinking black Gestapo cars. Just as it's important to walk leisurely toward German soldiers rather than guiltily spinning around or trying to escape them, our training taught us to hide in plain sight. There might be spies, but a crowd of distracted people, all concerned with their own security, is generally safer than standing out in a clearing.

Zofia and I form a little screen around the cover. With the stream of people passing by us, Mateusz inserts his rod into the sewer cover and lifts it aside. People glance at him, but continue on. Dropping to my knees, I step into the hole, my boot finding the first rung of the ladder. As I'd hoped, one woman is annoyed she has to maneuver around us, but no one pauses to inquire—or take a photograph. Zofia follows nimbly, and then Mateusz, pulling the cover after him. We're in!

I turn on my torch and immediately we're confronted with a narrow red-brick tunnel, the shape of a pointy egg, less than four feet high, freshly sprayed with shit—the stink unbearable. Mateusz pulls his kerchief over his nose.

Zofia kisses the cross on the amber rosary tucked into her blouse. Why not? If this is what we're up against, Mother Mary help us.

I hand my torch to Zofia, pull a stack of felt pads from the top of my bag, give each of them two. "I made these for everyone." No need to mention that I stole the felt from my art class.

"Hmmm." Mateusz is quick to figure them out. He ties the strings at the back of his knees, bends to test the position of the pads in front. "Nice."

"*Dziękuję,* Ala." The pads not only cover Zofia's knees but also part of her shins. She looks up from tying them. "Hey, what about our torches?"

Once more, Mateusz shows his inventiveness. I stand still while he ties the handle of my torch to the front straps of my rucksack, pulling a piece of string he's added to prevent it flopping down. I try not to smile as the kerchief across his face blows in and out with each breath.

With our rods in hand, we take our agreed formation with me leading. I brace my knees against the walls on either side of the shitty rill, stretch my arms forward, ram my rod into the redbrick wall ahead of me and haul myself forward. *Cholera jasna!* I'm immediately grateful for my knee pads, but the hardest part is wrenching the rod off the wall to start again.

I puff out a breath of fetid air. "All right?"

"Yup, it's working."

"Onward, into the slime!"

Our progress is slow, but I can see the merits of the iron bar. What else does this man have up his sleeve?

After an hour, with Zofia hard on my heels, my arms and knees are screaming at me, and I'm having a retching sensation that's so frequent, my diaphragm's aching. How on earth did Marysia think these canals would make a transport route?

The tunnel curves subtly to the left, continues on a downward slant for some time until it widens and the rod no longer jams against brick. I signal a pause and sit back on my ankles.

"How are things back there?" Now I can turn my shoulders to look at them.

"It's not a good place for a picnic," Mateusz says, his voice making a nice echo.

"Not for dancing, either," Zofia says. "Too slippery and too many globs of hair."

Ugh. She's right. I hear her drinking from her leather pouch and wish I'd also strung mine across my shoulders instead of jamming it near the bottom of my bag.

"Want some?" She reaches over my shoulder, and I squirt the salty-sugary rescue water into my mouth. Heaven! Then I hear a distant sound. "Anyone hear water dripping?"

"Yup. At first it was a patter, but now it's more like—"

"A small waterfall," Mateusz says. "Not more of the brown stuff, I don't think. It must be raining up above. Probably a street grate ahead of us. Hey, we can all have a bath."

Zofia roars.

How can such a small body make that sound? But I don't shush her.

"Zofia? Did you bring a towel?" Mateusz asks.

I smile, but I'm wondering if we'll be crawling in brown water up to our thighs, or if, as the map suggests, rainwater filters through a parallel tunnel system, separate from the sewers.

We decide we don't need the rods anymore, and I pass mine back to Zofia, who jams it into my bag, while she passes hers to Mateusz, who does the same for her. He's left to his own ingenious devices. These two clowns have been good so far. Not one whine or complaint.

When we finally come to the intersection, I take the tunnel leading upward to the right, which the map said would lead to the Old Town. This one's newer and bigger than the first, and I'm careful to mark our change in direction with chalk arrows on the brick ceiling.

"I can almost stand up." I turn around to see Zofia stretching, her bent head touching the roof of the tunnel. It might be possible for Mateusz and me to stoop instead of crawl. Would that help my aching shoulders and knees?

"Just don't fall into that!" he says. The central canal is deeper here and filled with filthy black water running downhill. From the regular splashing sound, we must be close to the rain grate. I roll my shoulders, look about. On both sides of the canal are narrow ledges that we could shuffle sideways along instead of trying to straddle the water. I shift my knapsack to my front so the curving wall doesn't throw me off balance. The others follow my lead and we move much more quickly until my left foot smacks into a tight nest on the ledge. I hear a crunch, and my heart leaps into my mouth. I can't get my foot out. Shining my torch down, I let out a piercing scream.

"What is it?" Panic in his voice.

Zofia puts a hand on my arm and peers around me. "Her foot's stuck in a . . . rib cage. Looks human." Somehow, she manages to squeeze by. She bends low and pries the ribs aside, scattering spiders, smashing bones with her gloved fist. My hands are trembling. So much for my cold blood. Still, her quick, methodical movements calm me. When I can free my boot, we kick the bones and spiders into the canal.

"Do you want to continue?" Mateusz's voice is gentle.

"It's a good time for a tea break," I say, letting Zofia lead us to a dry spot. Mateusz helps me off with my rucksack, and the three of us sit cross-legged on the ledge, far too close to the black water. As we're pulling off our gloves, I hiss a warning at Zofia as she's about to tug on a soiled gloved finger with her teeth. Laughing, we do our best to clean our hands with soap and squirts from our water pouches.

"Do you really have tea?" Mateusz's scarf is down, and I'm suddenly conscious of the ironic curve of his mouth.

"What did you bring? Wine?"

"I thought about it."

I smile, but I'm not quite over the shock of the rib cage—the fear of being caught in a trap, something set on purpose to deter us.

Mateusz tilts his head. "I thought you'd stepped into the black brook of death."

I nod, remembering my unearthly scream. Sliding the flask from my bag, I unscrew the cup and pour him tea. He takes a sip and passes it to me. The gesture unnerves me, and I hand the cup to Zofia, chewing loudly on my left.

She drains it, and handing it back, says, "Once my father made us go three days without drinking anything."

My eyes widen.

She pushes a stray lock under her beret. "He had these tests for us. Another day we had to stay up for three nights without sleeping. The worst was when we had to fast for two days while he marched us on a long mountain hike."

I turn shocked eyes toward Mateusz, who nods before biting into his sandwich.

"He had a special test for my mother. He'd scream at her, 'Kneel!' It didn't matter where she was—in the kitchen, living room, even in the street, she had to show her obedience to him."

I put my hand over my mouth, then move it to Zofia's bouncing knee. "That's terrible." I'm afraid to ask what would happen if her mother refused. Maybe she never refused. People are strange—war or no war. But she's speaking about him in the past tense. "Is he still alive?"

"Unfortunately, yes."

There's a lot I don't know about my two cell members. I listen for the dripping water sound. The rain must have stopped because it's quiet save for the stinking stream in front of us.

When my stomach grumbles rudely, we all burst out laughing.

"Eat!" Mateusz hands me half his sandwich and I take it. All I have is a bun with garlic and fat. I unwrap it and offer it to him, but he shakes his head, and then I offer it to Zofia, who takes a bite and hands it back. "Your stomach's still singing. You eat the rest."

I rub my rumbling belly. Most days I give in, but some days I'd rather fast than eat all that ham, roast beef, cheese, even fruit Lotka brings home from her lunches with the doctors, one of whom I suspect has been ruinously courting her. It means that Mama's grass and potato soup is no longer the basis of my diet. Frau Hüber lets her keep a bowl of whatever she cooks for her, and at our liaison meetings, Marysia feeds us as only she can: sometimes pickled carrots with caviar smuggled from the Russian-held area across the river.

"Delicious mushrooms." I smile at Mateusz, packing up his bag.

"He has a secret mushroom patch." Zofia leans across to wiggle her caterpillar eyebrows at him.

I place a hand on her arm to still her. "Thank you for what you did back there."

She rocks dangerously back and forth. "Someone actually died in this tunnel!"

"Then we better move on." Carefully, I get to my feet. My mind begins sorting the possibilities: Maybe someone was killed down here. How long does a body take to decompose? And who or what undid the skeleton? Or did they do the separating before? These sewers make a good hiding place for a corpse.

With me in front, we continue up the canal, Zofia and I playing along with Mateusz's macabre humor as we keep a lookout for the skull and feet. When the climb gets steeper and more slippery, I know we're close to the end. I turn to the pair behind me.

"No noise from here on in."

I wonder if they're as tired as I am. My face feels greasy and strands of my hair stick to my cheeks, yet I avoid touching myself with my gloves and hope Zofia has managed to keep hers out of her mouth and eyes. Almost there. To myself, I recite one of the sacred lessons I've learned: never say it's over until you're safe at home base.

The tunnel widens to a small clearing at the bottom of a ladder, the occasional drip of water coming through the holes in the cover. The tension's almost visible as we wait, listening for footsteps, the special rattle of the German trucks, snarling motorcycles, anyone speaking German. When I raise my index finger, Mateusz climbs the ladder and lifts the sewer cover, swiveling his head around. At the sound of marching, his shoulders jump abruptly, and so do ours. Quickly and quietly, he lets the cover down, motions two fingers walking. A dragon patrol.

Did I take the wrong tunnel? We're supposed to exit onto a quiet residential lane outside the gates of the Old Town. I look at my watch. We've been down here for over three hours. The Old Town streets will be swarming with carts, bicycles, everyone going about their business as best they can in a prison city. I look at these two scallywags making faces at each other. If we can only get past this next trial.

Our ears tune to the sounds above, and Mateusz indicates that he's going to try again. He lifts the cover and then loudly scrapes it aside, launches himself out of the hole, and slides the cover back on. What is he doing?

"*Dzień dobry.*" Another man's voice.

"*Dobry.*" Mateusz's voice. Two pairs of footsteps heading away from the manhole. What follows is too muffled for me to understand, but it sounds like Polish, not German. I look at Zofia. She shrugs. Then Mateusz's voice comes in loud, clear, in a rough accent.

"Don't worry. We're almost finished, so you can stop complaining."

The man says something and we hear retreating footsteps. I bite my lip and wait. Minutes later, we hear Mateusz swearing loudly as he lugs the cover aside. His smiling head appears with a small white cloud above it. I almost laugh—I'm so relieved to see his face.

"We need to get some more tools," he yells gruffly. "You better come up."

I raise my eyebrows, show two fingers marching.

"You missed the beautiful ladies," he says.

I make Zofia tuck her braid in her jacket, roll her trousers down, take off her green booties. She scrambles out.

"And you," Mateusz yells down the ladder. "Hurry up!"

I choke down erupting laughter, pull my cap down, climb up, and reach for his hand. The cover back on, the three of us walk to the end of the lane, where we pause under a hedge of lilacs. Mateusz digs his cigarettes out and offers them around. I shake my head, but Zofia pops one between her lips.

We mill about, almost like any group of sewer workers. Despite the smoke and the scent of lilacs in the fresh air, our stench is intense. Mateusz and I check the soles of our boots, scan each other's filthy faces, wet trousers, stained gloves tied to our waists. Then we turn to look at Zofia, who has magically remained clean.

"What?" she says. "Why are you staring?"

Mateusz trims his smile, averts his eyes. I step away from the lilacs and point down the empty lane at the familiar spires of the Old Town gleaming in the steamy air. We can't be far from Castle Square. The others join me, Zofia throwing an arm round my shoulders. "We made it."

"Let's call this the Rib Route," Mati says.

I laugh, then unthinkingly, reach up to wipe a streak off his chin.

He smiles his wide smile. "Next trip, we cut our time in half."

⚓

MY BOOTS GET a good rinsing under the garden tap, and I climb the stairs with heavy, socked feet.

"Hello!" Mama and Lotka are muted in the kitchen. "I'll be there in a minute." I was careful to wash my face and arms with soap, but now I remove my socks, cap, blouse, trousers and place them in the bag I've hidden behind the living room sofa. I hurriedly pull on the skirt and blouse I took from the bag, aware of the barnyard smell still clinging to me.

Mama's just putting the kettle on the stove when I enter. She throws me a startled look as though she's just remembered she has another daughter.

Lotka's setting out plates for the cheesecake at the center of the table. "Renka! I'm glad you're home." She comes forward to kiss me. "Mama made a fantastic *bigos* stew. We're celebrating my good news. Go wash up and I'll dish out a bowl for you."

In the bathroom, I take no chances. I strip and quickly scrub down, including washing my hair, which I'm convinced is where the shitty smell's coming from. For good measure, I brush my teeth, spray myself with some of Lotka's cologne, and wonder if her good news is about a proposal from this doctor who's been wooing her with cheesecake. I'd like to meet this man, find out what his intentions are. Why didn't she bring him to dinner?

I walk around to Mama's chair, and she allows me to kiss her cheek. "*Cześć*, Mama." If I still stink, she'll be the first to tell me, but I pass the test and take a seat before the steaming bowl Lotka set out for me. "Sooo, what's this good news?"

The two of them exchange a glance. "It's about my work," my sister says. "I've been selected to train as a surgical nurse. And I'll be paid. Just a small amount at first, but when my training's over, I'll make even more."

"Lolo!" I reach across to kiss her and detect a faint scent of roses. "How did this happen? Where are you training? Tell me all of it."

Her face animated, she explains that she'll be moving to the much larger University Hospital under the tutelage of a respected surgeon. "It was getting worse and worse at Infant Jesus. It's terrible seeing children dying like flies and nothing I can do to help. Now I know I'll be making a difference."

Chewing a forkful of *bigos*, I remember Małgorzata, on the verge of completing her medical training, lamenting that Infant Jesus had hardly any money under the General Government. Why keep Polish children alive? In contrast, University Hospital, reserved for the use of German citizens, Volksdeutsche, and German military, has rich coffers. They even support a medical floor for women who cater to the sexual appetites of Nazi officers—mostly young Polish women who've been abducted by this terrible machine the Nazis run for their own comfort while they tirelessly invent ways to destroy ours.

My sister's joy brightens her blue eyes, brings out my smile. "I'm happy to see you so happy."

She nods. "They're hiring more Poles now. Danuta will be trained as well."

I pause with my fork in the air. "Danuta?" Lotka's close friend seems an unlikely choice for a German-run hospital. Her mother was murdered in an early Gestapo roundup of Polish teachers.

"She's an excellent nurse. You have to understand that, for us, sick people are just sick people, Renka."

My instinct is to argue the point. Instead, I rest a hand over Lotka's. "Some lucky people will be saved by your expert care."

Mama looks at me over her new glasses. "Don't forget, Lotka will be bringing home a salary. Thanks to her, our lives are changing for the better."

I nod, waiting for the criticism of me that's sure to follow. It doesn't come.

In some ways it's true that things are getting better. My mother closes her eyes as the cheesecake lands on her tongue. I believe Mama's glasses have also contributed to her lighter mood. Lotka knows an eye doctor who was able to get them for her.

My stomach makes a satisfied noise. *Hypocrite, Irena.* The bowl of *bigos* is scraped clean. Oh, well. When's the last time I had pork sausages?

"Where were you today?" So, I'm not being spared Mama's criticism.

"I had classes. Then I helped out at the fish warehouse, packing fish." Wrong smell, but I say it anyway: "Very smelly."

Lotka sends me a skeptical glance.

"Did you bring anything home?" Mama cuts a slice of cheesecake, sails the plate like a ship toward me. "Fish? A few zloty?"

"I—"

"Renka's still studying, Mama. One day she'll be a famous artist."

Saved by my sister's lies.

THIS SPRING NIGHT, Lotka and I agree to keep the bedroom window open to let in the sweet air—as was our habit before the war. It's been two years since the Siege, but part of me still expects to hear the eerie whine of the Stukas, the blast of a bomb. As for the Gestapo invading our household, there are still moments when Lotka is afraid to enter our bedroom alone and I have to accompany her, assure her there's no one hiding. And, occasionally, she wakes me in the middle of the night to stop me shouting in my sleep.

Lying on my side, facing her, I try to resist pummeling my sister with a hundred questions.

"I thought you were going to tell me about your engagement to some handsome doctor."

She laughs. "No. No engagement, no marriage proposal."

"But you like him."

"He's an excellent doctor. Respected by everyone and so generous with the nurses."

A slippery answer, but I press on. "What's his name?"

"Tarnowski—Dr. Kazimierz Tarnowski."

"Hmmm, such an aristocratic name. Do you call him Kazik? Kazzie?"

"Irena! No more teasing."

Laughing, I turn onto my back, and feel the achy stiffness in my shoulder from yanking my body through the tight tunnel.

"And you?" she says. "Fish packing! You stank of something else when you came in."

"I know." If I could, what would I tell Lotka about my day—the suffocating sewer journey? Nauseating shit in every color? The terror of being lost in an underground maze? Mateusz's wide smile?

She sighs. "I suppose Marysia's up to her old tricks. Promise you'll be careful, Irena."

I croak out an evasive sound.

"But you see how the Germans are rebuilding the city?" She perks up. "The Napoleon Cinema's open again to everyone. Food in the markets, telephones working. Naturally, there are things I don't approve of—the *łapankas* are terrible, but they wouldn't be happening if people stopped stealing or breaking the laws."

"Are you serious? Lotka, people steal because they have no money to buy food. The *łapanka* raids are all about culling the Polish population. Do you know what happens to those people they drag into their trucks?"

"Don't fight, Ren. Please."

I humph and punch my pillow, groan when one tender knee knocks the other one.

We lie in awkward silence before she starts again. "I'm thinking how the money I earn can help us. We should get the piano tuned so Mama can start giving lessons again. We should all get our terrible teeth seen to."

I breathe myself to a soothing voice. "These are all wonderful ideas, Szarlota—in peacetime. But we're still at war—all of Europe is at war, and I can't pretend otherwise."

"I know you don't see it my way, but I want peace in our country, too." Lotka sits up, a pale form in her white nightgown. "Just look at the French. Did they fight until Paris was a hole in the ground? No. They were spared the bombings because they had the sense to negotiate a peace."

"Negotiate? Where did you hear that?" Livid now, I spring upright. "Mr. Godlewski said the French surrendered everything."

"So it's not perfect, but people are eating; and, Renka, artists are still painting."

"Well, those they haven't killed yet." Mr. Godlewski's question seethes in my brain—*Pluck or peck, Irena?* I picture the walled neighborhood in Warsaw—intentionally built as a prison for Jews. Are they at peace? Then there's Elsa, abducted by German soldiers into sexual slavery. Is she at peace?

"That pig Göring bombed the shit out of Britain, and the British are still fighting," I say, on the attack again. "And guess who's leading the British bombing raids on Germany—Polish fighter pilots. They're not giving in, Lotka!" Out of breath, I fall back onto my pillow.

My gentle sister rarely raises her voice. When she does, it unravels me. "Just listen to yourself! Are you still civilized, Irena?"

Mama's rapping on the wall finally stops us.

Ten

Toronto, November 2010

I find comfort in nature's ultimate recycling depots—like this one, St. John's Cemetery and Necropolis, a vast burial ground buttressed by ancient maples, their thinning branches stretched so high, I have to lean far back to see the wind rustling the twigs.

At the gnarled feet of trees, my sculptures tell the story of the people changing underground. A blip in the infinite universe stops beating, starts a new rhythm, never ceases to exist—life, death, life, on and on forever. It's simple science, and it steadies me—like a guardrail beside a precipice.

On my way to inspect Stefan's plot, I stop at Sophie's sculpture, run my hands up the smooth spires twisting together in a shiny zeppelin knot. I worked so long to make it perfect that she died before she saw the finished piece. *Hello, Soph.* I'm happy that my work comes alive in cemeteries. I wave to Mati's sculpture a few rows away. *Irena and I will be back soon.*

Flanked by sprawling beeches, a mossy path leads to the back of the cemetery. This is sloping terrain, little green hillocks leading down to the valley and the winding river beyond. I'm nervous about designing a sculpture for an incline, but Stefan's plot is almost level, with just two root knuckles buckling the low grass. Morning sun slants through the trees. As I slip my hand into the thick diagonal of sunlight, it traces a yellow border around each finger. My feet clear a circle in the leaves.

"Hello, trees."

A decrepit ash tree falters to the left, but on the south side, a catalpa extends pendulous brown seedpods, almost touching my hair. I stand beneath the lowest branch, willing the tree to touch my head. On my toes, I'm about five centimeters too short. Rummaging in my knapsack, I yank out the crazy-quilt cap Sophie bought me. Jamming it on, then fluffing it higher, I try again: a breeze initiates a swooping seedpod, and there it is—contact.

I do what I've done with each sculpture: stroke a tree trunk with my right hand, pat the bark five times. Then I wait for whatever alchemy comes. If I'm lucky, it all mixes together—the tree's invitation, my hands in the soil, the stories I hear from the dying person. In my mind, an image will appear, a revolving 3D drawing of the grave sculpture. Hard to explain. "Talent," my professors at Emily Carr called it. "Freaky shit," Frank called it.

While I wait, I examine the ground Stefan will inhabit—sandy yellow, like much of the soil in this part of the city—prepped by glacier, then water, then crustaceans, then human bodies.

I scan the gravestones. Stefan will have *Frederick Lurie, b. 1824–d. 1852* to his left, an Irish potato famine gravestone, spring-green lichen edging the angel wings. To his right, a shiny gravestone in gray granite: *Mary Balfour Cegielski, 1923–2005*. Stefan's second wife.

Crouching by the elephant leg of the catalpa, I take a close-up with my camera, check the picture, see them: two black flat-head coffin nails and a gnawed bone tucked beneath a root. The trio of artifacts, almost an arrangement, feels disturbing. I take a gulp of leafy air.

The back of my neck is where it usually starts, a faint cooling. From this point on, every breath counts toward waiting.

DRESSING FOR THE windy cemetery, I forgot about the tropical heat of the health center. By the time I arrive at Stefan's door, I'm sweating. He's in his wingback chair, dressed in designer jeans that can't possibly be comfortable, his slippered feet on a matching ottoman. "Hi, Stefan."

Confusion crosses his face.

"I'm Jo Blum, back to interview you for your grave sculpture."

Something triggers his memory, his eyes light up, and he makes that courtly inclination of the head. "Jo. Welcome. You look happy today in your yellow jersey."

I'm blushing and smiling again. The room's as I remember it. Only, instead of freesias, pink tulips bow their heads over the lip of the blue vase. In November. A benefit of owning a landscaping business, I guess. I pull up a chair, position the recorder on the table.

"I went to your land today—the burial ground. It's a beautiful spot. I guess that's why you chose it."

"Oh, yes. And Ola's nearby. I can't remember now. Is she next door?"

My turn to be confused. "I didn't . . . I'll look again when I go back." He must be in his own time—a dementia straddling 1940s Poland and 2010 Toronto.

I smile, and he points his finger at me. "*She* was a true soldier." His body quivers with excitement. "You know we fought together in the Polish Underground." The last fifty years of his life with Mary dissolve in the presentness of Ola and wartime Warsaw. He clasps his hands, speaks directly to the recorder. "In school she used to make fun of our teachers. She could copy their voices exactly, especially our French teacher. You know how they talk through their noses."

I frown. Almost a little recitation.

"She was always braver than me. I was afraid to break the rules. I was afraid to stand up to my father."

"Tell me more."

"He was . . ." A shadow flits across his eyes and silence pours over everything, burying the moment.

"Was Ola a rebel?" I prompt.

"She was. She fought for years with the Armia Krajowa. She was so young, but she knew what to do. It wasn't easy living in occupied Warsaw. You could be betrayed."

"By whom?"

He flings me a sidelong glare. "By everyone, even your own side."

"And you were part of the Armia Krajowa, too."

"Oh, yes. We worked together in the sewers."

"That must have been difficult."

"Horrible. The smell—you can imagine. And the tunnels were four feet high in places. Sometimes we walked through sewage up to our waists."

Interesting. An exact repetition of what he said last time. His memory for the distant past must be on autopilot.

"She died, you know. Somebody threw a hand grenade down."

"Oh. I'm so sorry." Silently, I count to five. "Were you with her that day?"

His eyes look through me. "No. That day I was far away." He makes a grim line with his mouth. "I couldn't save her. I didn't even save her from my father."

A little lamp lights up inside me.

"You needed to do that? Save Ola from your father?" Our eyes meet and he turns away, but not before I feel his wound.

In my interviews with Rudi, even in my casual conversations with Sophie and Mati, I learned to wait for that moment when something surfaces like water from a secret well. Something ugly, but definingly human. Stefan's look fills me with dread.

Aloof again, he crosses his feet on the ottoman. "War," he says, and takes a sip of tea. "It was hard for everyone. Your family must have suffered, too."

A soft creature flip-flops in my belly. Is he aiming at my Jewishness again? I curb my instinct to correct him.

"Where are they from?" he asks conversationally.

"Oh, no." I laugh. "I'm asking the questions, remember?"

He laughs, too, as if acknowledging his own trickiness.

An older man saunters in, carrying a new garbage bag. "Hello, boss. How are you today?"

Stefan gestures at me. "This girl here is digging up my past."

Girl, woman, person.

The cleaner nods. "You the gravestone maker?"

Gravestone, sculpture. I stop the recorder and smile.

"Maybe you make me one, too?" His tone and a roll of his shoulder suggest something lewd. The two men laugh. Time for me to go. I pack up my notebook, recorder, flask.

Stefan smiles politely. "I'll have someone call about your next visit." The boss. Like he's back in his office again.

"I'll call you once I've checked my calendar, Stefan. Have a good lunch."

In the lobby, attendants are setting pots of white chrysanthemums and pink hydrangeas around the lobby. I check the register again: Cynthia, Roland's wife, visited yesterday. No sign of the man with the maestro hair.

Outside, I stop under the giant white pine, smell her nutty bark, pat her gray grooves. Green needles, more like fronds than needles, brush my shoulder. I think we made headway today. That thing about not saving his wife from his father. For a second, a window opened. But a second might be all I need to get that spark at the back of my neck.

Walking to the subway, I button my jacket, tuck my hair under my cap. This commission's proving more complicated than I thought. I googled *Alzheimer's*, found out it's a progressive form of dementia with memory lapses, mood changes, sometimes aggression.

In my sculpting interviews, both Mati and Rudi were talking men, capable of carrying on well into the wee hours. I followed them into memory caves, sometimes coming up against stone walls that seemed to shock them—even though they were reviewing their own lives.

Even with Bradley, nothing was ever linear. All their lives spiraled forward and back like waves, picking up the past and flinging it forward into the present, raking it into a future they hadn't yet lived. Often, the spirals had to do with patterns they'd never noticed before, like Mati's surprise at the repeated randomness of his survival—turn left and die in a bombing; turn right and make it to safety. Or—get rear-ended at a busy Toronto intersection, meet the driver, and form a thriving engineering company with him. My grandfather's life was a sea of blind luck—until lung cancer.

And my grandmother? Last night when I was emptying her giant ashtray, I was surprised by bits of charred paper among the cigarette stubs—ashes of an envelope flap, a melted scrap of photograph.

Eleven

Warsaw, June 1941

Tired from my sleepless night, I'm almost run over by a pair of German motorcycles carving a careless passage through a crowd of people. *That's all I need.* I'm already late for my meeting with Marysia. On Puławska Street, a soldier takes a last bite from an apple and throws the core into a mob of street children, watching in amusement as they claw over it. Also entertained is a young woman who grins and flirts with him. How I hate these people.

In Saski Park, I slide up beside Marysia on the bench, where she's rocking a baby in a pram. Not her baby, but my troop leader has many ways of transporting secret material.

"Clear."

"Clear." We exchange kisses like family, and I take my tattered sketchbook from my rucksack, my hiding place for the map I copied then marked with notes of our successful passage. She slips the folded paper under the blanket beneath the baby's head.

"You look tired, Ala." She smiles at the sleeping infant. "How was the party yesterday?"

"Very good. The children enjoyed themselves, and the celebration ended with everyone getting home safely. Of course, having to play all those games was hard on the parents." I turn to smile at her. "But they're ready to do it all again for the next birthday."

While we talk, I draw the baby's perfect miniature features, the curled fingers and dimpled hands.

An aged couple dodders toward us and stops at the pram, the woman oohing and aahing over the sleeping baby and my drawing. It makes me nervous, but Marysia patiently lies to them until they say goodbye. When they're out of the park, she puts on a pair of glamorous sunglasses, ties a scarf around her hair.

"Let's walk," she says, standing up, and we start a round of the park. "There's news, Ala. Pani's bakery has been forced to close."

Blood drains from my face, but I stretch a smile. "Just the bakery or her special pantry, too?"

"The whole place."

"Too bad." Thanks to Marysia's instincts, our liaison group stripped the hidden classroom of any evidence months ago. Afterward, it looked like a kitchen pantry lined with sacks of flour and tins of yeast. Still, it had a too-neat air about it, a smell of secrecy. "And old Pani?"

She hesitates. "Staying at Pawel's house."

My eyes scrunch tight. No! I try to look relaxed, just strolling through a park in terrorized Warsaw while my brain's buzzing with this catastrophe. If Pani Nowak's in Pawiak Prison, we're all in danger.

"She's a tough nut to crack. But there's a leaky pipe somewhere. It's the only way the damage could have been done."

Ice trickles down my arms. "How much do you know about Zofia's family? She told such a bizarre story about her father."

"You mean about him being at Treblinka?"

My mouth gapes.

"He works there. Her mother, too."

"Are they . . . ?"

"No, they were hired." She adjusts her sunglasses. "They're German, Ala. I wondered if she'd tell you."

German! I'm tempted to tear off my jacket, my cap, completely ruining my disguise. "Another turn round the park?"

"The baby has to eat soon. I only have a few minutes."

I glare at her. "You could have told me."

"She's trustworthy."

Our gaze follows a truckload of armed soldiers racing by. On this side of the park, we're not far from the walls of the Jewish ghetto. My mind drifts to the Freeman family, but Marysia's voice orders me back.

"Carry on with what you started. Make inroads throughout the city."

Gunshots blast from inside the ghetto walls. It's impossible not to cringe. The baby wakes and starts to cry. Rocking the pram as though she's ready to launch it down the path, Marysia's tone is brusque. "As usual. *Cześć*, Ala."

"*Cześć*." I take a deep breath. I can never forget that Marysia's my superior officer.

Who do I share this devastating news about Pani Nowak with? Long ago, it would have been Lotka. Or my liaison troop. On our last sewer journey, Mateusz talked about the AK's failed attempt to blow up a German supply train. The entire cell was tortured and executed. Rumors about a mole flew fast and far. I'll have to watch Zofia.

ꝕ

THIS IS BY far the highest, widest sewer we've been through—the Spa, Mateusz named it. He's standing with one boot on the bottom rung of the ladder. Zofia and I are holding our breath, but not because of the stench. About to exit from our fourth scouting mission, we're being thwarted by sniffing, snarling dogs. Mateusz lets go of the ladder, and we retreat. Growls and scuffling, followed by the cry of a cat or other small animal. Then the sound of two men laughing—*"Guter Hund, Essie!"*—before their boots march back to stop right above us.

We all grimace. I get Zofia's attention, signal all of us back farther in the direction we just came to a wider shelf where we can wait. Along the way, I chalk the ceiling with a danger sign—stylized skull and crossbones, add the outline of a German shepherd dog. A wry smile—my drawing classes are coming in handy.

We speak in low, tired voices. "We'll have to wait for 'Clear.' I give it forty-five minutes."

"What if they're still there?" Zofia widens her eyes.

"I know it's been a long day, but if they're still there, we'll have to go back to an alternate exit."

Mateusz nods, signals with a twirl of his index finger that he's going to relieve himself. We're used to this necessity now, Mateusz being courteous whenever Zofia or I need to crouch.

Lifting my rucksack, I take out my map and torch and a bag of mint leaves. Chewing mint leaves or wild gingerroot is one of Mateusz's helpful tips for nausea. We pick them growing wild in the cloister gardens of abandoned churches. When he returns, I pass around the last of the dried sausage and bread Marysia gave me.

"What else have you been hiding, Ala?" Mateusz does what he always does: keeps his for later, while Zofia and I devour ours. You can eat anywhere when you're hungry with miles to go before you can stop. Leaning against the wall, he smiles his wide smile. "Does anyone have any knitting or crocheting to keep us busy?"

Zofia grins. I think about drawing. I started carrying a small sketch pad and pencil on our sewer journeys.

"What if we all say our favorite places to travel?" Zofia smiles in the dim light, her voice exuberant.

"Traveling out of this sewer is number one for me," Mateusz says. "Number two might be a trip to Moscow, now that our comrades are fighting on our side." He looks at me pointedly. "Are they or aren't they?"

I shrug. "Hard to say." Last June, Germany's invasion of their country was a knife in the back for the Russians. Yet not that long ago the two were allies intent on dividing Poland between them.

Zofia puts her hand over her mouth. “Once I traveled in a truck full of pigs. Me and my cousin, Yulia.”

“Swine pigs?” I ask, wanting to rule out the Nazi kind.

She nods. “We were living in Poznan after the invasion. It’s a very German town. I wanted to get away from my father, and Yulia ran away with me. Our last ride was with a pig farmer, who dropped us off just outside Warsaw. We lived on the streets in the Old Town until Elzbieta found us.”

“Your cous—”

Mateusz catches my eye, shakes his head.

Zofia moans. “She was caught in a *łapanka*. I don’t know what happened to her.”

Silence descends.

After a while, Zofia picks up her thread. “I asked my mother to look for her in Treblinka. Her job’s in the commandant’s office, keeping records. She didn’t find Yulia’s name.” Her voice gets fierce. “My father could probably find out; he works for the SS, but he told Mama, ‘Why should we waste our time. She deserves whatever she gets.’ ”

I have a strange sensation like the ground tilting.

Mateusz shifts against the wall, gives Zofia his open, sympathetic gaze. I pull out my sketchbook, and my pencil moves as it did in the dark cellar—forming the curve of a cheek, the wisps of hair behind an ear, the tranquil hands in his lap. At the back of my mind is the shock that Zofia communicates with her mother in the Nazi terror camp of Treblinka. That her mother shares this communication with her SS husband. As a trained liaison member, Zofia should know what not to reveal. But she has an indiscreet voice. Mr. Godlewski’s advice comes back to me: *Better sure than sorry. Find out more.*

When our wait’s up, I walk alone to the exit and stand listening beneath the sewer cover. The dogs are still there, a woman’s voice speaking in German to two men, most likely the same soldiers with their dogs on a leash. *Cholera!* Perhaps someone reported people climbing out of this sewer? I turn back to give the others the bad news.

THE LIGHT FADES earlier now, and I'm tripping over my own feet as Mateusz and I stumble home—hungry, exhausted, but mostly disappointed that this spacious sewer route has been a dead end. In the tunnel, he asked me to show him my zigzagging alley route home, which could take him most of the way to his rented room.

"I see what you mean," he says, surveying the empty alley. "No room for the black cars. Compared to the canals, the garbage smells"—he sniffs—"flowery."

"Are you always so serious, Mati?" I feel the blood rush to my cheeks. I've changed the whole tone of our conversation.

"My parents were experts in how to worry about everything." He shrugs. "I learned to laugh."

"You lost them too early."

His family lived in Kraków, where his parents worked at Jagiellonian University as cooks. Even so, they were swept up along with the professors in the first purge of educated Poles. It strikes me we have this in common—I've lost a parent and he's lost both.

We carry on, ducking and diving through the narrow alleys behind buildings.

"About Zofia," he says. "Maybe it's out of order for me to say this, but she worships you, like she did with Elzbieta."

I nod. Is it just Elzbieta's execution that makes my gut twist at the mention of her name?

"Zofia's father licks the Nazis' boots, but she's loyal to us. That's what I see."

I meet his gaze as we march elbow to elbow. "It's good to hear your assessment." There, I've turned the conversation back to formalities.

I raise a hand to my tired eyes.

"Don't rub your eyes, Ala." He digs me in the ribs.

I giggle like Zofia before I get ahold of myself. "All sorts of things got mixed up today." Because we couldn't exit close to St. Anthony's, I wasn't able to change into the fresh clothes I hid in the cloister. I sigh. "Father Joseph's garden has that little fountain where I planned to scrub my face, and now I can't even do that. Poor priest."

"Executed?"

"No one knows. The dragons raided his church when the organist went crazy, singing and banging out the Polish national anthem. Almost a year ago now. Normally Mother wouldn't miss Sunday mass, but she had a headache that day. My mother's friend Basia brought us the gory details."

"Elzbieta's family used to attend that church."

That twist again. "Everyone was massacred except a few people. Basia crawled behind a stone effigy of a saint."

"And the priest?"

"They never found his body."

"Hmmm. I like your word *dragons*, Ala. Mind if I steal it?"

"I give it to you freely, Mati." I stop beside a garbage pile, point toward an intersecting passage between two buildings. "This is where you have to turn off. Go straight, and you'll come to the main road."

"*Cześć,* Ala."

I have to look away from the tender look he gives me. I hurry off, determined to smother the unsettling feelings in my chest. This can't be happening now. When we were younger, Leah and I swore that we'd never marry. Passionate love was reserved for our film idols, not the real boys we knew. My present plan involves seeing the Allies triumph over the Nazi war machinery and helping the AK liberate and rebuild Poland; my plan for the future involves making films and art and marrying for practical reasons around thirty. I'm not sure where love comes into anything.

On Krakowskie Street, I pick up my pace when the gray walls of University

Hospital rise ahead. Is Lotka still working? Her hours are strange these days. Even so, I imagine walking up behind her on her hospital ward. *Surprise!* We'd laugh and hug each other.

A sharp pang shoots through me. That could only have happened in the past. I tell myself that my shitty boots and greasy face would be most unwelcome in a sanitary hospital, but that's only half the truth. My sister and I speak carefully to each other now that we've agreed to disagree. We might as well be on an ice floe that's slowly splitting apart, drifting us from each other.

My mind wanders back to Marysia and my urgent need to speak with her about Zofia. My industrious liaison leader has landed a job in the central post office, where officially she's a clerk; unofficially she reads any letters with suspicious addresses such as Gestapo headquarters or work camps. When needed, she and her team visit the culprits—dangerous, but necessary work to roust out Poles who denounce resistance fighters or Jews in hiding. With her tall stories and disguises, Marysia's ideally suited for this work.

Across from the hospital entrance, I give a start—my sister is coming down the stairs with a tall, graying man. She's in her dashing new uniform, a navy and red cloak round her shoulders. He tenderly adjusts it. Lotka looks up at him with one of her dazzling smiles, and I half expect them to kiss. Instead, they wave goodbye as a tram rolls up.

When I see her edging into the crowded tram, I turn my back. I don't like the feeling of spying on my sister.

Twelve

Warsaw, November 1941

In Saski Park, I follow a swirl of dry leaves rising in a funnel of wind, wrap Papa's scarf closer round my neck, check my watch again: almost ten. Marysia's never late. Where is she? Nothing to do but wait and pretend to be absorbed in the art book on my lap. Of course, when I grabbed it off my bedside table, I did not consider that it might be banned—the Hitlerow being averse to this terribly degenerate, immoral form of modern art.

An immense woman waddles toward me, carrying two heavy shopping bags. Her hair is such a brilliant orange color, I have to stick my nose in my book to stop a burst of laughter.

"*Cześć*, Ala."

"*Cholera jasna!*" I move over on the bench.

Marysia pulls out a cigarette, lights it. "The big cheese is very pleased with your progress. Asked me to be sure to tell you."

I nod, wave smoke out of my face.

"I looked into your worry about Zofia. It's true, she writes many letters to her mother." She reaches into her blouse and hands me a sheet of paper. "I made a copy of the latest one."

I open it between the pages of my book, scan it quickly. It's Zofia's intense voice: *Happier than I've ever been, extremely blessed with God's work, loads of important friends.*

I glance at Marysia. "Important friends. You think that's us?"

She taps her cigarette ash onto the ground. "That would be nice."

I go back to the letter. *Promise me you'll find help. If I could be there to protect you, I would joyfully shoot him ten times.*

I stare at Marysia.

"Don't worry, I blacked out that part before I sent it through."

I continue scanning until the end: *If I don't see you again, I'll see you in heaven. Love you love you FOREVER.* I glance up at Marysia. "Protecting her mother from . . ."

"Must be her sadistic father. You could ask her, you know."

"I can't ask if her mother's being—"

She shrugs. "All the letters I've seen are like this. Absolutely nothing about her work on the farm. No hints about what she's growing."

"Poor kid. She's completely on her own."

"Better to be on your own than with a family like that." She grinds the cigarette under her heel.

"What else?" I give her the look Mr. Godlewski taught me: tight lips, clenched jaw, wide, unblinking eyes focused on hers.

"Don't try that on me, Ala. Yes, her mother drops hints about what's happening in that disgusting place—though her letters are censored. That's as much as I'm going to tell you."

She gets up. "I hope this puts an end to your suspicions. Here, I brought you a few things for your next trip." She hands me one of the bags. "Say hello to the chickens." Then she nods in the direction of the ghetto wall, gives me the Godlewski look: "Go straight home."

On top of the bag is a package of fluffy white buns. Hungry now and nursing a reckless, contrary mood, I make a detour onto Twarda Street, where the ghetto wall stretches all the way round to Chłodna. This morning, I avoided

Lotka by staying in bed until she left. Then I rushed out without breakfast before Mama could pester me.

Loping up Twarda, I torture myself by thinking of Leah—that last time I saw her at her window while I turned away the young mother reaching for my loaf of bread. My heart winces.

Months after that, when Marysia explained why the tall, thick walls were being built, I risked a return to the Freemans'. First, I walked to the little park, thinking I'd check for a message in the brick wall. I froze in my tracks. The entire wall was gone, along with the thicket of fir trees, everything paved over except for a patch of grass. Parked in the center was the dragons' bread van. I casually circled the park, noticing the antenna attached to the van's passenger window, swiveling as it searched for the source of the secret radio waves that so maddened the Gestapo, they chopped down anything that might be blocking them.

I pause mid-step. Perhaps it's the word *Gestapo* prickling the back of my neck. I take a breath, lean against the wall of a dilapidated building. When I think it's safe, I wait more, letting my eyes and ears work while my mind wanders back to that last day at the Freemans' flat.

The shiny black door beckoned me; I lifted the lion's head knocker. When the door opened, a bearded man with a belly the size of two pumpkins frowned down at me.

"Can I speak to Leah?"

"There's no Leah here." He was about to close the door when I rashly put my hand against it. "Do you know where they've gone?" Through the half-open door, Mrs. Freeman's paintings still dotted the hallway walls. At the end of the hallway, a woman stared at me with large frightened eyes.

"Dupa wołowa," the man said and slammed the door shut.

Stupid ass, yourself.

There was no point going back. Today the penalty for helping Jews is execution. Bending to tie my bootlace, I listen for breathing close by. Standing up, I scan the area around me: men and women scuttling by—all of them pictures of poverty and neglect, a dragon truck roaring out of an exit in the wall, commotion in the back. That sense again that someone's watching me. Mr. Godlewski's voice in my head: *Right, Renka, best be off.*

I cross back into Saski Park, where the trees are scattering their leaves, ramble toward Dworska, where the Jewish hospital has purposefully been left outside the walls of the ghetto, hug closed storefronts until I make a hard left, pausing in the familiar alley to take in the reek of rotting . . . something. Have I lost my follower? No faces in the bombed-out windows at the back of a once thriving Polish bank. Good. I turn sharply sideways, push my bag ahead of me, and squeeze into the narrow gap between two buildings. Anyone passing in the alley will be visible, but I won't. Anticipating a mouthful of fluffy white roll, I send the bag forward, breathe in, twist around two rusting pipes, and come face-to-face with a small, filthy child.

"Shhh, shhh." A pull on my hand. Long, reddish, matted hair covers most of its face. When it brushes the hair aside, I see the sores around the blue eyes, a head too big for such a tiny body.

"Irena." The cold hand tugs my own. "It's me, Davey."

Mother Mary. I squeeze his hand. "Davey? I didn't recognize you."

He manages a smile.

"How long have you been following me?"

"I saw you in the park," he says, scratching his neck, "but you were with that lady. I followed you, but I kept losing you. I need food." His grip on my hand tightens and he starts to cry, but he quickly checks himself and rubs his sleeve over his face. "Can you help us?"

"Of course, Davey." I pull him close, feel how cold his skin is. "Where's Leah? And your mother and father?" I dig out the package of rolls.

"They took Papa away long ago. I don't know the name, but people say it's a bad place." He takes another shaky breath before he gives the rest of the news. "Leah is better now. We have rooms on Sienna Street. But Joel . . ." He shakes his head.

"Oh, no, Davey. Did he . . . ?"

He nods. "My mother's very, very sad."

I shake my head. But Leah's alive. She could be standing below that electricity wire I saw hanging above the ghetto—the one with the sparrows lined up and free to fly over those walls. He quivers against my side. "You're such a brave boy. You dug under the wall to find food or you came over the top?" I tear open the package, take out a roll.

"Under." He sniffs, shivering in the cool wind. "They put wire and glass on top. Do you have a handkerchief?" I give him the yellow kerchief Mati gave me. He blows long and hard, his eyes on the roll in my hand. "I used to crawl out once a week, but then another family moved in with us and I started going every day. Some nice Polish ladies give us stuff, or . . ."

I nod. I've been tempted to steal an apple myself. "You must be hungry." I hand him the roll. "Does Leah come out?" Imagine seeing each other again!

"Just me and the small kids."

I unwrap Papa's scarf and tie it round his neck. "Better?"

He nods. He's about to drop the roll into a small sack when I stop him. "Eat. There's more for you to take home."

With difficulty, I peel off my jacket and jersey in the tight space, drape the woolen jersey round him while he chews very slowly. Water. I remember Papa's wine pouch in my jacket, squirt the rescue water into his mouth. Swollen gums, missing teeth. "How old are you, Davey?"

"I'm eight."

When do children get new teeth? I stick my hand in Marysia's bag, touch gold: in addition to the six rolls, there's a meat spread—do they still keep kosher?—cheese, pickles, an orange, a small jar of honey. Then torch batteries, a new folding knife, half a bar of soap—an old Polish magazine with an article on painter Beata Bohdanowicz—that was sweet of Marysia—Leah and her mother will love it.

I offer Davey some cheese, but he refuses, content with chewing the roll, and the novelty of squirting water into his mouth. Little by little, I piece together his story.

Dr. Freeman was taken by the Gestapo when they were still in the big house.

Soon after the wall was built, they were forced into the ghetto. At first, they had a nice flat on Sienna, there was food in the ghetto markets, and they had money to buy it. There was a nurse in the ghetto who Mrs. Freeman knew. He doesn't know her name, but she helped Joel. Then the Germans trucked in more and more people from all over Poland who were sick and hungry. Soon his family was ill with typhus—his mother, Leah, Joel, but so far not him. Joel was two when they took him out to the Jewish hospital. Mama couldn't go with him. She cried and cried and got weaker and weaker. Leah was very sick, but the nurse helped her. Mama's still not right. Sometimes she can't sit up. He finds food, and Leah finds medicine and other things. I take it all in—each sentence a cut or a punch.

It takes effort to stay in the present, in this gap with the rusty pipe and the small, hungry child gamely answering questions. My mind keeps picturing the Freemans' living room with its black piano, books on every surface, above all, my exuberant friend, surrounded by her adoring family. Davey's last sentence sends ice up my spine.

"The trucks come every day now to take people away."

Any day, Leah could disappear.

"Thank you, Davey. I want to help. I'm going to write a message to Leah in code." I pull my sketch pad from my jacket pocket. "You know what that is?"

"Like detective comics?"

"Yes, kind of. Leah is going to be Gabin and I'm going to be Wit. Who do you want to be?"

"Mordechai Anielewicz."

Cholera. I was sure he'd choose Superman. Marysia's given me news of Jewish resistance within the ghetto; Davey's just given me the name of the leader.

I wink at him. "He's fantastic, isn't he? But don't say his name out loud. You can give him a comic book name, and you pick a comic name for yourself, okay?"

He nods, thinks for a moment. "What if he's Captain America One, and I'm Captain America Two?"

"Wonderful. We'll call the ghetto the jungle and outside here is—"

"I think the ghetto should be the zoo, and outside here is the jungle." A smile on his grimy face.

"Done. Promise you'll never use my real name with anyone except your family. I'm Wit, all right?"

"And Mama?"

"Mama is . . ." Tears well in my eyes. "Let's make her Queen."

I finish my message to Leah while he goes through Marysia's bag. There's too much for him to take all at once, so we plan to meet again tomorrow. The Freemans' situation is grim, but I'm buoyed by this chance encounter. I'll find ways to help; Leah and I can communicate again, maybe even meet. The possibility feels like sun beaming from behind a dark cloud.

"What section of the wall is the hole you go in and out of?"

He shakes his head. "It depends. Sometimes it's a sewer tunnel."

I stare at him.

THE VAULT IS chilly and so is the mood. No one wanted to be called out for an emergency meeting tonight—after curfew, in the freezing rain.

Marysia, Zofia, Mati, and I sit around a gas heater, mugs of tea that I brought in two flasks warming our hands, but coats, gloves, scarves useless against the cold breeze that mysteriously blows through the cavernous bunker.

"What's happened, Ala?" Marysia shakes ice from her brown fedora.

My gaze travels the circle. I should have planned a first sentence, at least. I clear my throat, make a shaky start.

"Two days ago, I was followed by an eight-year-old—thin, hungry, dirty—a Jewish boy who had dug himself out from under the ghetto wall. His sister is my best friend. We met when I sat beside her in the Jewish section of my art class." Their eyes hold mine.

"She and I were part of Marysia's Mokotów Guide troop. I lost track of the family two years ago. Yesterday, we exchanged messages. Her two-year-old brother has died. She thinks her father was sent to Dachau about a year ago. They have no idea if he's alive. Her mother's dying." I want to add, a more loving mother to me than my own mother, but I can't. My voice gets hoarse as I talk about my closeness to Leah, our shared dreams, her family like a shelter in a storm for me.

I watch Mati and Marysia cringe in the way people do when someone they care about peels themselves raw. Zofia regards me with fierce, dark eyes. I take a breath. "I need your permission and your help to get them out."

There's a long silence in which Marysia closes her eyes and turns her head away as though she's in terrible pain. Zofia draws her rosary from her blouse and caresses the cross; Mati steeples his hands in front of his mouth.

My fingers search for Leah's last message in my pocket: "'Wit, yes or no, you have made us happier than we've been since we got here. Courage, my friend.'"

I brace myself for Marysia's response—*Are you crazy? Do you want us all to die before a firing squad? What makes you think these people are important enough for us to risk our lives?*

Finally, she sniffs and turns to me. "I need more information. First, do they have typhus?"

I'd hoped she wouldn't ask.

She lights a cigarette and Mati and Zofia take that as their cue to light one, too.

"Joel, the youngest, died of typhus. My friend had it, but a Jewish nurse helped her recover. Her mother's still recovering. Her brother's never been sick at all."

Marysia nods. "I know the nurse—Ala Gołąb-Grynberg." She drags on her cigarette, squints at me through the smoke. "If you could get them out, where would they go that's safe?"

"Their former housekeeper in Włochy, Kasha, was ready to take them into her home, but something happened. Soon after, the Gestapo forced them into the ghetto."

"Something happened? That doesn't sound secure enough."

"I know."

"Have you thought about how to get them out—all the way to Włochy from the ghetto?"

"Yes. Through the sewers."

Mati raises his eyebrows, nods thoughtfully.

Marysia gives me her Mr. Godlewski stare: "There are too many unknown elements, Ala. Transporting Jews through the sewers endangers the entire resistance. I'd need the colonel's go-ahead even to explore the possibilities. You've never taken untrained people through a tunnel before, you don't know if they're still infectious, if they're strong enough. We don't know if we can trust this housekeeper or what kind of safe house she has to hide them. Have you considered that taking one family out of the ghetto is unfair to all the rest clamoring to get out? Helping everyone in the ghetto is an impossible task. Have you and your friend discussed these problems?"

I look at my hands clasped in my lap—the nails bitten to the quick. Then I look up at this woman who's coached me through the most gratifying, most dangerous years of my nineteen-year-old life.

"We have. Her brother often uses the sewers to get in and out of the ghetto to find food. Before she was sick, she hid in the sewers twice to escape a *łapanka*. It's not the same as traveling through a tunnel, but it shows a readiness to be in a dark, narrow space. I believe the nurse could verify if they are all well enough and no longer infectious. As for Kasha, I have her address, and I'm prepared to investigate her situation, character, property—all the usual checks. The journey will need careful planning, and I would ask Zofia and Mati to help me escort them. If they refuse, I will take the family myself, one at a time."

Marysia grunts, looks inquiringly at Mati and Zofia.

"We should get them out," Zofia says, as though it's the most obvious thing in the world. "I'm on Ala's team."

I send her a grateful smile, turn to face Mati.

"There's the question of time." His eyes are focused on the ground. "The

Germans are accelerating their murders in Treblinka, emptying the ghetto faster." He looks up at Marysia. "Once you get the go-ahead, we'd have to move quickly." His eyes settle on mine, and I feel an entire army behind him.

Marysia gives him a wry smile. But her look when she turns to me is grave. "You haven't answered my final question."

I bury my chin in the hollow of my hand. As long as I delay my response, I can delay her decision. Eventually, I raise my head. "I can't say if it's unfair to rescue one family. I can only say that these people are my family. I love them as much as my own."

Marysia puffs out her shirted chest. "I make no promises, Ala." She checks her watch; I check mine—it must be almost light outside.

"I'll contact the colonel immediately. I'll also get in touch with the nurse and send a Włochy cell to check on the housekeeper. If the answer's affirmative, you'll have forty-eight hours to prepare your route and your team. If the answer's negative—all of you, obey orders!"

Thirteen

Warsaw, December 1941

Still groggy with sleep, Mati, Zofia, and I start our separate routes to the Blessed Mary drop box. Will there be a go-ahead for this mission or a sharp brake that sends me plummeting?

The air's crisp after last night's snowfall, although most of it has melted, leaving dustings on the roofs of my city. Departing the Old Town this morning, I come out onto a wide avenue with its bombed-out buildings still crookedly standing, black maws where windows used to be, and flapping in and out of one, a white sheet like a flag of surrender. I pause and look around. No soldiers behind me. The street's bustling with trams, people hurrying along with baskets, wheelbarrows. No soldiers to the left. There—on the corner, an armored truck's backing up, dragons ready to jump out and amuse themselves. *Mother Mary!* It might be a *łapanka*. I slip in among the crowd waiting for a tram.

Almost our third year of Nazi occupation, and there's no letup. If anything, their stranglehold grows tighter as they squeeze the life out of anyone they suspect is working against them. But the dragons' worst evils are reserved for Jews. I cross my arms to stop myself from biting my bitten nails. The sentence

Leah and I wrote on the slip of paper I buried in the wall in that graceful park—*We will see our children's children*—rises like a brandished sword.

Today, swaying at the back of the tram along with all the other overheated Polish bodies, I can't help seeing omens everywhere—first, the decimation of the brick wall; then, last night's nightmare; just now, the raid. And into the midst of all this, I'm desperate to drag Mati and Zofia—two resistance colleagues who've become my friends. Maybe the colonel will say no.

Pluck or peck, Renka. Mr. Godlewski's voice in my head. But look what happened to him.

My stop's coming up, and I inch through the packed tram quelling a strong impulse to shout "Poland is still alive!" or some such thing that will get us all killed.

It's a short walk to Blessed Mary, where Mati and Zofia will meet me behind the chapel. Now that so many churches are closed, their grounds, cloisters—even crypts—make good places for clandestine meetings, but you have to be careful. Couples or black-market smugglers are often conducting their own private trysts. The drop box lies in a man-made grotto with a statue of Mary carrying her infant son in her arms. It's small, painted white and blue, and kept fresh by girls and women who go there to pray to have a child or not to have a child—a continuously seesawing female predicament as far as I can tell.

My heart's singing a hopeful song as I walk down the little hill. I move toward the kneeling stone, bend to heave up one end—nothing. Then I try the other end, and there it is—a folded square of white paper. I won't read it until Mati, Zofia, and I are together.

I find them with their hands in their pockets, leaning against the yellow brick wall of the chapel, their faces turned upward to the sun. They make space for me and I show them the piece of paper. "Ready?"

It's in Marysia's favorite Zakopane code, and just three words long. Mati and I bend our heads together. "First word—Yes." Zofia gives a little squeal. "Second word—Begin. Third word—Immediately." I sound breathless as I speak. "There's still time to change your minds."

"I'm afraid you're stuck with me," Mati says.

"Me too." Zofia reaches for my hand and I reach for Mati's. For this sliver of time, with the sun beaming on our faces, I'm happy.

IT'S EVENING BY the time I get home, and I haven't eaten anything except the boiled potato Davey gave me. He watched, smiling, as I gobbled the whole thing—grains of sand, peel, and all. It was a supreme act of gratitude from a child whose most precious currency is food. Thinking about it, my eyes tear.

I hang up my coat, take off my boots, and walk toward the voices in the kitchen, where I'm surprised to find Lotka home so early. She's been working the late shift at University Hospital, but here she is with her arms around Mama, who's looking both angry and tearful. *Cholera.* I should have told them I'd be gone overnight.

"Hello, Renka." Lotka looks up while she massages Mama's back.

My mother's downturned mouth greets me.

"I'm sorry. I should have telephoned." I really have no excuse—we have a phone now, courtesy of the hospital, because Lotka is often called in for emergency work.

My sister shakes her head at me. "Mama's not feeling well. I'm glad you're home." She gives me an arch look. "I told her you were with your Girl Guide friends all night."

"Yes. I was." I put down my knapsack. "What's wrong, Mama?"

Lotka walks toward the icebox. "Have you had dinner?"

I shake my head, sniff the air.

My mother gives me a glimmer of a smile. "We saved some *bigos* for you."

I pull up a chair near her. "I'm sorry you're not well, Mama."

A sniffle. "You warned me," she says, blotting her eyes. "I should have listened to you."

I look at Lotka, who raises her eyebrows, then I turn a sympathetic face to my mother.

"What happened?"

"It's that vile woman next door." She's upright now, her usual indignant self.

"Frau Hüber?"

She gathers her indignation, flings it in the direction of our neighbor's window. "Who does she think she is? Just because she has a German name. My great-grandfather—your great-great-grandfather—was a Prussian count. If we hadn't lost that ring, I would have shown her."

I'm still confused, so when Lotka puts a bowl in front of me, I look to her for help.

"Mama was at the market and ran into Pani Hüber. She was with some of her German friends."

My mother's fist hammers the table. "She had the nerve to pretend she didn't know me. I was standing right in front of her in my new hat. I said good morning twice—in Polish and in German—but she looked right through me as though I was nothing!"

"That's terrible. You're well rid of them," I say, digging my spoon into the rich stew, which Pani Hüber may well have contributed to.

"And that son of hers is an imbecile. I'm returning the big pot she bought me. She can take it and . . ." Lotka and I wait for any number of possibilities, but our mother's run out of steam.

"I'll put the kettle on," I say, taking my empty bowl to the sink. An electric kettle shines brightly on the counter. "Where did this come from?"

"I bought it for us. It's a brand-new model from—" My sister has the grace to stammer. "It's imported from Italy, actually. They don't make them here yet."

Mama's eyes glint. "We don't need her charity. My daughter earns enough to buy us things of the highest quality."

I raise an eyebrow at Lotka—*Italy?* That other fascist country we're fighting against? She ignores me and turns on the radio for Mama's after-dinner classical music program.

My stomach satisfied, I decide to take a bath. I fill the bath with hot water, put in two drops of Lotka's flower-scented bath oil. It's only when my tired muscles are beginning to relax that I think of my meeting with Davey and guilt overwhelms me—but not enough for me to get up out of this wonderful, curing, hot water.

He is a remarkable child. He'd been waiting for me as we planned, in the narrow gap between the run-down buildings. I felt a surge of joy and fear when I saw him, his eyes outlandishly large in his thin face. His hair had been cut as I'd instructed Leah. I'd given them soap, and his face was clean. He was wearing the wool jacket I'd bought for him at the clothing bazaar in the Old Town.

I said, soldier to soldier, "We have the go-ahead, Captain."

He threw his arms around my waist. We had a momentary cry before getting down to work. I went over the list I'd sent Leah: what to wear in the sewers; bring money or jewelry Kasha could trade; bring anything tiny of sentimental value—nothing more. We reviewed his plan for the three of them to enter the sewer. I reassured him that if they could just get past that first section, beyond the ghetto walls, the tunnels would get much wider and higher.

"Fallback to plan B all arranged, Wit." He gave me an adult nod. If they're betrayed or caught, one of his orphan soldiers will leave me a message in the gap by dawn the next day.

I handed him two bags of food to last the next two days—I need them to be strong. I also gave him a note for Leah: *We'll see our children's children.*

Just before we said goodbye, I pulled the dented tin soldier out of my pocket—the one I'd taken from the hole in the brick wall behind their house years before. "This is yours," I said. "I've been keeping it for you."

His small chest rose and fell in a great sigh. His hand closed around the toy, and he jammed it into his trouser pocket.

I stood watching as Davey threaded his way out of the gap; I followed him in my mind across the park to the hole in the ghetto wall, where he'd disappear. Tomorrow the Freemans will lie low. No point taking any risks before the night of the mission.

The ring around the bathtub takes ages to clean. I've gotten so used to rationing—food, water, electricity—I forget I can take a bath whenever I need to. Another Volksdeutsche family moved into the building across from ours, which means that our caretaker is guaranteed coal to heat our two buildings. Once again, I'm benefiting from the dragon occupation while other Varsovians, like Mati and Zofia, are lucky to get any heat. Maybe I should move out—leave Mama and Lotka in peace, out of danger from my AK exploits.

At night in our bedroom, I begin packing one of Papa's hiking rucksacks—bigger than my school satchel and with many canny pockets for flashlights, batteries, a gift of drawing pencils and a small sketch pad for Leah and Mrs. Freeman. For Davey, most of a Superman comic I found in the bin at the back of our building.

I'm counting knee pads when Lotka walks in with her freshly ironed uniform on a hanger. It sends me back to the scene on the hospital steps, and I take a tentative step toward renewing our friendship.

"You look ravishing in that uniform." I slip the knee pads into the rucksack and hope she doesn't ask me about them.

"It's a bit fussy," she says. "Dr. Tarnowski likes his nurses to wear the uniform inside and outside the hospital. He thinks it sends a message of hope and compassion."

"I suppose it does."

Careful not to wrinkle it, she hangs it on the hook behind the bedroom door. "I change into a surgical smock for operations. It has a waterproof apron. A few wipes and it's clean."

"So you like this bloody work?"

She smiles. "It's a dream come true, Renka. I'm learning so much. And the pay will go up as my skills improve."

"And the good doctor—is he still in love with you?"

She surprises me with a serious face. Sitting heavily on her bed, she brushes her hair off her forehead. "He's very sweet to me. Of course, he's much older, but I don't mind. You haven't met him, but everyone says he's very handsome—and he's cultivated, highly respected as a surgeon by everyone, even those outside medical society."

The disapproval I feel melts into tenderness. My sister's face has taken on a quiet radiance—maybe that's what it means to be loved. I reach across to take her hand. "I'm happy to hear this news, Lotka. And you—do you love him?"

"I do. I never thought I'd find someone who cared for me who also understood my dedication to nursing. Most doctors wouldn't."

"It had to be a doctor?"

She smiles a lopsided smile.

I squeeze her hand, but a tinge of fear takes root in my heart. Will they marry during this escalating war? What will happen to Mama?

"And you, Irena. Are you in love with anyone?"

"Me? Mother Mary, no! I don't have time." Yet I feel the blood rushing to my cheeks.

Her pressure on my hand is warm and strong and forces me to meet her gaze. "We're young women living in terrible times, Renka. We deserve some happiness. That's what Kazimierz said to me—'You deserve to be happy.'"

My thoughts immediately fly to Leah and her family. They also deserve to be happy. I withdraw my hand, and rising, pick up my comb from the dresser. Dragging it through my hair, it occurs to me that I'm doing what makes me happy, too. If I can get Leah out safely, I'll be the happiest person in the world. I look at Lotka in the mirror, waiting expectantly for my response.

"Yes," I say. "We do what makes us happy."

SASKI PARK IN December is a maze of bare trees, black from last night's snow. Early this morning, as I pulled on my boy disguise—Papa's cutoff trousers, warm vest, cap—I was shocked to find the trousers tighter around my hips, shorter in the leg, the vest stretched across my breasts. I thought I'd stopped growing. With all these meals I've been gobbling, I'll have to find a new disguise.

I pull up my cap to scan the park. The benches are too wet for sitting, but the winding pathways are full of people trudging in winter coats, seemingly oblivious to the high wall close by. The old man with a cane shuffling toward me turns out to be an actual old man and not Marysia. Where is she? I skirt the edges of the park until I hear a low whistle. Not our usual code. When I turn around, there's a mustachioed man sitting in a truck, smoking a cigarette with the window rolled down. Could that be—? I saunter up. The back of the truck is filled with bedsprings, an old stove, other metal things I can't make out. My idea is to ask for directions, but he starts the engine. "Get in."

Marysia's voice. I climb in beside her and she rolls up her window, takes off down the street, turns a corner, and parks in front of the old furniture factory.

I let go of my iron grip on the dashboard. "That's not your real mustache, is it?"

She lets out a cackle. "Big day tomorrow, Lieutenant. How are you?"

"Petrified. What did the nurse say?"

"The boy's fine. Weak, but all right. Leah's no longer contagious; she's still recovering, though."

"And Mrs.?"

She pauses to scratch her mustache. "She says she's very changed."

I feel a stone plunging inside me. "What do you suggest?"

"Take the boy. Leave Leah and the mother."

The stone hits bottom, sending ripples through my body. I turn away to roll down my window, roll it up again when I've given myself time to breathe.

"I can't do that."

"I'll be frank, Ala. The colonel is eager to see if your cell will succeed. If you're able to conduct untrained citizens through the sewers, especially the distance you're proposing, that would be a great service to the AK and our country. If you fail, if you or any of the members of this mission—Kasha or the aboveground team, your two cohorts—are caught with this family, we hope the Germans execute you swiftly."

I nod. That's only to be expected. I'm struggling to focus when Leah's voice rings clearly in my head: *We* will *see our children's children*. I close my eyes. She's always been braver than me. I shift so I'm facing Marysia, wait until her gaze meets mine.

"We won't fail," I say.

My old Guide leader squeezes my arm.

"Tell me about the aboveground team."

"They volunteered, Ala. Your old cell—Małgorzata and the rest—some of them were in Leah's Guide troop, remember. They've been collecting clothes, food, bedding to take to Kasha. Małgorzata was able to gather some medicines. Once you reach your destination, an armed team will take over from you and escort the family to Kasha. Memorize this password."

She hands me a slip of paper that makes me laugh until I choke.

Fourteen

Warsaw, December 1941

A winter wind kicks up as Mati yanks up the sewer cover. I wonder if he feels this same sense of unreality that's fogging my brain. Am I looking down into a sewer, or am I watching a film of myself staring into a deep black hole? And Zofia—is she a shadow in my dream, or is that her climbing down the ladder, nimble as a cat?

Mati signals me to follow. Tonight, all of us are carrying more than usual. I have two rucksacks—one for me, another for Mrs. Freeman and Leah; Mati will hand Davey his own rucksack. And Zofia has extra food and water. I fumble down the swaying ladder, notice how much warmer it is down here. Tying on my knee pads, I wish I could say I felt anchored, a solid human instead of a ghost. Mati wrenches the cover back, and when he's down the ladder, I shine my torch along the shaft—narrow, redbrick, about five feet high, with a small rill cut into the concrete for the flow of waste. I take a breath.

"One section at a time—that's our focus for this mission," I whisper, keeping my voice steady. "Let's go meet them."

Zofia kisses her crucifix, takes the lead as planned. Following, I pull my kerchief over my mouth and nose. Mati's in the rear, and soon Zofia's crawling forward at such a pace I almost can't keep up. My two bags, one on my back, the smaller one hanging from my front, unbalance me, and I feel like an elephant in a small boat. I expect Mati to crack a joke, but his mood is almost somber, and I wonder if, like me, he's said goodbye to the family he boards with as though he might never see them again.

I kissed Lotka and told her again how glad I was that she's in love with a man who loves her. I gave Mama a painting I made of Papa long ago—smiling in his knitted vest. It made her cry. I'll be back in twenty-four hours, I told Lotka. To Mama, I said my usual, "See you later." She brushed my arm with her hand—the first time in years she's touched me tenderly.

With Zofia, Mati, and I chewing on our own thoughts, an hour passes quickly. Months of sewer exploration have built calluses on my knees and shins, have taught me to crawl with elbows slightly bent, neck straight and floating. I give myself a mental pat on the back, aware that I no longer feel like a ghost—that my straining body's making me real.

"The route ahead looks clear." Zofia's throaty voice. "Almost no shit or garbage—no bones so far, either."

I let a nervous laugh escape—turn it into a cough. "Should be a good return trip with our cargo." *Uh-oh.* Mr. Godlewski's voice in my ear: *No celebrating until you're safely home, Renka.*

We're getting close to the intersection where we'll meet Leah and her family. It's been a long time since I've felt this kind of excitement. Side by side digging trenches, Leah and I thought we could hold back Hitler's forces, but part of us was thrilled just to be laughing and talking together. Our plans for the future grew elaborately, yet always central was the idea of living as painters in France, and along with that, of taking as many lovers as we wanted, of being poor—in a romantic, French way, which was somehow different from being poor in Poland. I'm ashamed that I never invited her to our flat. Mama and Lotka would never have approved, but Leah knew enough about my sorry home life that we never talked about it.

"Can you see the intersection, Zofia?"

"Not yet."

The tunnel's widening. My bags no longer scrape the walls. Almost there.

"I hear something," Mati says.

We pause, quiet our breathing, listen—children's voices, a muffled blur. Sobbing.

My gut clenches.

Zofia switches off her torch, slinks forward. When she reaches the intersection, she suddenly flattens herself against the ground. I back up. She rolls into the curving wall of the tunnel, signals me to move ahead of her.

In the darkness, I can just make out a figure, slouched in the entrance to the ghetto sewer, legs and feet stretched forward into our tunnel. Leah? A small body lying across her legs, sobbing head in her lap.

"Hello?" I wait, but there's no answer.

"Gabin, it's me Witold." I hear a chuckle behind me. *Cholera!* I forgot to tell Mati and Zofia about the code names Leah, Davey, and I have been using. Leah's head peers out from the tunnel entrance.

"Wit! Is that you?" Loud enough to scare the crows.

"Yes. Keep your voice down. I'm turning on my torch."

Davey's head pops up. A pair of blue eyes rimmed red in the circle of light.

"*Cześć*, you two." I shine the torch into the tunnel behind Leah. "Where's your mother?"

Davey chokes on a cry. Leah strokes his hair. "She's not here." Her voice echoes in the tunnel. "She pretended she was coming. Then, at the last minute, she made the boys push the cover over our heads."

Mother Mary.

"Davey heard her say goodbye, didn't you, *bubala*?"

He sobs into his sister's knees.

I crawl to them, shrug off my rucksacks with Zofia's help, and sit back on my heels.

"I'm so sorry," mouthing it softly to get them to quiet down. "Can you come forward? This tunnel's much wider and higher."

Mati and Zofia back up, while Davey scrambles toward me, landing in my lap.

"Hello, Captain." I clasp him tightly. "That's Zofia behind me. And Mati behind her."

He waves a hand over my shoulder. When I show him his rucksack, he lets out a yelp. "Captain America Two!" On the front of the bag, in red, white, and blue, I painted the letters *C.A. 2.*

"Climb over. My friends will show you what to do with the gear in your bag." He wriggles around to join them.

I take a breath before turning back to Leah—milky pale, hair short, almost blond instead of red. Sunken blue eyes. Yet she's bigger and taller—like me, she's grown in the years since I've seen her. She slides forward, folding herself into an awkward crouch, but when she lifts her head, there's that wry smile. "We meet again, old Witold." I reach for her shoulders, feel bone. When our eyes meet, neither of us cries.

"Zofia and Mati know me as Ala. Call me that, okay? Are you hungry?" Stupid question. I pull out the pillowcase filled with sandwiches for three of us, equipment we'll need for the journey.

"A few special things for our trip, mademoiselle."

"Are we heading to Paris?"

"*Oui.* By Sewer Express." I hand her a torch, help her circle it round her upper arm with the elastic sling Mati invented. When I pass her a red beret, she laughs, arranging it over one ear.

I smile, shake my head. "You'll need to cover your whole head." I tug the edges of the cap down, conscious of a need to touch her. While she ties on the knee pads, folds the kerchief round her neck, slips her hands into the much-too-large gloves, I explain the plans for the expedition. Five to six hours of travel, if all goes well—lunch and breaks in between. She fusses with her kerchief, and I wonder if she's paying attention.

"Carry your water pouch across your shoulder, like this. See? Now you can squirt water into your mouth whenever you're thirsty."

She takes a small bite of the cheese sandwich, puts the rest back in the food bag.

"Leah." I put my hand on hers. "Eat as much as you want. You'll need your strength."

She studies our interlaced fingers. When she looks up, her eyes are welling with tears.

"I'm sorry about your mother." I squeeze her hand.

"I can't hear you," she shouts. For a moment, I think the beret's too tight around her ears. But she turns her left ear toward me. "I can hear a bit in this ear. Nothing on the right. It happened when I was sick."

I stare at her. *What she's been through!* I point a finger at her chest, then at mine, cross one finger over the other.

She smiles, gives me a Guide salute.

It's time to get going. It might be hours before anyone suspicious notices Leah and Davey are missing, but I want to put the ghetto behind us. I turn around to see Mati and Zofia have kitted out Davey like a pirate—one kerchief knotted around his head, another jaunty around his neck. I give them a grateful smile. "This is my dear friend Gabin. She's become deaf in her right ear, so we speak into her left. Gabin, my co-conspirators—Mati and Zofia."

She waves hello, and Davey clambers into his sister's embrace, hugging her tightly.

I squirm into position near her left ear. "In this group, I'm known as Ala. We use these names when we're working. That's how we should address each other in front of other people. Never use our real names." Davey nods sagely, but Leah gives me a wry smile.

"We're going to get started," I say. "Mati goes first, then Zofia, then Davey—"

"Captain," Mati corrects me.

"Sorry—Captain—Gabin next, and I'll be last on this leg of the voyage. Watch how Zofia does it. Follow her. If you need to stop, raise your hand, and I'll signal the group."

"I have something." Zofia extends two balled fists toward Davey. He touches the back of her right hand, and when she opens it, there's a small, smooth pebble in her palm.

"For good luck," she says. Shyly, she offers Leah the other one.

"Thank you." Then Leah takes Davey's hand. "Kiss Mama," she says, kissing her fingers and throwing the kiss upward. Davey whispers something into his fingers before flying them up and out. I raise my eyes to the tunnel ceiling, send out a long breath of gratitude.

We set out—a mismatched camel caravan—and it takes no time for Davey to scoot along like a windup toy. Leah's knee pads keep slipping. We pause several times to tighten them before Mati has an idea. With his knife, he makes three small holes in her trousers on either side of her knees and at the back. When he sees how thin she is, he gives her his second pair of knee pads, larger than the ones I made for her, doubles them up, and loops the ties through the holes in her trousers. Leah catches me smiling proudly at him, pretends to gaze at the ceiling.

"There. That should hold them in place."

"Thank you, magnificent Mati," she says when he's done.

Used to moving faster, I'm finding it hard to slow to Leah's pace. I keep bumping into her feet. In our planning, Mati, Zofia, and I talked about the need to reduce our speed, to rest more frequently, but somehow, we've forgotten all that in the excitement of starting. I don't want to fall too far behind the three camels at the front—but I'm getting a sense of how weak Leah is. She's cheerful, but her breathing's labored. I scold myself into slowing down. Eventually, one of them will look back and notice how far behind we are.

"He's beoooootiful, Ren." Her voice echoes down the tunnel.

"He can hear you, you know."

"Am I being too loud?"

I reach forward to tap her on the back. "Gabin, you have to call me Ala in here. For safety. We'll take a break partway through the second tunnel; then we can talk. Another half hour or so." Or longer, at the rate we're going.

"How's your family, Ala? What's this cloak-and-dagger group you're part of? I bet Marysia's the ringleader."

I've forgotten she can't hear.

But I don't know what she *can* hear, so I tell her about Mama getting snubbed by Frau Hüber, the complex features of their friendship-of-convenience, the high-and-mighty Hüber's dyed yellowy-green hair. I have a laugh at poor Mama's expense, but since the Gestapo specializes in ornate methods of extracting information from unlucky captives, I say nothing of my AK work. It's wonderful having Leah laughing with me, even if it's only the idea of her laughing with me. I launch into the tale of Lotka's work at University Hospital as Leah gives a little cry. My breath catches, but it's just Davey crawling back to find his sister. They embrace.

"My *bubala* Captain," she says, ruffling his hair. We all sit back on our heels, Leah takes off her beret, and in the torchlight, I notice beads of sweat on her forehead.

He holds on to her hand. "We're waiting for you," he says.

Leah uses her kerchief to mop her brow, turns to me. "Is it almost time for my tablets?"

I check my watch. "You could take the first ones now."

Małgorzata was able to "find" Leah's typhus medicine through her contacts at University Hospital. Ever since their troops became infected while invading their dear friend Russia, the Germans have been petrified of a typhus epidemic. And if it happens in the general Polish population, where will they find slaves to carry out their plans for making all of Europe a playground for Nazi Germany? It means typhus medicines are in ready supply if you know who to bribe.

Leah takes a tiny bite of her sandwich, swallows two white pills with squirts of water. The whole time, Davey kneels at her side, anxiously gazing up at her.

I look behind them into the dark tunnel. It feels like we've hardly moved at all, and we have so far to go. Panic worms its way up my chest. This is completely different from Zofia, Mati, and me darting in and out of Warsaw sewers, game for any crisis. I watch brother and sister smiling sadly at each other—still immersed in the world they've escaped from—a world unfamiliar to me. What made me think I could simply patch them onto mine?

I hear Mati and Zofia before I see them.

Mati's gaze rests on the small boy whispering into his sister's ear. His brown eyes meet mine and he shrugs, smiling his wide smile.

"I think it's time to switch places," he says.

And that's how we carry on until we reach the second tunnel—Mati in the rear with Leah ahead of him, me leading, with Davey in front of Zofia—our rejigged caravan making better time. Leah's pills have quelled her fever, and by the time I crawl out of the old tunnel into an intersection with the newer one, I hear her chattering away to Mati—"My mother's a painter, too, but Irena's the real artist. Have you seen—"

"Oh, wow!" Davey scurries ahead of me, stands up straight with ample room above his head. In the dim light, the new tunnel's wider, higher—but with a steadily running black canal burbling down the middle. I grab the back of his collar as we find our feet on the slippery side path. "Stand against the wall."

"It's slimy," he says. "And stinky."

"Pull your scarf over your nose and stay away from the edge!" I point my torch at his leather-soled shoes. I should have bought him proper boots.

"Slippery!" we hiss as Zofia and Leah emerge.

"I can almost stand up." Leah starts a joyful smile, but then she clutches her chest, retching.

Zofia and I reach for her elbows and lead her against the wall, get her to sip water and pull her kerchief up.

As soon as Mati arrives, he pulls out his bag of dried mint leaves. He and I are the only ones too tall to stand up straight. His shoulders hunch against the curved ceiling. We watch as he rubs the dried leaves into his kerchief before retying it over his nose. A sneeze, and then he gives a thumbs-up. Leah and Davey follow his example.

I reach into my rucksack for the orange peels I've been saving from Lotka's weekly fruit surprises; I offer around the shriveled curls—oranges all the way from Spain, that other fascist country. "Here, chew on these when you feel nauseous. Tiny bits at a time."

We all take a moment to roll our shoulders, stretch our necks, let our knees revel in relief. I get a different look at my old friend as she and Davey lean against the wall, whispering and chewing peels under their minty kerchiefs. There's a shakiness about her—more than nerves. Reason reminds me that she's been ill, and now without her mother, maybe her bluster's gone for good. Mati, Zofia, and I break off into a group and stare gloomily at the dark canal.

"How deep do you think it is?" Zofia's eyes like headlights.

Mati wrinkles his forehead. "Three, four feet? I thought I saw a tree branch floating by."

"At least it's not that wide." I reach into my rucksack. "Let me look at the map."

Mati shines his torch on the section I've squared off.

"It doesn't say anything about depth, but following this line, you can see our tunnel's connected to this one that flows all the way into the river."

"Cholera jasna!" Zofia rolls her eyes.

"Exactly," Mati says. "No swimming unless you want to end up in the Vistula."

We take a moment to confer about safety. When we're done, I gather everyone, with Leah close on my right so she can hear.

"All right. You may have noticed that the ground's very slippery. It's fantastic that we can walk upright here, but we have to move slowly. See how Zofia does it?"

Zofia takes short, slow steps, landing each foot deliberately. Davey mimics her in his little shoes, but he doesn't have a gripping tread. When Mati offers to walk beside him, screening him from the canal, they hold hands and pretend they're tightrope walkers. Leah, Zofia, and I share smiles of gratitude for Mati.

"Magnificent man," Leah says.

Zofia lifts her chin and laughs. But a question enters and niggles my mind:

What makes a kind man so different from a kind woman that we must pause to appreciate him?

It takes a while to get used to the foul smell, the smooth slipperiness of the tunnel floor, but we're finally making progress. Leah is being magnificent in her own way, paying attention as we pick up our pace even as she bombards my back with questions.

"How did you three meet? It seems that you're in charge, Ala. Is that right, Zofia?"

Zofia laughs, but gives nothing away.

"What's that?" Davey's boyish voice echoes from up ahead. We pause to watch an object bobbing along in the canal—something that looks bizarrely like a whole cauliflower.

"Hitler's brain," Leah says.

"That explains so much," Mati says, and we all laugh.

We're slowly slip-sliding down the sewer corridor, savoring the little joke, when a bubbling erupts from the canal. Instinctively, we hunker against the wall, and I almost expect a monster to rise up and snatch us in its jaws.

"Goebbels belching," Leah says dryly, and that sends us into paroxysms again. I keep my eye on the water, though. Is it rising? Little waves ruffle the surface. We carry on for another ten minutes while I watch the black water splashing up the rim of the corridor before it drains back into the canal. I look at my watch—nine o'clock.

"Time for a break," I say. Murmurs of relief. We huddle in a line against the wall. I slip out of my rucksack, slide up to Leah. "Breakfast, lunch, supper? I'm not sure which."

"The word you're looking for is brupperunch, Ala." She smiles, but I see the fatigue in her eyes.

"Time for your injection, my friend."

Mati and Zofia prop Davey between them, help him get his food bag out. My team and I have grown used to picnicking along the banks of a shit river. I'm hoping the stink won't discourage Leah and Davey from eating.

I tug off my gloves. "Cheese or chicken or cheese and chicken?"

No surprise that Leah starts with a slice of pickle, followed by another slice of pickle and half a chicken sandwich.

"You're doing very well."

"Am I?" She takes small bites, chews slowly. "Davey's wonderful, isn't he?"

"Yes, and so is his sister."

She sighs, gives me a sidelong glance. "What will happen to my mother?"

I'm ashamed to say I haven't thought of Mrs. Freeman since we started out. "I don't know." The possibilities for horror are endless. I'm taking a bite of my sandwich when a splash of black water ripples over the edge of the canal, stopping just before my boots. *Mother Mary.* Are Zofia and Mati noticing the rising water? I wriggle up against the wall, pull my feet closer in, and lean across to see what they're doing: all three amiably munching away. No need to panic Leah. I find her sad blue eyes. "It must have been awful in the ghetto."

"Don't call it that. For us, it was a home. A terrible home my mother made as beautiful and safe as she could for Davey and me." She sinks her forehead into her palm.

I lay my hand on her back. Would my mother do for Lotka and me what Mrs. Freeman did for her children? I'm surprised that I have no ready answer.

When Leah's eaten, I remove the bottle of hydrogen peroxide from our first-aid kit, a wad of cotton wool. Małgorzata stole this maroon leather case for us. I clean my hands, wishing that Lotka were doing this instead of me. "Ready?"

She nods. When she rolls up her sleeve, I clean her arm with the hydrogen peroxide, fearful now that I might hit bone given how pitiful her arm is.

I take out the syringe, stick the needle into the little glass bottle nestled in the case, upend it the way Małgorzata's diagram showed me, and slowly pull out the plunger.

"Take a breath." I flick the syringe to remove bubbles, plunge it into her arm, wondering if her thigh would have more flesh.

Not a squeak from her. She rolls down her sleeve, smiles at me. "Ala

Gołąb-Grynberg told me it was a Polish prisoner who invented this for the Germans—penicillin doesn't work against typhus."

"Really?" I put away the syringe, unwrap a chicken sandwich. Chewing on my mouthful, I ponder what would have happened if the Polish prisoner had refused to cooperate. War offers excruciating choices. There'd be more dead Nazis, but Leah may not be crouching here beside me.

A babble of voices makes its way closer to us—Mati following behind Davey as he races toward Leah. "Slow down, Captain." Davey kisses his sister, while Mati crouches on my other side. When I turn to look at him, he nods at the canal.

I follow his gaze. "What are you seeing?"

"The other sidewalk is higher than this one. See how dry it is?"

"Yes, but is the water rising?"

"I think it rises and ebbs depending on what's flowing into it. The other side's higher than this, so it stays dry."

"What's your idea?"

"If we can cross to the other side, we can move along much faster."

"And how do we get across?"

"You and I and Zofia can jump across. It's only three feet."

I raise my eyebrows, incline my head at the pair snuggling on my other side.

"I'll carry them."

AFTER OUR LITTLE break, Mati explains his idea, but Davey's the only one who's keen—mostly because he's going to ride on Mati's back. I suspect that Zofia is afraid for Leah. She's seen the fever weakness and also the shaky trembling that plagues her. Still, even with the extra time we've allotted, we're behind schedule. Aboveground, we have a team waiting for us—including Kasha's household. We can't endanger them further. I make my case for speed, and Leah and Zofia reluctantly agree.

Mati's gangly legs make the crossing with ease. And here, even with brown clusters floating in a sewer canal and AK soldiers armed for killing above, my mind takes the time to wonder if he's a good dancer.

"It's dry," he says. "But, I think, it's not as wide as the other side. Be sure to land leaning forward." He leaps back to our side, skidding into the slimy wall. "Okay, Ala. You go first and I'll follow with Gabin."

Me? *Cholera.* I've been admiring Mati's grace instead of observing his jumping technique. *I can do this*, I coach myself. Avoiding Mati's eyes, I remove my rucksacks, hand them to him. One, two, three—I make a leap and land with one foot on the rim of the canal, arms windmilling forward, fingers reaching for the wall. Not the best, but now I'm safe on this side. When Mati throws my rucksacks over, I catch them neatly, call over to bolster Leah.

"This is the beautiful side!" But, of course, she doesn't hear me.

Across from me, Mati crouches while Zofia helps Leah climb onto his back. He stands strongly while she crosses her feet around his middle, arms around his neck, face against his shoulder.

I'm thinking that neither of these two jokers is cracking a joke when Zofia yells, "Wait!"

"Don't look, Gabin!" Davey shouts as Mati steps back from the canal. Floating toward us, four stiff legs in the air, is a dead animal—hairy and bloated. A dog? Jaws open in rigor mortis. I duck my head. How did a dog get in here?

Naturally, Leah does look.

"That's got to be Himmler," she says firmly. "Those yellow teeth give him away."

Mati laughs, hoists her higher. "Ready? Hold tight."

I stand aside to give them room. He launches across, teeters one foot on the edge with Leah hanging over the canal.

"Leah!" Davey's panicked voice.

With both hands, I grab Mati's shirtfront and yank him forward. The three of us crush against the wall until Mati pivots to the side. The only one laughing is Leah.

"Phew! That was exciting. Could we do it again?"

"Are you mad, Gabin?" But I'm smiling—that's my friend, that's the blustery voice I've been missing. We give each other a tight hug while Mati pats each of us on the head.

"You're next, Zofia."

Zofia takes two strides up the slippery side before jumping and landing on two feet, arms outstretched like a gymnast. The four of us laugh uproariously.

"Hey!"

Cholera. We've forgotten Davey.

"We haven't forgotten you!" I wave at him, standing small and forlorn across from us.

Mati leaps back, crouches down as thick water burbles up over their side of the canal. But Davey won't get on his back.

"I'll fall in," he cries.

Mati picks him up, hugs him tightly. Davey's arms strangle his neck.

"Not so tight, Captain."

Leah, Zofia, and I stand ready while Mati makes the leap. As soon as Davey's on the ground, he runs into his sister's arms. Finally, the five of us are safe on the other side. Rucksacks back on, we set off with Zofia in the lead, cautious at first, but bolder as we get used to our secure footing.

Mati was right. It takes us no time to reach the new intersection. I'm pondering the possibility that Leah has gained strength from her close call over the canal, while Davey seems exhausted. I hadn't bargained on him spending all his energy holding up his sister with his valiant heart. Neither they nor the nurse said anything to us about her deafness, her tremors. But she's held up. Almost there. *I know, I know.* Don't say it's over till everyone's safely home.

Walking side by side with Leah, we link arms, and I'm eager to begin a proper conversation. But then she asks, "Are you getting along any better with your sister? You used to be so close."

How do I answer that? Instinct tells me to avoid any mention of the good doctor who showers Lotka with rich presents. "She loves her work—cutting up people and stitching them back together. It's her salary that's keeping us fed. I suppose I'm grateful."

"You suppose. I thought University Hospital was for Germans only."

"Apparently not. She says they help everyone. I think she's very good at what she does."

"I bet your mother's holding her above you all the time."

I nod. "But I was remembering when my mother worked at the Education Ministry before the invasion—how she paid for my painting lessons with Professor Rank. Those materials cost so much. I've never even thanked her."

"Well, do it, Ren. You never know."

I squeeze her arm. "That reminds me. I brought some drawing materials for you and your . . ." The memory of Mrs. Freeman halts me, and the moment feels too fragile to correct her use of my name.

Her turn to squeeze my arm. "The professor—you know he was rounded up with the other men? He might be in Dachau with my father."

"I didn't know." Despite Leah's news, the image of gleefully sarcastic Professor Rank brings a smile.

It was in his Saturday art classes that I felt free to break the rules I learned in my high school classes. He had a wildness about him that was so liberating, I felt confined by my own skin. Yet I was afraid of bursting out, of not having walls to stop me from floating away. Then came the war, and all that changed. By trying to break us, the dragons created monsters of freedom. Marysia and the AK burst through boundaries every day. Not doing so is like killing yourself slowly. My friend Mr. Godlewski was the first to teach me that.

Leah slows. "Your Mati told me he lost both his parents in the first roundup."

"He's not mine, Gabin."

"He's utterly and completely yours. Anyone can see that."

I'm about to protest when, from the corner of my eye, I see something swimming in the canal—a snake?

Davey screams and clutches Mati's legs—a long-tailed rat scrambles onto our pathway and shakes itself off. Mati quickly lifts Davey and carries him past the slickly wet animal. Has Leah seen it?

"Here's another one," Zofia says, kicking it into the canal.

I feel Leah tensing beside me.

"And another." Mati steps on it and I hear a squeak. "Into the canal with him. You're safe up here, Captain."

It's not the first time we've seen rats in the sewers, but never this many. We carry on until the squeaking sounds become more of a chorus. When a rat scurries across her boot, Leah screams as though she's been shot. *Mother Mary.* We can't be caught this close to the exit.

We gather round while Leah tries to calm herself. "I hate them!"

I give her some water and two of the Bayer aspirin, but she's a quivering mess.

"I hate them, too." Zofia stands on Leah's other side, stroking her arm.

Mati steps away and motions me over; we shine our torches ahead of us in the tunnel. Rats are darting in and out of holes at the base of the walls. Davey buries his face in Mati's neck.

"It's because of what they carry," Mati says as we kick several of the scurrying animals into the canal.

Of course—lice. And lice carry typhus. Another loud screech from Leah. We hurry over to find her kicking out her feet, brushing off her arms as though they're crawling over her. "Get them away from me."

Zofia touches Mati's arm. "You carry Gabin; I'll take the Captain."

But Davey reaches for me. I slip out of my rucksacks and hand them to Zofia. Mati helps Davey onto my back. When he hugs my neck, I hook my arms around his knees.

"Can't we go back? Please?" The fear in Leah's eyes makes me worry she's about to bolt. I step in close.

"Gabin, Mati's going to carry you. We're almost at the end, and Kasha's waiting in her cozy home. We have to keep moving."

"They'll be all over me!" Beneath the sound of her ragged breathing, there's a rabid squealing going on.

"Mati won't let your feet touch the ground. And Zofia will make sure they don't come near us."

She climbs onto Mati's back while Zofia and I kick the scrabbling animals out of their way. Zofia has the idea of covering Leah's head and throws my jacket over her. Then she wraps a kerchief around Davey's eyes, but he tugs it off.

Zofia goes first, kicking and swearing under her breath. Even so, every third step my boot squelches a squirming body, almost toppling me.

I hate rats, too. Mr. Godlewski once asked why I called the Hitlerow dragons instead of rats, as most Poles do. I don't remember what I answered, but seeing this plump army I understand their logic clearly: living things require food. Dragons, on the other hand, are incomprehensible to me—killing other creatures to increase their stores of gold.

The minutes pass slowly. On my back, I feel Davey's steady heartbeat, hear the pleasing sound of his snoring. Poor Captain. He's finally getting some sleep.

Squelch. "That fat one was my father!"

Oh, no! I was hoping Zofia wouldn't bring up her Nazi parents.

"I made up a poem about him. Would you like to hear it?"

I whisper, "Not now, Zofia."

But Mati says, "Yes, a poem, please."

"It goes like this: There once was a man from Lvov, who was more like a pig or a hog."

Maybe Leah's deafness will work in her favor this time.

"His family, he hated, but in fact, they were fated to hate him, so they fed him to the dog."

A moment of stupefied silence before Mati coughs out a laugh. "Sorry, Ala."

Seconds later a voice speaks from beneath my coat. "What's so funny?"

I hesitate. "Something Zofia said."

The number of rats becomes a nightmarish swarm. It's impossible to take a step forward, and now there's something else—a smell so bad, I'm heaving.

I ask Zofia to check the map in my rucksack, while I shine my torch at the walls and ceiling. There should be chalk marks indicating that we're close to the exit. Zofia has her kerchief over her nose, and her eyes are watering.

"Do you smell it?" Mati says softly, moving close.

"You don't mean the shit in the canal," I say.

He shakes his head slowly. I see dread in his eyes.

Leah stirs on his back. "What's happening? Is it time to get down?"

I keep my tone calm and firm. "No. Keep the jacket over your head. We're just checking something."

Mati and I have a conversation with our eyes. "I'll go take a look," he says. He turns to Zofia. "You hold the Captain. Ala will have to take Gabin."

Davey lets himself be folded into Zofia's arms, his lids quivering in sleep. When I pass him over, I see his fingers are curled around the dented tin soldier.

We quickly transfer Leah before she can protest, and I back her up against the tunnel wall to help support her weight. "It's fine," I say. "Mati's going to confirm what's up ahead."

She rests her head against mine.

When Mati comes back a few moments later, he and Zofia huddle round me—Leah now fitful and heavy in my arms. We'll have to risk that she'll hear everything.

"There's a body floating in the canal," he says softly. "Shot in the back of the head." He smooths the red scarf over his face. "He's wearing a Gestapo uniform."

I squeeze my eyes shut.

"It looks like an assassination—AK or some other group."

I take this in. The dragons will be searching for him. "We have to chance it. I'm going ahead to meet the ground team."

When Mati takes Leah back, she groans. "What's going on, Ala? Is it bad?"

"No, no. We're close to the exit, so we have to be extra cautious, that's all."

To Zofia I say, "If I don't return, backtrack to another exit. Here's the map."

"I'll go," she says.

I shake my head and reach inside my rucksack for the envelope I've been guarding. Then I tie my scarf tighter over my nose and mouth and hand over the pack. "See you soon."

"Don't look at the canal," Mati says as I turn away.

I think I'm going to plough forward, but I've underestimated the work Zofia's been doing clearing a path through the swarm. They are every size and shade and some are clawing up my trousers.

I beat them off with my gloves, but it's hard to stop myself from screaming and running back to the group. By the time I get to the corpse, I have to struggle to remember my objectives—get to the exit, meet the AK team, verify their identity, transfer Leah and Davey to them safely.

It's the boots I see first, or at least the back of the heels. He's floating face down. *Thank you, Mary.* Yet, I can't help glancing at the bloated body, or what I can see of it, crawling as it is with vermin. Once past that pleasant scene, the ground clears, and I sense a cooling in the air. It's still night, still winter out there. I look up. There they are—white chalk arrows high on the wall in both directions, and a new symbol I don't recognize. If that's a danger warning, it's not the usual skull and bones.

I climb the rungs, careful not to make a sound. Listen. Wind in the trees? I remove the white feather from the envelope in my pocket, push it through a hole in the sewer cover. Footsteps. I scramble down a few rungs. A larger dark feather appears through the same hole. So far, so good. I move back up as the cover's yanked off. A face, covered in a black scarf, leans into the hole. "You're late. Where are the others?"

Not so fast. "Where are the swans?" I ask pointedly, glaring at the impatient man.

"Eaten long ago," he says. "Now hurry."

Password checked. Hope pops into my heart. I retreat into the rat-filled tunnel and, when I'm close, call out to Mati and Zofia. They thrust their way past the rats to the base of the ladder. Mati lets Leah down gently.

"Is it safe to take this off my head?"

I touch her arm. “We’re here. This is the end of the sewer journey.”

She takes off the jacket, keeps her gaze on my face, but I avoid it.

The cold air’s wakened Davey, and I kiss him goodbye. “Friends are waiting up there to take you to your new home.” He reaches for Leah.

“In a moment, dear one.” She gives us each a kiss. “Thank you.”

A voice hisses from above. “Send them up!”

To me, she whispers, “We’ll see our children’s children.”

But I can’t see her. My eyes are blind with tears.

Fifteen

Toronto, November 2010

In the buttery morning light, Irena and I are leisurely cleaning up the kitchen, a process in which we create a whole new mess. My grandmother dips her fingertip in the jar of honey, licks it clean before closing, reopens the jar, and, grinning, looks up at me. "You going to see that old man today?"

"Just a few hours." A pang of guilt. I've been pushing Stefan, trying to get him to move forward in his story. Guilty also because I hate to leave Irena alone. Maybe today something Stefan says will break my block. "I'll be back around two. There's chicken and potato salad in the fridge."

She rolls her eyes. "I will try my best to survive." She turns to leave the room, but the window's slammed by a tremendous blow. I duck, look up to see a hawk flying off with a small bird in its talons. On the window, a smear of blood, grease, and gray feathers.

I hurry over to Irena, leaning against the doorframe, her hand over her mouth.

"You're shaking." I hold her in a tight hug. "Thank God the window didn't break."

We stare at the bloody feathers sticking to the glass: dove or sparrow, like most of the birds at the bird feeder. Once again, I wonder if the bird feeder is in fact a trap for the doves and sparrows, an invitation to a feast for the falcons and hawks flying in from the Don Valley.

My grandmother shrugs. "Life."

AT THE HEALTH center, Stefan's sitting up in bed, entranced by my story of the hawk and the sparrow.

"My grandmother just said, 'That's life.'" I set my tape recorder on the table. "I don't know. I'm wondering if we should get rid of the bird feeder."

"Keep it. It's good for the sparrows and the hawks."

"You think so?"

"You're feeding them both." His hands smooth the blue blanket.

I give him a quizzical look. "Is that like 'Doing good is important'?" It's a saying he returns to often, but he sidesteps my question.

"I tried to be a good father. I think I was a very good husband."

Finally, he's talking about Mary.

"I gave her everything she asked for—she had a good life." He sighs. "I worked hard to build my landscaping company, and now, you see how successful it is."

"It is."

"I started over. You see how I made a better life?"

I nod. But there's something I'm missing. "I saw the garden your company made to honor the women murdered in the Montreal Massacre. Those fourteen red oaks—stunning."

He shrugs.

"During those war years, you and Ola did so much—rescuing people from the Nazis. You don't think that was doing something good with your life?"

"I don't know." He pulls the blanket up around his chest, and in a faltering voice, begins his familiar narrative, rhapsodizing over Ola's sacrifice, her bravery.

"They shot her coming out of a sewer. That's how she died."

"Oh?" I'm about to add, *Last time you said it was a grenade that killed her*, but he's closed his eyes and is sinking into sleep.

Gray has cast over the promise of the morning. I get up, stretch, walk over to the photo gallery on the wall. Mary Balfour Cegielski has dark hair in a classic sixties helmet bob. Legs crossed neatly at the ankles. Stefan, seated on her right, wears a scarf tucked inside the neck of his shirt, the two boys stand at attention behind them in a stance that makes me wonder if they were in the cadets. Something else I didn't notice before: a cane on the arm of Mary's chair.

I close my eyes, try to conjure Stefan crawling through a sewer tunnel, but instead of Stefan, Irena appears in the tunnel, her face oily with brown streaks. *Jesus.* A moment passes before I can shake the picture, and then behind me comes Stefan's voice, shouting manically in Polish. Or is it German? I hurry back to his bedside and shrink from the spittle flecking his lips, the blue eyes icy with malice. Yet he's not focused on me.

"Stefan," I say stroking his hand. "*Proszę, proszę*," soothing him in the little Polish I know.

His nurse walks in briskly. "Mr. Cegielski!" She shakes his shoulder. "Hello, Mr. C.!" He turns toward her, his breath coming in short gasps like a child after crying.

"Should I go?" I say, turning off the recorder.

"He's okay. He yells like this a lot. Strong lungs, eh?"

Stooping close to his ear, I whisper, "Goodbye, Mr. C. See you soon." I put the recorder in my jacket pocket, jam my notebook in my pack. What was he so angry about? Our next meeting, I'll have to ask him to translate. I walk quickly down the hall to the elevator. Suddenly, it's crucial to feel my muscles working, the brush of wind on my young skin.

ON THE COUCH in front of the TV, Cheriblare and Irena are watching Blue Jays baseball reruns. I flop down beside my cat and pat her velvet head.

"Shh! Bautista," Irena says, pointing to the batter.

Cheri and I widen our eyes, turn to watch as Bautista bats out. Irena hits mute, sighs, and offers her cheek for a kiss.

A warmth fills my chest, and I risk adding a hug. "How's the triptych coming?"

She opens her hands in a gesture of resignation. "It's doing its own thing."

"Can I see?"

"Not yet." A smear of yellow on her neck beneath her soft bun. "What about that old man's sculpture?"

"I'm getting nothing. Not one little buzz." Stefan's aggressive shouting came from a place more like hallucination than dream. Still, my questions seem to have missed the mark. I'll review the recording tonight—sometimes a phrase or tone of voice, a pause or sigh speaks more than a whole paragraph.

"Take some drugs," Irena says. "They helped me when I was stuck."

I laugh. "Sophie told me about your acid trip." I cross my eyes. "Luckily, I get all the psychedelic effects without LSD. At least I usually do. You want anything?"

She makes a measure with her thumb and forefinger. "Maybe just so much brandy."

"Coming up," I say. "We'll celebrate you going back to oil after all those years of acrylic."

"Oil is like cream. Also, the smell makes me remember."

When I return with two glasses, she's snoozing, her head on the back of the couch. I smile at her plumped-up cheeks, turn off the television, routing Cheri from her seat. I'm doing a good thing. *Interesting.* Weren't those Stefan's words?

In the kitchen, I make myself a smoked salmon on rye, miss my smartphone, and get up to find it in my jacket. Reaching into the pocket, I glance up at one of Irena's paintings hanging above the entrance to the basement. It looks, as it always does, like a gray shrunken head squeezed into a warped oval. Actually, it's a painting of a tunnel in a Warsaw sewer. For the first time, I pay attention to the red streaks bordering the painting, a splotch of bright yellow at the far end of the tunnel. The name *Ala* is scribbled in the yellow flare. I pull up a chair, stand on the seat, and take the painting down. Blowing on the dusty glass, I rub my arm across the painting. Close up, the letters read *Ola*.

Heart pounding, my feet propel me to the living room, the painting before me like a tray. On the sofa, Irena's in a side slump. I rush forward to check if she's still alive, but her soft wheeze reassures me. The painting hangs heavy in my hands.

Irena and Ola. Ola and Stefan. Stefan and Irena?

Sixteen

Warsaw, December 1941

The morning after the mission, I'm lolling in bed trying to understand what it is I'm feeling—numb tiredness, yes, but also shimmers of joy mingled with a shadow of doubt. Leah and Davey are out of that segregated prison, but will they be safe at Kasha's, and for how long?

Mati says Britain's losing thousands of lives to the German bombings and their relentless torpedoing of Allied aircraft carriers. The three of us talked of nothing but war on our long journey out of the tunnels. Names like Moscow, London, Norway flew us up into the warring world while we slogged from Włochy's sewers back to Mokotów, fueled only by fatigue. I've heard that occupied France has a strong underground resistance, but others in that country enjoy the benefits the Vichy government pays to betray them. And across Poland, news of executions clogs the resistance channels—traitors executed by the AK and other resistance groups; resisters betrayed and handed over to the Gestapo for interrogation, torture, and execution.

I snuggle deeper under the warm covers. In the grand scheme of this war, Poland seems small and insignificant—giant Russia on our east—ally or enemy, it's hard to say. Then to our west—Hungary, Romania, Bulgaria on Germany's side. And Italy! My mind pairs the busts of Michelangelo and da Vinci that once sat on Leah's bookshelf with an image of Mussolini. I'm laughing at my joking brain when Lotka tiptoes into the room.

"Are you awake?"

"Yes, no." I smile at her. "I've been pondering why some people are wonderful and others are terrible. Are you off to work?"

"I have to get to the bank first." She sits at the end of my bed, glowing in her white uniform, her navy cape around her shoulders. "You look tired. Where were you all night?"

Snatching two friends from the clutches of beasts. Of course, I say no such thing. The last time I fretted about the Freemans, she said, "They have lots of money, Irena. They'll get by." Add to that my AK oath of secrecy, and I think up an acceptable answer.

"Guide work."

"You mean Armia Krajowa work." She shakes her head.

I don't respond. While many of its activities are clandestine, the Armia Krajowa is no secret to Poles, those with us or against us.

"Does this work include sleeping with your colleagues?"

I send her a questioning glance. For a nurse, Lotka's rather prim about such things. I look at her more closely. Her face looks splotchy, and I wonder if she's been crying.

"I'm sorry." She rubs her forehead. "Things are complicated at work."

I reach for her hand and she grips mine with an unexpected force. "I'm worried about you, Renka. You can't trust Marysia. I don't like the way she dresses like a man and orders everyone about. Isn't it true that you don't even know her real name?"

I raise my eyebrows to cover my alarm at my sister's distress.

"I don't want anything bad to happen to you. And I can't keep making excuses for you. You know Mama doesn't like being alone at night. If I'm working a night shift, you should be here."

"I'll try." I give her a sly smile. "At least you're keeping our family going. Can we expect any happy news in the near future?"

My teasing brings tears to her eyes.

"Lolo. What's wrong? You can tell me."

She lifts the corner of her cloak to wipe her eyes.

"Won't you be late for work, Lotka?" Mama yells from the living room, where lately she's been practicing piano with her coat and hat on and the window open, so Frau Hüber can hear.

My sister and I share a despairing smile. When Lotka rises, I throw off the covers and pull on one of Papa's thick jerseys. Before I run to the bathroom, I give her arm a squeeze.

"I believe he does care for you, Lolo." I brush some lint from her cloak. "I'll be home for dinner; let's talk more tonight."

While I'm running a hot bath, I hear Mama and Lotka saying goodbye, and feeling that I haven't said enough to comfort her, I stick my head out the bathroom door, wafting steam into the kitchen. "I hope you have an uneventful day."

Mama shoots me a stern look. "Don't use up all the hot water. I have washing to do."

In the bath, I massage my red knees, hold my breath underwater to ease my neck and shoulders, but my mind's a hive of questions: What are Leah and Davey doing this morning? I forgot to give them their gifts. Is it too risky to get them to Kasha's? And Mati? I'll see him later today, along with Zofia. The message I left Marysia at our Mokotów drop box was short: *Mission Complete*—even in code it looked impressive. Plans were, we'd meet at the Vault for a debriefing if our mission was successful. I think we can safely say it was—black canal, rats, and assassinated Gestapo officer notwithstanding. I splash my face with the cooling water.

Rattling my mind is also Lotka's warning about Marysia. My sister wasn't at the liaison meeting where our leader assigned us code names, shocking us with the news that she'd been using her alias, Marysia, from the very start of being our Guide leader.

AFTERNOON SHADOWS PLAY across the grassy mound concealing the Art Academy bunker from the world. A casual Sunday stroll across the grounds, and I could easily miss this recessed door behind the spruces. I press the head of a nail, hammered into the gap between the frame and the heavy door. It's attached to a cable that rings a bell inside the Vault.

"Ala!" Garbed in her elegant man's suit, Marysia takes my arm as we head inside. The three bars of the gas heater are on, there's a beautiful new carpet on the concrete floor, and why am I surprised to see Zofia doing a headstand on it?

"It helps my back," she mumbles, toes aiming into the air.

I send Marysia a grin.

"We'll get started when everyone's here. There's tea," she says, walking to the tall canteen on the table.

Zofia topples her feet to the ground and I sit beside her on the thick carpet. "How are you?"

"Very glad to be out of the rat tunnel."

I cover my eyes with my hand. "Don't even say that word."

Marysia hands us each a mug, and I marvel at how quickly I've moved from swallowing mouthfuls of food beside a shitty sewer to being squeamish about drinking from a cracked mug.

Careful not to spill the tea, I get up to explore the massive paintings stored against the bunker walls. Zofia accompanies me, and we stray in the direction of a large open crate. I focus my torch on an oil portrait of a pink-faced, goateed man with a lacy white cravat.

Zofia peers at the canvas. "He's very pretty."

"Look at that lacey detail. Eighteenth century, probably." Peering closely at the delicate brushstrokes, I think of Mrs. Freeman's gift of paintbrushes and feel her absence like a cavernous wound. What could I paint to honor her sacrifice? Something will come to me; something I don't expect.

"Look at this!" I follow Zofia's voice down the corridor.

My mood lifts when I see, painted across the concrete wall in broad white strokes, the name Beata Bohdanowicz. I smile. "She's a Polish artist Gabin and I admire."

Marysia joins us and I wonder if I could tell them about Leah's slashed painting when she says, "We recently got word—she was murdered in the Nazi death camp at Auschwitz."

My hand goes to my heart. They're destroying everything I love.

"The Gestapo took all her paintings from the upstairs galleries. That's why we made the wall banner."

I stare at Marysia. "You mean members go into the boarded-up galleries?"

She gives me a wry smile. "Where do you think we got the carpet?"

I don't return the smile. There's something she's not telling me.

Shivering, we make our way back to the heater when the little bell rings. Marysia unlocks the door, and, expecting Mati, I'm surprised to see the colonel accompanying him into the Vault, a pair of dark spectacles on his nose and a white cane in his hand. Mati turns his head and winks at me, and my stomach does a somersault. Zofia and I return to our positions on the carpet while he lifts two folding chairs into the circle. We wait for Marysia to start, but it's the colonel who speaks first.

"Congratulations on your successful mission." He nods at the three of us in turn. "I can assure you that your ability to transfer equipment and personnel from one part of Warsaw to another—underground—will be invaluable to the resistance." He steeples his fingers. "At this point, the Germans are unaware of the sewer method of transport, so we must be extremely careful to keep this information secure, far away from any suspicious ears or eyes. Now, tell me, how was your journey?"

Mati and Zofia look to me, and so I begin with Mrs. Freeman's sacrifice and, without naming any of them, talk about Leah's surprising deafness and Davey's intrepid courage. The colonel listens quietly, but I can tell it's not what he wants to hear. I turn to Zofia for help, and she jumps immediately to the rats. Mati describes the dead Gestapo officer, and I see Marysia glancing nervously at the colonel.

"Will you look into it?" he says, leveling an order at her with his eyes.

So he doesn't get the impression that it's all been a promenade along a boardwalk, I describe crawling through the low first tunnel. Mati follows with the slippery canal pathway. When Zofia tells him about the dead dog, his eyes bulge, and he shakes his bulldog head.

Good. He's starting to get an idea of what it's like. "Five and a half hours," I say. "Not counting the trip back to Mokotów." When his gaze meets mine, I hold it until he turns away.

"We'll say nothing more of this," he says.

I nod. "Thank you for your confidence in us, Colonel."

He leans back in his chair. "It's young people like you," he says, "who'll keep the resistance alive. Have you seen the new AK symbol, the *kotwica* anchor? He draws the letter *W* in the air and, rising from that, the letter *P*.

Zofia and I look at each other. That's the sign we saw at the exit, not far from the body with a bullet in its head.

MAMA'S BY HERSELF when I get home. I'm not hungry, and I'm eager to be alone to ruminate over the colonel's news, but she's in a talkative mood, so I sit at the kitchen table half listening.

"I've been thinking I might return to work," she says. "Not at the Education Ministry, of course, but I could give piano lessons again—some people have money for such things. Your sister earns a good salary, but she can't spend all her money on us, she has other needs now. Good heavens, Irena, you look terrible. What have you been doing?"

I smile at her. *If you only knew.*

When she wobbles toward the radio to turn on her music program, I wonder if she's been drinking. An Italian opera's playing, and Mama's humming along when the radio goes dead.

"Oh, no. See what you can do, Irena."

I get up to fiddle with the knobs when the sound blasts back on. A news bulletin. What now?

"This is a message from your General Government. The United States of America has declared war on Germany, Japan, and Italy. In response, our Führer has been forced to make a declaration of war against the Americans. This unfortunate action is necessary to come to the aid of our ally, Japan. America threatened Japan's rightful claim to land in Asia, and our ally responded by successfully sinking nineteen American warships on the island of Hawaii! There are few casualties on the Japanese side."

Grinning broadly, I turn to face my mother's wrinkling forehead, her hand holding her neck.

"Mama! It's good news! The United States has finally entered the war." I raise my fists in the air. "The Americans are our official allies."

"I don't understand. They're far away. How does this matter to us?"

I try to explain why having the world's richest nation on our side is a good thing, not only for Poland, but for the whole Allied war effort. I think I'm getting through to her when there's a quiet knock at our door. Not our proper coded knock. I turn off the radio, put my finger on my lips. Another knock, different this time. I motion for Mama to go into her room, close the door.

Tiptoeing down the hallway, I put my ear to the front door, dreading the sound of German voices. Instead, I hear whistling—the first bar of "*Siekiera motyka.*" I hold my breath. There it is again. Could this be . . . ? I whistle the next bar in response.

I open the door and see Mati standing at the bottom of the steps.

"Wait here," I say. "I'll just tell my mother."

I pull on my coat and stumble down the stairs. What is he doing here? Maybe he wants to celebrate the good news with me. But coming to my home! That's not AK protocol. I follow him out of the gate, down the side street, where we pause.

"I had to come," he says, his face deadly serious. "It's your sister."

"Lotka?"

"Sorry, Ala. I'm not sure what happened." A big exhale. "Fryderyk and I were on our way to the fish market, the one by the river. We were passing University Hospital when there was a big commotion."

I clutch my throat.

"The Gestapo took your sister."

"How do you know it was my sister?"

"For a horrible moment, I thought it was you. You look alike. But Fryderyk said your sister was a nurse. His friend Małgorzata knows her."

My next thought is for Mama. If something happened to Lotka—*Mother Mary!*

Mati interrupts my thoughts. "We should go to the hospital. Make inquiries. It happened not long ago."

I run back to the flat to tell Mama something important's come up and not to open the door to anyone but me. Or Lotka. Mati and I catch a tram, and all the way I puzzle over what this commotion could mean—a *łapanka*? I can't remember if Lotka's working late tonight. It's probably all a mistake. At the hospital, I'll go inside and ask for the surgical department. She'll be upset with me, but at least I'll know she's safe.

We hurry up the stairs just as a group of nurses files out the main door, and one of them is Danuta, Lotka's friend, being supported by another nurse.

When she sees me, she falls into my arms. "Irena! Lotka!"

"Tell me what happened."

We find a bench and the two of us sit while Mati and the other nurse stand beside us.

Danuta takes a breath. "At the end of our shift, Krystyna and I left together, but Szarlota was late, so we waited for her at the bottom of the steps. When she came out . . ."

I put my arm around her shaking shoulders.

The other nurse takes up the story. "When she saw us, she waved. She was halfway down when these Hitlerow tore up the steps to grab her. She took one look and ran back up the stairs."

Danuta's face is a red mess. "I screamed, 'Let her go! Let her go!' but—"

The other nurse interjects, "I shouted at them, too. A crowd was gathering on the street and people ran out of the hospital to see. One of the rats ran at us with a pistol, but the other one called him back. It was so frightening."

"She was crying and kicking, fighting them. Poor Szarlota."

"They threw her like a sack of potatoes into their car and took off in that direction."

Mother Mary. Not Pawiak.

I ask the question that's been running through my mind: "Does Dr. Tarnowski know?"

"I don't think so." Danuta eyes me warily and I wonder how much she knows about him and Lotka. "He was in surgery when I left. But someone will tell him."

"Thank you for talking to me. You've been very helpful."

Danuta's hand covers her mouth. "My God! What are you going to tell your mother?"

I shake my head. "I'd like to talk to you again. Are you still at your old address?"

She nods. "It's just my father and me left."

I remember now that her mother disappeared in that first raid on teachers. I can only guess what happened to her brother.

She searches my face. "Do you think they'll let her go?"

"I can't say."

Mati and I watch the two nurses board a tram. I'm breathing hard, eager to smash something, but Mati says, "You should go home. Tell your mother."

I pull away from him. "No. I have to go to Szucha Avenue."

He grabs my hand. "Really? You're going to march into Gestapo headquarters?"

"She could be in Pawiak. I have to find out."

"We will." He tugs me closer, whispers, "Let's remember our training."

"You don't understand! They took my sister."

I'm trying to remain upright, but only Mati's arms are holding me up.

I can't remember how long we stood like that. How he brought me home. But he's come in with me, and now I'm frightening my mother by keeping my hand on her shoulder, insisting she stay seated.

"Mama, this is my friend, Mati."

She tries to spring up, pushing her hair into place. "I'll make some tea."

"That's all right." I press down on her shoulder, pull out a chair beside her. *Just say it, Irena.*

"Mama, I'm sorry, I have bad news. They took Lotka."

She looks at me blankly.

"The Gestapo." My voice sounds wrapped in fog. "As she was leaving the hospital, they seized her."

Her mouth works wordlessly, and I think she's going to faint.

Before I know it, Mati's at my elbow with a glass of water. I hold it to her lips and make her sip slowly, watching the color return to her face and neck. When I try to rise, my arms and legs are too heavy to move.

Inside, the red-black chaos blots out any thoughts except one: I'll find her. Then I'll kill as many of them as I can.

Seventeen

Toronto, November 2010

"Jo? You bring me a nice cup of Red Rose."

Irena's awake again.

I need time to examine the little sewer painting more closely, so I leave it on top of the heap of plastic bags in the broom closet until I can take it out again in private. I'm not sure whether to ask Irena about this *Ola*. I'm not sure why secrecy seems in order.

"I'm feeling for spaghetti tonight," she says when I hand her a mug of tea.

I slap my thigh. "No way! Guess what's on the menu? Spaghetti Bolognese."

"Fancy-schmancy." She trails off to her studio. The brandy's obviously forgotten. Probably a good thing.

At the store, our local pasta maker had sliced the air with her hand: "*Exactly* three minutes in a rolling boil. No more"—vertical slice—"no less!"—horizontal slice.

Dinner should be a simple task of heating up the sauce and boiling the spaghetti.

Minutes later, I carry my coffee flask and the painting to the workshop I've been setting up in Mati's woodworking shed. At the counter, I pull up a stool and turn on the gooseneck lamp, focusing it on the little painting. I clean the glass, and the colors leap out; so does the name, *Ola*.

Could this be Stefan's Ola? First he said she died when someone threw a grenade into the sewer as she was climbing out. Today he got confused and said someone shot her. Which version is the truth?

There must have been thousands of Olas. It's a common Polish short form for Alexandra. Stefan's Ola could be a completely different woman from Irena's. I sip the hot, sweet coffee, zip up my fleecy. It feels like too much of a coincidence.

The painted sewer tunnel looks freakish—light and dark gray and uterine in shape. How did they move around in there? Neither Stefan nor Mati is a small man. And Irena's tall, too. Still, it's an interpretation. Imagining myself in that tight space, the orange-yellow blast at the end seems to roll toward me. That blotchy red along the border? Is that blood, or just Irena's technique for making the gray interior stand out?

I get up and walk to the sink counter, where the mold of Bradley's sculpture stands; I tap the wax positive. Still tacky. There's no way around it. I'll have to ask Irena who this Ola is.

A CANDLE FROM Sophie's vast collection flickers on the dinner table. Entranced by the shadows on the cupboard doors, Cheri bobs her head up and down.

For once, dinner's a success, and we end the night clinking our brandy snifters.

"To oil!" I say, a little drunk.

My grandmother's eyes shine in the soft light. What a difference these six weeks have made. Her cast is off, she's gained weight, and some of it's from eating healthy meals. Tomorrow, by the grace of the Sunnybrook social worker, we have a physio coming to the house—partly, I suspect, to observe the state of things. But I'm not worried. A warm glow connects my grandmother and me, and the silences that separated us these past weeks now feel generous. I remember the sewer painting, but now's not the time to bring it up.

AT NIGHT, WITH Irena turned to Mati's side of the bed, snoring like a buzz saw, I'm propped on two pillows in my single bed, earbuds in, listening to Stefan's hoarse voice shouting in the recording. I don't understand what he's saying, but he sounds demented. I reach for my iPad. There's got to be a voice translation program, but they're not always accurate. Another mystery to ask Irena about. Roland's caution about his family's privacy taunts me, and there's my confidentiality agreement with Stefan.

I play the recording—only a few minutes long—over and over. What happened to the cultivated Stefan full of old-world charm—kissing my hand, complimenting me on my clothes, joking with his nurses? One afternoon we'd laughed so hard a nurse came in to check. He's never asked to see a sketch of his grave sculpture, never asked what form or shape it might take. As though telling his life is the real point of this collaboration.

Cheriblare chatters in her sleep, the way she does when birds are close. Unplugging my earbuds, I sink deeper into the pillows. This blustery November night, I'm conscious of arriving at a singular point in my life: losing, first, Martin my father, then Mati, then Sophie. And now Frank. "But I still have Irena, and she has me." I say it out loud to ward off any demons trying to take her from me.

When I was downplaying the damage of Frank's betrayal, I inhaled too many cigarettes—after years of quitting. Now I have cravings again. I get up, drink a glass of water, and quickly email Tahira, asking if her husband, Farzaad, might be willing to listen to the recording. He's a professor of German literature at York. If I pay him as a professional, and we can come to an agreement about confidentiality, I reason that I won't be breaking my contract.

Why Farzaad spoke German was a confusing mystery to me, but when I asked Tahira a question that always interests me about couples, the mystery was solved:

"How did you and Farzaad meet?"

"At uni," she smiled. "He was my German tutor."

"Ohhh, Tahira!"

She laughed. "His family's from Hamburg."

"I thought he was Afghan."

"He is. His parents were accepted into Germany as refugees during the Soviet-Afghan War. My family was accepted by Canada."

Satisfied with collapsing decades of conflict into this singular point of migration, we finished our tea and cookies. The memory makes me smile.

When I click play again, the volume's on high: *Something, something, HUNDE!* Gripped by the savage tone, I picture gnashing teeth, purple lips foaming at the edges. Scuffling sounds overlay the shouting, and finally, there's the nurse's voice, "Mr. Cegielski!"

Footsteps falter in the hallway outside my door. "*Babcia?*" I stop the recording, throw off the bedcovers.

My grandmother's standing in the doorway holding on to the frame. Her soft bun has come undone and her eyes stare dazedly.

"What is it?" I spring off the bed, move to put my arm around her shoulder. She shoves me away, loses her balance, and almost lands on the floor before I grab her under the arms and hold her in a tight hug. "I'm so sorry. I forgot to turn the volume down."

Her squirming settles. She wipes her eyes. "I need some cigarettes."

We link elbows, walking slowly to her sitting room. When she's seated, I light her shaking cigarette holder, take my usual place, and zip up my fleecy.

"Want one?" She offers me the pack.

"Sure." We smoke in silence.

Stubbing her cigarette out with a twist of her bony wrist, she turns to face me. "I heard."

"I know, it was too loud."

She reaches for another cigarette, inserts it into her holder.

"Polish or German?" I ask.

"German."

"He was shouting."

"Of course. He is an SS." She drags deeply, holding the cloud of smoke in her open mouth before she swallows it.

"You mean he's talking to a Nazi?"

"No." She stares at me.

"He was a Polish soldier."

"I want to hear the whole thing."

Panic seizes me. Why is Sophie not here? Or Mati? "I made a promise not to share any of the interviews with anyone. I signed a contract."

"He is shouting at prisoners!" Irena jabs her cigarette at me. "Interrogating them."

"He could be repeating what an interrogator said to him, right?"

"No." She places the empty glass on the side table.

"You sure?"

"Of course. I know this voice."

I scrunch up my eyes, give my head a shake. "That's impossible. You only heard a few seconds."

"At the camp, there was an officer—hysterical screaming like this one—*HUNDE, HUNDE!*"

I scrape my chair closer. "What was his name?"

"I don't remember." She strains to cough.

I fetch her a glass of water. "I don't think we should talk about this now. It's late."

She pushes the glass aside. "You go to bed. Erase everything. Make your smooth, nice story."

"That's not— Let me get some brandy." When I come back with the bottle, she lights another cigarette. I zoom in on the purple veining of her hands, her long fingers, the nails bitten like my own when I'm brooding over something. *What the fuck have I done?*

She takes a gulp, swallows hard. "It was a joke in my barracks. Every time he screamed, 'DOGS, DOGS!' we screamed, 'PIG, PIG!' But only in our heads. And we made a step like this with our heels." She lifts her bare heel and pounds the ground.

I feel an urgent need to excuse myself, run to my room, and pore through my hundreds of emails. This is way more than she's ever told me about the war. I know Mati was captured by the Russians, that he jumped off a train in Białystok and eventually found his way to Sweden. When I was in high school, reading about the Second World War, I remember Sophie telling me Irena had been in a German prison, but I didn't register that word as a Nazi concentration camp.

"The other one was much worse." Her voice is dreamy, as though she's walking through a dappled forest. "Quiet." She makes a thin line with her mouth. "No lips, but more died in his barracks than ours."

"No lips are always bad," I say.

Stupid joke. Roused, she shoots me a dagger look.

"That one liked to watch the blockova beat the girls. When one of our friends in that barrack died, he made the others lay the body outside the doorway so they had to step over her."

Jesus. Everything sharpens and slows like a car coasting toward a rushing train. *Stoppp!*

"This one yelling in the recorder . . ." I begin and pause.

"He was the interrogator. He was clever. He gave us things—bread and tea. Let us sit by the woodstove because we had no heat in the barracks. That worked better than beating." Irena smiles sadly. "I hear this voice every night."

I bolt to my feet. Kneeling in front of her, I lay my head on her knees.

She doesn't touch me. "What did he tell you?"

"That he was a soldier in the Polish Underground. He guided people through the Warsaw sewers, like you and Mati did."

"Really? What is his full name?"

I hesitate.

"Did he give you his code name? What cell did he work in?" She starts to cough, and I look up.

"I don't know. He hasn't told me that yet."

She dismisses him with a flick of her cigarette holder. "Let him tell his story. Maybe he gets captured and tortured by the Gestapo."

I feel myself recoil. Yet I say, "It's just such a weird coincidence."

Her blue eyes pierce me. "You bring that voice from my war life; then when I explain," she sputters, "you don't believe me."

I try to embrace her, but she shrugs me off. "I want to sleep," she says, her voice sagging with fatigue.

I pick up the ashtray in one hand, her empty glass in the other. "I'll bring you some water."

In the kitchen, I lean my head against a cupboard as the jug fills. How could I have been so careless? She hates hearing German. Just a few seconds of the recording and she's dragged back into the horrors of that camp.

When I return, she's in bed. I put the jug on the bedside table, wait to see if she'll ask for her sleeping pill, which I'll have to refuse her, given the amount we've drunk. She doesn't ask.

I bend to straighten the covers, as I always do, before kissing her good night.

"Just go!" she growls and rolls to Mati's side of the bed.

Part Three

Eighteen

Warsaw, May 1942

Young trees are doing their best to leaf again. Through the kitchen window, the signs of approaching summer charge me with hope—though once again, I haven't been able to get Mama out of the house. Her reasons for not leaving are always the same: "Lotka might come home and find us gone." Or "I'll stay here in case Lotka forgot her key." My heart breaks whenever she says my sister's name, and then it takes me a while to regain that venom that keeps me looking, keeps me determined to find her and destroy her abductors.

The long months Mati, Zofia, and I spent tapping into Marysia's intelligence network confirmed that Lotka's not in Pawiak, nor has she ever been. Neither is she in Mokotów Prison. Our only clue so far is a conversation overheard in Gestapo headquarters. A trusted cleaner reported two officers joking, making indecent remarks about a Polish nurse. *Cholera!* I clamp my hand over my mouth to stop myself from moaning. Picturing Lotka, terrified in a Nazi brothel, has become a scene my brain likes to shock me with. Still, I need to know more. My mother's sad sniffling draws my attention.

"I don't understand how this could have happened to us," she sobs.

My stomach clenches. This complaint starts a woeful liturgy she recites day after day.

"My Szarlota's a respected nurse. She cares about everyone." She wipes her nose with the handkerchief Mati gave her—the one she's washed and ironed ever since the night Lotka was taken. "Who would want to hurt her?"

Unspeakable answers populate my mind. "I'll put the kettle on," I say. "A nice cup of tea will make you feel better."

"You promised to find her, Irena."

Mother Mary. I am planning to meet Elsa this afternoon. As an insider working in a Nazi brothel, she has access to a lot of information. Walking one day with her boyfriend, Elsa was spied by a truckload of soldiers, who rounded a block to come back for her. Janusz fought them, but they beat him so badly, he lost an eye. Desperate to rescue her, Marysia spread the word to several of her liaison cells. It was the first time I'd ever seen Marysia cry. I'm guessing Elsa chose to be an AK informant as a way of getting back at her assailants, and now she's graduated to a ward in University Hospital. A few years older than me, Elsa was in the same German-language class as Lotka. Even as a senior Guide, she seemed unbreakable.

"Anyway," Mama adds, "what could *you* do? You don't know anyone important."

That rattles the cup on my saucer. Nineteen years old, and I still feel her disappointment like a punch. Under Marysia's guidance, I started work in the sorting room of the post office. It's true it doesn't pay much, but it gives me access to suspicious mail. My hope is I'll come across something that leads me to Lotka.

Mama moves the vase with a sprig of lilac to the side of the table, and I notice the tremor in her hand—so much more pronounced today.

I arrange a smile. "I've been thinking I could get more hours at the post office. And, Mama, I notice you've been practicing more regularly. Are you ready to give lessons again?"

"I don't know." She frowns at the peeling paint on the kitchen walls. "The house looks so drab. I fixed the piano, but it needs a proper tuning."

"I'll find a tuner. He'll be happy to tune a piano for Agata Iwanowska. It shouldn't cost too much."

Her gaze skims my old skirt and blouse. "You'll need new clothes if you want to rise in your post office job. We could use some of the money Lotka saved in our Deutsche Bank account.

Carefully, I set her tea in front of her. "Our account? You mean she saved money for us?"

"Well, the account's in her name and mine. We went together to open it, and the manager was so nice to me." She bursts into tears. "Lotka provided everything I needed—even piano music."

I lay my hand over hers, and she doesn't pull away. All those things Lotka did, I took for granted; I stopped paying attention to the cakes and earrings and new dishes. I give my mother's hand a squeeze. "I'm so glad you have your music. They can't take that away from you."

Her eyes soften before she withdraws her hand. I feel an immense release, as though a window briefly opened before it closed again.

"If you like," I say, "we could make a visit to the bank." I have no idea what my sister's salary might have been, and I'm eager to find out how much money she saved.

⚓

THIS IS WHERE I have to be extra careful. Dragon soldiers cluster around the main entrance to University Hospital. Two officers break from the group and come bouncing down the stairs. Perhaps they've been *inspecting* one of the girls.

The Nazis are fussy about the health of their senior officers, so they house selected women in a ward, where they feed them well and regularly check them for venereal disease. Under guard, the women are escorted to parties and private homes, but sometimes they have visitors at the hospital. Even with these sanitary provisions for their entertainment, the Hitlerow still find time to attack girls on the streets. Women have never been safe in this war. Luck is what we depend on. Luck and weapons. The colonel's promised to let us keep some of the guns we steal.

I'm waiting for Elsa at the back of the hospital when a wolf whistle spins me around and I see an armed guard in an SS uniform in the open door to the morgue. Elsa's standing in the background. *Mother Mary!* I'm turning to run when I hear her hiss, "Ala! It's okay." She waves me inside.

The three of us hurry up the back stairs without being stopped by anyone. On the third floor, she enters a door marked *ZUTRITT VERBOTEN*, which is jammed open with a book. The guard marches past us to the main doors at the opposite end of the ward.

"Relax, Ala," she says. She jerks her thumb at him and gives the signal that he's AK. "No one's going to bite you." She checks her watch. "Not for the next twenty minutes, at least. Have a seat." She pats a wide bed, and when I'm seated on the edge, she draws a wheeled screen around us.

"Is it about your sister again?"

"Is it safe to talk here?"

"Safer than anywhere else. The matron and nurses are too disgusted to set foot in here. And the officers arrive by strict appointment through the main doors to the ward. We always hear them coming."

"We?"

"The other prostitutes are out working."

"Is that what you call yourselves?"

"Since I can't call myself second lieutenant in here."

I feel my face flush. "It's dangerous work you do."

"That *we* do." She inclines her head toward the guard.

I nod. "I'm asking if you could check again to see if my sister's in a brothel."

"I've been checking from the start of her disappearance. Our leader must have informed you of my findings: as of May 1—no sign in any of the Warsaw districts."

"I don't know how wide your net is, but could you check outside the city, near the provinces?"

"What makes you think she's in a provincial brothel?"

"A hunch. She's not anywhere nearby."

She gives me a long, pitying look. "I'm sorry about your sister. I sometimes saw her in the hallways. Of course, we ignored each other."

Where's this leading?

"Is she younger or older than you?"

"Older."

"But you're taller." She inclines her head. "Even so, you could almost be twins."

I raise my eyebrows. "You think they wanted me?"

She takes a moment to consider, shakes her head. "No. I think they wanted a nurse, and they grabbed a pretty one."

Somehow, I'm relieved. If Lotka's not in a brothel, she might be better off. Unless they're using her as a camp nurse.

She takes a pack of cigarettes from a locked dresser beside the bed, offers me one. "You've heard the rumors, of course. About her and Tarnowski."

"Fill me in," I say, waving aside the cigarettes.

"They were very discreet, so I have no direct evidence. But whenever I saw them together, I wondered if they were lovers. Danuta might know more."

"What do you know about the doctor?"

Before she can light her cigarette, there's a clatter outside the main entrance. A woman's voice. "My God, I'm tired. Anybody home?"

Elsa motions me to hurry, and I follow her into the common toilet, where she checks all the stalls.

"I have to get ready for my colonel," she says and tugs her dress over her head. "Sit in the far stall. If she comes in, close the door." At the sink, she quickly washes her underarms, neck, and breasts with a flowery soap. In the long mirror, in this white light, her mouth is a grimace, the blue eyes hard black dots. But she's well fed.

"Tarnowski's a slippery one," she says softly. "He's the surgeon of choice for the Hitlerow. But the Polish College of Surgeons reveres him as well. Old money, old name, some mystery around the death of his wife."

"Oh?"

"I can't tell you more."

"Thanks for this intelligence." I hesitate. "I'm sorry to have to ask you, but my monthly pads disappeared off the washing line. Could you help?"

Her mouth gapes, and she shakes her head. "Wait here," she says, pulling on her dress.

I hear her go into the ward, and a moment later she's back with a washable pad, a whole box of the new throwaway kind from Germany, and a package of Turkish cigarettes.

I give her a grateful smile and offer her one of Lotka's silk scarves that I've brought as a gift.

Her lips twist wryly. "Scarves aren't essential in this line of work. I spend most of my time taking my clothes off."

I shrug. "You could strangle one of them with it."

"My colonel might enjoy that." She leads me into the ward, glances at the woman sprawled on the bed near the back entrance. "You'll have to leave by the main door. Good luck."

I tie the scarf around my hair. My dirty rucksack's all wrong for this little adventure, but at least I'm not wearing Papa's trousers. Leaving the ward, I walk past the guard and enter a hallway where a white-coated man makes kissing sounds when he sees me. Veering sharply into the next ward, I'm met with a line of women lying in their beds, babies beside them in little cots, two nurses attending to a crying woman. I smile, wave at a surprised nurse, and keep walking until I get to the exit. I have no idea where I am, but I start down a staircase and then another until I get to what I believe is the street exit, which opens onto a fenced-in garden attached to a kindergarten. I'm making for the gate when the guardian turns in my direction, eyes popping out of her head, followed by a toothy smile. "Charlotte!"

I make a run for it.

MUCH TO MY surprise, my first whole chicken smells wonderful roasting in the oven—a gift from Mati, who came upon the hen and her sister pecking among the refuse in an alley. True, my potatoes are overcooked, but I'll mash them and sprinkle them with breadcrumbs fried in fat, the way Lotka used to do. Boiled peas and a vinegar cucumber salad with dill from St. Anthony's cloister garden round out this meal I've made. Danuta will bring dessert. After dinner, I'll take her aside to see if she can open a door in my search for my sister. Danuta's also bringing a surprise visitor for my mother, posing now in her kitchen doorway, all lipstick and perfume.

"Mama! You look beautiful," I say.

"Is it just Danuta or is Mati also coming tonight?" She rubs her lips together.

"You like him, don't you?" Now that I've asked, I'm embarrassed. Mama's not the best judge of character, but recently, I have a compulsive need to hear what others think of Mati.

"I'll never forget how sweet he was to me that night. And he brought me mushrooms last time he came to see me. You know, he reminds me so much of your father when he was young."

Oh dear. I think Mama feels safe around my cell's newly promoted captain. I smile because Mati also makes me feel safe. But Marysia eyed me curiously when I asked her about Mati visiting me at my home.

"Aren't there mostly Volk living there now?"

"Just two families. And the others, especially the caretaker, are strongly on our side."

"I see no harm, but make sure you stick to teatime conversation. Especially in front of your mother."

"Mostly mushroom conversation. He has a calming effect on her."

She tilted her head. "And on you?"

"He's a fantastic liaison officer, Marysia. You know that."

She sighed and shook her head. "This is going to be very interesting."

When the knock comes, I straighten my skirt, brush the crumbs off my blouse, and wink at Mama.

As soon as I see Danuta and her father, any reservations I had about their allegiances disappear, and it seems only natural to welcome them into our home. Pan Galik can't be much older than Mama, but his skin is gray and there's a crushed look about him. It must be terrible living with the knowledge that his wife was shot and buried in a mass grave she and her fellow teachers dug themselves. As a truck mechanic, he was considered much less threatening and far too valuable for the Wehrmacht to dispose of. Until he was suspected of sabotaging Nazi vehicles. According to Marysia, the Gestapo broke his shoulder to ensure he'd never work again.

Mama's lit a few candles in the kitchen to mask the shabbiness of our home, but with these two, any pretense is ridiculous. Danuta warmly embraces my mother and formally introduces her to her father. He bows to kiss Mama's hand, and she's charmed. Danuta and I exchange a smile. This will be good for both of them.

While they talk, Danuta carves the chicken and I remove the potatoes and peas warming in the oven. She looks at her father, relaxed at the table. "You don't know how long it's been since he's been out. Since anyone's invited him."

I smile and nod. "Mama, too."

Conversation flows smoothly while we eat, and I marvel at the healing properties of roast chicken. I find myself grateful for this company that feels like family—a different kind of family from my resistance sisters and brothers. Even so, now that we've gobbled Danuta's poppy seed cake, it's time to return to the menacing world outside this flat. Thankfully, Mama invites Pan Galik into the living room for coffee and a piano recital, allowing us some privacy while we wash dishes.

"I'd like to talk to you about my sister."

"I'll do anything to help you find Szarlota." Tears well in her eyes and she wipes them on her sleeve. "You might be wondering why I took the job at University Hospital." Her brown gaze is forthright.

"I know why Lotka did, but yes."

She slowly dries a plate. "I hesitated about training there because I knew they treated German citizens and Nazi soldiers. It felt like a betrayal of my parents. But your sister convinced me I could do good for the Poles in Warsaw as well as for my father. He's all I have left."

I nod. That sounds like Lotka.

"My brother was killed at the front on the first day of the invasion. You know about my mother."

We pause to listen when Mama's mazurka drifts in from the front room, and then Danuta continues the confession I believe she's been wanting to make for years.

"From the start of this job, the pay—and frankly, the other benefits—have been wonderful." She leans in to whisper. "My father needs medicine for his arthritis and for his heart. I have a contact at the hospital chemist who makes sure I have what he needs." She hesitates. "I don't always feel right about the work I do—I have a team that rounds up Polish street kids. I make a record of them, check their health, and then they're sent to a camp for orphans. I visit the camp from time to time to check on them."

Davey's dirty face pops into my mind, and I think of his pals who risk their lives daily, crawling under the ghetto walls or out of the sewers to find food. What happens to their families when they're kidnapped?

Danuta notices my alarmed look. "At least they get fed and housed there, Irena. The simple fact is, without my income, we'd starve and we'd have nowhere to live."

"What role did Tarnowski play in hiring you and Lotka?"

She sighs. "At first, he was fantastic. I was eager to be part of a surgical team. The work was challenging and more interesting than regular nursing. But after several months of training, the German matron said they had to choose one of us, and Szarlota showed more promise. But it felt like they didn't trust us together, and I was sent to the social work department."

I take a moment to digest this. Of course they wouldn't trust the two of them together. Hiring Danuta was an odd choice to begin with given her family background. Working with the orphans was definitely a demotion, yet it sounds as though she's well paid.

"My sister often came home with food and gifts," I say. "I'm assuming they came from Tarnowski. Is that right?"

"She swore me to secrecy, Irena. But I suppose that means nothing now."

"Please, tell me everything. I can't bear—" My voice catches, and she lays a hand on my back before she continues.

"They were in love, and I think they were lovers. He took her to cafés, even cabaret shows. He bought her so many expensive presents, she was embarrassed to take them home. She kept them in a trunk at the hospital. After she was arrested, I went to look for it; it's still there, but the matron wouldn't give me the key."

"You think she was arrested? What for?"

"Well, because of her and the doctor becoming too close. He looked so sad when she was taken."

"Really?"

"It's the Nazi General Government that runs the hospital, Irena. They hire Poles, but we're very low on their scale of importance."

"Even someone like Tarnowski?"

"It's more complicated than that. Szarlota confided that the German surgeons don't like him. They complain that he's an arrogant Pole, but she thought they were jealous because he often gets the most interesting cases. Even during my training, I noticed he was having patients referred by high-ranking Nazi officers. You see, they rely on his work, but he's still a Pole who has to be put in his— Oh my!" Laughing, she lays her hand on her chest. "I haven't heard my father sing in years."

We dry our hands and hurry to the living room, where Mama is playing and Danuta's father is singing a famous old love song in his quavery tenor voice—"*Miłość ci wszystko wybaczy*." Danuta sits on the sofa while I stand in the doorway, listening to the words *Love will forgive everything*, and wonder if that can ever be true when you're living in a war like this one.

IT'S BEEN A fruitful evening in many ways. While Mama and Pan Galik say a long goodbye in the warm May air, I yank Danuta's shawl off the hook and step back a few paces from the doorway.

"I'd like to talk to Tarnowski myself," I whisper, handing her the shawl. "Could you introduce us?"

"Oh, you won't find him at the hospital, Irena. According to my chemist, the hospital brass has disciplined him—forced him to take time away from his surgery without pay."

Nineteen

Warsaw, June 1942

"I'm quite sure it was that Wozniak person. How can you trust a girl who comes and goes all hours of the night?"

"No, not her. It has to be Malinowski. Remember the remark he made when the ghetto walls were going up."

Mother Mary. For the major part of our tunnel journey, our talkative transportees have been arguing about who betrayed them and the teenage brothers they were harboring.

Zofia and I came upon them by accident when we were transporting electronic apparatus from Mokotów to the Vault. I swear their white hair stood up straight when they saw us, and while Zofia and I managed to keep our composure, that was only after we'd both bleated like goats.

As we near the end of our rescue mission, I make a note of all the suspects' names they're debating. When the dust settles, Marysia and her intelligence cell will make a visit to their address. The couple has been hiding in the sewers for ten days, eating the groceries they'd just picked up.

"Pan, Pani!" Zofia cautions them. "We're nearing the exit. You must be quiet now."

The handover goes without a hitch, and it's only as we're walking back through the high tunnel that I understand how good we've become at this risky business; how efficient the aboveground teams are and how many safe houses we've created—all from this little project Marysia put me up to a year ago.

As soon as the cover closes above us, Zofia and I break into muffled laughter.

"Can you believe them?" she says.

"I know!" I wave my hands about in airy conversation. "As though they were promenading through the sewer, just doing a little window-shopping."

Her big man's laugh erupts before she can stifle it. Then she crosses herself. "Those poor brothers."

I inhale the fetid air, puff it out in a long breath—there is no laughter without tears anymore.

"Let's take the new Spa Route back," she says, fingering the amber rosary round her neck. "I'm meeting Fryderyk by the Marconi Fountain; we need to plan tomorrow's transport, and the Spa comes out near—"

"I know—the Fort. Please be careful. Better wear your sweet country girl bonnet."

That sends us into giggles again.

These days, Mati and Zofia often travel without me on guiding missions through the sewers, and Fryderyk's almost finished his sewer training. He's shy, and has terrible eyesight, and I worry about him losing his spectacles, but under Zofia's tutelage, he was very useful transporting stolen gold on our first mission together: a Gewehr 43 sniper rifle that Mati swooned over when he heard about it; an older Karabiner 98k; and a Spanish-made pistol I'm coveting for myself if the colonel approves. Still, I'm not sure the Vault is the safest place to hide them. My worry runs along a track with stops reaching back to childhood; it pauses now at the old Fort, where Elzbieta was executed.

"How well did you and Mati know Elzbieta?" I ask.

Zofia's luminous eyes seem to read my mind. "We were part of her study group, and we all worshipped her. She's a saint now."

I nod.

"Mati liked her," she says.

My breath catches.

"But not the way he likes you."

Mother Mary. Am I that transparent?

She drifts ahead of me in the tunnel.

I let my mind off its leash, and it makes a dash for Mati. I could go on pretending that the tumbling in my stomach when I hear his voice—or even when I spot his jacket in a distant crowd—is simply hunger pangs. But what a ridiculous time to be feeling like this. The work we do is dangerous. If we start a little fling and one of us is killed—or worse, captured! No, I can't let that happen.

Tucked beneath these protests is my guilt about Lotka. It's my sister who should be married by now, or at least engaged. Mama could have— *Cholera jasna, Irena!* What's the point of what-ifs?

I look up to see Zofia slowing down for me.

"You're quiet today, Ala. Any news about your sister?"

Zofia's risked so much to find Lotka, to save Leah. She even softened up a slimy Pawiak guard—enough for us to bribe him. His search through the prison records and cramped cells proved Lotka wasn't there. And yet, I answer Zofia with only a few vague details from my meetings with Elsa and Danuta. Why does my old mistrust of her persist?

"I could ask my mother to look for her at Treblinka."

I pause to smile at her angelic face. "I know you mean well—"

"Since my father died, she's been telling me things."

"Slow down. Your father died?"

"Shot himself in the head. At least, that's what they told Mama. Don't be sad. He was a beast."

"Still, your mother must be—"

"Free! You know what she told me? When we were living in Poznan, she plotted to kill him because of what he did to me."

I lay my hand on her arm, and she curls into me like a child.

"I wish I could feel free."

ENTERING THE SWASTIKA-ADORNED doors of the Deutsche Bank, with its uniformed German guards, an enormous photograph of the Führer disgracing the wall behind the bank of tellers, leaves no room for speculation—my mother and I are in Nazi territory.

I've done my best: one of Lotka's newer dresses and a pair of my mother's clip-on earrings form my guise of respectability. But Lotka's and Mama's feet are much smaller than mine, and as we stand in the queue, Mama's gaze falls to my battered brogues—all I have apart from my sewer boots. Mercifully, her lips clamp shut. In her navy suit and hat, she looks ready for a military drill.

As we approach the young man sprouting a copycat Hitler mustache, I fear the drill might become real, but Mama ignites her charm with pursed smiles and dignified dips of her head, greeting the teller in halting German before switching to Polish. The switch so alarms him, he has to call another teller over.

They scan Mama's bankbook and identification card with frowns and whispers. Then they make us wait while one of them knocks on the door marked *STELLVERTRETENDER BANKDIREKTOR*.

Mortified, Mama smiles and bows at the people behind us in the queue.

A moment later, a short blond man in a double-breasted suit stretched over his belly marches out to examine Mama's documents. More frowns and whispers among the three men, followed by a trip to another door marked *BANKDIREKTOR*.

A shiver runs down my spine, and I quickly scan the exit route, which ends with the two rifle-carrying, pistol-wearing guards at the door.

Through the glass behind the wicket, we watch the men pace outside the director's office. *Is this about Lotka? Or me?* I glance at Mama, who's pretending she's not with me.

When the director's door eventually opens, they walk in, and five minutes later walk out in brisk fashion, accompanied by the fearsome-looking director. He pauses on our side of the glass, raises his spectacles to stare at us, and waves.

"*Frau, Fräulein*." He dips his head. "*Guten Morgen*." Then he disappears back into his office.

I exhale. The Polish-speaking teller sheepishly approaches us. "You wish to make a withdrawal?"

I let Mama do the talking.

I am stunned at the size of Lotka's monthly salary. Did the hospital pay her that much more because she was a surgical nurse? I'll have to ask Danuta.

When the teller returns with a stack of *młynarki*, the General Government's version of our Polish money, Mama sends him a steely look and counts the notes. My heart cheers her little act of defiance, but my shock returns as I watch the teller writing a new deposit and balance in Mama's book.

I point to the previous deposit. "This was made by University Hospital last May?"

His smile makes me squirm. "*Ja, Fräulein.* Is it your holiday money?"

I'm on the verge of sputtering "*But my sister no longer works at University Hospital*" when I actually bite my tongue and wince at the sharp pain.

On the tram home, I almost expect my mother to sit in the German seats, but she flounces to the back, her bag of loot slung over her arm. All the way to Mokotów, I ponder the improbable: that Lotka might have gone on holiday and forgotten to tell us.

AT HOME IN her bedroom, once she's taken off her heels and hung up her suit, Mama has a violent fit of weeping. I sit beside her on the bed, attempt to touch her, but she fidgets away.

"I miss Lotka so much," she sobs.

"So do I," I say, and mean it.

When she curls up on the bed, her back turned toward me, I hover my fingers over her hair, but my cowardice gets the better of me, and I leave her to her grief.

After a hasty supper of leftover *bigos*, I present her with the Mozart I found in the box of used sheet music at the Chopin shop.

"Aah," she says, leafing through the music. "Will you be seeing Mati tonight?"

"Yes." In fact, Mati's not the only one I'll be seeing, but I say nothing more about the person Marysia's sending us to visit.

Her mood changed, she turns to smile at me. "Please give him my best."

I'm not used to this new Mama, and I wait for a callous remark about my clothes, my hair, or just about my being. But, saved by Mozart, it doesn't come.

In the courtyard, another miraculous thing: Mr. Godlewski's plum tree is sending out a green shoot from its stump. I crouch to admire it, and his face floats up before me.

Pluck or peck, he said. Am I still pecking? Or have I caved in to life under our occupiers?

On Marszałkowska, I check a shopwindow reflection for any followers, see Mati crossing the road toward me.

"Ala," he says. "Long time no see."

I smile, my stomach performing tumbling tricks. We worked together in the sewers only last week.

He lights a cigarette, smiles at me through the smoke.

"My mother sends you her best."

"That's very kind of her. How did she get along with Leopold?"

"Famously!" It was Mati who recommended the piano tuner. A white-haired man, probably old enough to be my mother's uncle, he arrived stooped over his black bag, kissed my mother's hand, and said, "Agata Marianowska! I heard your Chopin E minor concerto at the old Philharmonic Hall. You must have been no more than sixteen."

Mati throws his head back in a warm laugh. "That old fox." He shakes his head. "Please give my best to your mother and tell her I have some wild mushrooms perfect for pierogi."

"No one in our house is going to make pierogi from scratch, Mati."

"Are you inviting me to dinner, Ala? I'll be happy to show you how."

"Cheese or bacon?"

"My mushroom-bacon pierogi are . . ." He smooches his fingertips, and I laugh from my belly. How is he able to make me feel like a happy child?

"I hope you're not afraid of dark cemeteries," I say. "We're going to Old Powązki."

He shivers his shoulders. "There's a good mushroom patch in the seventeen hundreds section, but I've only been there on a bright day."

On the tram, we sit arms touching, and I put my hand out the window to feel the warm breeze. The night feels blessed. We're comfortably quiet until we get off at the cemetery stop, and following Marysia's map, walk past the main gate to the break in the wall. I help him unsnag his jacket as he squeezes through. "Stand still."

"How did you get so good at this unsnagging business?"

Shaking with laughter, I hang my head, and when I look up, he leans in and kisses me. "I've been wanting to do that for so long. You don't mind?"

"No," I say. He takes my hand and pulls me through the gap. And that's how we run down the Avenue of the Distinguished, barely noting Poland's famous and illustrious, carpeted now in grass and shadow.

By the time we get to Małgorzata's safe house, it's pitch-black. I turn on my torch to check the map, look around the crowded graveyard. *Mother Mary, how can she live here?*

"I think this is it," Mati says, prying aside a mat of vines. We wait, staring up at the bewigged statues of dukes seated beside angels atop the massive crypt. I stand apart from my liaison captain, but he reaches over to stroke my cheek with the back of his hand. At exactly ten minutes past ten, we see a sliver of light at the edges of the high wooden door. I give a low whistle—the first five notes of

"*Siekiera motyka*." From inside the door, the next five notes follow. When the door slowly creaks open like a scene from *Nosferatu*, I squeak and grab Mati's arm. Małgorzata, wrapped in her winter coat and fur hat, stands inside the doorway. Holding Mati's bare arm, I'm suddenly aware of our summery clothing.

Her eyes dart from side to side. "Are you sure you weren't followed?"

I look at Mati. Then I lie and say, "Clear." Surveillance is impossible when you're running, and pausing to kiss every few yards. As we enter the earthy-smelling crypt, Mati blurts, "Are you sure you can't come out? It's a beautiful summer night."

"No," she shudders. "It's not safe for me."

The tremor in her voice confirms Marysia's suspicions: she sent us to test her impression that Małgorzata's mind has been broken by her close call with a *łapanka*.

She leads us into an antechamber with a gray stone altar at its center covered in pillows and bedclothes. "Here," she says, pulling them off. "Wrap these around yourselves and cover your heads. You don't want to lose body heat too quickly."

Mati takes a woolen blanket and wraps it around both of us. Then Małgorzata throws the other one over our heads and shoulders. I stifle the urge to giggle.

When I poke my head through the gap in the blanket, the sight of her face jerks me into reality. "How long have you been hiding here?"

"Since the *łapanka*. Exactly fifty-five hours now."

I shake my head. There's a pall over her, her eyelids puffy and black as though she's been punched.

"Thank God you got away," Mati says.

"I bit him. Then I ran like the devil and rolled under that row of lilacs behind Canon Square."

Mati goes still, shakes his head. Then he smiles his wide smile. "We brought you some food, and water, a magazine. And a thermos of hot tea."

"Thank you." Steam rises as she opens the thermos, pours herself a cup. "They're trying to kill me," she says finally. "I told Marysia months ago that

I was being followed." Her teeth crush her upper lip. "Now they try to grab me in the *łapanka*. I had no choice but to go into hiding."

Mati and I exchange a glance. Apart from being an AK officer, Małgorzata's now an experienced doctor, laboring tirelessly in our underground clinics as well as at Infant Jesus Hospital. Countless times, she's helped her resistance colleagues with medicines and advice.

I keep my voice soft. "Do you know who's following you?"

"Of course not. If I knew, I would have told Marysia long ago."

"Gestapo?" Mati says.

"Well, they're the most obvious. But what reason would they have to target me?"

I can think of several, but I try a different tack. "Have you talked to your sister recently?"

"Edyta? I haven't heard from her in over a year. She moved to Kraków, married a Volksdeutsche. I wasn't invited."

Of course. Once Małgorzata joined the resistance, her sister wanted nothing more to do with her.

"Any sign of Lotka?" she asks, her hands clasped round the warm cup.

A spasm twists my gut.

"I'm sorry," she says. "Your sister was always very kind to us at Infant Jesus. So different from my sister, who only cares about her own safety and bank account."

I nod again, remembering Lotka's despair at the pointed neglect of the Polish children in her care.

"About once a month, she'd drop off a pile of dressings or surgical tools. Ointments or other medicine. We'd chat. I think she did the same for her former nursing colleagues."

Like a fish unused to air, I open, close, open my mouth. "Do you mean she took things from University Hospital and gave them to you?"

"I don't know why you're so surprised, Ala. Medical people share things all the time."

"Even under enemy occupation?" I fix her with my Godlewski stare.

She blinks a few times. "Oh. I see what you mean."

Mati tilts his head at her. "You're thinking that's why Lotka was taken?"

Małgorzata covers her mouth with her fingers. "Or why I'm being hunted."

But that doesn't sound right to me. There's something I'm missing. I let the blanket slip off my shoulders, get up off the cold stone.

While Mati gently explains to Małgorzata that this crypt cannot be her long-term hideout, and that we have a more practical house with a hidden attic space, I walk to the back of the antechamber, where a second door usually leads to the burial room. A deep crack, made by an axe by the look of it, splits one side of the locked door, but I can't see into the dark chamber. I close my eyes, allow my mind to conjure Lotka's troubled expression the last time I saw her.

What did she say? "Things are difficult at work." No—"Things are *complicated*." Was Lotka continuing her strategy of consorting with the Hitlerow as a means of protecting the people she cared about? On the other hand—

"Tell Marysia whatever you want! I'm not leaving here!"

In the light of his torch, I meet Mati's stunned gaze.

DURING OUR MERRY travels to the cemetery—now a disappearing idyll—I told myself if Mati wanted to kiss me again on our way home, I'd give in to the rising wave that made me want to break myself on him.

Małgorzata changed all that.

"What do you think?" he says, marching at a brisk clip past the tilting obelisks.

"Marysia might be right," I say, struggling to keep up.

"She's terrified."

"Yes, but is it justified?"

"Ala," he says, pulling at the roots of his hair. "I saw Edyta two days ago in Canon Square."

Twenty

Toronto, November 2010

Irena's been avoiding me all morning. No demands for sugary cups of Red Rose. No chummy breakfast together. Even Cheriblare is barred from her studio: "Shoo, shoo!"

And we were just starting to be easy with each other again. I'd like to erase the last twelve hours, press start, begin again. But what kind of chemical erases the sounds and images of her camp experience?

To say that I'm ashamed doesn't capture the drowning sense I have—heart and lungs too heavy to lift me from the black water. I push my bowl aside. The spoonful of oatmeal with yogurt, honey, and blueberries might as well be newspaper in my mouth.

Last night, I heard her toss and turn. She was up to the bathroom three times, and when the early light summoned me around five, I found her already in the kitchen making toast. The ashtray I'd cleaned before going to bed was half-full this morning. I don't think she slept a wink, and neither did I.

I drag myself to the sink. I have no one to blame but myself. How is it that I know so little about my grandmother's life? Sophie must have told me things. But I was so absorbed in worshipping Irena Marianowska, the great artist, I never asked the questions that plague me now. Over cocktails, at social evenings in this very house, it was Mati who recounted his war history with such fatalistic humor, my young, eavesdropping ears might as well have been listening to *The Count of Monte Cristo*.

I busy myself with scouring the oatmeal pot. If Irena ever talks to me again, can I summon the courage to ask the questions I need to, and stay for the answers, and stay for the after-answer effects?

I pause in my dishwashing to look up a word Irena used in her story of the beaten girl—*blockova*. They were prisoners chosen by the SS to guard and police their fellow prisoners in the camps. Some of them were vicious. *Shit Galore!* Already, I'm flinching at the images my mind's composing. I suppose this is what Sophie tried to protect me from. But I'm in it now, Soph. A tide's pulling me out, and I have no choice but to swim even farther from shore.

To make matters more interesting, now that I've triggered Irena's camp memories, it doesn't feel safe to leave her alone. I call Tahira to see if she could look in on her, and she offers to skip her class, but I say, "No. Just give her a call because she may not pick up if she knows it's me." *Shit Encore.*

What's more, given that Irena's accusation contradicts everything Stefan's told me, I have no choice but to ask him in person, "Hey, Stefan, were you ever in the SS?"

How's that going to play?

Before I leave the house, I place a pot of tea on the counter. Against it, I lean a note with a caricature of my own mortified face with my hand over my mouth, and a big *SORRY* in a cloud above my frizzy hair. *See you this afternoon. Call if you need anything.* A row of leaping hearts.

AS I WHEEL into the health center parking lot, my head's pounding. Not all of Stefan's stories are lies. His wife, Mary, existed; his son and his landscaping business are real. But if Irena's right, such a big lie throws the whole life into question, implicates everyone who ever knew him. Ola could have been on the side of the Nazis, too. Maybe she wasn't killed by the Germans, but by the Poles.

I decide to walk up the four flights to Stefan's room so I can pause at each landing to summon courage. Farzaad agreed to translate the recording, but right now, I need something from Stefan himself. Something definite like a confession or denial.

Out of breath, I knock on his door.

No answer. I take a step into the room. A nurse stands at the head of his bed.

"Look, Mr. C., you have a visitor." She waves me in. "He's not feeling so good today."

"I can come back," I say, but she mouths "It's okay" before she leaves.

Stefan's lying on his side, facing the window, hooked up to a monitoring machine.

I put my jacket on the back of the chair. "Sorry you're not feeling well."

He looks up at me, a tight smile of recognition. But the eyes are sunken, the cheekbones jutting against taut skin. How could someone change so much so quickly?

I look through my backpack for my recorder. Can I go through with this? Rummaging deeper, I draw out the blue and silver box from Kolata. On the way here, I stopped to buy Irena's favorite dark chocolate ginger truffles. Stefan could use one. So could I.

He glances inside the box. "No, thank you." He rolls over onto his back. "Some water, please." Up on one elbow, his hair standing up in greasy peaks, he shivers as I hand him the cup.

"Stefan, I listened to our interview from yesterday." I stay focused on his protruding wrist bones as he sips the water. "There was lots of shouting in German."

"Thank you," he says, handing back the cup. Then he sinks back into the pillows and closes his eyes.

"I know some Poles spoke German . . ." *Jesus, Jo. Get to the point.* "Stefan, I'm sorry to ask you this, but did you ever fight with the Germans? I mean on the side of the Germans?"

He keeps his eyes shut. "Ola and I," he whispers.

"Yes, I know about Ola and you working in the sewers, but did you ever work with the Nazis? Were you in the SS?"

When he turns his head, his blue eyes impale me. "What more do you want of me?"

Cold sweat trickles down my arms.

He holds me in his gaze until I sit down. Then he shuts his eyes again and begins a rasping breathing.

Perched on the edge of the armchair, I find my breath syncing to his, like a child asleep in a parent's arms. When the nurse comes back to check his vital signs, I get up to leave.

At the elevator, I'm surprised when Roland and a woman exit the open doors.

Roland's hands are jammed into the pockets of his long black coat. When he says nothing, I extend my hand to the woman. "Hi, I'm Jo Blum."

"Nice to meet you, Jo. I'm Cynthia."

She's short and slender, with long black hair and a nervous smile.

"Dad always looks forward to your visits," she says.

I hesitate. "I think he had a rough night."

"Yes, we heard," Roland says, looking down the hallway toward his father's room.

"How's the sculpture coming?" Cynthia asks.

The bing of the elevator startles me. "It's coming along fine." Waving goodbye, I back into the closing doors.

Running into Cynthia and Roland has recast the tone of the last hour. I walk to the washroom, where I wash my hands, press my damp fingers to my cheeks, trying to reconstruct the moment I asked Stefan about fighting on the German side. But my anger and suspicion have receded, replaced by guilt and shame. And I never even turned on the recorder. Something Frank once said comes back to me: he called me a reverse vampire, poking the dying to reveal their secrets. What did I accomplish today other than frightening a sick old man?

In a daze, I walk to my bike, pausing to look up at Stefan's window. Irena's been stabbed by a voice she hears in her worst nightmares. That's my doing. And because I didn't quite believe her, I had to prod Stefan.

Twisting my backpack onto my back, I set my route southward to St. John's Cemetery. If this is a simple case of mistaken identity, I could resolve things with Irena and still complete Stefan's sculpture. But if Irena's right?

People are never simple, Jo.

Right.

Cycling soon settles me, my bike grounding me in a rhythm that takes me out of my head. I shortcut through subway parks, dip into the Don Valley, then back onto streets teeming with people—old, young, bent over phones or swinging to earbud tunes. I move fast, not meeting the eyes of a hijabied woman weighted by an immense briefcase, nor those of a young woman in heels so high, her feet are perpendicular to the ground. A tight-suited man whizzes by, talking on his phone while weaving in and out of traffic on a longboard. It's delicate choreography, and I'm part of it—connecting by respecting the privacy we've drawn around ourselves.

AT ST. JOHN'S, the trees tower above the wrought-iron fence. No sun today. The sky could be a rough northern sea swirling pale blue patches between gray clouds. Meandering to the section where Stefan will be buried, I stand with my back against the old ash tree, look at my hands. All my fingernails are demolished to the quick as of last night.

Did I really expect Stefan to answer my questions? In my imagination, I try out a scenario: accidentally playing him the recording of his Nazi voice.

But that feels cruel. *Can you be cruel to a Nazi?* He's a frail old man. Irena's old, too. Her memory falters when it comes to names of things; decades often collapse into days. I have to mend things with her.

I arch my back into the trunk of the dying tree, feel the crusty folds of the diamond bark against my shoulder blades. The tree passes a shudder through me, and I hear a seesawing. Then a crack. Startled, I look up as a fracturing branch lands a spray of twigs on my head. "Ouch!" My teeth clamp down on my tongue, shooting pain through my whole body. A dusty haze clouds my vision. I can't see out; only in. Black lines intersect, zoom across a pale screen behind my eyes. I fumble for my sketchbook in my backpack, draw quickly, my arm moving across the page like an electric tool following its own coded path. Dismayed now that it's done, and shivering, I gape at the drawing.

THROUGH THE BIG south windows, I see my grandmother painting in her studio, her back to me. *She's still alive.* I let myself in through the kitchen entrance. Cheriblare weaves a welcome between my feet, and I stumble to the table with my bags of groceries.

"Hello, I'm home!"

No answer. Just Ella and Louis swinging in Irena's suite. Lifting Cheriblare into my arms, I kiss her soft head. My grandmother has every right to be angry with me. Irena would never lie. She might be silent, she might forget, but she'd never twist the truth to her advantage.

With a plate of apple cake as my peace offering, I knock, slide open her studio door, inhaling the rich infusion of oil paint and turpentine. When I stick my head in, I can't help grinning. My grandmother's wearing her ancient painting smock, splotched with years of oil and acrylic, not just on the front, but the back, too, because she wears it buttoned either way.

"I brought you some *szarlotka*," I say, placing it on top of the wooden chest. I'm flooded by a longing to walk up behind her, put my arms around her waist, tell her once more how sorry I am for mistrusting her.

She half turns, dips her brush in a can on the long table beside her, returns to her canvas.

"Not now."

IN MY WORKSHOP, I stare at my sketchbook. I made three drawings at the cemetery after the first image of Stefan's sculpture came through the haze. I drew in a panic—scared that the strange broken cross would evaporate, that the noisy faces might dissolve. I pull a stool up to the counter and begin filling in the lines.

The faces are mobile, like the stone faces carved high up on the entranceways to medieval cathedrals. Lips stretch in leering smiles, eyebrows frown over bulging eyes, cheeks balloon into hard apples. But everything is tiny like a family of grotesque dolls. Too late to stop the sculpture now. This thing bubbling in my head has its own life, determined to be made whether I want to make something for Stefan Cegielski or not.

At supper, Irena and I slump at the kitchen table, neither of us hungry for food. I slice my sausage into thin rounds, stare at the potatoes hardening on my plate. Irena pokes her fork into her broccoli, never lifts it to her mouth. Then she pours herself another glass of wine and takes a gulp.

"I'll eat something later," I say, taking my plate to the counter.

"Me too," she says, pushing hers aside. "I want to rest in my room."

Which means she's going to smoke. I put the leftovers in the fridge. She pauses in the kitchen doorway.

"You want to smoke?" she says, arching her eyebrows.

My heart does a little leap. "Yeah. You go ahead. I'll bring the wine bottle."

Ensconced in our wicker chairs, the side table with its heavy glass ashtray between us, I sense the battle waging in our minds. Every cigarette, every sip of wine feels like conversation, but something's wrong, smudges of feeling like screens between us. I pick up my sketchbook on the seat beside me, open it to my recent drawings.

"I can't go ahead with Stefan's sculpture. But maybe you want to see what images finally came to me this morning." I hand her the book. A moment later my phone chimes in my pocket. *Roland.*

"I'll be right back." I hurry into the kitchen.

"Hi. We wanted you to know—Stefan passed away at six thirty this evening."

An unexpected pang. "I'm so sorry." Even though I knew this was coming. Even though he might be a Nazi. *Might have been a Nazi?*

"There's still some detail we have to figure out about the funeral," he says, his voice thickening.

Please say you're canceling the commission.

"Why don't you come by the office," he says. "Cynthia and I would like to see the drawings for the sculpture."

I swallow hard.

Alone at the kitchen table, I hang my head in my hands. No tears, but still that aching pang. Farzaad's translation has to reveal the truth.

As I enter the sitting room, Irena glances up. "Make this sword sculpture for me. It's very beautiful," she says, the sketchbook in her lap.

Sword? I step forward, peer over her shoulder at the cross, fractured at the crux, sharply splintered, without a Christ figure.

She blows smoke into the air. "In Warsaw, there was a church with a stone statue of St. George, but his sword was broken after the first bombing. He had just the handle left in his hands. So we made a new sword from whatever we could find—wood and old iron."

"You know I drew that for Stefan," I say, lifting the book from her lap. The thought of Irena having Stefan's grave sculpture makes me nauseous. But also the thought of Irena dying. *Not yet.*

"That phone call was from his son," I say. "He died a few hours ago."

She exhales vigorously, tips her head back against the chair, and gazes at the ceiling. "You going to the funeral?"

"No. How could I?"

"You can make a sword like this for my grave." She inserts a fresh cigarette into her black cigarette holder.

"It's not a sword; it's a broken crucifix."

"To me it is a sword," she says, thrusting herself forward, a flare of gold in the blue of her eyes.

"It came to me after you told me he was an SS officer."

My grandmother flicks her old Dunhill lighter.

"I asked him," I say.

"And what did he answer?"

"Nothing." But his blue eyes had impaled me.

She sweeps her cigarette holder in an arc. *See. I told you.*

"I'm so sorry you heard that recording." I grimace. "I was very careless."

She falls back against the headrest on the chair. "I miss my Mati."

"Me too."

Our eyes meet and we smile glumly. My grandmother wipes a tear with the back of her hand, and I wipe my sniffling nose with the back of mine. Radiating between us is a warmth that almost fills the hole in my heart.

"I'm getting Stefan's recording translated," I say.

"Why?"

"He lied to me. I want to know the truth."

"Don't be foolish," Irena says. "In a war, everybody lies."

"Are we at war now?"

She looks at me, smoke screening her face. "He can't hurt you anymore."

Hurt *me*? I try to read her expression, but it's her silence that speaks, and what I hear is sympathy. I lean closer. "I understand that he hurt you, but how was he hurting me?"

She shakes her head. "Will you make a sculpture for my grave?"

"Of course I will. But not this one. I can't."

She stubs out her cigarette. "That man was a soldier. He was a *sadystyczny* killer. I was a killer, too. And your grandfather."

I begin to protest: she and Mati could never be sadistic killers, but she sits up straight, her floppy sweater falling off her shoulders.

"I was in charge. I had to say who the traitors were. The ones who were talking to the Germans, telling them our meetings, giving them our names. We had to stop them. Mrs. Powanska—she was one. She was in her kitchen with her father. We shot them both, of course. This was necessary."

"You, personally, shot them?"

She folds her arms across her chest.

"How many?"

"Many." She doesn't blink. "It was my job to find them; usually I was there when we killed them."

"Shot them."

"Not always shooting. Sometimes we ran out of bullets." She stretches her legs and crosses her ankles.

My hands grip the arms of the chair. "It's not the same thing," I say quietly.

"Nothing is the same thing," she says, her voice rising.

I get louder, too. "You and Mati were protecting innocent people. Stefan was murdering them!"

"You know nothing!" she snorts. "Go make some Red Rose! And bring some *szarlotka*!"

Twenty-One

Warsaw, 1943

The boy is scrawny, like so many of us these days. Bony knees, bony elbows, and hair too long. I bend over him, resisting the urge to lift a ragged lock off his face.

I wish Mati were here, but he and Fryderyk are scavenging for guns and ammunition today. Anyway, this is my job and Marysia's, not Mati's.

Last year, when the colonel promoted me to the rank of major, he also asked me to join the intelligence wing of the AK. I jumped at the chance that gave me to dig deeper into Lotka's disappearance. For almost two years now, every lead has been a dead end, every rumor, an enticing idea and nothing more. Yesterday, I found myself having to leaf through my old sketches to animate her face and hear her gentle voice.

In the last weeks, my intelligence training has progressed from underground classrooms, where I learned disguises, playacting, methods of interrogation, and the defensive use of weapons, including knives and firearms, to the dangerous streets and even more dangerous homes of Warsaw citizens.

As intelligence officers in the AK, Marysia and I have a complicated series of actions to follow. First, as post office workers, we open suspicious mail, often addressed to the Gestapo or General Government. These letters, written by earnest Polish citizens, sometimes denounce smugglers or warn of AK sabotage plans, but there are also vengeful or petty people who denounce their neighbors on a whim for suspicion of harboring Jews or other innocents the dragons are determined to annihilate. Marysia and I keep a close watch for anything that reads like a denunciation of Kasha, the Freemans' housekeeper and guardian of Leah and Davey.

The second task Marysia and I must perform is to approach the ones denounced, in disguise, and warn them of the danger they're in. Since the letters are often anonymous, there is detective work to find the denouncers. Once we find them, the AK higher-ups ask for evidence, and once we verify that, they usually approve our actions. We move swiftly to deal with the traitors. It's one way we save lives and keep AK secrets from the Hitlerow.

It was a fellow Scout who reported seeing Piotr and his mother walking through the dreaded doors on Szucha Avenue, unaccompanied by Gestapo guards. Marysia and I broke into this pitiful apartment as soon as the mother left for work this morning. When we came through the back door, the boy screamed, and Marysia probably hit him harder than she should have. He's finally coming around.

"Piotr? Here, sip some water." I hand him the cracked cup. He takes it with a shaking hand.

"What happened?" he says, touching his head.

Today, Marysia and I are heavily disguised. I point to our AK armbands. "I'm Ilsa and this is Helena. We came to talk to you because you're in danger. The Gestapo is following you. Do you know why?"

"No. Are they outside?"

"Maybe." Marysia steps in front of him and the boy's eyes widen, his thin shoulders start to shake. "We know that you and your mother visited Gestapo headquarters." She glares at the boy, jabbing a cigarette at his face. "What did you tell them?"

"Nothing. I told them nothing. Honest."

I keep my voice soft and calm. "But you did go there."

Piotr hangs his head and starts to sob. "I didn't want to. Mama made me."

Marysia pokes his shoulder with her finger. "Why would a nice Polish mother make her son visit the Nazi secret police?"

Piotr turns to me with pleading eyes. "She knows I'm a Scout, but I don't tell her about delivering messages. That's against Scout rules. She thinks I just sell newspapers."

"Good man," I say. We wait while he struggles to put his story together.

"I forgot a message in my pocket. I'm really sorry."

Marysia tears at her hair. "She found it? Your mother found a secret AK message because you were stupid and lazy and forgot?"

I shake my head at her. "It's easy to forget when you're in the middle of a war like we are, isn't it, Piotr? Did you read the note?"

He nods. "It wasn't in proper code. I could understand most of it."

Scouts are trained to memorize written notes, people's looks and conversations. I smile at him. "Go ahead. Tell us what it said."

He clears his throat. "The coat belongs to Szarlota Iwanowska, nurse at University Hospital."

Lotka? *Mother Mary.*

"To obtain the coat and its contents, hide in the hospital among friends."

Dizzy, I look around for something to hold on to. Marysia, too, is staring at Piotr as her hand roots for a notepad and pencil in her knapsack. The boy repeats the message.

Strange. Not real code. Lotka's actual name and the place she works. A major betrayal, and yet, not a true denunciation.

I take a deep breath, walk around in circles for a bit. Then it strikes me.

"Piotr, which drop box did you find the message in?"

He looks puzzled. "It wasn't a drop box," he says. "An AK lady gave me the message on Oleska Street. She told me to deliver it to the Blessed Mary drop box."

"How do you know she was AK?" Marysia asks.

"She showed me the armband in her pocket. And she spoke Polish."

Marysia and I exchange a glance. "Was the message addressed to anyone?" I ask.

"No." Our agitation is making him nervous. "I have to use the toilet," he says, squirming.

Marysia whirls on him. "Not now!"

I lean forward and place my hands on his shoulders. "So, Piotr, your mother took the message to the Gestapo and you went with her. Who took the message from you?"

"A Gestapo major."

I nod. "What did he ask you?"

"He wanted to know where the drop boxes are in Mokotów. I told him that wasn't my route."

"What else?"

"He said I have to make a list of all the Mokotów drop boxes, and he would send someone to my house tonight."

Mother Mary. "Piotr, this is a hard question. Did the officer hurt you or your mother in any way?"

His narrow chest begins to heave again. "Mama asked him for a reward for bringing in the note. She asked for a better apartment with a new heater for winter."

Jesu Maria.

"The man slapped her and she cried."

"Did he hit you?" Marysia asks.

Piotr shakes his head. "He said I was brave for bringing him the note. He said I should carry on my job as a Scout like normal." Then the boy covers his face with his hands and howls. "He said if I didn't do what he asked, they would tear Mama's hair out and beat her to death in front of me." He turns to Marysia with terror in his eyes. "Where is she now? Do you have her?"

When he pees all over the chair and floor, I quickly step away. Marysia motions to me and we move to a corner of the room.

"No AK soldier would write a note like that," she says, lighting a cigarette.

I wave away her smoke. "Unless they wanted to hurt Lotka and betray all of us."

"Nothing's impossible these days."

"What do we do with him?" I ask.

She shakes her head. "They'll torture him and he'll talk. Too many others will die." Then she hands me the Luger.

"You do it," she says. "I'll distract him."

I look at the shivering boy. He can't be more than fifteen. The old gun hangs heavy in my hand, and I start to shake.

"Ala." Marysia grips my arm. "He's useless to us now. We're protecting the network."

A roiling black chaos storms across my chest. While I struggle to catch my breath, Marysia grabs the gun from my hand.

"Wait," I say, and walk toward the boy sitting in his own urine, stand at a distance in front of him, and call his name. Marysia shoots him from behind so as not to frighten him.

We are, each of us, guilty of crimes. But we don't look back. Only forward. Now we have to deal with the mother.

THE DRAGONS ARE quiet tonight. Of course, this means bad things are happening to people in dark places.

At the Vault, Fryderyk, Zofia, and I set up easels, as we've been doing lately. We're an art class meeting to paint together now, a necessary subterfuge. The dragons are becoming more desperate in their search for resisters with the AK ranks swelling and the Wehrmacht shrinking. To the east of us, the Russians are hemming in the German army, and to the west, only weeks ago, Italy surrendered.

Today, I need to get my cell's thoughts on Piotr's note about Lotka. And we have to find a new hiding place for the guns Mati and Fryderyk stole. It's Mati's opinion that the Vault gives us a false sense of security. I agree.

"My bird is the best," Zofia says, twirling around with her canvas. "It actually looks like a bird, and not like a dinosaur, like Fryderyk's."

"Dinosaur, bird. Same thing," he says, chasing her round the easels.

With her hair in pigtails on either side of her head, Zofia looks about twelve. She lands a pirouette in front of me. "Should I get an easel for Mati?"

"Don't." No sense tempting fate. If Mati doesn't return from the sewers tonight, his empty easel will haunt us. I put the tiniest dab of paint on each palette—why waste good paint?

I won't start the meeting without Mati, though. No one's seen him since he left to conduct two AK members through the sewers this morning, but it's not unusual for delays to happen.

"We're living on the edge of a precipice," I say to quiet Zofia and Fryderyk, "and you're chasing about like headless chickens."

"On the edge of an earthquake," says Fryderyk.

"On the edge of a hurricane," Zofia returns.

"On the edge of a tiger's mouth," I whisper, placing my finger on my lips.

"Oh. That's the best one, isn't it?" She nudges Fryderyk until he grabs her and holds her still.

I shake my head. You'd never guess that we're soldiers waiting for our exiled leaders to give the go-ahead to rise up against the invaders. My heart swoops like a swallow when I think about walking freely through my city, about the death camps opening their doors and the prisoners—*Jesu Maria*—the stories we've heard seem incredible. But I believe them. We start every meeting now with a salute to Anielewicz, Davey's hero and a leader of this April's Ghetto Uprising. For one month the ghetto warriors rattled the dragons. Now its burned-out buildings are full of ghosts.

I stir the green paint on the palette, mix it with a bit of brown for the tail feathers of the stuffed partridge working as our model. Through the labyrinth of my intelligence network, I hear that Leah and Davey are still safe in hiding.

By the grace of Mary, I pray that Mrs. Freeman died long before the Germans laid waste to the village behind those walls.

Where is Mati?

I wind my way to the back of the room, where the guns are hidden, tilt a tall canvas forward inside its wooden crate. There's the Karabiner and Gewehr. The pistols are well hidden behind a small canvas leaning against a bigger one. But Elsa's locked dresser at University Hospital would be a better hiding place. No one would think of looking there. I reposition the Karabiner between two large portraits and cover them with canvas cloth.

Zofia walks up beside me and strokes my arm. "Don't worry, he'll be here soon."

I smile at her, tuck a dark curl behind her ear—and freeze.

The sounds of heavy boots running above us. German voices. *Cholera!* I signal to Zofia and Fryderyk to make a run for it. I reach for my rucksack, but boots are tearing down the ramp, crashing through a hole in the ceiling of the Vault. We jump to our easels. Two German soldiers appear before us, rifles pointing at our hearts. Then two more guards, followed by a Gestapo officer, taking his sweet time. I make my feet move, step forward with my wet paintbrush in my hand.

"Good evening, Herr Officer. Can I help you?"

He ignores me. We're all suspended, brushes in midair. He begins to stride about the room, examining the canvases on our easels.

I blab like a fool. "I'm the teacher. These are my painting students."

His silence controls us. He slows at Zofia's easel, stands so close to her, he's almost smelling her face. Fryderyk mustn't move a muscle. Zofia's young, and she's Zofia, so we protect her. But she's got iron in her blood.

He issues an order and two guards begin a search—shooting open the filing cabinet, emptying old crates onto the floor, lifting the carpet, and smashing things with the butts of their rifles.

"Fräulein Professor!"

His voice so startles me, I squeak like a mouse.

"Let me see you draw a portrait of her. At once."

Zofia grasps his mix of German and Polish before I do, turns her stool and positions herself so I can see her.

"I'll make a charcoal sketch," I say. I don't want to give them a reason to shoot any of us, so I add, "The paper and charcoal are in the drawer over there."

He flicks his head in the direction of the drawers, takes out a cigarette case. One of the soldiers walks me to the shelves at the back of the room. I gather a sheet of paper, grab a box of charcoal sticks. Suddenly the soldier is flipping through the canvases in the bins. The exact place the guns are hidden. I run to his side and wave the supplies in his face. "I have everything."

He turns and looks at Zofia, angelic on her stool, then at me. It's only half a second, but there's an agreement between us. Or between him and Zofia. If I could replay the second, I wouldn't be any surer about what just happened, but something like nerves touching nerves. He uses his gun to point me to the center of the room. A muffled sound reminds me that we're expecting Mati at any moment. If he comes past the main entrance, he'll see the Gestapo car. There must be a dragon guarding it. But if he rings the bunker bell at the back, he'll walk right into this little scene.

Why didn't I try to paint her with the oil palette? Pride. I'm good at charcoal portraits. Not so good with oil. My hand's shaking so much, I'm smudging every line I draw. Did the soldier see the guns? I'm sure he did. Then why didn't he sound the alarm? The fluttering in my veins suddenly settles. I'm not afraid anymore. I almost laugh out loud at the absurdity of our situation. I glance at the officer on his stool. He isn't watching me. He doesn't care what I draw.

I begin to understand that he's waiting for Mati, or for someone else. How do I warn them? My scratches fill the silence. One of the soldiers clicks his heels. Fryderyk is frozen at his easel. Does he have the same dread I do? Only Zofia is relaxed, a smile playing about her mouth as I keep drawing and smudging and drawing and smudging. *Cholera.* Now she's twitching her eyebrows like dancing worms.

As always, the eyes are the most difficult for me to get right, and Zofia's eyes especially are so dark, large, and luminous, like a Caravaggio painting. I'm almost done. Just a few stray tendrils of hair. I thought we'd been so careful, each of us checking we weren't followed here. *Not careful enough.* When I'm finished, I stand back, regard my work. A breeze wafts in from somewhere, and the hairs on the back of my neck stand up. The sound of a window being smashed. Someone's up there on the higher floors. Someone they've missed. *Please, not Mati.*

Whirling about, the officer issues swift orders, and then he and two guards rush back up the ramp. Sounds of gunfire.

"*Hände hoch!*" yells one of our guards, and we quickly raise our arms.

In the rooms above us, shouts of "*Halt! Halt!*" More gunfire. More boots pounding in the direction of the big front doors.

For what seems like an hour, we stand with our arms and hands raised above our heads. The tingling pins and needles give way to excruciating pain.

The officer returns, striding confidently down the ramp, and I wonder if they've caught the person they were looking for. *Not Mati!*

"Nobody moves, nobody leaves," he says. My eyes meet Fryderyk's above the top of his easel. The officer looks at my sketch of Zofia, then back at me.

Outside a car engine starts up, a shout, a rifle shot followed by another and another. Tires squealing. The officer removes his revolver from his holster. A minute later, a new soldier skids down the ramp.

"How many?" asks the officer.

"One, Captain." *One*. Was that Mati doing the shooting? Or was he being shot at?

"Class is over." The captain takes a step back and aims his gun at Zofia's head, swings sharply, and shoots the portrait, one smoking hole between the eyes, the bullet lodging in the wood of the easel. "No more classes, no more meetings," he says. "We close this place for good. If you're seen near this building again, you'll be executed immediately. *Versteht ihr?*"

Like obedient children, we all nod. Then we troop up the ramp in single file to the first floor, rifles pointed at our backs, our partridges left to their own devices.

Outside the main door, with the barricades torn or kicked out, the body of a German soldier sprawls face down on the path, blood pooled under his jaw. I count the remaining soldiers and conclude the dead man is the one who saw the guns. A jeep pulls to the curb—a driver with one heavily armed soldier aiming directly at our group. They must have signaled for help. Zofia, Fryderyk, and I still have our hands in the air. I feel the chill and remember our jackets in the Vault. Have I left anything important in the pockets? In my bag?

When I see the black, wet patches under Zofia's and Fryderyk's arms, a calming thought passes through me. *Soon, we'll all be dead.*

The captain barks some orders. Then he gets into the front passenger seat of the jeep. Two soldiers lift the dead man and dump him in the back. My eyes are drawn to the gun still holstered at the dead man's hip. The car pulls away, the officer baring his immaculate teeth in a wide-mouthed yawn.

Our guards order us to lower our hands and send us off with a volley of painful kicks and slaps. Why are they letting us go?

Where's Mati?

Twenty-Two

Warsaw, 1943

Walking quickly down Pilicka Street, I pause when I hear a footfall directly across the road from me. I'm forced to zigzag back and forward, pausing in dark doorways to escape the skilled trackers following me. I finally succeed when a tank comes between us and blocks me from view. Quickly, I try a door in the old furniture factory behind me; it opens easily, and I fall into a room filled with shadows. As I step to my right, my foot snags a chair leg, stumbling me onto a table with a loud bang. I hold my breath while my eyes take in the outline of a wardrobe, a long sofa. When no one barges in, I push as much furniture as I can against the door with its lock hanging useless on a hinge.

My head is all foggy confusion. For reasons I don't understand, my team has become so important to the Germans that they let us go.

Mati, where are you?

Zofia and Fryderyk, where are you?

My hands are trembling. I absolutely cannot cave in now. Negotiating the edges of furniture, I find a path to the front of the factory, stop before a window in the wall. Crouching below the sill, I look onto Malczewskiego Street.

A tank, maybe the same one that screened me, rolls by. No other movement. No, wait! There's the long-legged shadow pacing near the corner on the other side of the road. I'm grateful for the door beside the window with its heavy latch and many locks. That might keep him back for a while, but I have to find a weapon of some kind. If only I had a gun.

Exhausted, I choose a chair leg for my defense, unspool a bolt of heavy material, and retreat to a sofa, where I lie down and cover myself. But sleep doesn't come. We lost four guns tonight. And to think that unlucky soldier didn't turn us in when he saw them hidden. Was he an angel, a spy, or just a confused young man? What's much clearer to me is the depth of my feeling for Mati. I'll die if anything bad has happened to him. When the sofa springs dig into my spine, I try lying on my side, facing the door, but my eyelids begin to droop. How is it possible to be gloriously in love even as danger circles everything I care about?

AS DAWN STREAKS the dirty windows of the factory, I take in my surroundings. I'll need a disguise if I want to get home without being followed. What would Marysia do? There's no shortage of flocked material or cushion stuffing, but where do I find a pair of scissors or a knife? I search the drawers and cupboards, and discover a large man's jacket with patched elbows and a straw hat—that should draw stares on a dull October day.

When I'm done, I have a flocked maroon cap on my head, stuffing inside the waist of my trousers, and the heavy jacket ending just above my knees. All of which makes me waddle. With coal from the fire grate and spit, I smear my hair and eyebrows, dab some on my cheeks and upper lip. Without a shiny surface, I have no idea what I look like, but as long as I don't look like the person I was last night, I'll take this chance.

Barricade gone, I lift the latch and push. The back door swings silently onto the early-morning alley. I slip outside and keep up as brisk a pace as my guise will allow. When I reach Mokotów, I walk all the way to the end of our street, turn the corner, then swerve sharply into the alley between two buildings, climb over a high railing with just one fist shaken at me, until I make it through the loose board in the back fence and into our courtyard.

I give our knock, and my mother opens the door to our flat, her eyes wide with terror.

"It's just me," I croak, my throat dry from breathing so hard. I step into the kitchen and stop in my tracks.

"Mati! Mother Mary, what happened?"

Mama's voice is stern. "Don't touch him."

The skin on his face and neck is scarlet. Yellow blotches on his right arm and hand. The other arm and hand are covered in a wet pillowcase. Burns! He mustn't see me cry.

He tries to smile at my ridiculous getup, but grimaces instead.

Take a deep breath, Irena. We have painkillers. Lotka brought us all kinds of medicine from the hospital. I hold Mati's gaze for a moment, and then I hurry into my bedroom. In a biscuit tin, on top of the wardrobe, I find packets of pills and capsules. Lotka was brilliantly organized—labels on everything. I tear open a packet of morphine pills on my way to the kitchen. I'll have to crush one in water.

Mama and I gently cut his clothes off with a pair of scissors. His legs and lower torso are unmarked. First degree on his face and neck, second degree on his arms and his poor hands.

When Mama's out of the room, he tries to tell me something. A name? When she returns, we move him step by slow step into my bedroom. He lowers himself onto Lotka's bed. Mama's ripped a wet pillowcase into strips. She lays them across his arms and face.

"Let him rest. He's starting to feel the drug."

In the kitchen, she sits at the table, her head in her hands. I think she's going to cry, but she doesn't. My mother's behaving like a soldier.

"He came in about an hour ago," she says.

"Alone?"

"I couldn't understand what he said. Something about grenades or gasoline."

Grenades. That could mean the dragons knew about his sewer job. Or did they randomly choose a sewer to bomb or burn? And what happened to the people he was guiding?

My mother takes a closer look at me, draws her brows together. "What in God's name are you wearing?"

Without explaining, I pull out the stuffing and head to the bathroom for a quick wash. "You get some rest," I say. "I'll watch him."

Washed and dressed in my own clothes, I put the kettle on, cut a slice of bread and a slab of cheese, and wolf that down. What do I feed Mati?

Standing at the foot of his bed, I look at his long, sleeping body: his hands and face covered in the white strips we soaked, his black eyebrows singed above the strange mask. My heart breaks when I realize that I can't touch his head, his hands; he can't touch me. I choke down sobs, but can't stop tears streaking my cheeks. I sink into the chair, close my eyes, and doze on and off until midday, when I hear Mati cry out.

"It's okay, Mati." I kneel beside the bed, resist the longing to stroke his hair. I give him another dose of morphine and a bit of sugar water. He moans in pain until the drug takes effect. Then, finally, he slips into a deep sleep.

I'M GUESSING THAT it's been a beautiful day, but I can't be sure. Late afternoon, I left Mati with my mother while I sent a drop box message to Zofia. Since then, Mama and I have spent all our time trying to ease Mati's pain. I wish my sister were here. I've said those words a thousand times since she disappeared. *But Lotka, we could really use your help now. Where are you? Are you alive?*

Mati seems a bit better even with our amateur efforts. He sits up, drinks some cold chicken broth from a cup in Mama's hands. I can tell swallowing anything is painful. Yet, after a few sips, he puts two fingers to his lips—begging for a cigarette.

"Absolutely not," I say, and he looks like he's going to cry. Mama soothes him by spooning more broth into his mouth. When she finally goes to bed, I pull the chair closer to his bed and we gaze at each other, blinking slowly like two cats.

"We need a way to talk," I say.

Mati winks his left eye. *Ouch.* Even with his burns, he makes me smile. We devise a simple plan.

"Grenades?" I ask.

Slow head shake.

"So, gasoline."

Nod.

I take a deep breath, hold it for a moment. "Are the others alive?"

No. Mati closes his eyes, takes a long breath in and out.

I lay my hand gently on the bed beside him. "I'm sorry." He doesn't open his eyes. "Do you want to stop the questions, my love?"

He squints at me, shakes his head.

"You were followed by a dragon?"

He shrugs.

"But someone tried to kill you and your transportees."

His eyebrows rise, eyes widen. *Ouch.* He draws breath between his teeth.

I'm desperate to tell him about the meeting at the Vault, but I restrain myself. It's more important to know his story first.

THE MORNING LIGHT comes first to the black telephone pole outside the bedroom window, outlining it in yellow paint. It's only the third day after the tunnel fire, and Mati has slept all morning, lying on his back with his arms stiff and bandaged, like a stone effigy. Every five minutes, I open our bedroom door, afraid to look at him, but needing to make sure he's still alive. Mama does it, too. Without Lotka here, I don't know how much morphine to give him.

What Mati has related is a horror story—with strange holes and missing pieces: Contrary to our intelligence, the two AK colleagues, one man and one woman, were completely unfamiliar with the tunnels, so Mati had to lead. They moved fast. Everyone was cold and eager to get out before light, but at a point where they could stand to rest, they carelessly switched places, and for a short while Mati ended up last in the convoy. When he called for the man at the front to stop, he said, "I've got the hang of it. Let's keep going."

As they neared their exit point, the woman thought she smelled gasoline. They looked for the warning chalk marks on the walls, but there weren't any, so they walked ahead at a slower pace. When they stopped again, Mati asked them to smell their clothes, shoes, and hands. They were filthy, but had no smell of gasoline, and there was no slick feel of it in the water. Mati decided to proceed because they were close to the end, and turning back would have been more dangerous than pressing on. A few minutes later, an explosion ripped through the tunnel, a red and yellow fireball shooting toward them. They were like trapped animals.

I had to make Mati stop at this point. His bottom lip had begun to bleed again, and we were both in tears. We took a break. While I made him some cold tea, my mind painted the redbrick oval of the sewer tunnel, the orange-yellow fireball hurtling at me. I find it's better not to block these images. Drawing them in my mind, choosing the best paint colors, keeps me calm. I carried the pot of tea into the bedroom, and Mati continued his story.

The fire consumed the two at the front, licking at the walls around him. He lunged forward with his hands to beat at the flames covering the woman. The tunnel was a furnace filled with smoke. He couldn't breathe and started to retreat, pulling the woman along with him, but she quickly succumbed to her wounds.

Somehow, he turned around and, crouching low, walked back until he came to the intersection. Only then did he notice his burned hands; only then did the pain begin.

"Rest now," I say, but his eyes follow me as I pace back and forth at the foot of the bed. I need a clear head. I need something to eat.

In the kitchen, Mama offers me a bowl of her potato cabbage soup. Do I look as hopeless as she does? I force a smile. "It's good. Salty." I'm careful not to look at the bones. The broth is heavenly, but I never ask where she gets the bones, or what animal they are.

We fall silent for a while, but any second now, I'm expecting a barrage of questions.

Instead, my mother yawns, covers her face with her hands.

"I have to get help for Mati's burns," I say. And then I yawn, too.

IDIOT! I FELL asleep at the table. Voices murmur from Mati's room. Mama and someone else. What more can go wrong? My chair scrapes the floor as I stand, and the voices stop.

In the bedroom, Danuta is bandaging Mati's hands with gauze. I glare at Mama.

"I remembered she worked with Lotka," she says.

Danuta smiles at me. "*Dzień dobry*, Irena." She continues her wrapping. "This will keep the blisters from opening. I'll leave some bandages and ointment. Your mother did the right thing."

Mati winks at me.

"Surprisingly, your eyes aren't injured." She frowns at Mati. "Does it hurt to breathe?"

He shakes his head slowly.

"Can you talk? Is your throat burning?"

Mati tries to speak and croaks like a bullfrog. I laugh, then gasp when his lower lip starts to bleed. Danuta dabs at it with a cloth.

Mati's bandaged hands are neat and clean. His handsome face looks less like raw meat. Mama brings a bowl of cool bone broth and begins to spoon some into his mouth. Despite the recent horrors, it's these small kindnesses that make me weep, and I have to leave the room.

After, Danuta sits across from me at the kitchen table. "He'll be okay, Irena. But it will take time." She gives me instructions for washing my hands before touching him, changing his bandages, applying ointment. "And be careful with the morphine. Start to halve the pills, then halve those. It's easy to get addicted, and it's in short supply."

I nod. "Thank you, Danuta. I've been missing Lotka's knowledge."

She lays her hands on the table. "I'll come back in two days to check on him."

I'm grateful, but I would have preferred Małgorzata to be treating Mati. She was one of us after all, and I could trust her completely. But she took her own life months ago. At least, that's how it appeared to Fryderyk, who found her lying on that gray stone altar with her veins emptied. Was Marysia right after all? Or, in fact, was Małgorzata targeted by the Gestapo?

When we get up to say goodbye, Danuta puts a hand on my arm. I draw closer as she whispers, "Remember the trunk of Lotka's gifts I told you about? It's gone."

I raise my eyebrows.

"There's a new nursing matron." She shrugs. "Maybe the old one took the trunk with her. Things are a lot stricter at the hospital now. They're cutting my orphans' program next week."

I open my mouth, but don't know what to say. On the war front, things are not going well for the Germans, and every part of me wants things to get much worse. Still, I'm hoping Danuta's had the sense to collect a store of the medicines her father needs, and that she's saved money the way Lotka did.

Which reminds me—"About Lotka's salary. It seemed like an unusually large amount each month."

She nods. "Even as trainees in Tarnowski's surgical program, we were paid a higher wage than ordinary nurses at Infant Jesus. But that was true for all the staff at University Hospital. Your sister was more like a surgical assistant than a normal operating room nurse, so I imagine her salary was quite high."

"I see." When you consider the influence Tarnowski had, and that he was in love with her, I suppose it all makes sense.

"Has Tarnowski returned?"

"No. But I'm not surprised. They're getting rid of all the Polish staff anyway."

After she leaves, I decide to check the drop boxes. Mama has a higher purpose now, and her fussiness has returned full-bore. I take a rambling route to the elementary school drop box, where I find a coded message from Zofia. She and Fryderyk were followed, but they evaded their pursuers by hiding in the sewers for two days before leaving from separate exits. *Well done!*

Trudging home, I stop to look at the sky, striped in lilac and orange at the horizon. This war can't last forever. I have to believe that when the Rising comes, we'll kick these dragons out of our country. I have to believe the British will send help.

At home in the bedroom Mati and I now share, I make a confession to him.

"I feel sick about the death of our colleagues, but, Mateusz, I'm so happy you're alive." I want him to hold me. I want to kiss his neck.

He smiles, closes his eyes. I close mine, too, and feel as though we're embracing in the airy space between us.

"I have something to tell you," I say. "You know we were going to discuss moving the guns at the meeting?"

He nods.

"We never got started. We were waiting for you when four dragons surprised us. Mati, they brought a Gestapo captain. He made me draw a portrait of Zofia."

Mati chokes on his mouthful of tea.

I describe the events leading up to the stolen jeep, the dead soldier.

"It doesn't make sense," he says. "Why would they let you all go?"

"I don't know. They shot at the man in the car as he was driving away. He could be wounded."

He nods. "The people I was guiding gave me a warning: the Germans are on the hunt for an escaped AK prisoner, code name Wojtek. Apparently, they're desperate to find him."

Beyond the window of our bedroom, night has fallen. I draw the curtains. "There's more. Something very strange happened."

"My God. More strange than drawing Zofia in front of the Gestapo?"

"While I was getting paper for the drawing, one of the soldiers looked through the canvases by the wall. I can't imagine he didn't see the guns, but he said nothing. Not a peep."

"Maybe he missed them."

"No. He looked at the canvases, then just for a fraction of a second at Zofia, then me. No words or hand signals. Just a zing of understanding between us."

"A zing? You sure it wasn't a zong?"

"Be serious, Mati. What's going on?"

He sighs. "I don't have answers. I just have suspicions—"

"Suspicions about what? *Who?* Are you thinking it's Lotka? You are. You think she talked."

"Ala. Come here, please." He lays his head on my belly. I look down at his beautiful, singed hair, the bandages on his hands. I won't touch him. I won't be nice.

He looks up at me. "We don't know what we'd be capable of in her shoes. We think we'd be so brave, but, really, we can't know." He takes my hand, puts it on top of his head. "Have you heard from Zofia and Fryderyk?"

"They got away." I smooth his hair.

"Ala, I'm afraid there's even more bad news." He pulls me closer. "Marysia's missing."

Twenty-Three

Toronto, November 2010

Irena's still upright in her long coat, but her boots seem too heavy for her feet. It takes us a long while to walk from the St. John's main gate to Mati's gravesite.

Inside our home, my grandmother fills every room with her rich voice, her cigarette smells, the colors of her paintings, her blaring jazz music. Outdoors, she's a small, old woman. For reasons Sophie and I have never figured out, my grandmother objects to public smoking. Seated comfortably on our folding chairs, we're facing Mati's sculpture, inclining our heads with the moving glints of sun on metal and glass. I spent a week carving his name in Helvetica on the plinth.

"You never called him by his first name, Pawel?"

Her gaze softens and she smiles a secret smile. "From the beginning, he was always my Mati."

A man in a tweed cap stops at a grave opposite, tugging the leash of his fat dachshund. Irena is seduced. Her sweet dachshund, Lupi, died soon after Mati did. She clucks and the dog waddles over to sniff her hand, dragging the man along.

"Amazing sculpture," the man booms, nodding his cap toward Mati's grave. "Truly, amazing. You should come back on a night when there's a full moon—amazing!"

Irena raises her eyebrows at me. When the man's down the path, we burst into giggles. Joy floods my heart. Am I forgiven?

"This is a good sculpture you made for Mati," Irena says.

I beam. To think I was hesitant about coming to the cemetery today. Not just the cold, but all that revelation about shootings and she and Mati being killers. Buoyed by her praise, I risk a question I've been hoarding in my encyclopedia of Irena questions.

"I saw the name Ola in your painting of the sewer explosion."

"Which painting?"

I pull out my phone and show her the photograph I took, zooming in on the name *Ola*.

She sighs. "She was my brave friend. In the war, we called her Zofia." She touches the screen with her fingertip. "I wrote 'Ola' because it was shorter."

"She died in this tunnel?"

"No. I made a terrible mistake about her." My grandmother tugs back her woolen cap to scratch her forehead. "I made so many mistakes during that war."

I'm impatient to dig deeper, but I think I might have my answer: Stefan's Ola could have worked with Irena during the war. So what happened to Stefan? How did he end up in the SS when Ola was in the Polish resistance?

Irena points her chin at Mati's sculpture. "We had a good life. I'll make no more paintings."

It takes me a second to understand. The thought of Irena dying sends icy darts through me. I decide not to block them. "I want to make you your own sculpture," I say. "It will be *amazing*!"

She laughs her gurgly laugh. "What story will you tell about me?"

"What story do you want me to tell?"

"Your mother was very good to me," she says.

Surprise. Irena rarely says anything complimentary about Sophie at all.

She digs a small trench with the toe of her boot. "She saved my life many times."

My shoulders stiffen.

"She had a hard life, alone," she says.

"But she wasn't alone. She had you and Mati. And me, I guess."

"That's not what I mean."

"No?"

My grandmother leans toward me, exasperated. "Mati and I were like this." She twines her middle finger over her index finger. "Your mother was alone. What's his name—your father—ran away when she was pregnant."

"That's not true. Martin left when I was five. He went on a pilgrimage to a monastery in the Himalayas. That's what Sophie said."

Irena shakes her head, tucking her coat under her knees.

I look up at a cloudless blue sky. *Why is she telling me this old stuff now?* "Besides, Sophie always seemed so self-sufficient."

Irena stares at me over her sunglasses.

I turn away. I haven't seen Martin since the day Sophie and I hugged him goodbye at the airport. I remember him tearing up a bit, ruffling my curls before turning to kiss Sophie, she and I staring at the passenger entrance long after his denim jacket disappeared.

My grandmother stirs. "She was a stubborn girl," she says. "Mati could make her listen, but I never could."

"And bossy," I say, wiping the back of my hand across my eyes.

Irena laughs. "My daughter was in love with her work, running around the world, interrogating women prisoners."

I wince. "Don't say it like that." Sophie's many academic articles were often quoted. She coauthored a seminal book on women in Canadian prisons.

Irena hunkers down into her coat.

Near us, two leafless sister maples cast their leggy shadows. "Well, at least she had her friend in Melbourne," I say.

Irena toggles her head back and forth. "And I think someone in Chicago."

Something else I didn't know about my mother. Sadness seeps into me from that deep well.

My phone chimes in my pocket. Farzaad. I walk quickly down the rows of angels and sinking stones toward my mother's grave.

"Hi, Jo," he says. "I thought I wouldn't get to your recording for a few days, but I got bored with marking papers, so I opened the file, and, wow . . ."

I wonder what he's found. "This man was very old and had dementia—so he'd go back into his war past, like into a fog or something."

"My grandfather does that a lot with Afghanistan."

In the brief silence that follows, the two of us plunge into multiple understandings.

"So, look," Farzaad says, "I'll email the transcripts by tomorrow morning. And, Jo, you know—be prepared for the translation."

"For sure." I pause in front of Sophie's sculpture, press my lips against her name, then wend my way back to Irena.

A sad smile tugs at my grandmother's lips, and I know she's been talking to Mati.

"What time is it?" she asks as I pack the thermos into my backpack.

"Late. We stayed too long."

I run my palm over the dents and mounds in Mati's sculpture. Irena brushes a fingertip kiss across his name. Then we gather momentum for the walk.

Arm in arm, we navigate the pebbles in the path, me leaning into my grandmother to balance the weight of the chairs over my other shoulder.

No word yet from Roland or Cynthia about Stefan's funeral. It's been three days.

But by morning, Farzaad's translation might be sitting in my inbox like a letter bomb.

When we get home, giving in to my badgering, Irena has a mug of miso soup from the Japanese café. Too tired to have her tea and smoke in the sitting room, she goes directly to her bedroom for her afternoon nap.

I check my mail. Nothing yet from Farzaad, but there's a message from Roland.

Can we meet tomorrow to discuss the sculpture?

Shit! We arrange for him to pick me up at the Oakville commuter station. Might as well ask him about Stefan in person.

Ꝓꟺ

I CARRY THE hatbox and thermos; Tahira carries the cookies. Inside my workshop, I turn on the overhead lights, plug in the heater. When we're seated at the counter, I switch on the gooseneck lamp and take the cover off the old hatbox. "You've got to see this." I lift out the yellowed nun's cap. "This hatbox was in Irena's closet. I think they brought it from Poland back in the nineties."

"Of course," Tahira says.

I smile. No need to explain the fall of communism to someone doing a master's in international relations. "There was a nest of old lady hats and inside them, I found this."

"It must have been important for them to keep it so long." She spreads out the veil, turns the cap over. "Handmade, perfect stitching. Who's the nun?"

"I'd love to know. Never heard about a nun in the family—maybe someone on my grandfather's side."

"There's something—" She peels back a seam, shows me what she sees: *S. Iwanowska* in blue curlicue embroidery.

"Iwanowska. That's Irena's maiden name."

"Maybe *S* was Irena's sister?"

"No. She was an only child."

"Maybe a cousin or aunt?"

"I have no idea." One more thing to ask Irena when she's in a good mood. I'm replacing the veiled hat in the hatbox when Tahira touches my arm. "Have you noticed anything wrong with Irena?"

I take a deep breath. "She's been remembering horrors from her past."

"Oh." Her eyes tell me these are paths she's traveled, too.

IRENA'S STILL ASLEEP when I look in on her, the amber rosary she's been sleeping with twined round her wrist. Leaving the door slightly ajar, I head to Mati's office, wondering if my grandmother knows that her neighbor, Tahira's husband, is a young German man.

I open the top drawer of the filing cabinet, and soon newspapers, photo albums, and files are spread out on the oak desk. In the mix, I find Irena's Polish army medal in a red satin case—the *Virtuti Militari*, the highest military medal bestowed by Poland. I run my finger over the white eagle at the center of the Maltese-style cross. It's never occurred to me to ask: What did you do to earn this?

Perched on the edge of the desk, I go through the big photo album of Sophie and Jo pictures. Sophie as a young woman, laughing, raising a wineglass to the camera, a bearded older man with a cigarette in his hand standing beside her. I run a finger over her face. *My mother.*

There's a photo of me, a chubby toddler, prancing while Mati holds my hands. A posed shot of Sophie and me with Martin, his arm around Sophie, me on my mother's lap. It's been a long time since I've seen his face. That curly dark hair, thinning at the forehead, big glasses, serious mouth, like he's thinking, *I'm a father and husband and that's extremely important business.*

Cheriblare wanders in to stare at me until I pick her up. I set aside the photo album and she spreads her furry self on the yellowed, laminate pages.

I turn my attention to the newspaper articles and pamphlets about my grandparents' work in the Warsaw Uprising—just the ones written in English. Comfortable in the office chair now, I learn about Mati fighting hand to hand with the Germans, Irena and her fellow soldiers pulling drowned bodies from the Warsaw sewage canals, the two of them crawling from cellar to cellar during bombings. Such bravery. Yet, the biggest surprise I glean is that thousands of other Poles, civilians as well as resistance fighters, performed similar acts of bravery.

The second drawer bulges with clipped reviews in various languages, interviews with Irena Marianowska, the resistance painter, and photos of my grandmother and her artwork.

I open an old issue of *Vie des Arts*, winter 1984, turn to an article titled "An Intimate War: The Art of Irena Marianowska," with a full-page color photo of *Mokotów Angel*. In the introduction, the writer summarizes Irena's heroic work in the AK and the fact that she was a military prisoner at Ravensbrück concentration camp from October 1944 to February 1945. So that's where she was held—where Stefan might have been an interrogator in the SS. That gives me something to work with.

With two file folders in hand, I move to Mati's recliner. The pale green corduroy chair is threadbare on the arms. How does Irena bear his absence? Through all my childhood, the edges of the world ended where my grandparents ended. Inside this country, everything looked normal and good. I was aware that within the Polish community, they had a special rank—people bowed and kissed their hands. It wasn't until grade five when I'd taken one of Irena's paintings for show-and-tell that this same country took on a layer of madness. The image of red arms and hands reaching up through the ground, decimated buildings leaning back, blasted by some force in front of the painting, sent squeals of "Yuck!" and "Gross!" through the classroom. Even the teacher averted her eyes. But I knew it was beautiful.

A file falls off my lap, scattering articles across the floor. Gathering up the clippings, I come across a full page from the *Toronto Star*. There's a photo of me standing beside Mati's grave sculpture, looking radiant, younger, even though it's only five years ago. Sophie must have clipped it for Irena. The article's not only about me—Shereen Patel interviewed three other artists who've made sculptures for gravesites. It's not until I come to the last paragraph that I'm blindsided: *Making art must run in the family. Three of these four artists have a close relative who's also an artist. The internationally renowned painter, Irena Marianowska, is Josephine Blum's grandmother.*

My heart dives. Stefan was an expedient man—hiring people he thought would make him appear fair and unbiased. Was I hired so he could tell a bullshit story to make himself look good?

Or did Stefan hire me because he was trying to reconnect with Irena? I feel myself edging a deep quarry.

Queasy now and ashamed of my cowardice, I finally open my laptop.

There's Farzaad's email.

I download the two transcripts and click on the English translation. The words hurl themselves at my eyes:

> BITCH!
> WHORE!
> UGLY, POLLUTED SLUT!
> *Five seconds of coughing.*
> *Six seconds of silence.*
> Don't hurt her. STOP! OH, PLEASE STOP.
> *Five seconds of hard breathing.*
> FILTHY, STINKING DOG!

Twenty-Four

Warsaw, July 1944

The tide has turned, and everywhere joy whirls round me like a dancer. When I look at Mati spooning mushroom soup into his mouth—his skin puckered and pink in places, but healed, my only thought is *How lucky I am to love this man.*

"Hold on," he yells as the table shakes and a deep rumbling rolls toward us from beyond the river, clattering my knife to the floor.

Yowza! Mati and I whoop at this long-awaited sign—until we see Mama clutching her neck in terror.

"It's okay, Pani, it's not an earthquake." He beams across the table.

I rub her shoulder. "It's just the Russians coming to help us, Mama."

"The Russians?" Her tone is so incredulous, Mati raises a wry eyebrow, waiting to see how I'll answer.

For weeks now, the urgent question ricocheting among Warsaw's AK members has been how soon we'll get the signal to rise up against our occupiers. The second, equally urgent question—on which the first depends—has been whether the Soviet army will assist us in the fight. Now here they are, somewhere just east of the Vistula. And if they're that close, surely the Rising we've labored for, longed for, each hour of the five years we've lived and died under these Nazi dragons, must be close. The thought darts quicksilver up my spine. Even so, I toss a glance at Mati and decide to stick to the facts.

"What we're hearing, Mama, is shelling between the Germans and the Russians. They're fighting each other and they're not that far away."

Instead of settling her, the news makes her whimper. "What will happen to Lotka? Where is she? You still haven't found her." Her tears reproach me, and this time I have no ready response. Among all the shiny summer moments—our fighting Allies finally setting foot in northern France this June; a picnic in Arkadia Park with Mama and Mati where I caught my first fish—my sister's been a pale shadow at the back of my mind.

Mama drags herself up out of her chair. "I'm going to pray in my room."

"I'll make you some tea," Mati says, but she looks at him as though he's a stranger and waves his offer away. His face falls, and I feel terrible that he's sandwiched in this battle between my mother and me, especially given the peace he's brought into our home these past months.

"Let's go for a walk," I say, reaching for his hand. "I've been wanting to ask you an important question."

I say a quick goodbye to Mama and follow him out of the flat to the landing, where he pulls me into an embrace. "If you're going to ask me to marry you, Irena, I will probably say yes."

Laughing, I thump his chest with my fist. There's been no formal engagement. Between us there's just a strong intent to marry and a private feeling that we already are. We're standing like this when a clatter from above forces us apart. Down the stairs from Mr. Godlewski's old flat clomps the charming Frau Hüber and her mustachioed son, both dragging heavy suitcases.

Mati and I depart the shadows to wave them goodbye and are greeted with averted eyes.

Once they're in the courtyard, he grabs my waist and lifts me in the air. "You know what this means?"

"Yes!"

The Hübers must have got the order to leave Warsaw immediately, along with other Volksdeutsche and German civilians. If we heard the rumblings to the east, the German garrisons in Warsaw heard them, too. Now the whole bloody machinery is aware the Polish Underground is about to rise up; they just don't know when or where. I squeeze Mati's hand as we step into the sunny courtyard. Soon, soon!

"What were you going to ask me?" he says, casually putting on a pair of green sunglasses.

"As a matter of fact, I was going to ask what you're going to wear when the time comes. But I see that you're going to look quite glamorous. I won't ask where you got them."

"Don't. Many of the soldiers in my regiment have top boots, but I haven't found any in my size. I have an old military jacket from Fryderyk's father and my black regiment cap. We'll be issued helmets at our muster stations. How about you?"

I sigh. "Well, since Zofia and I aren't designated combat soldiers, but nurse and courier—"

Mati snickers, but stops when he sees how upset I am. "I know; it's not fair."

"Not fair! There are whole battalions of women combatants in the AK, while Zofia and I—"

"It's true. Zofia has many skills, but nursing isn't one of them. As for you . . ." He brushes a strand of hair off my face. "I want you to be safe."

"I won't be relegated to the kitchen, Mati. I've waited too long for this."

"The kitchen!" He covers his face in mock horror. "Of course not. Let's agree your talents lie elsewhere."

I try knocking him over with my shoulder, but he pulls me toward him. "You'll need a helmet," he says, his fingers on my neck.

"And a Browning pistol. Can you get me one? It's impossible to get bullets for my old Luger."

He laughs. "You're dreaming, Ala!"

Nattering and teasing, we walk down Puławska Street arm in arm—until we encounter two SS soldiers about to block our path.

"*Halt!* Where are you going?"

My eyes scan the street, landing on the brass plate of Dr. Jankowska, and before Mati can answer, I blurt out, "To the doctor," pointing to the building ahead of us.

"She's pregnant," Mati says, and lays a hand on my flat belly.

The dragon scoffs, and I curse Mati's playfulness. To our horror, they insist on accompanying us. Inside the building, we climb the stairs and I randomly turn left. Down the corridor I march, hoping the doctor has a nameplate on her door. She does, and when I knock, it's opened by a gray-haired woman in a white coat, the sight of our companions barely widening her bespectacled eyes.

"Come in," she says calmly, and the dragons shove us forward.

"Does this woman have an appointment?" the big one asks. I quickly show her my ID card.

She walks to a desk and consults a large register. "Yes, and she's late. I'll be closing for lunch soon. Come this way, Pani," she says, taking my arm and guiding me to a small examining room. "Lie on that table, and you"—she points at Mati—"wait here." As she's closing the door to the examining room, she hesitates as if she's just remembered there are two SS soldiers in her office. "Will that be all?"

My heart lurches when I see them approaching Mati, but it's a bluff, and they troop out, slamming the door.

We're about to thank her when the doctor puts a finger to her lips and points to the telephone on her desk. Then she looks through a peephole in her office door, opens it, and motions us into the corridor.

"Goodbye. And please be more careful on the streets."

Outside, Mati shakes his head at our close call; I shake mine at the miracle of Dr. Jankowska.

Ahead of us on Puławska, SS soldiers are searching people at intervals. It's time to head back. We veer off toward Belwederska as an explosion erupts north of us near the river. We pick up our pace.

Stay calm, I tell myself. *Mati hasn't got the message to put his company on standby. Just get yourselves home.* I can't tell my mother anything about the imminent Rising, but I have to initiate my plan for her safety. If she'll only listen to me.

WHAT A DIFFERENCE a few hours have made. Supper has been a gloomy meal with each of us grinding away at our own hapless thoughts. It's time to broach the subject of going into hiding, so while Mati turns on the radio to listen as he washes the dishes, Mama and I carry our tea into the living room. Her coolness sets the tone for me, and I stand while she sits on the sofa.

"Look at me, Mama."

Her eyes look up in alarm.

"You remember the planes at the start of the war, and the terrible Siege when they shelled the city. We hid in the cellar then. The fighting between the—"

"Irena!" My prepared speech is disrupted by Mati rushing into the room. "Come quick, both of you."

Over the radio, a passionate Polish voice is shouting, *"People of the Capital! To arms!"*

My jaw drops, and I turn to Mati, who slowly shakes his head.

Not the AK! Then, who? I raise my eyebrows.

He shrugs. "KRN?" That's the National Homeland Council, a shadowy group backing the Soviets and Papa Stalin.

"Strike at the Germans! Help the Red Army. Send them information and show them the way into the city."

Mama stares at us, and I wonder if she's about to faint. Mati pushes a chair behind her.

A moment of scratchy silence passes and then the whole broadcast begins again.

"May the whole population rise like a stone wall around the KRN and the capital's underground army!"

I plop down beside Mama, confused by yet a third repetition of the broadcast. What happened to Bór, commander of the AK combat forces, or Colonel Monter, leader of the Warsaw AK? Are the Soviets giving orders now?

Mati turns off the radio and sits down beside me, his head in his hands.

Out of the blue, Mama levels the full force of her anger at us. "I knew it! You two are part of this ragged army!" Her palm slams the table. "Too selfish to leave good enough alone. You're the wicked ones dragging us back into starvation."

Goaded by my own mother, I forget my years of training. "*This* is our last chance to fight for our freedom! For Poland's freedom!" I feel the heat in my face, and I'm afraid to look at Mati, who must be appalled that I've let our secret out.

"You're not fighting for me!" she shouts, her face livid.

That tears my heart, and when she breaks into sobs, I do nothing to soothe her.

Her arms reach toward the kitchen window. "What will happen to all the people out there when the bombs drop? When they shoot us in our homes?"

"Not if we win," I say, all my doubt and fear, pride and faith thrown into that one sentence. "You heard the radio. The whole Soviet army's behind us!"

My mother rocks back and forth, her arms wrapped around her body. "I want Lotka! I want my daughter back!"

Unable to bear her weeping anymore, I leave the flat.

CURFEW DOESN'T NORMALLY stop me from venturing out at night, but our recent visit to the doctor makes me cautious. That, and the old despair of fighting with my mother. On impulse, I walk up the stairs, tap at the door of Pani Hüber's vacated flat, and wait. No footsteps, no stealth presence. I turn the handle, and the door opens with a squeak. Switching on the light illuminates the remains of their recent flight: a baronial armchair, too heavy to move; empty wooden crates strewn about; in the kitchen, a cup of curdled tea, and in the sparkling new fridge, a full bottle of milk, a bounty of apples, potatoes, and onions. Thank you, Pani Hüber! I find a string bag wedged at the back of a drawer and fill it until it needs two hands to carry.

Since April, Mati and I have been stockpiling tins of canned pork, beans, peas, and pickled cabbage in the cellar we used to share with Mr. Godlewski. His name in my thoughts makes me smile. How I miss that old man.

"Irena?" Mati's voice springs me to my feet. I open the door and call down the stairs, "I'll be down in a minute." Before I switch off the light, I skim the empty room once more. It offers no assurances for my doubts, no comfort for my fears.

Mati stops pacing when I reach the bottom of the stairs. "She's gone to bed with a headache." His face has a blotched look and he's not meeting my gaze.

I grab hold of his elbow. "What's wrong, Mati?"

He lays his hands on my shoulders as if to steady himself. "While you were gone, there was a knock at the door." The softness in his eyes and voice makes me dread the worst. "When I went to look, the courier had disappeared, but I found a message stuck in the letter box. It's in code, from Zofia."

"And?"

"She's found Marysia's body."

WE MEET IN darkness in Canon Square: Zofia, Mati, and me, with Fryderyk standing guard around the corner beside his borrowed rickshaw bicycle.

The scaffold stands in the middle—a tall, roughly built gallows, its dark wood at odds with the brightly colored houses behind it. When we're close enough, Mati squeezes my fingers. I call up all my courage to raise my eyes and look on the body hanging from the noose, see that it is unrecognizable as a person, as a woman, as Marysia.

With money from the colonel, Zofia bribed the German guards who were standing nearby; they had the decency to move to a distance. The three of us mount the stairs, and Mati reaches up to cut her down, while Zofia and I reach up to catch her, a task a child could do, now that she's so small. We cover her in the sheet I brought, and while Mati carries her body to the waiting rickshaw, Zofia and I embrace fiercely, too shaken to cry. Her amber rosary is wrapped around her right wrist, and I feel the crucifix pressing on the back of my neck.

Zofia's luminous eyes find mine. "She's an angel in heaven now, Ala."

I sigh. My grief feels bottomless. *Where would I be if not for you, Marysia? For years I clung to the comfort that you'd always be here; you were only eight years older than me.*

In a silent cortege we follow Fryderyk to Powązki Cemetery, Mati pedaling while I sit sideways on his bicycle seat, one arm around his waist. Zofia rides ahead of us.

At the cemetery, the dark form of the colonel waves us to the proper location, and our little procession comes to a stop in front of the grave he's dug—in fact, Marysia's father's grave. Her father was a decorated soldier from a previous war, and we're burying Marysia on top of his moldy coffin. Zofia and I quickly gather ferns and leaves, sprinkling them over her shroud before Mati shovels the dirt back over her. No hymns or prayers apart from our falling tears. Heads hung in silence, we bury ourselves in mourning and our memories of her. Raising my chin, I sight row upon row of grave sculptures iridescent in the moonlight. She'll be forever surrounded by frozen angels, and I'm certain she would have hated that.

To my right, the colonel blows his nose. "Soon we'll have our country back," he says, "and I'll make sure she gets the medals she deserves."

"And her name on this gravestone," I say, suddenly angry at the miles of

Gothic lettering swaggering through this forest graveyard, loudly proclaiming the lives of fallen generals—all of them dusty footholds for young trees now. Yet I recognize their names from our history books.

Mati throws his head back to look at the sky. "She would have loved this moment before the Rising."

"She'll be with us when we march into battle to reclaim our city." The colonel stamps his feet to shed the soil from his boots.

I glance up from the grave at my feet and notice that Fryderyk and Zofia are tightly clasping hands.

I'm not ready to join you, Marysia.

I don't believe in heaven or hell, but many times I've imagined how I'd paint the feeling of them. My portfolio of hell paintings grows larger by the day, while my heaven is just one image—Mati and me walking beneath the trees in Arkadia Park on a spring day, my arm circling his waist, his arm around my shoulders.

Part Four

Twenty-Five

Warsaw, August 1944

Tuesday, August 1, awoke and turned its back on the blue skies of July. A cool drizzle coats my jacket as I stand waiting for the tram that will take me to my meeting with Zofia.

There's no mistaking the mood in the city. Ahead of me in the queue, a group of young men in oversize raincoats fidgets and chatters excitedly. In front of my cold nose, an old army rucksack can't conceal the tall, thin shape wrapped in newspaper protruding from the top. *Cholera!* These boys may all be carrying weapons under their bulky black raincoats.

My hand smooths the bump of my stomach—bandages and medicine collected from Infant Jesus and the remnants of Lotka's rainy-day first-aid kit from the top of our wardrobe. The idea for this subterfuge came to me after our narrow escape from the SS two days ago.

When the tram arrives, the boys gallantly make way for me, several of them winking conspiratorially. I hand the conductor my fare; he waves it away with another devious wink.

I head to the back of the tram, my hand unconsciously protecting my stomach, but when the ruckus at the front turns to loud cheering, I look over my shoulder. The boys are all sitting in the front seats reserved for Germans and Volksdeutsche. I give in to a loud burst of laughter.

The thousands of German civilians and administrators, who've lived like the aristocracy these past five years, have fled Warsaw. Good luck to them as they search for a place to hide. The SS remains to torture us, along with the retreating German army battling their former Soviet colleagues not far from the east bank of the Vistula. I'm hoping this Russian army cuts across to the west bank with the greatest speed—for the sake of Mati and his company, for the sake of these beardless, raucous, grinning boys in front of me.

As we rumble along the tracks this afternoon, it feels like Christmas Eve in August—the city vibrating with anticipation for tonight's Rising. At exactly twenty-four hundred hours, the fighting is set to begin. I squeeze my eyes shut. Will I remember what it's like to be free? Despite the steaminess of the tram, the thought raises goose bumps on my arms.

As more people get on at each stop, it becomes unbearably hot, and I'm tempted to undo my jacket in what feels like collegial, Polish company. Between the balancing bodies, I recognize two women from my Guiding days. Our eyes meet fleetingly, then look away. The tram sways and everyone shifts the burden they're carrying—sacks lodged between feet, green carrot tops sticking out of a pail probably stuck inside a larger pail, and between the bottoms, something crucial like a coded message or transmitter. Fanning my face with my hand, I try to breathe in something other than the smell of woolen coats in summer, or the sweet mothball perfume of ancestral army jackets. Many of my fellow Varsovians are heading to the city center, as I am. To avoid suffocation, I decide to get off early and walk through the rain.

Outside, it's immediately fresher, and I'm glad now for the warmth of my jacket. I check my watch—just enough time to reach the Polish Bank building on Holy Cross Street. Cutting through an alley, I slow at the sight of two young people kneeling beside a stucco wall. The sound of my footfall spins them around, but reassured, they wave and continue painting what I soon discover is a black gallows, with something hanging from a noose.

Shuddering, I hurry along. The couple has been busy: two more hanged swastikas dangle farther down the wall. A long sigh escapes me. Mati would have appreciated their humor.

He and I said goodbye this morning as though we were rushing off to our jobs at an office. As company captain, he left early for his muster station in Mokotów, and I to my final courier delivery. I feel oddly transparent without him—not quite my solid self. At the last minute, he got an order to release me from his company. I'm glad someone higher up saw sense. Insurgents may need to be escorted through the sewers. At this critical moment, the military wing of the AK is scrambling to oversee all its fighting companies throughout Warsaw and the suburbs. They can't be escorting vulnerable people and risk getting lost themselves. If I'm to be useful in this battle, the sewers must be my territory. Even though it means I likely won't see Mati tonight.

The tram's Christmas mood has spread into the city center. When I look around, I almost expect to see lights strung up. Bicycle rickshaws, cars, and trams are speeding to their destinations. I check my watch again. People carrying heavy bundles, children running to keep up with their mothers. No, this mood feels different. There's a frantic effort to the pedaling legs of the rickshaw driver passing me. I keep my eyes moving as I pick up my pace: the usual SS presence studs both sides of the street. A loud disturbance up ahead. I pause to take in an empty pastry shop window—all its wares sold or moved days ago. A girl's scream, a shot. Another. I look. Black boots kicking the bodies. Twisting away, I come face-to-face with one of the tall black lampposts lining this wide street. Tied to its waist is a sign: ONLY FOR GERMANS. More gallows humor. The crowd scurries across the street to avoid the scene of the killing; I scurry after them.

Mama left for Wola yesterday with her friend from the secret masses.

"It won't be any safer in Wola, Mama," I argued. "It's just another district of Warsaw."

But she insisted her friend knows a church that hides people, and, what's more, they still have a priest who says mass in the crypt.

While I carried her suitcase down the stairs to the train platform, she had the grace to tell me that she'd tried to remove all the money left in Lotka's bank account in order to give it to the church—but the bank would only give her half.

It doesn't matter. Money's only good for bribery now. We rely on our wits, and whatever the AK is able to provide. Nothing new for Mati and me, but wouldn't it be wonderful if the British and Americans made the airdrops they've promised?

Seeing my mother off at the train station raised my childish hope that we'd rekindle some warmth between us before she left. Instead, her icy gaze raised a gate between us and kept it firmly shut. No kiss, but she didn't fight me when I held her hand just a moment longer than was needed to say goodbye.

"ALA! THANK GOD you're here." Zofia's pigtails look incongruous with her high-collared military jacket. She grins at my rounded middle, and we embrace briefly.

The gruff AK constables who check my pass are impressed that it gives me access to any facility I need to enter, but the pass doesn't stop them from leering at Zofia and me. I follow her into the building, where she dashes down two flights of stairs. We're stopped by a second group of constables, and then enter a long concrete cellar ringed with hospital beds. Women and men with red crosses on their armbands flit about in the dim light.

"You're really a nurse now?" I say teasingly.

She stops in her tracks and stares at me. "*Cholera*, Ala! You don't know?"

My pulse quickens.

"They changed the start time to seventeen hundred hours."

"That soon?" Mati and his company must be standing by in Mokotów.

We hurry to the end of a double line of cots. "Apparently Bór got news the Russians have broken through the German ranks."

"What?" But it makes perfect sense. Without Russia's tanks, artillery, and planes, or battle-hardened army, we won't survive long against the Wehrmacht. Our commander must strike now.

I smile weakly. "I hope I'm the only one who didn't know."

"I have to get back to work." She grimaces. "They're training me in removing shrapnel, stopping bleeding—that sort of thing. But, Ala, I'd much rather be with you in the sewers. Could you do something?"

"I'll try my best. Before I forget . . ." I open my jacket and unpack the rolls of bandages, the penicillin, morphine, and aspirin packets knotted into a string of Mama's scarves around my waist.

Arms full, she looks around. "I'll make sure the director gets these. What are you going to do now? Do you want to stay here?"

"No. I have to report for duty." My assignment and its location aren't news I can share with Zofia, but I have to make my way to Warecka Street as quickly as possible.

ALL THROUGH MY sewer journey beneath the city center, my heart calls out to Mati. Close to the exit to my last tunnel, the first shots ring out, and I turn my ankle, splashing my boot into shit. I check my watch. *Early.* Not quite five. Someone's itching to pull a trigger. When I gently shake my foot, my ankle feels intact. I climb the ladder, breathe, listen.

After a while, the shooting seems to die down, and I put my back against the sewer cover, hoist it an inch, and peer out. The air feels warmer, drier, and I'm glad I left my coat with Zofia. No running boots or quiet bodies on the ground, but the slow breathing Marysia taught us fine-tunes my hearing, and I pick up machine-gun fire echoing from the direction of the Telephone Exchange, where the SS has a large base. That's followed by single shots from a rifle or pistol. *Mother Mary!* That might be Mati's company.

When the firing stops, I haul myself out of the hole and land on the curb of an empty-looking Marszałkowska Street. Staying low, I zigzag across the wide boulevard until I squat in the middle behind the barricade of an overturned tram. As I'm catching my breath, I find myself beside two young boys with grenades in their hands and adult-size helmets on their heads.

"Run!" one of them says, pointing to the end of the barricade.

"Irena," the other one says, his blue eyes shocked into panic. I just have time to recognize Davey's features when the unmistakable clanking of a tank shakes the ground beneath my knees. The boys put their hands over their ears, and I do the same. The clanking gets louder and is followed by a blinding explosion that slices off the top third of the tram. Glass and metal rain down on us. The boys shake themselves off. Alarm all over his face, Davey unbuckles his helmet and hands it to me.

"No!" I shout over the ringing in my ears. I make a crouching run for the end of the barricade, where a group of armed men in red and white armbands huddles in the doorway of an apartment building.

"Keep going!" they yell, waving at the building farther down.

I reach the next doorway just as another deafening explosion shatters the spot where the men were grouped. *Jesu Maria.* How many of them were there? I hope the families in that building are safe in the cellars. My answer comes in the gathering darkness—the screams of the wounded, and then a barked order, "NOW!"

I take it as my signal, and, keeping close to the walls of buildings, manage to get to the nearest alley, too small for any tank to enter. Despite the sounds of fighting blasting from every direction, I'm overcome by wonder. Davey Freeman is alive, and he's fighting with the resistance. That is a thing to rejoice. And my old friend, Leah? Where is she on this first day of the Rising?

Leaning against the back wall of a building, I begin to feel a burning heat in my shoulder. I check for a wound. A cry from the roof yanks my gaze up, and I see that the building's on fire. Flames shoot from windows as an ancient couple, each carrying a bundle, ambles past me as if to say, *We've lived through this before, no point rushing.*

Tearing past them, I carve a safe distance between me and the burning building. When I pause to look back, a person falls or jumps from the roof and crashes to the ground. I check my watch. I'll never make it to my destination on time; my cargo will just have to stay put.

I'm not far from home now, and cursing the catastrophic tank, I take the route I learned from Mr. Godlewski years ago. But it's no longer a shortcut. I'm delayed by falling concrete and shattered glass on the ground, by fleeing families. Squeezing through the back fence an hour later, I'm pleased to find all four buildings of the Sobieski Residences still standing. I breathe a sigh of relief until my dazed ears pick up a full orchestra of voices. From pillar to hedge, I steal toward the central courtyard and stop in my tracks—a group of civilians is spread out on the grassy knoll by the water tap. Small children, a baby, young mothers, old men and women—all caught in the suddenness of the Rising. It hits me that thousands of Warsaw citizens knew an uprising was imminent, but they couldn't have known the exact day or time.

An old man in a beret calls me over. "Don't worry, miss, you'll be safe here. Only a few more hours, and the Russian tanks will come barreling in, then we can all go home to our beds." He laughs and pats the head of a small girl nestled in her mother's lap.

His confident ease makes me smile. "This is my home," I say. "Give me a few minutes and I'll bring down some food for everyone."

A rousing cheer.

"Could someone help me?" I call out.

A young girl jumps up and follows me to my flat. I turn on the light switch and nothing happens. Of course they've cut off the electricity, and probably the water, too. No matter, I have my flashlight. Inside, the flat is eerily still, everything as Mati and I left it this morning.

"My name's Ala," I say.

"Hania," she says.

I quickly find the candles and matches, and set one on the kitchen counter.

The sack of twenty-five small red apples is where I left it this morning. "How many people are out there?"

Hania doesn't hesitate. "Twelve. Thirteen if you count Marius, the baby."

I give her a quizzical look, but she's not wearing an AK armband.

"Just a moment," I say and step into my bedroom.

When I return, she smiles at my AK armband and the major insignia sewn onto Papa's military cap.

We count out twelve apples. In the fridge, the milk's still fresh, as is the half loaf of bread. I decide on cheese sandwiches and, efficiently, she slices while I assemble.

"The old people in the other building gave us some water and milk for the children, but the lady in C building told us to leave or she'd call the police."

Laughing, we carry out the plates and candles and pause at the sight of even more people crowding the courtyard, several of them wounded.

A few faces nod acknowledgment of my AK status, but food is the critical issue, and soon an old *baba*, aided by Hania, is cutting the apples and sandwiches in half.

As the sky flares with crackling bursts of light, I approach a wounded boy, who sits up when he sees my AK insignia.

"Please, don't rise. Just tell me your name."

"Second Lieutenant Aleksi Dabrowski." *Legs bloodied, maybe shrapnel in the flesh.* I marvel that he's made it into the courtyard, and at the same time, curse myself for not keeping some of the medicine and bandages I gave to Zofia. I give him a squirt of water from my pouch, and he sinks back onto the ground. What have I got to help him? Mama always makes sure we have clean sheets and a secret store of vodka, and I have my sharp pocketknife. *Jesu Maria.*

I sit beside him on the ground. "What's your company, soldier?" *Pupils dilated.*

"A-Division, Company C."

So not Mati's. "You're a brave man," I say, holding his wrist. *Hot with a slow heart rate.* "I'm going to check for injuries, okay?"

"I had a flamethrower," he says, dreamily. "Took out a machine gun and four Hitlerow."

I smile. *No abdominal wounds. Arms okay.* But his legs have been gouged by shrapnel and he's lost a lot of blood.

"Rest now. I'll bring you a blanket." My words seem to have brought back the drizzle, and he squirms as the rain hits him.

"Major— Pani, please don't go."

The drizzle turns to rain, and I call for Hania.

"Tell them to go inside. Flat number one is mine, and upstairs, I believe flat number two is empty."

People gather themselves and troop into the building. The old couple from B building opens their curtains to watch. In a little while, they walk out into the courtyard with a bundle under their arms.

"Our old camping tent," the man says.

"That's so kind, Pan, but I don't think we should move him," I say.

"Don't worry, we can make a roof over him," the woman says, and they set about in their raincoats, putting up the poles and draping the canvas over us.

A little while later, Hania runs out carrying a blanket and my sister's raincoat. I slip it on gratefully and lay the blanket gently over Aleksi.

"They're cooking up a storm in there," she says, jerking her thumb at my flat.

"I have cabbage and carrots," the old woman says. "I'll take some up."

I look up at Hania. "The stove isn't working, is it?"

She shakes her head. "They made a fire in the fireplace with wood from that big armchair upstairs and all the empty packing cases."

Just like in the days of the Siege. I smile. What would Pani Hüber say to that?

Hania gazes at Aleksi breathing shallowly on the ground. "I can stay with him if you want to step inside."

I shake my head. "I'd like to cut away his trousers, see how bad the wounds are. Can you ask if anyone has any pain tablets? And bring a clean sheet."

Aleksi lies depleted under the canvas tent, candlelight glowing from my building, the sounds of children and laughter carrying into the dark courtyard. The rain has slowed, and as night deepens, I find myself strangely at peace. I can't remember the last time I felt the red-black chaos engulf me.

Aleksi murmurs awake, and I say his name, stroke his arm. With my pocketknife, I cut along the seam of his trousers, and I'm met with a gruesome sight. Black metal and grit in red and yellow flesh. Infection setting in. *Mother Mary.* Judging from the blood-soaked trousers, the other leg could be as bad. There's nothing I can do here. Transferring him to an underground hospital would be ideal, but it's too risky. The best thing is to go there myself and bring help back. I'll tell Hania.

Near the door of the flat, the smell of food simmering makes my stomach growl. How long has it been since I've eaten? The next instant, rifle shots ring out close by, followed by the sound of shattering glass, the belch of fire, the acrid stench of burning gasoline. Inside the flats, the clatter of household noise stills for a long moment, then resumes.

Through the gates beyond the courtyard, I make out two AK soldiers taking aim and firing down the road toward Marszałkowska. A tank engine screams, grinds to a stop while the boys cheer. Their cheers are answered by machine-gun fire, and retreating, they crash through the gate, into the courtyard.

"No!" I rush at them. "Don't bring the fighting here. Civilians and children are sheltering in these buildings."

But two more boys with AK armbands come thundering through the gate, completely unarmed. One of them is Davey, and this time, to the surprise of his troop mates, he runs straight into my arms.

"Bar the gate!" I yell at the others. "There's a chain."

"Don't worry," Davey says. "The tank's stuck on the corner. This street's too small."

"But they can still come after you or blast that long gun at these buildings!"

They exchange looks. "Maybe," one of them says. "But Davey and Janusz set it on fire."

I stare at their grinning faces, smell the gasoline coming off them, and laugh. "Good work, men."

A tall red-haired boy slings his rifle over his shoulder. "What food do you have here?"

I direct them to the flat, and a moment later clapping and cheering erupts from inside. Davey stays behind, following me when I move to check on Aleksi.

"Do you recognize him?" I ask.

He shakes his head. "Maybe one of the others can. We're all from different platoons. Most of my company was killed in the tank blasts."

"That's terrible." When I try to clasp his hand, he shakes me off. Then he says, "Leah got married to an old man."

"She did?"

"Yup! He was hiding at Kasha's, too. He had a contact, got some fake papers made, and they left last January. Their plan was to get to America."

"And you?" At twelve, he's still part boy, but in the set of the jaw, the carved cheekbones, I see the man approaching.

He shrugs, looks up at me with defiant eyes. "I stayed behind to fight."

I smile, but I think how hard it must have been for Leah to leave without him.

His fellow fighters stream out, Hania in tow with plates balanced on her arm, and we sit on the concrete verge of the garden, eating the most delicious meal I've had in ages.

None of the other soldiers recognizes Aleksi, but Davey volunteers to get help from the cellar hospital on nearby Puławska. His red-haired mate seems eager to accompany him.

When we've licked every last smudge of the vegetable stew from our plates, Hania and I go inside, where I'm greeted with applause from the plate cleaners wiping the dishes with the AK *Information Bulletin*.

"The children are asleep in your beds," Hania says. "I hope it's okay."

"It's not safe in here anymore, Hania. Everyone should go into the cellars.

I'm sorry, but there's a Panzer tank on the corner. If it's still operational, it could blow us all to dust."

The women rouse the children and follow me outside and into our cellar. Pleased with their accommodations, they set out the bedclothes and pillows from upstairs. The men decline to follow. With the two remaining AK fighters, they form a loose gathering around Aleksi's tent, passing cigarettes around, taking sips from Mama's bottle of vodka.

I stand a bit apart. No stars out tonight, but I'm cheered by flashes of yellow bursting the night sky from the Old Town, from across the river where the Russians must have captured Praga by now.

As if in answer, a scratchy voice begins to sing the old battle song "*Warszawianka*," the Song of Warsaw. Normally a fast, marching tune, when you sing it as slowly as the old man does, it's rife with melancholy and longing.

In this sweet courtyard bubble, a familiar refrain repeats in my head: *Come home to me, Mati.*

Twenty-Six

Toronto, December 2010

Roland picks me up at the Oakville station, a forty-minute train ride from downtown Toronto. In the car, I glance at his face—sometimes there's little mourning for the very sick and very old. Everyone wants an ending.

"I'm sorry about your dad," I say, noticing the lines of grief straining his face.

He grunts something inaudible.

After a restless night, I woke with a bilious headache and the words of the translation flashing like cue cards before my eyes. I glance around the car. What would be the best place to throw up in Roland's Volvo? Glove compartment?

"Could we stop for coffee?" I ask.

"We have an espresso machine at the office. Would that be all right?"

"Great." I roll down the window, hoping the cold wind will numb my nausea.

By the time we arrive at the wrought-iron gate, the logo of Cegielski Landscaping crowning the top, my nausea's settled, but the headache's still a hammer.

Everything in the office is sharp white, even the low leather sofa.

"We're all relieved," Roland says. "He had a long run."

So no sorrow, just relief? I push my hair behind my ears. Today I feel its fussy weight like a hood I want to throw off. *Where to begin?* I clasp my hands in my lap.

"The last few interviews, Stefan spoke mainly about the past. Ola and the war."

"I know. Like my mother and our whole life on Taylor Street meant nothing."

He has his back to me, waiting for the machine to finish my espresso. "And yet, they had a very long marriage." He swivels around. "My mother died eight years ago—but you know all that."

I nod. "I guess the death of his first wife was devastating—the way she died."

"Excuse me?"

"Ola's death. The hand grenade . . . ?"

"Ola was his sister."

I smack my forehead. "I'm so sorry. I misunderstood."

"Jesus. You scared me." His voice catches, and he excuses himself as he pushes open the glass door.

When he returns, I have my jacket on. "Maybe I should go."

"No, sit. We'd like to see the sculpture."

"Before I show it to you, may I ask you a few questions about your dad?"

He hands me my espresso in a white ceramic cup and saucer. "Sure. Fire away."

"During the war, did he— What did he do during the war?"

"He was an officer in the Polish army in exile—in Britain. He never said much about it. My mom's war stories are the ones I remember. They met in Scotland near the end."

"And Ola? What happened to her?"

"That part I know because my dad's mother came to visit from Poland when I was a kid." He leans against a concrete pillar, its upper half strung with little succulents poking out of sphagnum moss. "She told us that Ola had been in the Polish resistance. Apparently she saved many people's lives. She got ambushed by the Nazis one day. I think she was shot."

So that part may be true.

"Her name's in the Warsaw Rising Museum."

Like Mati and Irena. "Have you been?" I ask, placing my cup on the low table.

"Oh, no. Dad told me about it."

The door opens and Cynthia hurries in, glancing at Roland. "Hi, Jo." She smiles and sits beside me on the sofa. I offer my condolences.

"Jo's asking about Dad's army career," Roland says, frowning at me. "What's all this about?"

"Your father told me several times that he was one of the resisters in the Polish Underground. That he fought with Ola against the Nazis in Warsaw during the Occupation."

"That doesn't surprise me," Roland says, stirring his coffee.

Maybe it's the strong coffee, but my headache's gone. I turn to Cynthia. "I shouldn't be asking you these questions now. I'm sorry." I could stop right here, but I don't. I turn again to Roland. "There is something else. Is it possible that your father fought on the German side? As an SS officer?"

His eyebrows shoot up. "Where'd you get that idea?"

Bringing Irena into this feels wrong. "He said things in a recording, in German, and I had it translated. I brought you a copy. His mind was in the past, shouting at prisoners."

Roland looks at Cynthia, who shakes her head. "That's not possible," he says.

A wave of anger crests in my throat. "Do you still want to see the drawing?"

I stand, holding the cardboard tube between my palms, turning first to Cynthia, then to Roland.

He looks down at the soft gray carpet, rocks on the heels of his boots.

"You're accusing my father. That's pretty serious, not to mention tactless." He takes a step back. "You know, we knew you were Jewish, but we didn't think it mattered."

"Didn't think what mattered?"

"That you'd be making a gravestone for a Polish officer."

I feel myself planting my feet farther apart. "My grandparents are Polish, heroes of the resistance. Both were captured. I never discussed that with Stefan."

"Why not?"

I meet his eyes. "Confidentiality. Your father's story ran so parallel to my grandparents'. Maybe it was his way of reinventing himself."

He throws up his hands. "Who knows?"

His father's voice raves in my ears: *BITCH, WHORE!* I jut my chin forward. "Are you certain he wasn't in the SS?"

Roland's mouth gapes. Cynthia hurries over to him. "There's that photo of him and your mom on their wedding day."

"That's right. He's in his Polish army uniform. They're in Edinburgh or somewhere, standing on the steps of a church." Roland folds his arms tightly against his chest, looks at Cynthia. "I don't feel the need to prove anything to her. Besides, everybody's dead."

"Not everybody," I say, thinking of Irena. Moving quickly, I pull out the roll of paper, spread it out on the white marble table, pressing the dab of soft clay at each corner to hold it. Cynthia breathes in sharply. The three of us look down on a slender black crucifix, fractured at the crux; the Christ figure is missing, replaced by a sinuous curve of knives. I think the knives are beautiful—the handles densely carved with little faces, the blades etched in delicate filigreed designs.

For a moment, they stand dumbstruck; then Roland says, "I'll get someone to drive you to the train station."

"I'll get a cab," I insist, rolling up the drawing.

"I'll have someone call," Roland says, striding out.

Cynthia walks up to me. "You must know it's a hard time for him. His dad hasn't recognized him for a long while. He treated him like a stranger at the end."

"I am sorry." I place an envelope on the table. "I'll leave you the recording and this copy of the transcripts."

"Please don't," she says, her hand on my forearm. "The past is passed."

I don't reach for the envelope. "It's important. If you do read this, be careful; he's shouting at women prisoners."

"No, that doesn't sound right," she says, clutching the front of her blouse. She opens the door, and I follow her out.

On the way to the reception area, I glance down a white corridor and stop mid-stride. Hanging on the far wall—the focal point—is Irena's *Mokotów Angel*. I stagger down the hallway and stare up at the print—the body lying half out of a manhole in a pool of blood, and walking away, his back to the body, a soldier. The perspective, level with the street, makes the viewer an intimate witness. I close my eyes, take a deep breath. When I turn round, Cynthia's waiting at the end of the corridor.

"One of Dad's favorite artists," she says, nodding at the painting. "Polish. He has a big collection of her work."

I swallow, open my mouth to say nothing.

She says goodbye, taps on Roland's office door, and slips in like a thief so he doesn't have to see me.

"I'll wait outside," I say to the receptionist.

"I find it creepy, too," the receptionist says, wrinkling her nose.

THE STATION PLATFORM'S crowded with fans in Toronto Maple Leafs jerseys—moms, dads, little kids, including those already lubricated for their evening in the big city. I keep my back to the platform wall, head down, hair veiling my face. My body's cold, but my face is burning, my head swimming in a brine of questions with answers I'm afraid of hearing.

Switching from train to subway at Union Station, I blend in with the moving tide. Accompanying me is the image of *Mokotów Angel* hanging on the wall in Stefan's landscaping office. My feet stop in the middle of the platform.

When did Stefan become a collector? In Canada, it's mostly the Québécois who admire Irena's art. Françoise Bisset, her longtime art dealer, might know.

The smell of cinnamon and baking accompanies me down the stairs, courtesy of Bus Stop Bakery on the upper level. I step toward the platform edge as the subway squeals into the station, and score a seat beside a man with long dreadlocks.

At my subway stop, I watch a teenage couple exit the doors, his arm around her shoulders, hers around his waist. I register a familiar feeling—no one to turn to. It squeezes my heart. I walk home with a question in my head—How long has it been since anyone touched me with that casual intimacy?

Cheriblare hurries to the front hallway as I ease my boots off. "Hello, I'm home!" I sing, bending to scratch behind her ears. "Where's Irena?" I whisper, and add, "Did she show you her triptych?"

Cheri gives me her signature blare.

"She did? Lucky girl!"

I pick up a red and white courier envelope from the hallway table, turn it over—addressed to me. Now what could this be?

Following the TV sounds to the living room, I find my grandmother watching *Grey's Anatomy*, a bowl of something on her lap tray.

"Hi. How was your day?"

"Terrific. Tahira came and brought soup."

"Smells divine! I'll join you in a minute."

In the kitchen, I pour myself a glass of wine before opening the envelope. Inside is another envelope labeled Barton, Barton, Lewinski, and Cohen. The letter is curt and courteous:

The commission for Stefan Cegielski's grave sculpture is withdrawn. Thank you for the work you've done so far. The Cegielski family has decided to have a conventional gravestone. Please submit an invoice for all work completed to the law firm. All recordings, images, and any other materials created or gathered in the course of the interviews with Stefan Cegielski and family must be returned . . .

Roland didn't waste any time.

I read the letter again, and this time it feels vengeful. Something I should have anticipated given the great big lie at the center of Stefan's life. I swirl the mulberry-colored liquid in my glass. Maybe they're hiding something else. Or were they as shocked as I was by the recording?

I try a calming breath in and out, flinch when a branch taps the night window—tap, tap, like a ghost wanting to come in.

Screw them. I'll keep copies of everything. They can cancel my contract, but they can't erase my memories of Stefan or his voice on the recording.

I won't let it go. That black crucifix with its noisy knives has to mean something.

Twenty-Seven

Warsaw, August 1, 1944

Sacrificing the young oak tree with its wild August canopy anguishes us all, but we agree it's necessary. Pan Bukowski from B building has a handsaw, and the recently arrived AK group takes turns going at it by the back fence as if they're sawing through Hitler's leg.

The German garrison towed away the burned-out tram car, eliminating the main barricade on Marszałkowska, and tonight, while the little ones are asleep in the cellar and the Germans are in their beds, we're rebuilding it. We've seen the damage one Panzer tank can do to our army and homes; we can't allow any more rumblers to enter this main thoroughfare.

Hands on her waist, a skeptical AK soldier, recently injured, limps around, determined to order us about. "Those barrels are useless. We used sandbags in the Old Town—so much better at absorbing bullets and they don't catch fire."

I stretch a smile. "Good for you, Lieutenant. You find the bags and sand, and we'll follow your suggestion."

We form a line and haul the tree with its tangle of branches to the center of the street, wedging it on top of the barrels, bedsteads, an ancient leather sofa, slabs of concrete from decimated buildings, even bales of hay from who knows where. We work in silent harmony, moving round each other effortlessly in the dark, young and old hurrying to the heavier tasks. I try to remember the last time I smiled so much.

Standing apart to survey our handiwork, I turn to the old man beside me. "Not very high, but at least it's thick and wide."

"And inscrutable," he says, showing missing teeth. "It should halt the Huns for a while."

I smile. Come morning, they'll tear it apart again, but not before we pick off a few of them with rifles and gasoline bombs.

"Come morning," he says, as though he's heard my thoughts, "the Russian troops will be in Warsaw and we can hand over the job to them."

"Not the plan, old man." A young AK corporal saunters up, cigarette aglow. "It's our capital, our country." He thumps his chest. "We're thousands of Poles in the Home Army, and we'll keep leading the fight." He winks at me. "We just need more weapons and ammunition."

I look at his handsome face and let a sigh escape. *Mati, where are you?* With Mama in Wola, I've been looking forward to the two of us having the flat entirely to ourselves. The things I had planned to do with him! But now, overnight, the Sobieski Residences have become this unlikely way station for soldiers and civilians caught in the Rising.

Once the barricade is established, I return to our cellar to check on the women guarding the children. Since I've been waving new arrivals into the cellars for hours, I'm surprised when only one dozing woman and two sleeping children greet my arrival.

"*Cześć,* Pani. Where is everyone?"

She points to the whitewashed wall of the cellar and I point my flashlight in that direction. A large hole knocked in the brick leads to a dug-out tunnel beyond.

"They've been going back and forth between the cellars," she says.

"Mothers and children?"

"*Tak*, and the soldiers."

Brilliant. It could be an easier way to move about the city than crawling through the sewers; certainly better for transporting weapons and ammunition. Or wounded soldiers.

ABOVEGROUND, THE SUN is rising even as blasts of artillery flame the dark sky. Burnt umber, scarlet, cadmium yellow bursting through ultramarine. I rub my sleepy eyes. Day two of the Rising has announced itself. A whimpering wheedles its way to my ear. Aleksi! Too busy with the barricade, I've completely forgotten about him.

I lift the flap and startle a young man with his head on Aleksi's chest. He lurches up when he sees me.

"How is he?" I ask, but one look at Aleksi's pale, placid face tells me that he's died in the night. I check for a pulse anyway. "I'm so sorry." My body tries for a comforting gesture, and can't make any. I've got to get some sleep. "What's your name, soldier?"

He hesitates, pulls his cap on before looking away.

"Adolf."

Poor kid. I give him a consoling smile. "Will you help dig his grave?"

The boy accompanies me outside, and we stand before the gathering group of AK soldiers. What can I say to bolster them?

I take a deep breath, moisten my dry lips. "Fellow soldiers, our colleague Aleksi has died from his wounds."

A groan scuttles through the young men.

"He fought bravely for his city and his country. Who will make a cross with his name?"

A hand goes up.

I look about the courtyard. "We'll bury him here in the garden bed. You two, ask around, see who has another shovel."

While they're busy, I return to the tent and search Aleksi's pockets for anything worth saving. Overnight, a fine blond beard has sprouted from his unlined face; his narrow chest so peaceful now that his bluster's gone. My mind wanders unexpectedly to Lotka. Danuta. We could use a nurse. Even Zofia. I'll get permission to bring her here. Nothing in his trouser pockets, but in his right breast pocket, a folded photo of a woman who could be his mother. No writing on the back. In his left breast pocket, two unspent rifle cartridges. *Good man, Aleksi.*

ON THE WAY to Warecka Street to meet my cargo—a mission impossible to complete yesterday—I ask myself, *Is this what I imagined I'd be doing in the Rising—providing shelter for civilians separated from their homes, from their young children; burying young men in the courtyard of my building, watching ordinary women perform fishes and loaves miracles with a few potatoes, onions, and carrots?* And now I'm off to meet this mysterious Wojtek, who I've been assigned to guide via the sewers from his imperiled hiding place to a secure one—if such a thing still exists. I tighten the straps on my rucksack.

The truth is I'm glad to be back in my tunnel trousers and boots, with the added comfort of a loaded Luger in my left pocket—bullets courtesy of Mati's platoon. It makes me feel more like an insurgent and less like a housekeeper. The wordy message from the colonel couldn't have been clearer: *As regards Wojtek, he's triple-A important to our current project. Get him whatever he needs, do as he says, and protect him with your life.*

I suppose I should be flattered.

I managed two hours' sleep on my bedroom floor, the voices of my fellow Varsovians nattering outside—soothing babies, cobbling food together, some crying, some gossiping, some flirting, everyone talking about how the Russians will quickly overcome the vastly outnumbered German soldiers remaining in our capital.

Glancing up at a clear blue sky, I rub my tired eyes to be certain of what I'm seeing. Draped over the second-floor balcony of a residential building are the white and red bands of the Polish flag. It's a shock to see it lifting jauntily in the breeze as though it hasn't a care in the world, as though it hasn't been banned from its home country for almost five years.

I made the decision to travel aboveground this second day of the Rising. If I'm to guide this precious cargo through the sewers, I need to know where the fighting's worse, where the dragons have their strongholds and which neighborhoods and streets the AK have liberated. That word sends my heart leaping. We are liberating ourselves! Still, the last thing I need is to guide this triple-A Wojtek into the hands of the Wehrmacht, weakened and threatened as they are.

Tight knots of AK soldiers huddle behind barricades on the main streets, aiming pistols and rifles, lobbing grenades at dragon soldiers armed with heavy machine guns. I stop when they say stop, run when they say run, and get down when I see them diving for cover.

Unpleasant discovery number one: my preferred alley shortcut is barred by a collapsed building, but undeterred, I clamber over the rubble to discovery number two: rows of corpses laid out on the ground. Mostly women civilians judging by the feet in heeled sandals; some small children—all covered in flapping newspaper. An AK soldier is laying bricks on top of them to stop the pages from flying off. I spend fifteen minutes helping him.

"You the last of your platoon?" I ask.

He shakes his head and silently, methodically bends to his work as if his life depends on it.

ON NOWY ŚWIAT in the city center, I come across fierce fighting, a building in flames. I'm not sure which side of the street is ours and which theirs, and I'm about to retreat in search of a sewer grate when I hear "Ala! Over here, Ala!"

I follow the voice and look up at a soldier behind a rifle in a second-story window of the Prudential Insurance building.

He waves his arm toward the back of the skyscraper, and, when they signal, I follow two AK soldiers scrambling across Napoleon Square behind a series of barricades. The ping of rifle fire whizzes above our heads, and I'm conscious of the soft, helmetless melon atop my neck.

They guide me to a doorway at the back of the massive building before returning to their posts. When I show him my official pass, an armed soldier lets me in and tells me to wait under the stairs. How am I to get to Warecka? I should have stuck to the sewers. I crouch down and wait for direction. In the static quiet that follows a shuddering blast, I hear boots running down the stairs above me, cringe into the shadows beneath the staircase.

"Where is she?"

A voice I recognize. I stumble out to meet Fryderyk in full combat gear, a rifle and ammunition slung across his shoulders, rimless spectacles covered in a light spray of dust.

He takes off his glasses to polish them. "What are you doing here, Ala?"

I raise my eyebrows, pin my gaze to his.

"Oh." He takes my arm and we climb up to the second-floor landing.

"I need to get to Warecka."

"I think I can help. We captured this whole building an hour ago." Amazed at the words that have come from his mouth, he rubs his unshaved chin.

"So things are going well?"

"Yes. We're driving them out of their cubbyholes. But civilian casualties are high."

I tell him about the rows of bodies I saw. "Are we doing enough to protect them?"

He sighs. "The problem is the Germans don't seem to be making any distinction between us and the regular population. They blast their homes with artillery; snipers pick them off as they're crossing a street with their kids—the same as they do with us in our uniforms. It's a slaughter, Ala."

"You think they're purposefully targeting civilians?"

"Looks that way."

I bite my lip. *They're breaking the basic rules of combat.* A shell lands nearby, and the building shudders. People should be staying in their cellars, but everyone's trying to get to their own homes, their own families. Human nature.

"Have you seen Zofia?" he asks. "How is she?"

I take my water from my rucksack and offer him the flask.

"Yesterday. She's okay. Working in the cellar hospital in the Polish Bank building. Not happy about it, but safer there than out here."

"And Mati?"

I shrug. "Haven't seen him for two days."

He tugs at his rifle strap. "Speaking of cellars, we could get you closer to Warecka by taking you through the cellar. This building's more than a block long, and yesterday our regiment started digging into the cellars on either side. I have to get back to my post, but I'll show you the entrance."

I follow him to a dark, deserted cellar, electric lights everywhere, but none working, painted concrete floor and walls and a large safe that must have held and perhaps still holds bonds, certificates, stocks—the paper that used to make the world go round. This would make a good hospital if we had medicines and equipment. If our Allies made the drops they promised.

"I'll leave you here. I haven't been farther than this, so I'm not sure what lies beyond. But Warecka is only a block from the other side of this building. Good luck."

Ten minutes later, the long corridor comes to an end, and I see the beginning of an earthen tunnel. I shine my torch up, down, ahead. It's big, but is it stable? One step in and a clod of earth falls from above, hitting me on the head and obscuring my vision. I brush cold soil from my eyes. *Jesu Maria.* I should have stuck to the sewers. I plod on cautiously and mercifully without incident until ahead of me I hear—singing? My ears pick out the tune of "*Siekiera motyka*," the low laughter of men, composing rude new verses, no doubt.

I whistle the banned tune. "Hello?"

A torch shines in my eyes and I have to put up my hand.

"Well, well. Who have we here, using up our oxygen?"

"Major Ala Iwanowska. I need to get to Warecka without delay."

He's a thickset, imposing figure. With the light in my eyes, I can't make out a face, but a gentler voice says, "Lower your torch," which the first man does.

Both men have shovels in hand, half-filled sacks at their feet. "You have your identification?" says the first man.

I shine my torch on my pass, but don't hand it to him.

A low whistle. "Signed by Bór. I guess we better let this important miss through, Jas."

They step aside, and I have to squeeze by them. The kinder one calls after me. "It's fortified closer to the exit, but this part is newly dug. Move quickly."

Which I'm only too happy to do. Another ten minutes of breathing in the smell of freshly dug soil, roots like pale fans in the dug-out walls, and finally new voices up ahead, the sound of hammering, and a section reinforced with wooden struts in the roof and walls. The two carpenters are younger and one of them is a woman, who offers to show me the exit onto the street.

"I need a smoke," she smiles, "and we can't smoke down here."

The tunnel ascends gradually until we're in a wide rectangular underground room, paneled in beautiful old wood. "Part of an old palace," she whispers. "Can you believe it?"

We pause at the foot of a staircase leading up to the ground floor, and an appallingly familiar smell reaches my nose.

"Smells like a dead body," says my escort.

We climb cautiously, and I no longer need my torch. There's no door at the top of the stairs, and yellow light streams from above.

"Must be blue skies," she says, lighting a cigarette. "Too bad."

I nod. Blue skies mean the German bomber planes will more easily target our hard-won strongholds. My poor Warsaw.

As predicted, the floor of the landing, possibly Carrara marble, is laid with bodies. We've become good at placing corpses into neat rows; these are covered in rich curtains, bedding, a tapestry. I cover my nose with my scarf, and then I notice the feet. Bootless. The arms, shirtless. These are German soldiers, some still in their bloody jackets or trousers, some liberated from their black boots or gray uniforms. Still other bodies have AK armbands.

The woman waves at me, her nose wrinkling, and motions that she's going to climb the wide steps to what must be a grand entrance hall.

I point to the bare feet. "Could be Hitlerow," I whisper.

She pauses, stubs out her cigarette, and flattens herself against the bottom step. I watch her from behind a marble column. She creeps slowly up the next step, and suddenly a barrage of Polish and German shouting echoes through the entrance hall, accompanied by bullets ricocheting off the marble surfaces. The skirmish travels up and down the stairs, avoiding the woman's now bloodied body. Hand to hand, rifle to pistol, some on a balcony above the entrance hall, AK insurgents wearing the jackets, boots of the dead German soldiers, mixed with Polish army caps and helmets; the Hitlerow in their finery, but losing more men. I become still, small, and silent, my only movement my roving eyes and my bounding heart. Then it's over, and some bodies are silent, while others are in noisy agony.

AT FIRST, WARECKA Street seems quieter, the AK in firm control of the section I need to traverse, but after my experience in the palace, I can see why this important Wojtek has to find new lodgings sooner rather than later. I find the house and rap smartly at the door, giving the coded knock. Footsteps. The door opens enough to reveal the barrel of a revolver. *Okay!* I grip the pistol in my trouser pocket and give the password; the one-word response is exactly what I expect. The door opens just enough for me to enter before it's locked behind me.

"What took you so long?"

I whirl around. Before me are the changed but unmistakable features of Mr. Godlewski. I put my hand on my heart, and he does something I don't expect: he opens his arms wide, and I walk straight into his strong embrace. Then I do something I don't expect—I burst into tears and weep, and weep, and weep.

"You're bleeding," Mr. Godlewski says and leads me to a tiny kitchen at the back of the flat. I sit at a table while he presses a handkerchief to my forehead.

Twenty-Eight

Toronto, Mid-December 2010

Cautiously, like I'm defusing a bomb, I lift the plastic bin I placed over the book, set the bin aside on my workshop counter. Fear makes me linger over the cover. The stakes feel unbearably high, yet when I name them, they sound ridiculous: I'm terrified that this book holds something that could destroy my love for my grandparents, nullify the admiration I've had for them for over thirty years. I get up to search the pockets of my work apron. *Shit.* No cigarette butts.

Irena was bent on working in her studio this morning, which gave me a chance to whisk the book out of her bedroom beneath my fleecy.

My grandmother's cough has been sounding wetter, thicker, but every attempt at getting her to a doctor has failed.

"No fuss. I have just a cold," has been her stubborn argument.

Still, I went behind her back and got an appointment with her doctor, which was harder than begging for mercy in a Roman gladiatorial arena. Warm clothes laid out on her bed, a taxi on its way, I was all set to stand firm when my grandmother returned from the bathroom this morning and slayed me with her blue-eyed glare: *You think I'm stupid?*

We compromised: I agreed not to take her temperature, and she agreed to let me make her a hot toddy with lots of lemon and honey. I plugged in the new humidifier, vacuumed extra, and attacked the dust sculptures on the one shelf she never runs her duster over. The domain of dried flowers, seashells, ribbons, pebbles, and newspaper clippings inside of magazines and books, the shelf is where I noticed the glossy hardcover.

Perched on a stool, with Cheriblare in a box beside the electric heater, I flick on the gooseneck lamp.

Poland's Fighting Glory is the book Mati prized from my hands many years ago. Just as I remember, the black-and-white cover photo is a close-up of two soldiers in helmets: one handsome, stubble-chinned male; one pretty, apple-cheeked female. I turn the first page and find a group photo—like a 1940s movie still. A shiver passes across the back of my neck as I read the caption: *Home Army soldiers at a sewer entrance on Malczewskiego Street in occupied Warsaw.*

Pawel Marianowski (code name Mateusz/Mati) stands on the far left, a rifle hanging from one shoulder, a cigarette in his other hand. *So Mati was his code name!* Next to him is another young man, *Eryk Borowski (code name Fryderyk)*—blond, with round wire glasses. On the far right, *Irena Marianowska (code name Ala)*—tall, fair, those striking eyes. In the middle, a younger girl—smaller than the rest of them—with dark hair, a round, luminous face—*Alexandra Wenders (code name Zofia).* I sit up. Is this Ola? But what about the name *Wenders*? If she were Stefan's sister, wouldn't she be a *Cegielski*? Unless she was married, I suppose. But Wenders doesn't sound Polish.

I lean over the page. Is this what Mati was hiding?

Ola looks springy, like a cat. I scan the photo for a wedding ring, but she has her hands in her pockets. I lay my fingertip on the chest of an impossibly young Irena, her hand on Ola's shoulder like an older sister. They're all incredibly skinny. Probably starving. Irena wears a headscarf, just the blond hair above her forehead visible. A hollow indents each temple, shadows each eye.

Shirts with lapel pockets, pants tucked into boots—was this their uniform?

Only Fryderyk's pants are rolled up, exposing thin legs, a wry smile on his lips as though the cameraman has just said something funny; his shoulders are turned toward Alexandra. She's the star of the photo, a pair of slippers dangling from a string around her waist. And Mateusz! My grandfather's a total glamour boy, like a young Clark Gable with that dark curl over one eye. I sigh. Everyone loved Mati. It was impossible not to.

But no Stefan Cegielski. He convinced me that he worked with Ola—big lie number one, I suppose. *Shit.* What if Stefan was a Wenders, too? Did he make a quick-footed name change to Cegielski?

And why would he do that? I ask myself.

To save himself.

The answer bangs a gong in my head.

He was that kind of man.

Turning the page, I'm startled by a close-up of Alexandra's face—wisps of dark hair, a bit of braid showing behind her neck. Dimples. She could be eighteen, in her last year of high school. Even in the blurry blowup, the dark eyes are pits of seriousness in contrast to the babyish smile. The caption reads: *Alexandra (Olenka) Wenders, code name Zofia. Soldier in the Home Army, she guided civilians and soldiers to safety through the sewers. She was killed in the Uprising, a day before her twentieth birthday.*

A stone lodges in my throat. Was she killed in that sewer tunnel? There's something about this Ola. Stefan's voice whispers in my ear: *She was braver than me, she had a pure heart.*

I raise my eyes from the page and my ears tune to the sounds of the city: sirens; streetcars and buses; car radios; music now, coming from Irena's studio. I stand and stretch, my stomach rumbling. Irena must be hungry, too. Thank goodness I had the sense to freeze the chicken soup from the Bulgarian deli, and we still have some of Tahira's leek dumplings.

Cheri purrs in her sleep and I return to the book for one last look before dinner. Many of these photos were taken by the same guy—Jerszy Borowski. Fryderyk's brother? I flip the page and shudder. The risks he took. A top photo shows a row of young people lined up against a wall facing a firing squad. The photo below shows German soldiers looking down at the bodies fallen at their feet. Maybe one of those young people was Ola. On the page opposite, a small group of frightened Poles looks on as three Nazi soldiers kick a body on the ground. *Jesus.* How did Jerszy get these shots? Did he have the means to make prints, or did he smuggle his film out?

I should get going. The wind's picked up, and it's dark so early now.

But I turn the page again and come upon another photo of Irena—a two-pager. Her face is full-on to the camera, smiling; she's in a nurse's uniform, with adoring young soldiers huddled behind her. I smile. Of course—not a nun, but a nurse. Why didn't anyone ever say? She looks happy. I flip back. In the group photo she's quite serious. Here, her face is fuller and her hair isn't covered. I bend closer. Is that lipstick? On the bottom of the next page, I find a caption that says, simply, *Previous page: Polish Army soldiers with nurse Szarlota Iwanowska.*

Oh, fuck. The mysterious S. Iwanowska. I jump up to pace between the counters of my workshop, pausing to move back and forth between the pages. The resemblance is at first remarkable. But paying close attention I see Szarlota is more buxom than Irena, with a polished sheen to her hair and nails, a flirty upward glance at the photographer. *Who is she?* I flip back again. My grandmother, even at that young age, has her perennial big-eleven crease between her eyes.

PLUCKED FROM HER warm bed, an unhappy Cheriblare and I follow the pavers Mati laid in a perfect curve leading to the back door of the house. I could summon my pallid courage and ask Irena about this S. Iwanowska, but she's not at her easels as I pass her studio window.

Nervous now, I hurry inside and find her lying on the couch in the living room watching *Jeopardy*, a second toddy on the coffee table. *Oh, well.* Vitamin

C and warm liquid, and doesn't honey have antibiotic properties?

"Hi, *Babcia*. Chicken soup and Tahira's dumplings for dinner," I say, kissing her hot cheek. *Shit.* Maybe Tahira can convince her to see Dr. Chan, or else I could get Dr. Chan to come here. I have to do something.

We eat in the living room, a no-no in Sophie's time, and together, my grandmother and I get a shocking number of *Jeopardy* answers wrong.

"Soup is good."

Her voice sounds croaky. I sneak a look at her face—flushed—but she seems calmer, content after finishing her bowl.

In her sitting room, I give in to her having one cigarette, which, thank God, she doesn't finish, and lead her to the humid bedroom, where she flops on the bed while I administer two Tylenol. When she's tucked under her covers, I lay my palm on her forehead. She twists away, but not before my hand feels the wet heat of her skin.

"You know you're sick, *Babcia*. Why won't you let me take you to a doctor?"

"Because what will she do?" A coughing spell takes her, but after a sip of water, she sticks to her guns: "I stay in bed tomorrow, be better the next day."

AT TWO IN the morning, I feed her two more pills and change her damp pillowcase. Unable to sleep, I plan an early-morning assault on Dr. Chan's office. And if that doesn't work, maybe I could find a visiting nurse.

The glossy book's still in my workshop, so I open my iPad and google *Szarlota Iwanowska*, not expecting much. Well past the pouting selfies and corporate photos, I find the Polish site of the Warsaw Rising Museum and click on the English option.

There, I come across the same photo of Irena, Mati, Fryderyk, and Alexandra. I scroll down and there's Szarlota in her nurse's uniform surrounded by the soldiers. This time the caption says *Nurse Szarlota Iwanowska. Before the Rising, she was abducted by the Gestapo.*

A stab to my heart. Poor Szarlota. Is that why no one ever mentioned her? Yet she must have been dear to my family because they kept her nurse's veil; albeit, packed deep away. If she's on the website of the Warsaw Rising, though, she must have been in the resistance with the rest of them. I click on her photo. Szarlota looks as young as Irena, which makes her an unlikely aunt—more probably a cousin. Or half sister?

But that can't be. Sophie always joked about us being *The Only Baloneys*: Irena, Sophie, and Jo—three generations of girls, three children without siblings.

Twenty-Nine

Warsaw, August 2, 1944

"There's a first-aid kit in my rucksack," I say, feeling the sting of the wound for the first time. While Mr. Godlewski unbuckles the straps, I keep firm pressure on the handkerchief, glance about the drab room. The window's covered with a thick blackout curtain, planks of wood nailed to the frame like bars. How long has he been holed up here?

"I see you come prepared," he says, removing my little sketch pad before finding the first-aid kit.

"It's good to see you, too," I say, smiling at his scarred face, his arms and body leaner, more muscled than the vodka-soaked man Marysia assured me was long dead.

Antiseptic ointment and cotton pad applied, bandage tightly tied, he scans my body. "Any broken bones?"

I roll my shoulders, flex my arms and legs, absolutely do not wince at the sight of missing fingers on each of his hands. "Bones intact. I'm serving sandwiches and hot tea if you're hungry."

"Just tea," he says. "We should get going before things get more interesting around here."

"Where are we heading?"

"Back to Mokotów. I'll tell you more when we're close."

At the little table, with me in the only chair and he on a wooden crate, we hover over sweet, hot tea from my flask while he fills in the last few years, leaving some unexplained gaps.

I learn that the night he was dragged from our flat, he was imprisoned in Pawiak. The usual routine, he said, not pointing to the half-moon scar at the base of his neck, nor the circular burn marks on the backs of his hands. With bribery and the help of the AK, he escaped. But not for long. Recaptured, he was moved often—back and forth between Pawiak, an isolation cell in Gestapo headquarters, Mokotów Prison, the Fort.

"At the Fort, I came close to meeting the big guy," he says, pointing at the ground with his lopped-off index finger.

"But?"

He smiles. "Marysia found me. Got me out."

"Marysia!"

"You remember her disguises? She arrived as an SS colonel. Even I didn't recognize her. They had a Gestapo vehicle, forged papers ordering a transfer to Auschwitz signed by Reichsführer Himmler himself." He shakes his head in amazement. "She was one in a million." He stares at his empty cup. "At least now Dorota will have a place to visit her."

"Dorota?"

His brown gaze rests on mine, gentler than I've ever seen it. "The person she loved more than any other." He scrapes back his crate. "Help me move this table."

We slide the table, chair, and crate aside, and he throws back the worn carpet. I hold the trapdoor open while he uses two hands to pull out the heavy rucksack in the crawl space.

"Tools of my trade," he says, carrying it to the back door.

I eye the bulky bag and mentally rejig my route to Mokotów. No way that will get through the narrow tunnel I thought we'd take. I show him how to carry the water pouch across his body, tie the scarf around his neck. I can't do anything about the empty fingers of his gloves. *We'll make do*, I think, *as long as no surprises pop up along the way*, and laugh at my own foolishness.

THE AK SOLDIERS behind the barricade of charred church pews pay little attention as I shove the bag into the sewer entrance. At the foot of the ladder, we make ready to climb up into the wider storm tunnel running perpendicular to the narrow entrance, the red brick damp and smelly after yesterday's rain.

"This can't get wet," Mr. Godlewski says, indicating his hefty bag.

"Maybe you should tell me what's in there. So I can understand the risk."

"Shortwave radio equipment—transmitter, receiver, transformer."

My lips curl. Is that what he's been doing all these years? Sending and receiving messages? From Britain, I presume. Or has he been intercepting German messages?

"You have these instruments wrapped in waterproof material?"

"I have these instruments wrapped in my raincoat."

"That will do. We'll have to leave the novelty of swimming in shit for another time."

He laughs, and I feel wonderful. I'm doing something I know well, with a man who feels like family, a man I thought had died horribly. But here he is, still pecking at the ankles of the Reich. When I've hoisted myself into the storm tunnel, I turn around and help him lift the big bag. As he launches himself up, my torch lights up the burn marks on his scalp. *Bastards!* I remind myself that we've just left a section of the city center liberated by the Home Army. That instead of plucking out our own feathers in preparation for the pot, we're driving the dragons into the hands of our allies to the west and our allies to the east.

We start down the tunnel, and I have no time to worry about what the rain might have done to the black canal or whether my old friend will be able to keep up if I go at a faster pace because he's keen to catch up with my own recent history.

"How's dear Agata?"

When I tell him she went to Wola with a friend two days ago to pray in a church crypt, he laughs. But then he says, "That may land her in hot water."

"Hotter than in Mokotów?"

"This may surprise you, but the Führer and his henchmen aren't pleased with our success. When Himmler found out the Polish flag's flying over the Old Town again, he ordered the whole city destroyed, every man, woman, and child."

"I worried about that."

"Well, you should. We caught them with their trousers around their ankles, but by tomorrow, they'll wipe their arses, pull up their trousers, and get into their Stukas again."

"And Wola?"

"Let's hope your mother returns to Mokotów soon. You know, it's not so bad down here. Have the dragons discovered your underground network, Renka?"

"Yes and no. They know we use the tunnels to hide in, but they don't know that we're capable of traveling long distances through the city."

"That's good, that's good. And handsome Mateusz? How is he?"

"How do you know about me and Mati?"

"Word gets around, Irena. When Marysia first told me, we agreed you'd make a good match—one serious, one funny, one grumpy, one entertaining, one—"

"Okay, okay. I get the picture. So you approve?"

"I approve of whatever makes you happy."

"Aah. I'll try not to cry." And I almost succeed. Blinking back tears, I think, *He's not Papa, but like Papa, he sees who I am and still loves me.*

We carry on in silence for a long while, and I dare to imagine living in a liberated Warsaw with Mr. Godlewski as my upstairs neighbor. Mati and me cozy downstairs. And Mama? I can't picture Mama.

"You still drawing the war?" he asks.

"Oh, yes. Though there's hardly time for that these days."

It takes me a while to make the connection, but eventually, I'm the one with a burning question.

"That time in the Art Academy when—"

"Ah, yes. I was happy living among the Renaissance paintings before Captain Hauser sent me back to Byzantium. I heard he gave you and your team a scare."

I tell him about drawing Zofia, about the German guard who kept quiet about the guns we'd hidden.

"That's war, Renka: turn left and you walk into a land mine; turn right and you meet an enemy who looks the other way."

And when he looks the other way, you shoot him. "So that was you who stole the jeep?"

"That was me who shot the guard; that was me who drove away in the jeep. Any other questions?"

"Yes. How's your first sewer trip so far?"

"I'm impressed at how fast we're moving. Is it all like this?"

"Better. We're getting closer to the canal section. It's nice—you'll see." Nice and a bit slippery when wet. But he has good boots.

WE MARCH ALONG, and time unfolds in a dreamy fashion as though nothing worse than rain is happening in the world above us. We reminisce about Marysia and Pani Nowak. It seems safe to tell him about Małgorzata and Danuta—skirting, always skirting the question of Lotka. I'm afraid to ask, and he hasn't inquired about our search for her. What if he's seen her in Pawiak? Or heard about her in the basement cells of Gestapo headquarters? I couldn't bear to live with that knowledge. Once, I scratched my arms raw to stop my mind making pictures of her in the torture cells. The tunnel narrows, and I pick up the burble of water from the black canal. His footsteps slow, so I know he hears it, too. I need to prepare him.

"We'll break here. You can put the bag down, drink some water."

He lowers the bag, rotates his head, and rubs his neck.

I can tell he's itching to ask, so I tell him. "The last section's longer, but we can walk upright, even stretch our arms a bit."

"But?"

"There's a part where two other tunnels flow into the canal from either side. Imagine an intersection, a little bridge for the workmen to cross over one of the narrower tunnels. You have to, sort of, make a run across it."

He throws up his hands. "We'll cross that bridge when we come to it."

My sudden burst of laughter echoes dangerously.

I jump down from the storm sewer onto the pavement running alongside the deep canal. He shoves the bag near the edge and I pull it down slowly before it topples to the ground. Crouching at the edge to gauge the height, he makes a jump and lands a little too close to the canal for comfort.

"What's next?" he asks, panting. "Swinging from a trapeze?"

"Let me carry the bag for a while."

He waves me away. "I'm used to it."

And you've been through much worse.

Grates in the roof let in rays of sun that dapple the walls and silver the flowing black water.

He pauses to look up before I help lift the bag onto his back. *Cholera. How much does a transformer weigh?*

"Except for the stink," he says, pulling up his scarf, "this could be a little chapel, by a babbling brook."

I smile, let that image travel in silence along the long pavement ahead.

That same hush accompanies us through the next hour of walking, until he has to relieve himself, and I decide that even though Mr. Godlewski seems capable of existing on air, it's time for lunch.

I walk ahead to give him privacy and call back a warning: "Take off your rucksack first." Those transformers, transmitters, transistors, whatever they are, will sink like lead in the depths. I pause beneath a sunny grate, remove the lunch bag from my rucksack, curl into the curve of the warm yellow brick, and wonder what Mati's doing right now.

With my hand, I brush aside the blast of a tank gun somewhere above us. Not now. Unless that's a Russian tank. As a sharp ray of sunshine, or a fiery flash of gunfire, pierces the grate, I put on my sunglasses.

My cargo returns looking lighter, and crouches beside me. I offer him a cheese and pickle sandwich, the last of the warmish tea.

"You look like you're lounging on the Riviera, Renka."

I point to the roof. "You think that's a Russian tank blasting at the Germans?"

He takes his time chewing.

"Monter reported the Russian army was across the river two days ago. At least, that's the intelligence I heard." I bite my lip. "They must be here by now."

Reluctantly, he turns to me. "Monter was a little premature." On the verge of biting into his apple, he pauses. "The great Soviet army, which strangled the Wehrmacht in Russia, which has steadily pushed westward, trampling the enemy, is presently taking a siesta. I hope they wake up soon."

I pity the little apple his remaining teeth are mangling, ask my question anyway.

"What about the British? The Americans."

He throws the apple core into the canal. "As soon as they reply to my messages, Irena, I'll let you know."

When he rises abruptly, I wish I had one of Papa's old pipes to give him. Or one of Mama's hidden bottles of vodka. Anything to soothe this man who probably hasn't had any soothing angels since Marysia was captured. I'll remember for next time. I pack up the remains of our lunch, leaving nothing for the rats, although this tunnel is remarkably free of them. I'm disappointed by his news. How much ammunition does Mati's company have left? And Davey, and the rest of the insurgent army?

The hefty bag feels heavier when I lift it onto his shoulders. We stroll unimpeded down the dry brick sidewalk as though we're on a seaside boardwalk, but the mood of the sewer Riviera dims even more with the approaching August twilight. When we reach the crossroads of the three canals, I feel spent despite the ease of our journey.

"Well, here's the bridge," I say, shining my torch on the slender yellow arc. Brown sludge trickles in from the canal on the right, while under the bridge, a faster putrid-green rivulet streams into the canal from the left.

"You never told me how pretty it is, Renka."

"Like medieval Italy. But instead of the Arno, we have the black shit canal."

"So not *that* different from medieval Italy."

"Si, signore," I laugh, grateful that he's come around.

I test the upward arc with my boot. Not at all slippery. Tightening my rucksack, I take a run up the slope, over the top, and slowly descend the other side, arms raised in victory.

Mr. Godlewski applauds as much as the bag on his chest will allow.

Leaving my rucksack on the ground, I climb the bridge again, pausing before the top.

"Your turn," I say, my arms outstretched, knees bent in a lunge.

From his first step, I can see how unbalanced he is. Two strides, and he starts to topple into the canal, arms struggling for balance, his feet stuck near the top. I run up and grab the ungainly bag, and with all my strength pull him to an upright position.

"Now move toward me, slowly."

And that's how we reach the other side, with me walking backward down the slope, gripping the sides of the bag, and Mr. Godlewski like a vastly pregnant woman about to fall on top of me.

When his feet touch the pavement on the other side, he sighs. "Well, that was easy."

We make for the curved wall and he drops the bag on my feet. I yelp, and we laugh until our sides ache.

"Any more tricks up your sleeve?" he says.

"Just one last question before we reach the end." Forgetting my dirty glove, I brush the hair out of my eyes, feel the bandage around my head. "It's about my sister."

He nods even as his smile collapses.

"While you were in prison, did you hear anything about her? Any rumor, sighting, or . . . ?"

He meets my gaze. "I'm sorry, Renka. I never saw her. Never heard anyone speak of her or anyone who looked like her. I did ask. And I had to conclude that she has never been in any of the places I was held."

"Thank you. I suppose that means they took her to a brothel."

"A brothel?"

"That's what they do, isn't it? Like what happened to Elsa."

He looks at me pityingly. "I can't say."

I grab his arm. "You can't say or you won't say?"

He bends to pick up his bag. "Your timing's bad, Renka. I have to set up the equipment at the new place before morning. And your bandage needs changing. Let's go."

My chest is heaving with fears I've been afraid to name all the years of her absence. *Tell me!* I want to shout, but I twist my bag onto my back and let him walk ahead so he can't see my tears.

ꟼ

THE COURTYARD IS much quieter than when I left. Just a few old men and a child. A second grave in the garden, though. *Mother Mary.* I read the name on the makeshift cross, give thanks that it's not Mati.

Exhausted, I climb the stairs to the flat, expecting to find it bustling with activity. The door's half-open. No women or children in the hallway. The sounds of men's voices in the kitchen. I walk in and Mati leaps up from his seat. My eyes don't leave his for a second, but I'm aware of two young men leaping to their feet and hurrying from the flat.

"What's this, Ala?" he says when I'm in his arms, and he's touching the bandage around my head. "You got shot?"

I shake my head, rub my nose against his shirt, and smell the days we've been apart—the stains that could be blood, sweat, or loneliness. His kiss is tender and our bodies find their familiar holds and indentations before my mind pulls me back to Mr. Godlewski, Lotka, the Rising on our doorstep. *Not now.*

"Let me look at you," I say, holding him at arm's length.

"Just bruises. Come sit down. We should have a look at this hard head of yours."

We move to the bathroom and I sit on the edge of the bath while he removes the grimy, bloodstained bandage.

"Will I live?" I ask, looking up at him.

"For years and years, Irena Marianowska."

"Marianowska? So, you're marrying me, then. In this bathroom?"

"It's a new kind of wartime ceremony—if you love someone and you change their bloody bandage, that means you're married."

"I see."

We undress each other, counting bruises as we go, and decide that the one with the most beautiful bruises will have to clean up after supper.

THE NIGHT UNFOLDS as the day has—dreamily suspended between chaos and love. Lying on a blanket in my old bedroom, we recount these first days of the Rising in alternating waves.

"Only five left from my company, Ala. I lost fifteen men. One was only fourteen."

"Oh, Mati." I stroke his thick hair. "I saw Davey Freeman fighting."

"Not our little Captain?"

"The same. And in Śródmieście, Fryderyk helped me get to my cargo on Warecka Street."

"Fryderyk's still alive! And Zofia?"

"I haven't seen her since yesterday at the cellar hospital. You want to know about my secret sewer mission?"

"That depends. What do I have to do to find out?"

"Let me think."

He tickles me until I screech with laughter.

When we pause for breath, I tell him about Mr. Godlewski. At first, he can't believe that he's still alive, that he's the famous Wojtek, and that I've spent the day with him. Then he wants to know everything about him.

I tell him what I know, and feel his mood darken. But Mati's never sad for long.

"My regiment commander told me the Russians sent a reconnaissance team across the river into Warsaw. We're hoping they report back that the AK's in control of large sections of the Old Town and city center." He rubs his forehead. "Mokotów has been a harder battle, but our Baszta regiment is doing well; this section of Mokotów is ours for sure. And Wola—"

Where my mother is praying for Lotka.

"You'll like this, Ala. An all-women battalion in Stawki attacked the SS supply depot and killed all the German guards."

"Fantastic!"

"Isn't it? They were holding Jews there as prison labor, and when they freed them, the prisoners took them to a huge supply of food the Germans had been hoarding. Massive amounts of tinned pork, sausages, bread, eggs, wine, beer, oranges—"

"Okay, stop!" I laugh. But I'm picturing a group of young women like me, killing Germans and securing food for the whole of Warsaw.

And what have I done? The red-black chaos I thought had left me for good says, *And who have you killed?*

"Did you kill any Germans, Mati?"

"I hope so, Ala," he says, "but I made up that part about the oranges."

Thirty

Warsaw, August 1944

That can't be daylight nudging my shoulders through the blackout curtains. Our watches are somewhere in the bathroom, and our blue blanket feels like an island on the floor of the empty bedroom. Mati opens his eyes and reaches for me.

"I have to get to the toilet," I say, pushing him off. I search the closet for something to throw on. Wrapping the blanket around himself, Mati yawns, opens the door, steps out, and shuts it quickly behind him.

"Men!" I hear him say. "How long have you been here?"

I dress quickly in my uniform and wait until he says goodbye to them before opening the bedroom door and making a beeline for the bathroom.

Mati moves to embrace me when I come out. "It's almost ten," he says into my ear. "You hungry?"

"Ten!" We only have a few more precious hours together. I cobble together some breakfast while he gets dressed.

After we've eaten, we wander hand in hand out the gate to the sounds of singing and laughter serenading us from St. Kazimierz Square. By the white stucco church, we take in the Polish flag flying on top of the statue of

St. Kazimierz, little flags in the hands of children, women, and AK soldiers, men in clusters, smoking and arguing in the customary Polish way. I have a keen sense of déjà vu, as though I've been catapulted back in time. I turn to Mati, equally dazed at this scene.

"I wish Mr. Godlewski could see this," I say.

Someone's passing around a bottle, and when it's handed to me, I tilt it to my lips. *Brrrrr!* Homemade vodka. I smile and pass it to Mati.

He takes a swig, wipes his mouth, and passes the bottle to an old man, who salutes him.

Under a lithe aspen, a woman is selling the giant seed heads of sunflowers. When Mati offers her money, she waves it away with a toothless smile. "My thanks for freeing us."

He thanks her with a smile, followed by a head shake that I completely understand. Her words are like a rainbow that could fade at any moment. I tighten my hold on his hand as we continue round the square, crunching seeds between our teeth.

A man with an accordion begins to play a wedding polka, and when Mati clasps my hands, whirling me about in a big circle, people clap and cheer. Soon others join in, and the square becomes a blur of smiling faces.

Far too soon, it's time for Mati to join his new company. When I say goodbye to him, I try not to make a scene, but the memory of last night makes me cling to his neck. Instead of breaking apart, he holds me in a tight embrace.

"I'll be back soon, *kochanie*," he whispers in my ear.

I kiss his cheek, and because I'm afraid this may be the last time I'll ever see him, I turn away too quickly, turn my back, and walk away.

LONELY WITHOUT MATI, and missing the noisy demands of a courtyard packed with civilians, this evening I return alone to St. Kazimierz Square. The crowd has thinned, but the ones who've remained are a giddy mix of desperate drunks and somber celebrants, all of us exquisitely aware that for the first time in five years, we are free people dancing on free Polish soil.

I sit myself on the stairs of the church, sunk in my own thoughts. After a while, I become aware of a shadow close by, and looking up, see the familiar face of Mr. Godlewski. I happily join him.

"You risked coming out," I say, kissing his cheek.

"The dragons have more pressing concerns at the moment," he says. "I took a chance."

"You set up your equipment?"

"I did. But the news is disconcerting, Renka."

"Oh, no." I wait a long while before he continues.

"The British don't believe we've captured large sections of the city. They seem to have the impression that we're a small band of incompetent louts."

"How, who—"

"Can't you guess?"

"The Russians?"

"Apparently Stalin himself told Churchill that we're making it hard for them to liberate Poland. That there's no point sending aid, and, in any case, he won't give permission for the Allied planes to land anywhere near us. And the Americans have been given the same message."

Cholera. I'm glad Mati's not hearing this dismal news. I shuffle my feet on the worn steps of the church. We've just recaptured this ancient plot of land with our blood; Mati and I were dancing with light hearts just hours ago. The world seems upside down.

"What can we do?" I ask.

My old neighbor sighs. "We keep telling the truth. I'm hardly the only one in touch with our leaders in Britain. It shouldn't be such a difficult job to convince the Allied politicians that we're a valuable fighting force." He looks about the square, lit by candles and the smiles of Varsovians. "More valuable than the Soviets—since this is our country, after all."

I think about Aleksi, buried in the courtyard, about Mati and Fryderyk fighting in the city center, about Davey—who knows where—and the thousands of Poles anxiously expecting the Russian rescue of our country. "Will this madness ever end?"

"Of course it will, Renka. It always does. The problem is it starts again, maybe ten, maybe fifty years later."

"New leader, new group."

"Of course."

"So there's no escape?"

"Not in Europe; probably not in Asia or Africa."

"You think it's different in America?

He pulls his pipe from his breast pocket, lights a match, and as if that's the signal it's been waiting for, a shooting star arcs across the sky. *Chromium yellow sailing across cobalt, lapis lazuli, indigo, violet.* I rustle in my rucksack for my sketch pad and pencils. Upturned faces, lit from within and without.

"The Perseid meteor shower," my old friend says, blowing smoke that smells of plums in a haze around my head. "Early this year." When he turns his grizzled head to face me, I'm sure there are tears in his eyes. "Haven't seen one in years."

He lays a warm hand on my shoulder. "You and Mati should survive this mess, move to America, find out what it's like."

I smile and cover his hand with mine, feeling the gaps where his fingers should be. "I'll send you a report."

For the next blessed hour, every few minutes a star cascades to Earth, welcomed by a human chorus of *ooh*s and *aah*s.

He's about to say more when a distant cheer rises from behind the church. German voices, shouting. "*Sieh dir das an!*"

I shove my drawing into my bag. Mr. Godlewski tamps out his pipe, and we rise quickly, hurrying down the stairs toward the other side of the square.

"What were they saying?"

"Admiring the meteor shower." His head begins a subtle tremor from side to side. "They're never far away. I've got to get back."

"I'll walk with you. You were about to say something; do you remember what?"

A bear growl. "Of course I remember!"

We check for unwanted followers, but everyone, Pole or German, seems enraptured by the performance in the sky.

Rounding the shrubs at the edge of the square, I put a hand on his arm. "Are you going to tell me?"

He keeps walking; I hurry to keep up.

"Against my better judgment, I'm going to tell you what I know about your sister. I believe I owe you that."

My heart skips a beat, and my breath comes in bursts. "Can we slow down?"

"No. I have no desire to revisit Pawiak. This is going to be hard news, Renka."

"Is she dead?"

That halts him. "No." The look on his face alarms me.

"What? Has she been tortured?"

"I believe she's in Berlin."

"Berlin? In a labor camp?"

"Not in a camp. She and that Polish surgeon she lives with do very well. They perform operations on the highest levels of the German military, even on their wives. They make them look more—Aryan. That's what I've heard from my contact in Berlin."

"What are you saying? Lotka's being forced to work in a German hospital?"

"Not forced."

I stare at him.

"I hear they dine at Himmler's mansion."

"That's impossible," I say.

"I'm sorry." He walks ahead at a brisk pace.

"Wait! Are you sure it's her?"

"You wanted to know," he says, flinging it over his shoulder, abandoning me to the night.

Thirty-One

Toronto, December 2010

The bedroom smells dank, with an undertone of the eucalyptus oil I dropped into the humidifier last night. I open the blinds onto the frosty back garden, its tall hydrangea heads bobbing like gauchos in the wind. My grandmother's kicked off her blankets and wants to use the bathroom, but when I help her stand, she teeters back onto the bed and has to take a few wheezing breaths.

"Stay here," I say. In a corner of the closet, I find the folded wheelchair we used when Mati was ill.

"Take it away," she scowls. "Why are you reminding me of Mati's sickness?"

A fierce calm steadies me. "Just for today," I say firmly.

She lets me help her to the toilet. When she's seated, I close the bathroom door, pull my phone from my pocket, and call Dr. Chan's clinic again, managing to get an appointment with a different doctor for eleven thirty.

What do we need? Sweatpants, socks, nothing that might hinder her breathing. I strip the bed, change the sheets and pillowcases again, but in the bathroom, she's so weak and shivery, she has to hold on to the wheelchair to remain standing. Suddenly, getting into and out of a taxi in this weather seems out of the question. When I wheel her to the bedroom, I brush the stack of clothes I've readied off the bed while she burrows under the covers.

"I need to take your temperature."

"It's not necessary. I want to sleep now."

I could threaten to call— Who? Sophie's ghost? An ambulance? The police? *Yes, given her history, that should go over really well.*

"How about breakfast in bed? French toast?"

Propped on two pillows, she gives me a weak smile. "Just some Red Rose," she whispers, pulling a tissue from the box beside her.

Before I reach the door, she demands a cigarette.

"No! Not a good idea."

I see her hesitate, but some contradictory spirit in her finds strength. She pushes aside the covers to get out of bed.

"I'm going to smoke in my sitting room."

"Please don't, *Babcia*." I have to distract her with something. "How about a toddy?"

She nods, a fleeting gleam in her eye.

"I'll be back," I say, content with this small victory. "I have something interesting to tell you."

Slicing the lemon, twirling the honey, I'm ambushed by memories: Irena, Sophie, and me, sometimes Frank, sitting round Mati's bed in those last weeks, helping him die, yet trying to keep him alive—the distance between the two getting shorter and shorter. My fear gains urgency. What if Irena dies? She's been talking about dying for weeks. But she can't die now. We have to resolve this connection with Stefan; I have to get started on her grave sculpture.

The whistling kettle pulls me back. I don't suppose alcohol's the answer to nicotine withdrawal, but I have to keep her alive. I add another glub of brandy.

Once she's propped on more pillows, I tuck a napkin under her chin, and holding the mug beneath her nose, let her breathe in the lemony-honey scent.

"So, I was doing some research for your sculpture," I lie. "And guess who I found?"

She shakes her head, inhaling the vapor from the hot liquid.

"Szarlota Iwanowska."

A low gasp escapes her throat, she pushes the mug aside, spilling hot liquid onto the bed.

"You need to cough?"

Wild panic fills her eyes, her face reddens. I can't tell if she's struggling to breathe or livid with rage.

I grab my phone and call 911.

TEN IN THE morning, I'm focusing on the fact that Irena's alive, no longer parked in a hospital corridor, and breathing easier in an actual room-like cubicle. Her nurse adjusts the oxygen nasal prongs, hangs an IV bag, and smiles encouragingly at me.

"There'll be a doctor here soon," he says, checking the needle in my grandmother's purpling hand. Despite their difficulty finding good veins in Irena's arms—finally having to bring in Priya, the nurse with the star vein-poking skills—they've taken vial after vial of blood.

A damp weight drags at me as though I've eaten a rain cloud. It's not like we haven't been here before. But this is different. This is serious.

When the nurse leaves, I wash my hands again, stand near my grandmother's head stroking the papery skin on her arm. *Why did I have to surprise her with Szarlota?*

Shifting her weight, she coughs wetly into her hand.

Don't go yet.

I tell myself I can handle that fear. The other fear, I'm not ready for—being alone with only my sculptures and my ghosts.

A brusque woman pushes through the doorway with an ECG machine. I keep out of her way. Irena's still breathing heavily, her chest rising and then shuddering doubtfully like a toy with a dying battery. The technician departs as abruptly as she arrived; I go back to my vigil.

Even as we're surrounded by rapidly moving staff, tearful families, vomiting, moaning patients, an hour crawls by, emptying into an endless time loop.

We're finally rescued by the arrival of the doctor—calm, gray-haired, spectacled: the stereotype you hope for. I introduce myself and Dr. Aziz introduces herself.

"You're her granddaughter?"

"Yes."

"Any other relatives?"

"No. Everyone's dead."

She nods slowly, her brows rising above her glasses.

I help her rouse Irena to a sitting position. Dr. Aziz listens to her chest front and back, spends a long moment listening to her neck. When she asks Irena how she feels, my grandmother opens her mouth to speak, but says nothing; she just twists her right hand in a *so-so* gesture. When the doctor asks her name, Irena's eyes beg me to answer for her.

"Nice to meet you, Irena," Dr. Aziz says, and hovers an arm round my shoulders, steering me away. "We'll do an X-ray, but it sounds like pneumonia. That's what usually takes people her age. The ECG shows that her heart's weakened. Does she have a history of heart problems?"

Does she? "I don't know."

"There are signs of a silent heart attack."

She sees my frozen look and explains. "It's not uncommon in older people. It's good you brought her in."

"She's a heavy smoker," I say.

"Then she's been lucky so far." She looks back at Irena, passive on her bed. "I'm going to order some more tests. I think we need to rule out a small stroke."

Fuck!

"We'll get her on antibiotics right away." Her eyebrows knit, and I feel her urge to hug me. "She'll be moved to the seniors' floor as soon as there's a bed."

When she leaves, I move to stroke my grandmother's head—still busy manufacturing thoughts and feelings. She croaks something, and I bend my ear to her mouth.

"Cigarette."

"No way."

She finds the strength to glare at me.

The hour passes as her chest rises and falls with each loud breath. I search in the stack near the sink for a clean towel to mop her forehead. When I turn back, she's gone. I stare at a limp, silent body.

"Help!" I yell. "Help, my grandmother's dead."

A uniform streaks past me to the bed. "She's coding, I need help!"

As someone shoves me out of the room, I catch a figure performing CPR on Irena's lifeless body. Two more uniforms run in, one with a wheeled cart. Like a statue, I freeze outside her cubicle, unable to make contact with any of the crowd on that other planet behind the nursing station. A bearded man sets a chair a few feet away and motions with his eyes for me to sit. Then he brings me water in a Styrofoam cup. I sip carefully and recognize the jackhammer demolition in my ears as the beating of my own strong heart. Construction sounds are also coming from behind the cubicle curtains: clattering, huffing noises; a whirring machine; a woman yelling instructions, a man yelling back. Then it all goes quiet. People are speaking softly, less urgently.

That's it, then. She's died alone, without me even holding her hand.

A small woman with a mermaid tattoo on her arm slips through the curtains and looks around.

She sees me staring fixedly at her and takes a long breath in. "We got her back."

I jump up and grab her mermaid arm, but my only speech is sobbing.

She pats my hand. "She's going straight to cardio ICU."

A voice inside the cubicle says, "Fucking *A*-Team!" I imagine fist pumps and high fives.

"Thank you, thank you, thank you," I chant as they file out.

Soon, a porter, accompanied by a nurse holding an IV pole, trundles us to the ICU. Irena's frail body jostles on the bed, the IV needle like a leech attached to her hand, her eyes sunk deep in her gray face.

As we move through the ICU, we pass a cubicle with its ivory curtains half-open, and my brain records a forever-picture of a man, his skin stretched like plastic wrap over his massively bloated body. My mind forms a monstrous question: Is that still human? How much can a body take before it can't take any more?

Here, everything is calm and urgent. A nurse named Avi tells me Irena's going to be sedated for a few days so her body can recover. We exchange contacts and names, and then he's tending to her, his fingers moving skillfully along her frame.

"You want to get some rest," he says as I trip over the coat dangling from my arm. I won't leave, but I'll settle for a coffee.

Downstairs in the bathroom, I splash my face and pin my hair with my Staedtler. The café's painted banana and orange and it's packed. I buy a coffee and a giant muffin and walk in circles until a volunteer asks if I need help. I tell her I need a quiet place to sit. She directs me to a second-floor solarium. *A solarium!*

Seated on a bench under a honey locust tree, I run my hands over my face. *Sophie? Mati? Our darling Irena's in trouble.* Airy leaves cast a green light over me; reaching up, I brush the ferny fronds.

I should have called 911 days ago instead of mucking around in the past. All that fucking history. Why this need to rake it up and throw it over my body like dead leaves?

I leave the shelter of the locust tree and take the elevator up to the ICU, where I'm allowed to sit beside my grandmother and rest my hand on her arm, so recently healed, stronger after the physio's weekly visits. I'm glad she's not fighting me anymore, that she's here asleep. Or unconscious? What does being sedated actually mean? She looks suddenly years older. Acutely, I feel the narrowness of my education. How did I get away with so little science?

The monitor blinks and beeps like a screen in *The Matrix*, but the antiseptic smells and sounds—this odd, pregnant hush like the seconds before a hundred-meter dash—tell me I'm in the real world. And with that thought comes a question about Szarlota Iwanowska. When she heard the name, was that joyful surprise or utter devastation on Irena's face?

OUTDOORS, THE DAMP air's bliss after the desert dryness of the hospital. In the pale December morning, I understand that I've spent an entire day at my grandmother's side, only leaving when her nurse said she was stabilizing, that they'd call me if anything changed. Change being code for dying. I tell myself she's in the safest place possible and climb into a waiting taxi.

At the front door, a hungry Cheriblare welcomes me with a scolding head bump. I step in cautiously. The house has a weird, staged feel—like, *This is the set for a house where the family left in a hurry*. I wander through the silent rooms. On the foyer floor—a discarded scarf and woolen socks too tight to pull on quickly; in Irena's bedroom—a blanket wet from a spilled drink; in the kitchen—lemon halves on the table, a honey dipper pooling gold into a saucer. Old news from a distant time.

After Cheri's had her meal and extra treats, my mind makes plans to set my alarm, brush my teeth, undress, but my body throws itself onto the bed with my clothes on. The drop into sleep is immediate and deep. Sometime later, in a dream, someone I love is gently shaking my shoulder, kissing my ear. I squint my eyes open and see Cheri's furry body on the pillow beside me. I'm sinking under again when the phone rings. Françoise Bisset, Irena's Montreal art dealer.

"Hi, Françoise, it's Jo." Before she can say anything, I burst into tears, blubbering about Irena being in the hospital.

She gasps.

I tell my story, and my heart wells up again. "I should have taken her to the hospital sooner."

"*Chérie*, don't blame yourself. I know how stubborn she can be."

That soothes me, though it's hard to imagine anyone not giving in to Françoise's gravelly voiced charm. I ask why she's called.

"Actually, I have some good news. I'll call Irena when she's feeling stronger, but I'll tell you the secret now. The Musée des Beaux Arts is planning a retrospective of her work. They've been trying to reach her via email, telephone, but she hasn't answered. I'm so glad I got you because she hasn't answered my calls, either. Is it because she's been sick?"

How do I tell her about Stefan? About Irena's shock at hearing his voice? And now Szarlota.

"She's being transported back into her past," I say. "Into the war and all the people she knew back then." It sounds bizarre, even to me.

A sigh. "So she's still living in that terrible battle? But, Jo, you make it sound like she's been hypnotized, or under some enchantment. What's going on?"

Dear Françoise. Released from this weight I've been carrying, I spill out the story of Stefan's failed commission and Irena's accusation, ending with a vague description of the translation.

Except Françoise is not content with vagueness. "Abuse? What kind of abuse?"

I start with *BITCH*, and since my brain has ingrained Stefan's rant, move on to the rest. I hear her suck in her breath.

"So he was a con man. And in the SS, too. Then I'm glad he's dead. He can't bother her anymore."

"Actually, Françoise, you probably know him."

"I do?"

"Yeah. He was a big collector of Irena's work."

"His name doesn't sound familiar. Let me check my client list."

I spell it out for her and wait while a thrill races round a track in my belly.

"*Non. Non*, I don't see him."

"Oh. Could you try Stefan Wenders? Or a Roland Wenders?" That would confirm Stefan changed his name, and then I could check his army records.

"*Non.* Those two names are not on my list of buyers, either."

"That's so strange."

"But this whole story is strange. If he were still alive, I would say, why don't you call the police. Look, if you think it's important, I can check with my assistant. You don't know any of the paintings he owns?"

"I've only seen a numbered print of *Mokotów Angel*. His daughter-in-law told me he was a big collector."

"Ah. Does she have the same last name?"

A bell goes off in my head as I picture the visitor log at the Bennett Health Center. "Her name's Cynthia Nakamura."

A moment later, Françoise bounces back. "I have her. She has two acrylics from the seventies and eighties, one oil, very valuable now, five ink sketches. And—that's it." She sounds disappointed. "Any other names?"

"Try Mary Balfour." My mind's racing now.

It doesn't take long. "We have a jackpot. *Tabarnak!* She bought a lot, a lot. I'll send you the list."

"Thanks. Did you ever meet these two women?"

"*Non.* When these paintings came up for auction or for sale in my gallery, most buyers sent their agents. *Ben oui*, it's possible that this Nazi man came into the gallery himself. But don't send me his picture, please. I wouldn't like to think that I enjoyed his company."

"No." I cringe at the memory of laughing with Stefan. "I should get back to the hospital, Françoise."

"Please give Irena my love. By the way, now I'm curious about that letter from Germany. Did she say anything about it?"

"A letter from Germany?"

"Yes. A woman called from Germany asking for Irena's address and phone number. Months ago now. You know how private your grandmother is. I told the woman she could send her letter to my office and I would pass it on. Irena never mentioned it to you?"

The silence between us thickens as my mind shuffles images of a charred photograph in the ashtray—three bleached figures curled in at the edges.

Thirty-Two

Warsaw, August 1944

The Sobieski Residences are once more filling up with the wounded and homeless. It's day six of the Rising with no help from the Russians. I try to focus on the tasks in front of me, but wander about in a daze, dressing wounds with the last of our sheets and towels ripped into narrowing strips, conscious of our dwindling supply of clean water.

This time there's no Hania to act as my second-in-command, and everyone in this improvised settlement—civilians and insurgents alike—seems incapable of making a decision or lifting a finger. People lie about, some with their heads against the crosses of the graves as though they're waiting to die.

Mati hasn't returned from the city center, and, in a way, I'm glad. If he were here, I'd have to tell him Mr. Godlewski's bizarre news about my sister, which is impossible for me to accept.

I feel like someone centuries ago who's just been told that the Earth revolves around the sun: his accusation sounds like blasphemy; at the same time, it begins to make sense.

Bewildered, I stumble about wanting nothing more than to lie down in the courtyard beside one of the wounded soldiers or hungry civilians, my eyesight tinged with a strange blue light. From somewhere, a woman cries out, and I spin around to see a soldier bleeding from the chest stumbling through the gate. As he collapses, I run forward with my first-aid pail.

"Help me, please," I call to a man smoking a cigarette on the steps to our cellar. He looks up as though he hasn't understood a word I've said. Frantically, I raise my arms up and down as though I'm lifting something heavy, and he finally rouses himself. We drag the fallen soldier to an open space, and I see by the extent of his wounds and his fading eyes that he's not going to make it. Kneeling back, I hold his head in my lap and lean over to hear him whisper his name.

"Thank you, Jan," I say. "Thank you." And I hum the tune of the Varsovian over and over until his heart stops. A few people drag themselves over to say a prayer, and then we carry his body to the back of the courtyard, where yesterday, the work of digging up the paving stones began. We've run out of room in the garden.

As the light begins to fade, everyone looks for a place to bed down for the night. My flat is full of people lying head to foot. The problem is no one knows which parts of Warsaw are in enemy or AK hands—the fighting goes back and forth unrelentingly. Traveling through the cellars or even between attics, over rooftops, as many have done, is no longer safe. Once again, bombs are falling on Warsaw. For now, this small section of Mokotów seems to be holding, though at great cost to our fighting force, and to the thousands of civilians struggling to stay alive in our city.

Someone touches my shoulder, and I smile to see a woman carrying a baby in a sling across her chest. She offers me a slice of bread and water from her flask. Numb, I sit on the curb of the little garden cemetery, eating and drinking, when a horrifying thought crosses my mind—*At least with people dying all around me, there's no time to think about Lotka.* And with Mati away fighting, Zofia busy in the city with her hospital work, Fryderyk—*Mother Mary*—please let him and Davey still be alive, I have no one to discuss my sister with. And then I have an even grimmer thought: If Mama comes home, what do I tell her? I've thought of going to Mr. Godlewski's hideout to demand more evidence, but after my great delight in seeing him alive, he's the very last person I want to see.

"ALA."

After midnight, I wake to a gentle shake and see Mati's face leaning over me in the crowded courtyard.

I sit up drowsily. "You okay?" I ask. Caught up in the pleasure of seeing him, I forget for a moment the news I have to share. He helps me up, and we maneuver through the sleeping bodies toward the gate.

On the other side, the street is quiet and dark with just a few people huddled close to the wall, struggling to sleep sitting up. I look up at Mati's tired face. "Don't you think it's strange that so many people have put their trust in these residences to protect them—this rickety gate, the thin walls, the peeling cellars?"

He pulls me close, kisses my cheek. "It's a safe place because of you, Ala." He sighs. "I only have a few hours before I have to get back. I came to get you."

"Me?"

He explains that they need to get a platoon from the city to Mokotów through the sewers by morning. He can't guide them alone. When I ask for more details, he shakes his head.

"I'll tell you later. For now, the good news is we captured a tank in the city center, and a company in Żoliborz seized a truckload of guns and ammunition, including a machine gun. The bad news is the Germans have had time to regroup under a new SS leader."

"Who?"

"A General von dem Bach. There'll be more enemy troops, more weapons."

"I'll get my things," I say, turning away.

He grabs my arm. "What's the matter, Ala?"

I gaze up at the black sky and fight back the welling tears. "It's about Lotka." I tell him what Mr. Godlewski told me.

He frowns, looks down at his feet. "I'm so sorry, Ala."

"What?" I shake his arm. "You knew?"

"I didn't know, but I suspected."

"And you said nothing?"

"At first, I wasn't sure. I saw her getting into the Gestapo car. Before that she was crying and pushing them away. But in the back seat, she was smiling."

"How—"

"I checked with Fryderyk and he also thought he saw her smile."

"But—"

"There are other things, Ala. The money you said was deposited into her account. All the way up until the Rising. This doctor she worked with—Marysia confirmed he was a Nazi spy. He was probably using your sister."

"I don't believe that."

"We have to face the fact that she knew about Marysia's work, about Małgorzata, about Mr. Godlewski. Even Pani Nowak." He tries to pull me into an embrace.

I twist away. "Lotka would never do anything to harm me or Mama."

His gaze is gentle and kind. "I have to go, Ala. Are you coming with me or not?"

ⓟ

IN THE TIGHT sewer tunnels, I cry most of the way to the city center. When I'm not crying, I'm scrambling after Mati's heels, swearing at him.

"How could you let me go on believing she was a prisoner? *Cholera jasna!* All those months we spent looking for her. Zofia, me, everybody. You're a complete shit, Mati. Did you all know? That was cruel." I'm weeping loudly now. "How could you do that to me?"

He lets me cry and swear, but after several hours, he pauses at a rain grate.

"Are you finished, Ala?"

I smash my gloved fist into the brick wall. "Now I'm finished. But you have to promise me one thing: I never want to hear her name again. She is dead to me."

"I promise. How does your hand feel?"

AT FIVE THIRTY in the morning, we enter the sewers in the city center with the platoon—seventeen men and three women. I've given them some rudimentary sewer instructions—and like most uninitiated, they barely listen. We set off with Mati in the rear, and I'm happy he's that far behind so I don't have to talk to him. My hand aches, but I've wound it with rags and then squeezed it into my glove. No point complaining.

I keep up a fast pace because, as it turns out, there are wounded soldiers in the Old Town, and after this mission is complete, we'll need to return, find the wounded, and get them through the sewers to Zofia's cellar hospital back in the city center. Mati has arranged for stretchers—that means able-bodied men pushing and pulling the wounded. So two long trips this morning.

My camel train starts off full of jokes about the shit, until their knees and throats start to ache, and the disorientation caused by darkness and lack of oxygen begins to wear them down. Making matters more interesting is the booming noise from above—German Stukas strafing the streets, climbing to a higher elevation before they drop their bombs. Then shattering glass, falling concrete. The sounds echo through the tunnels like an oncoming train, our bodies absorbing the shock.

Like sewer rats, we keep moving through it all, and partway through our trip, I think I must be hallucinating when I hear a child crying. *Cholera.* That can't be. I slow down. There it is again. I speed up once more, and, at an intersection with a storm sewer, I come across a family of civilians. Soaked through. Father, young son, smaller son. The smaller son screams when he sees all the helmet-headed men in a line behind me.

"It's all right." I smile. "We're Polish soldiers." I look at the father, whose eyes are wild with confusion.

"Do you know the way?" the man asks hoarsely. "We're completely lost."

"I'll take you to Mokotów. Are there any more of you? How are the children?"

"The children are sick from the smell. My wife . . . We had to leave her. She fell into the canal. I couldn't save her."

Mother Mary. I give him my flashlight and water. Then I pass a message to the men behind me to pass down the line. "We're slowing down. Children in the line."

I suggest that the father carry the little one on his back, but the boy kicks and screams and will have none of it.

With water and a few sunflower seeds in their bellies, though, the family keeps up with me, but after an hour, the children are tired and we stop. The father strokes his little son's head. "We're almost there," he says. The child falls asleep, and this time we successfully tie him to the father's back.

"How long have you been down here?" I ask.

"Eight, maybe ten hours. I've lost count. We passed some other people back there. They said they'd been down here for two days already trying to get to Żoliborz."

Jesu Maria. This can't go on. I need help from experienced Guides: Zofia, Fryderyk, Mati.

At the Mokotów sewer exit, Mati agrees to escort the lost family aboveground to the Sobieski Residences before he rejoins his platoon in the city. Alone, I travel all the way back to the Old Town with only my raving thoughts: Lotka's devious betrayal, Mati's deceit, Mr. Godlewski abandoning me with not one word of comfort, Mama's misplaced loyalty to her traitorous daughter, her seeming hatred of me since the day I was born. All these grievances swirl in a tightening cycle until my head feels ready to explode.

Halfway to the Old Town, convinced that I must be going mad, I struggle to keep my wits by naming all the paint colors in the Winsor & Newton color chart—something Leah and I committed to memory as young students. With Leah now occupying my mind, her voice calls out to me all the way from that long-ago tunnel journey out of the ghetto. I hold on to it like a life raft: *We'll see our children's children. We'll see our children's children.*

WHEN I ARRIVE at the barricades in the Old Town, a nurse attached to this depleted, dogged company takes me inside the ruins of a building and shares some bread with a sort of fish paste and a flask of tea. While we're eating, a couple of out-of-breath insurgents rush into the building. Our eyes meet, and I'm surprised to recognize the old men.

Mr. Godlewski shoulders his rifle, a huge smile on his whiskered face. The other man is Leopold, the white-haired piano tuner who so charmed my mother.

"We meet again, Ala," Mr. Godlewski says, coming forward to greet me.

"You're fighting," I say lamely.

Pluck or peck is what I expect him to say, but he puts a hand on my shoulder. "We may be defeated, but we're not surrendering." He turns to Leopold. "You two have met, of course."

"Oh yes," Leopold laughs, his eyes on mine. "I was never sure if your mother understood what it was she'd removed from her piano. She'd been keeping that shortwave radio tube in the piano seat for months."

He and Mr. Godlewski have a good laugh. Then my old neighbor winks at me and the two of them are out of the hole in the wall and back into the fray as though they're running onto a football pitch.

The nurse beside me says, "Silly old men acting like boys. Just making more work for us when they're bleeding."

My heart skids from one competing response to another. In the end, I say nothing.

THERE ARE TWO wounded soldiers waiting for me—a young girl and a middle-aged man, and, with help from their platoon, we strap them onto stretchers and get them down the ladder into the sewer. Witnessing the descent, it strikes me that, in war, the impossible becomes possible through desperate invention. One soldier and I push and pull the stretchers through the sewers the short distance to the city center. Our journey leaves no room for chat or complaint. We just accept the groans of the wounded as happy signs that they're still alive.

At the other end, we're met by an AK armed guard who escorts us to the cellar hospital. I'm vaguely aware that there's an exchange of gunfire soon after we set out, but my brain says it doesn't concern me. I stay low and keep moving behind the stretchers. The rest of the route is clear, and, eager now to see Zofia, I skip down the steps of the once-grand bank, wondering how I still have the energy to move at all.

At the entrance to the hospital, my feet pause in confusion. I don't recognize the scene before me. Gone are the orderly rows of tightly made-up cots, the hushed silence. and professional, sanitary air. The unmistakable smell of blood pervades the space. It's everywhere, from the aprons of the staff to the black smudges on the ground.

"Is Nurse Zofia working today?" I ask an aproned woman hurrying past me with a bowl of pink water.

"Zofia!" she yells at a group huddled over a cot.

A woman looks up. Her face is masked and her hair's under a cap, but her eyes smile at me. "Ten minutes!" It's been too long since I've heard that husky voice.

The patients are a sad lot, and I try to keep out of the way of the busy staff. Drifting from one end of the cellar to the other, I hear the word *Wola* coming repeatedly from a young girl speaking to an older woman in the next cot. The girl is sobbing and the older woman holds her hand tenderly across the divide. I move toward them and introduce myself.

"May I ask if you have news from Wola? My mother's staying there at St. Augustine's Church and I haven't heard from her."

Silence. They exchange a look—then the older woman turns to me. "Pani, there's a slaughter going on in Wola. It's impossible to describe the hell. We barely escaped."

At that moment, Zofia appears and says something soothing to the women before guiding me away. My feet move mechanically after her. We climb the stairs to the vestibule of the bank, crowded with AK insurgents being fed by an efficient team of older women.

Zofia's hand on my arm. "Soup, Ala?"

Mugs of soup in our hands, we lean against a stone column, furtively scanning each other.

She looks battered, I think. She must be thinking the same about me. I push my scarf back from my forehead. "I can't believe my mother went to Wola to be safe."

"The news is terrible, Ala. Reports keep coming in from the wounded here: tens of thousands of civilians massacred by the Dirlewanger Brigade—SS commandos and Russian deserters. Himmler's orders were to burn everything, kill everyone. They must think it will stop us fighting." She throws her braid over her shoulder. "I'm so sorry to hear your mother's there."

Contradictory feelings collide in me as I realize the risks my mother took. "But those two women escaped."

She stares at me. "Yes. But first, they were raped. Then a group of them were made to march in front of a German tank toward the resistance fighters. Some of them died when the tank drove over them. I have no idea how these two survived."

She fingers the rosary around her neck. "Promise you'll shoot me before that can happen."

I throw an arm around her, pull her against me. The news about Lotka seems stale now, from a faraway time and place. It can wait until later. More pressing is the likelihood that Mama's died. My hand clutches my neck, as hers often did when she was afraid, and yet, I don't feel anything. I look at Zofia's matted hair, her liquid eyes, red with sleeplessness. What can I give her that's good news?

I tell her about the family in the sewer. "I need you, Zofia. Do you think you could leave your work here to help me guide people through the sewers?"

"You mean get my boots in shit instead of blood?"

"The choice is yours."

"I'll be happy to! Will you talk to the director?"

I smile, and tipping the last of the broth into my mouth, hear Zofia gasp.

"Ala? Why is your hand bandaged? Let me look at it."

"It's nothing."

"It's swollen."

I tell her I'm fine, but she insists on taking me back to the hospital. Once she determines I have no broken bones, she washes it with antiseptic liquid and rebandages my bruised knuckles. "Try to keep it clean."

I follow her arm as she reaches for a pair of scissors on a tray, and my gaze falls on a small tin soldier. My heart lurches.

"Zofia?"

She sees me staring at the toy soldier and hands it to me.

"Is he here?" I ask, clutching the figure.

"Who?"

"Davey. Have you seen him?"

WE SPEND THE next hour searching the cots and the upstairs rooms where soldiers are sleeping or eating. "Have you seen a small boy, big blue eyes, twelve years old? His name's Davey."

We find two young soldiers, one only eight, but neither of them is Leah's brother.

When Zofia reluctantly suggests that we look in the morgue, I recoil, but we are both determined to find him.

Outside the morgue, she pulls her mask over her nose. "There's a crew that takes turns burying them at night. They haven't taken today's batch yet. But he may not be here, Ala."

I cover my nose and follow her into a long room lined with filing cabinets.

Because of his size, he's easy to pick out from the others lying in a row on the ground. A note pinned to his shirt. *David Freeman. AK private first class. Anti-tank duty. Fought bravely. Died from gunshot wounds during battle on Warecka Street. August 7.*

His face and body have been washed clean. A kind person took some time with him.

"Our little Captain," Zofia says, weeping.

I grip the toy soldier in my good hand and grab for Zofia with the other. Hanging on to each other, we cry for Davey, for my mother, and all the others we can't name, for all the reasons we can't explain or begin to understand.

Part Five

Thirty-Three

Toronto, December 2010

A white plastic Christmas tree decorates a corner of the cardio ward. Green and red garlands hang along the edge of the reception desk, large red hearts pinned at each end by someone with a sense of humor.

Irena spent ten days in cardio ICU, surviving pneumonia and nicotine withdrawal as well as a heart attack, plus a whole week so far in this spiffy new wing. She's not the same Irena she was before I mentioned Szarlota Iwanowska; certainly not the same Irena she was before she heard Stefan's voice. But it's Christmas Eve, and there's much to be grateful for.

"Happy holidays," I call to the nurses behind the counter, and leave the box of Moroccan clementines with them.

In her room, my grandmother's sitting in her recliner, a blanket across her knees, hands on top fidgety, blue eyes clear and wondering who the hell I am. *Shit.*

"Merry Christmas, my darling *babcia*." I plant a smoochy kiss on her soft cheek. "It's Jo." She gives me a girlish giggle.

"Did you have a good night?"

"I don't know. Where am I now?"

"You're still at Sunnybrook Hospital. In this special ward for your heart. Very fancy."

I hang up my coat and pull up a chair beside her. "I brought you some presents."

"I have nothing for you."

"My present is spending this Christmas *Wigilia* with you—just the two of us."

"No one else is coming?"

"No, just me, for now." Why did I say that? As though Mati and Sophie might show up later.

Father and daughter shared a love of fine food and an appreciation for performance that festive occasions require. Irena and I, in our impatience and interior focus, could never match their initiative. But this evening, I'm channeling these two.

"Remember this?" I climb a chair and tape the worn tinsel star onto what I hope is the easterly wall. "So the Magi can see it."

My grandmother sips her low-fat eggnog, absent the usual glug of brandy. Her eyes are following me—a little too bright, a little bewildered, but amused at these antics.

"And now . . ." I connect my iPad to the little speaker.

As soon as the carol "*Lulajże Jezuniu*" sweetens the room, the light seems to change—less hospital harsh, more rosy, Bethlehem twilight.

On the wheeled table, I set about assembling our *Wigilia* meal, while Irena hums along to the lullaby, her voice as tremulous as this moment feels. I don't turn around to smile at her joy for fear of spoiling it.

It's a very modified *Wigilia* tonight: not the twelve-course version, but small portions of marinated pickled herring, beet soup with mushroom dumplings, cabbage rolls filled with fried potato and onion, baked haddock. Completely homemade by Starsky's Polish Deli.

"Sophie's Christmas napkins," I say, shaking out the red linen edged in gold, tucking it into the neck of her hospital gown. I'm greeted by a long yawn. Better hurry, or I might be eating alone.

When we're seated across from each other at the wheeled hospital table, I toast her recovery while she nibbles at the pickled *śledzie* on buttered rye.

"Pyszne!" she says as we clink—or try to clink—our Styrofoam cups.

I feel unreasonably proud.

We make it through the second course of beet soup before her spoon drops onto her tray. I wait to see if her eyes will close, but she takes a deep breath.

"In the war, we made this with cabbage. That's all my mother had. One year, just grass." She sucks in her breath as though she's dragging on a cigarette. "Our upstairs neighbor, Mr. Godlewski, was a good fisherman. It was forbidden to fish in the river, but he knew how to hide under the bridges so the Germans couldn't catch him. For *Wigilia*, he made the *śledzie*, and he brought the vodka—for the fish to swim in, he said."

We share a laugh at this jokey Mr. Godlewski.

"It was my job to get the bread from Pani Nowak's bakery."

"Nice bakery?"

She hesitates. "She was more like a spy than a baker."

"A bread-baking spy."

She nods. "Also, she made the vodka. My sister made apple cake or—"

"Your sister? You had a sister, *Babcia*?"

She gives me the *Fool* look. "Of course Lotka was my sister, a few years older than me. She made a very good apple cake. In the summer we picked blackberries and she made a kind of jam with sugar. It was nice."

"So Lotka was your sister." I reach behind for my knapsack and take out my phone, scrolling through the photos I took of the mysterious nurse in the glossy book. "Is this her?"

Her eyes skim the photos. "That one looks like her."

Why has no one ever mentioned a sister? "What happened to her?"

She shakes her head. "I don't know."

"She just disappeared?"

"Yes. One day she just disappeared."

Why am I so surprised? It was a brutal war, after all.

I try to imagine what Mati, Irena, and I would have done if Sophie had gone missing. As my grandmother slurps the last of her soup and smiles contentedly, my imagination roams over gruesome ground.

The Rising website said Szarlota was abducted by the Gestapo. What if we knew Sophie had been abducted, murdered? Wouldn't we have memorialized her in some way? Surely we would have talked about her when we were together. Her name would forever be in our conversation, especially on days like this, as my mother's has been in my mind all day today. It makes no sense at all that no one, not even the Polish old guard who came for parties and birthdays, ever once mentioned Lotka. As though she never existed.

Like a lens, my mind zooms out and focuses on Irena sipping her eggnog. Our eyes meet and we smile inscrutably at each other—me bewildered by the enigma of Lotka, my grandmother bewildered by who I am. I laugh, and rising, pull the table aside so I can give her a hug. She holds on to my arm as though I'm trying to strangle her.

"Let's open your presents," I say. "Then we can have compote and poppy seed cake. Okay?"

Bending to my knapsack, I pull out the gifts I've brought. "I found this in a secondhand bookstore. I know how much you love her."

"Frida," she says, running her hand across the shiny cover. "You love her, too?"

"Always have."

"She made herself into art."

"And made her art about herself."

A big sigh. "She lived through a different kind of war."

"You think?"

"Yes. That's what she painted. Like me."

We spend the next half hour head-to-head, turning pages. I love this feeling of being cocooned with my grandmother, hearing her painter's mind still lively and brilliant. When she starts to nod off, I set the book on the table and wheel it away with the barely eaten food.

"Want to lie down? I'll get the nurse."

Her head snaps up. "See if you can find Lotka."

WHILE MY GRANDMOTHER'S dozing, I take her nurse aside in the corridor. "Can we talk about how she's doing?"

She gives a little shrug. "She's recovering well. No one's talking about surgery."

"I know, but I'm concerned about her memory. It happened so suddenly. What's going on?"

"There's a resident on call today. You want us to page her?"

WHEN THE TEENAGE resident arrives, she's already read Irena's chart.

We hunker against the wall in the corridor outside Irena's room, and I tell her about Irena's time traveling, her forgetting who's dead and who's still alive.

"She's gone through a lot," she says. "It could be vascular dementia—the result of decreased perfusion to the brain, all connected to the cardiac arrest. I'll speak to Dr. Ahmed about an MRI."

"Could you? It just seems so sudden."

"You didn't notice anything before the heart attack?"

"Not really. I mean she's been very obstinate, uncooperative lately, but she's always been that way." I mean this to be funny, but she gives me a serious nod.

"So it might have started some time ago. You might not have noticed because you see her all the time. I'll make a note for the geriatric team to look in."

"That would be great." I'm relieved, yet worried. It's never once occurred to me that Irena's stubborn moodiness might be related to dementia.

AT HOME, I gobble the leftovers of our Christmas Eve meal, washing them down with a tart sauvignon blanc. Even with a glass of good cheer, the house feels abandoned and lonely.

"I should have got a tree. Right, Cheri?"

My cat crawls out to lie on my feet.

"I know you love batting the shiny balls, but I've always been two-minded about the annual sacrifice of evergreens."

I should have done what Frank and I used to do: hang boughs that bring the scent of pine and spruce into the house, or added Sophie's holly and poinsettia pots for color. But I've done none of that: at the hospital for hours every day, traveling back and forth, whacked out in front of the TV at night, or online turning down requests for new grave sculptures—I've burned through my entire store of Christmas merriment tonight.

I swirl the dregs of the wine around. Surfacing in my mind is my heart-to-heart-to-heart talk with Irena and Frida.

"She's never ashamed," Irena said. "She gets it all out of her."

I haul myself out of the chair, take the dishes to the sink. Christmas Day tomorrow.

Rambling across the foyer, crossing in front of *River Dream* shining eerily in the lamplight, I turn into Irena's bedroom. Tomorrow, I'll take her that red woven shawl Sophie brought from Ireland; Irena always wears that on Christmas Day. Maybe bring some more photos: Mati, Sophie, me, herself, the old Polish crew. See who she recognizes.

After a while I wander into Irena's studio, pausing before the covered triptych. Light from the wall of windows infiltrates the studio, silvery from the waning gibbous moon. Lifting the sheet, I walk it off the three adjacent canvases. I'm finding it hard to breathe—as though the painting's giving off something noxious.

Just drunk, Jo. No, not just drunk. *Scared.*

I turn on the lights. Like many of Irena's paintings, these have an icy-blue sheath, almost transparent. After a while, it comes to me that they're not abstract; in fact, they form one sequential painting—a chest-to-head self-portrait of a young Irena in an opulent fur coat. The portrait is split in three, so the parts of the face don't quite meld.

I step in close and notice the crosses in the background, larger and sparse in the first panel; so tiny by the third they resemble a swarm of insects. Small furred animals populate the corners and margins, a badger and a stoat—but upright, like people. I shake my head. So much detail. No wonder it's taken her so long.

Is that—? I nose the canvas and squeal at a small furred creature with Irena's human eyes. Disturbing. Also enchanting—a bit Chagall, a bit Hieronymus Bosch. I take a few steps back. Now the effect is simpler—a circular central portrait surrounded by pattern.

Fucking amazing. Wait till the Beaux Arts sees this.

As I turn around to leave, something makes me look back. Two blue eyes follow me—to the left, to the right. Stefan's eyes. And why haven't I noticed before? Lotka's eyes.

Thirty-Four

Warsaw, September 1944

Close to the end of the month, the September rains still haven't let up. My feet are never dry for long. Zofia and I have a new pair of sewer footwear: holes punched into the soles of shoes to let the brown water drain instead of filling our boots. My feet look like pale fish, and I hide them in socks when I'm not in the sewers, which is rarer and rarer these days.

When they can, Mati and Fryderyk join us in our constant ferrying of soldiers and civilians from the Old Town to Mokotów, but most of the time, they're fighting on our last remaining fronts: sections of the city center, and Mokotów. In Paris, near the end of August, when the French resistance defeated the Germans with the help of the French and American armies, we celebrated their victory and mourned our own entrapment with the same tears.

Only a few delusional people expect the Soviets to join us in this extended battle with the Hitlerow. Two days at the most is what we thought, and then the triumphant Russian army would come to our aid. Two months later, we're still alone, fighting tooth and nail, the Germans surrounding Warsaw and our supposed Russian allies—visible across the river—just waiting. For what?

Only three weeks ago, I came out of a sewer in a liberated section of the Old Town near Bielańska Street, and a string quartet was practicing in a semicircle before a spellbound audience. Today, pyramids of bricks, torn concrete slabs, and iron girders are all that's left of that entire area—the earth itself heaved up in waves at the atrocities it's witnessed.

These days, Zofia and I time our entrances and exits from the sewers according to the strict German bombing schedule: the planes start at six a.m.—flying low, strafing the streets looking for movement, dropping bombs every half hour, taking a break at midday for lunch, and continuing the bombing until seven p.m., when they retire for supper. Less predictable are the fire-belching *krowa* rocket launchers that sound like cows mooing.

Zofia told me she took a group past St. John's Cathedral in the Old Town, all the way through the sewers to Malczewskiego in Mokotów, and, when she returned to pick up the next group, the fourteenth-century cathedral was in flames. She wept then because she'd often stopped to pray inside that slender, delicate church. I cried for a masterpiece painting of the Virgin and Child that had graced the central altar from the 1600s, been stolen by Napoleon, was eventually returned to Warsaw from Paris, and is now burned to cinders.

Yet, as bad as the carnage is aboveground, it's got a fearsome familiarity: we've endured the Siege of our city and the bombing; we've got used to flames, smoke, ash in the air that makes it hard to breathe or see the sky. In contrast, the once-familiar sewers have become completely alien, grotesque, as fantastical as scenes in folktales: the SS has finally discovered that we're transporting hundreds of troops, civilians, and weapons through the sewers, and, to deter us, they've removed the sewer grates in the occupied areas and seeded the sewers with carbide gas, built barricades that flood the tunnels. And still people try escaping through them.

Zofia and I have drawn maps of the main sewer routes out of the Old Town, hammering or plastering them to buildings in the narrow warrens that remain. On the walls of the tunnels themselves, we've written instructions in chalk: *Turn right here. Go left if you want to die.*

MATI WANTS ME to cut back to one sewer ferry a day, but the need is desperate as the SS and their Russian conscripts gain traction, slaughtering civilians in the occupied zones—even attacking Wolski Hospital.

There is another reason I drive myself to the breaking point, and it's one I can't explain to anyone because I'm not sure I understand it myself: I must make up for my sister's betrayal. It's not just that I feel implicated in her traitorous actions—perhaps I was rash or careless with names or plans—I double down on my sewer missions to honor Marysia, Pani Nowak, and anyone else Lotka may have exposed, and I do it to negate her.

EVEN AT THREE in the morning, the bright yellow, burnt umber, and pale cream walls of the old buildings light up Castle Square. Mati, Zofia, Fryderyk, and I are all transporting separate groups of civilians and insurgents into Mokotów from Knight Street—the narrowest street in what remains of the Old Town. We've planned to leave in staggered runs, not far behind each other in case we need help. But already, our plan is faltering. Like a teacher on a school museum trip, I keep counting my six students, because even though we've divided them almost equally among the four of us, they keep changing places to be with friends or because they've heard Mati is a good shot or because Zofia's going first. Despite the obvious danger, they refuse to keep quiet.

Mati sidles up beside me. "Oh, come on, Ala. What could possibly go wrong?"

I throw back my head in a silent laugh.

What could possibly go wrong? has become our morale builder. The question's so horrifying, it makes us laugh uproariously.

Fryderyk and Zofia cleared the sewer entrance of barricades earlier—barbed wire coiled around a set of dining room chairs. There shouldn't be any impediments for at least an hour.

We climb down in darkness like a troop of mountain climbers descending a peak at dawn. Dangerous, but our lives depend on it.

The first tunnel slopes down at a sharp angle, but we're crouching rather than crawling, so it feels almost comfortable. Although I tried to split them up, my group has one complaining couple, then a man who's convinced he knows much more than any of us about everything, and three sturdy AK fighters, two males, one female.

My instructions were to carry only water and food for the journey, but my complaining couple is carrying two bulky packs each. When I asked them what was inside, the man said, "Valuables."

Much earlier than expected, my group comes upon Zofia's team nervously crowded before a barbed-wire barricade. I can't see past them, but I'm guessing Zofia's crouching down with her wire clippers, cutting a hole for the group to crawl through. When she hears me close behind, she stands and raises an arm in a flourish. *All clear.*

Thank you, gods. That means no body caught in the barbed wire—something we've encountered on previous journeys. The Germans have cleverly planted the barricades close to sewer entrances. That way they can shoot into the sewers from above, and any people struggling in the barricade have little chance of escape. At this time of morning, there are fewer patrols, but some desperate people risk traveling without a Guide at all times of the day. That's when the bodies pile up.

Zofia's group follows her lead and crawls through the hole in the barricade, leaving behind one blue cap, one woman's shoe, and several pieces of material hooked onto the barbs. It takes small, deft movements to pass through coils of bouncy barbed wire. Carefully picking off the cap and shoe, I hand them forward to the group hurrying to keep up with her. Then it's my team's turn.

"We can't get through that," the man with the two rucksacks says to his wife. "She'll have to make the hole bigger."

I hand him my wire cutter. "You have five minutes before it's our turn to go through."

When he keeps snagging his fine leather gloves on the barbs, his wife takes over and manages to increase the size of the hole, but still not enough for the bulging bags. Minutes later, I motion for my four team members behind the obstinate couple to move ahead of them.

"Keep tight, stay low; you don't want to raise your head. I'll go first."

The three AK soldiers get through without a problem. The man who knows everything does the same. The couple is having a heated discussion. When the woman removes the bag on her back and struggles through with just the one on her front, the back of her jacket snags and she cries out. Everyone freezes. A warm wind is wafting in from the open sewer grate behind us, and when I look up, a pair of eyes looks back at me. My stomach performs some acrobatics. I stare at the large gold eyes and the dog whimpers. Remarkable that it's escaped being eaten.

"It's just a dog," the man who knows everything says.

"I can't leave these bags behind," the man in the couple says.

"What's in them? Gold?" The two men glare at each other.

"My library," the man says. "You wouldn't understand."

"It will be light soon," I say. "Make a quick decision. There are two groups behind you."

The rest of us, including his wife, move on, leaving him to sort through his books.

In a short while, we reach the end of the downward-slanting tunnel, and our problems get more interesting. There's water. Up to my knees. Brown and dotted with things I'm glad I can't see clearly. We turn into a larger, newer tunnel, where we can plow through the water. I hear the man and his wife arguing, and hope he's left a bag or two of books behind—reading material for Mati and Fryderyk, who can't be far behind.

I'm pushing forward, the resistant water above my knees now, when something big splashes ahead of me. Please, not rats! I turn my torch on low and gasp. A naked man is speeding toward me—beard, hair in greasy strands around his neck, fording the water like a cross-country runner. When he's close, he waves his arms in warning.

"You're going the wrong way," he yells. "Go back!"

Behind me cries of alarm and anger.

"I told you she didn't know what she was doing."

"She's an AK major. She knows what she's doing!"

"You AK hooligans are the ones who caused this mess."

The naked man looks feverish. In the dark, his eyes have a wild luster.

"What makes you think it's the wrong way?" I ask, trying not to sound threatening.

"Of course it's the wrong way. The Holy Dove is never wrong."

"Where are your clothes?" a woman's voice asks.

When he tries to push past me, I move out of his way.

"You don't need clothes down here," he says. "Take them off."

I hear the woman's sharp intake and swivel around, motioning to the AK group to be ready. I feel for my knife against my hip. If he tries to attack us, I'll have to threaten or kill him.

"Now, just a minute," the husband says, and the man yells, "Out of my way, you fool!"

Everyone gives him room, and he splashes past us down the tunnel to surprise Mati and Fryderyk.

We try to collect ourselves, but a pall has covered the group. That civilians no longer trust the AK is not news. The same people who once cheered us on now blame the resistance for their starvation, the ruin of their homes, and the deaths of their families. In the city center, I overheard a couple complaining how much they miss the Nazi cafés and cabarets. It sears my heart, and I don't talk about it with Mati. He and his company are still fighting despite their dwindling ammunition, weapons breaking down, the lack of food and bombing wearing all of them thin.

"Go back! Go back!" The man's cries echo down the tunnel.

I look at the startled faces of my group and focus my attention on each of them. "If you want to get out of here alive, follow me," I say, and, turning, wade ahead.

Fifteen minutes later, we come upon a white chalk drawing on the curved tunnel wall: the wild man rendered by Zofia, an arrow followed by the words—*Keep moving forward!*

Comforted by the sign, we forge ahead in dogged silence, except for the loud splashing, while around us, the brown water keeps rising. I wonder idly if the couple's books are soaked through. I wonder if taking off our clothes isn't such a bad idea.

Hours later, another barbed-wired barricade later, we're soaked, but also sweating, the humid heat of the day adding to our thirst. I pause the group.

"We're very close to the final turn," I say. A low cheer. "You've all done well. Now, there might be one more barricade ahead." Groans and grumbles. "But you got through the others and you can get through this last one." We pass around water pouches because three people drank all their water early on and now have none left. But the sense that we could have a battle up ahead makes the rest generous.

When I make the final turn, I take a step and the water's suddenly up to my neck—I'm swimming. *Cholera!* They must have dammed the exit. Shouts behind me, and I paddle around to see panic.

"Quiet! Get rid of your packs if they're pulling you down." I help one of the AK soldiers, and the other two help the couple remove their precious library. *Poor man.* It would be like losing all my drawings.

Most of us are able to push our packs before us as we swim, but near the exit I make out the outline of a barbed-wire barricade. My heart sinks. Have the Hitlerow recaptured this section of Mokotów?

A few meters ahead, light from the open sewer grate filters onto the sharp barbs of the barricade, and the grumbling behind me grows.

"We should have gone back."

"That crazy man was right."

I point out that Zofia's group made it out—no floating bodies in the water.

"We can do it, but we'll have to dive through the hole in the barricade," the man who knows everything says.

I can only agree. I tell them that the tunnel rises sharply toward the exit and they won't have to swim much farther. But this is a challenge I've never faced before.

One of the AK soldiers volunteers to go first. He takes a deep breath of fetid air before diving under the water. We see his feet and legs kicking, and then he's through to the other side, smearing the water off his face.

He gives a thumbs-up. "Keep your arms to your sides," he says. "Use your feet to kick."

The man who was right goes next and gets through without a hitch. The woman in the couple is helped by the AK soldier, who shows her how to duck her head and hold her breath. Miraculously, she makes it through. Having forsaken all his bags, the woman's husband follows, and then the last of us make it past the barricade—mostly thanks to Zofia's group having cut and cleared the way.

We emerge into the light, a short distance from the barbed wire, and the woman in the couple begins wiping her husband's tears with her scarf; in turn, he cleans her smiling, crying face. Without a word, the rest of us take turns cleaning each other's faces, being careful around the eyes and mouth. It's a strange, animal moment that feels primal and peaceful.

At the sewer opening, I keep the others back while I climb the ladder, but there are no German troops in sight—just a mix of civilians and AK soldiers strolling by. I stick my head out, and Zofia runs up to me, grinning, her face shiny and clean, her clothes dry.

"What could possibly go wrong?" Zofia says, laughing.

Once we're out, Zofia shows everyone the buckets for washing up, and the library couple is the first to thank me for guiding them. Only slightly cleaner, they all hurry off, at liberty to roam these streets where so many Home Army soldiers have died trying to keep them free.

When I've washed and changed into the clothes I left with the sunflower seller, Zofia and I wander off in search of a hot drink while we wait for Mati and Fryderyk. It's her birthday tomorrow, and Mati and I have planned a little party in the cellar of the Sobieski Residences.

At the tea kiosk, we bump into a friend of Zofia's, who raises her fist in salute. "Day sixty of the Rising, Ola, and we're still alive!"

I smile at her, but a thread of fear is winding itself around my heart.

I BREATHE EASIER when Mati and Fryderyk finally find us. We're all wearily trooping down Malczewskiego when we're stopped by Fryderyk's brother, Jerszy, who waves his camera at us.

"Come on, just one photograph," he pleads. "All of you in a group."

"We're stinking and tired," Fryderyk says, shaking his head.

"Just one quick snap. I'll make you famous. You'll be in *Life* magazine."

Too tired to argue, we give in. He poses us near the sewer entrance. Crazy man. He's been taking photos all over Warsaw and smuggling the film out with sailors on the Baltic cargo ships.

"Ready, everyone? Look at the camera. Say, 'Freeeee!'"

With Zofia fidgeting like a dog with fleas, Jerszy has to take five pictures before he's satisfied.

Zofia and I say a quick goodbye to Mati and Fryderyk, who are scheduled to start back down the sewer ahead of us.

"Please keep a lookout for my rosary," Zofia asks them. "I think it came off at one of the barricades."

"See you in a few hours," Mati says, kissing me. Then he winks at Zofia and salutes me.

I roll my eyes at him, roll my eyes at Zofia—running on the spot, raising her arms up and down in the air. "I need to stretch my legs," she says. "Let's do a quick walk down Tyniecka like we did last night."

A few blocks later, we turn onto the street of tenement flats just as a truckload of heavily armed Hitlerow is emptying onto the pavement.

"Run," I yell, but they shout, *"Halt! Halt!"*

I pull at a gate, but it's locked. Zofia tries another—also locked. I have exactly two bullets in my Luger, and I know Zofia has two in her Browning. I squeeze between a brick wall and a tree trunk and fire. My first bullet grazes a building. They fire back, the bullets pounding into the wall and tree. My second bullet knocks one of them to the ground, unmoving. A red-black wave of nausea crests inside my chest. Then they're on me. Arms grab me from behind and lift me off my feet. I bite and punch the hands holding me, but that only spurs their brutality.

"Mati!" I yell, kicking and scratching. "Mati!"

An animal howl, and I twist my head in time to see Zofia in the grip of another soldier.

She raises her gun to her head.

"Ola! NO!"

A shot rings out as I'm lifted off the ground.

They throw me into the back of the truck. I try jumping out and a fist hits me across the face. Darkness.

Thirty-Five

Toronto, February 2011

Impatient and excited, the three of us are crowding the foyer of our house, anticipating the arrival of Françoise Bisset. Cheri's swooning in a sunbeam on the entrance rug; I'm pacing a bit, adjusting tulips in a vase; Irena's staring up at *River Dream.*

"Beautiful," she says, wheeling her walker side to side like a partner in a slow dance.

I move up behind her, put my chin on her shoulder. "You did that, you know. That's *your* painting."

"Hmph," she says. *Fancy that.*

Françoise arrives by taxi with a case of red Côtes du Rhône. That, and several types of cheese, olives, confiture, pâté from St. Lawrence Market (it wasn't far from the train station), two baguettes from Bonjour Brioche (just a short stop for the taxi).

"Fortifications," she says, and leans in for a long hug with Irena. I have to look away from the sight of them. Apart from Tahira, who welcomed Irena back with a pot of her lentil soup and the happy news that she was pregnant, no one's called or dropped by for a visit.

"You smell good," Irena says, and Françoise laughs her lovely, throaty laugh.

Much to our delight, my grandmother's longtime friend and art dealer is staying with us while she sorts out Stefan Cegielski's collection of Irena's paintings. She says that Roland wants to sell everything, as soon as possible. And that the Beaux Arts in Montreal wants her to catalogue all the pieces Stefan bought over the years so they can choose the ones they'd like for the retrospective.

I've put Françoise in Sophie's old suite, and, as she's unpacking, I tell her a bit about Irena's recovery.

"So first thing: she's not allowed to smoke or drink anymore, so the three of us have to find another way of celebrating."

"*Pauvre* Irena. To be punished for being sick—it's not fair. But don't worry." She smooths her generous hips. "I have to slow down myself, so we agree I'll only have a glass when I'm not here."

"Well, you and I—"

"Naturally, Jo! Tell me, how is she doing really?"

I sit on the bed and search for words. "Sometimes I don't recognize her. Sometimes she doesn't recognize me."

"It was like that with my father." She shakes out a long string of beads, lays it on the dresser beside the earrings. "But I had my sister and Rafael. It's a lot for you to handle on your own."

I shrug. Then I nod.

We share our experience of dementia, exchanging moments that shook us, like strange pebbles we've collected: Their bouts of anger. The mourning when the mind seems to know what it's losing. And the funny bits, like Irena's new penchant for undressing in the living room with the curtains open.

"How old is she now?"

"Eighty-nine this August."

"Ah, but she's lucky. My father was sixty-eight when his started. You'll need help."

I tell her about the stern angel, Nurse McDonnell, and her geriatric team. Françoise gives me a freesia-flowery hug, and we walk arm in arm to join Irena in the living room.

"You two catch up," I say, wedging another cushion behind my grandmother's back. "I'll put together some lunch."

Don't go, Irena's eyes plead.

I give her a wink. "Maybe Françoise would like to see the triptych. Why don't you take her to your studio."

"I would love that. Let's go while the light is good, *ma grande*."

WHEN THEY EMERGE from the studio, I can see by the look on Irena's face that she's smitten with Françoise. Whether that's in recognition of the role she's played ushering her art into the public sphere, or whether she's fascinated by the various shades of red in her hair, is uncertain. Françoise shows me how to make the perfect mustard-garlic vinaigrette, and my green salad adds zest to the meal she brought us.

When Irena wheels away for her post-lunch lie-down, I wrap up the cheeses, and Françoise leans against the kitchen counter with a coffee in her hand.

"*Elle est extraordinaire, ta grand-mère*."

"*Oui, je sais*. Any thoughts on the triptych?"

She waves her arms about her head in a way that makes me fear for her coffee and her hair. "One has to look at it for a long time, and from every angle. But, apart from *Mokotów Angel*, it might be her best work."

"She hasn't touched it since—you know—last December when she went into hospital."

"So it's done. I'd like to take some photos to show Stéphane at the Musée." She finishes her coffee, puts the mug in the dishwasher. "You know, the little sketches and watercolors are also very good."

"Aren't they? She makes one or two a day. I just keep pegging them to the line I hung in the studio." As she's about to leave the room, I catch her eye. "Françoise, have you ever heard Irena or Sophie or Mati mentioning Irena's sister?"

"A sister?"

I tell her all I know about Lotka, most of which is speculation. "Why do you think no one talked about her?"

She blinks at me over her glasses. "Well, families usually hide the black sheep. Someone they're ashamed of. But that doesn't sound like your grandparents. If she was taken by the Gestapo, she would have suffered terribly. That's not something to be ashamed of."

FRANÇOISE GETS BACK late from her meeting with Roland, tired, but bubbling with excitement. "Is she still up?"

"Oh, yes. It's *Grey's Anatomy* night."

"I'll say hello."

"No, Françoise!"

But she's already gone, and then back in a flash, looking stunned.

"I tried to warn you," I say and pour us two mugs of wine.

"She yelled at me! Put her hand out, like this. 'Don't come in!'"

"Sundowning," I say.

"Is that what you call it in English? My father used to swear at us, throw things. Then he was charming again."

We sit at the kitchen table cradling our mugs and she tells me about her encounter with Roland and Cynthia.

"It's a wealthy family, *non*? They have a Bonnard, David Milne, Ray Mead, even a couple of Picasso sketches. But they made it clear they want to wipe their hands of Irena's stuff." She takes a sip. "Of course, they have no idea what they're looking at. I tried to tell them that the retrospective will send the value into the sky, but they want to sell now, now, right away."

"They're embarrassed, I bet. Maybe angry or ashamed. They have all these paintings his dad collected, painted by a woman who was his prisoner in a Nazi concentration camp."

She rummages in her bag for her camera, sends me an ominous look. "I have something to show you. It's a bit *strict*, Jo. Okay? I looked at all the paintings. Apparently, there are more in the basement, and they'll show me tomorrow. But the housekeeper brought in a loose pile of unframed drawings, some on newsprint, some on good-quality paper; some dark pencil, some white on black."

"The housekeeper?"

"Oh, yes. Once they showed me where the paintings were, they left me alone, except for Madame Housekeeper, who kept looking in to make sure I wasn't stealing the silver."

"Sounds like Roland."

"I was leafing through these drawings, and I see my fingers have some black on them." She slaps her palm on the table. "*Chérie*, on the back of the drawings, just sticking together, I found these."

She turns on her Canon, and I shift closer to peer at the screen.

The charcoal sketches are all portraits of women. Most emaciated, some sick or possibly dying. All in long striped jackets, skirts or trousers.

"Fucking hell! Sorry, Françoise."

"No, it is fucking hell. There are twelve of them, some just quick lines, but . . ." Her head falls into her hand, and I take the camera from her. She sobs quietly while I rub her back. "You look," she says. "I'm going to the bathroom."

It's the tenderness of the drawings that tears the heart. Two women, possibly sisters, one healthier looking, the other all bone, both smiling. Arms around each other's shoulders. The head of an angry woman, hair shorn, eyes as big as saucers. A woman sitting on her heels, cradling a body across her lap, weeping, as Françoise did just now.

I run to my bedroom to get my laptop, pull my cable from my camera bag.

Back in the kitchen, Françoise has returned, and we connect the camera to my computer. In the time it takes to download the photos, we each drink a second mug of wine.

"I want these," I say. "I'll pay whatever they're asking."

"I don't think they've seen them, Jo. When I was leaving, Cynthia came out to say goodbye, but I never saw Roland again. I told her I'd be back tomorrow, and I never mentioned the charcoals. I left them in the pile, like they were given to me, with the pencil drawings facing up."

I stare into my empty mug and realize that it's not just the wine warming my blood. I'm still angry at them. Not just for canceling the sculpture, but for dismissing Irena's experience. As though a lie could erase the past.

I rub my fingers across my forehead. "There's only one explanation I can see. Irena makes these charcoals while she's in a Nazi camp with other women. Stefan is a guard or officer at the camp and steals them."

"And keeps them hidden for—what? Seventy years? Why? Wouldn't that be very dangerous for him?"

"It would. Unless she sold them to him, or gave them to him much later."

"You mean she could have drawn them from memory?"

I click on the new file of photos, and the twelve sketches spring to life on the larger screen. We scroll through them slowly, and as I meet Françoise's gaze, she shakes her head vigorously.

"Non. Absolument, non."

"I completely agree," I say. "Look at this detail on the bunk behind them. It looks like sacking—crosshatched. Their mismatched shoes. And the expression in the eyes on this one. You don't get eyes like that unless they're looking right at you."

"And the feeling. Each one is a little different. Like she was . . ." Françoise turns away, and I feel the welling in my own eyes. But I feel other things, too. Admiration. Gratitude. I want to know this shorn woman who is completely herself. Irena's captured her defiance, but as you often see in photographs, each eye is telling a different story.

Françoise swallows hard, digs for words to complete her thought. "She made a veneration of each woman's life. Like you see in old paintings of the Madonna."

I give her a grateful smile—for recognizing the wonder of these works. "When you go back tomorrow, can you ask what they want for the charcoals? They'll never sell to me, so just say you have an anonymous buyer. Please."

ꟼ

THIS MORNING, NURSING a hangover, I'm doing what my grandmother taught me to do whenever I was upset: I'm throwing myself into my work. Irena's relaxed across from me, rereading one of her Giles Blunt mysteries, engrossed in murder and mayhem; I'm coming up with ideas for her grave sculpture. Cheri takes one look at us and leaves with a flick of her tail.

I've avoided looking at the charcoals again, but those initial feelings will stay with me forever. Not in the way of Stefan's wrathful recording. The drawings are too beautiful for that, just as the women in the drawings are beautiful in their immaculate humanity.

I sneak a look at my grandmother. So far, she hasn't asked for a cigarette. Over several weeks, I've been mining her vast collection of cigarette butts, hidden in pockets, vases, mugs, and yes, the cuffs of pants. We are both being good.

Oops! Spoke too soon. She's looking under the wicker table. A search is underway for her big glass ashtray.

I head her off at the pass. "How about a bowl of strawberries and vanilla ice cream?" A new addiction she picked up in the hospital.

THIS EVENING, CUMIN Restaurant delivers our Indian food just as Françoise's taxi pulls into the driveway. She rolls her eyes at me as she enters, plunks her portfolio case in the foyer. "I'm going to take a shower."

That doesn't sound like good news.

I lay the food out on the kitchen table, conscious that, yet again, I'm wearing white to eat potentially staining food; and this time I've implicated Irena—hair in a high bun, sapphire earrings echoing blue eyes, she's in her flowing white caftan with sweatpants underneath. We both wanted to dress up for Françoise's last night.

In silent agreement, Françoise and I leave any discussion of the charcoals for later. Instinct. And not wanting to harm Irena. Instead, our conversation returns to Frida, and as long as we keep to other people's art, my grandmother has a lot to add. But as soon as Françoise asks about her triptych, she opens her palms as if to say, *I'm empty; I'm blank.*

All during dinner, in a spectacular feat of balance and grace, Irena gets zero stains on her white caftan, while Françoise and I, despite our napkins, drip and splotch. Our friend laughs uproariously. Happy, I clear the table, and while Françoise packs the dishwasher, I lead my grandmother to the living room sofa, help her get her feet up on the ottoman.

"I'll be back soon with tea and lemon biscotti," I say, impatient to hear Françoise's news.

"Is she living with us now?" Irena's blue eyes, hopeful.

IN THE KITCHEN, Françoise and I stay standing, alert to whatever turmoil is about to come.

"Well, I followed your instructions exactly, Jo." She sounds tired.

I take a long, patient breath in.

"I gave them my list of suggested prices for the paintings, and then I casually mentioned the charcoals."

"And?"

"Roland said, 'What charcoals?'"

"He did?"

She nods. "I went to the pile of drawings on the table. You know—no hurry.

I leafed through them, turned them over—no charcoals. They've removed them."

I'm aware of a splitting. Part of me is trying to stay afloat in a sea of agitation; the other part is sitting beside a skeletal woman, my one foot in a wooden clog, the other in a black shoe with no laces.

"I'm so sorry, *chérie*."

Too stricken to speak, I hang my head.

"But there is some good news." She smiles at me as I look up. "I went to the kitchen to ask the housekeeper for a cup of hot water—you know, they offered me nothing! On the way, I look around, and in the living room—on the Bösendorfer baby grand, *évidemment*—are the photos in silver frames: their wedding, kids, and one old one of Stefan and his wife, both of them in uniform. I will send it to you."

I make a move to hug her.

"Wait!" She lifts a folder from the table, hands it to me.

Inside is the charcoal sketch of the angry woman.

"They missed one."

Part Six

Thirty-Six

Ravensbrück Concentration Camp, Germany, October 1944

At dawn, the *Appellplatz* is always cold since it's in the shadow of the crematorium. We stand still for hours while the roll is taken and then hours after until my feet cramp and my back screams and the wind whistles around my shaved head.

This morning is no different except that I'm standing beside Rose, who's about to fall face forward. I inch my arm against hers to hold her up, and feel that Suzannah on her other side is doing the same, even though she has her little son beside her. The dogs are alert to the slightest movement, but we're in the fourth row, so there's somewhat less chance of being bitten.

Falling guarantees that Hilde will kick and beat Rose, or worse, let her dog, Grief, at her, endangering everyone nearby. In my peripheral vision, I can see that the burns on Rose's face look better after Marie's treatment. If she could just make it through this morning . . .

While I press closer and closer to her, trying to rise a little on my heels as she slumps, I count the black crows on the roof of the crematorium. There are twenty-two this morning, but that number keeps changing as they lift off or come in for landing according to some important engagement of their own.

Behind us, a woman's groan expires in a rattling gasp, and someone near her cries out. Before Hilde can pounce, another guard is at them, which at least means they won't be mauled by Grief. The sound of a whip slashes the air, although I'm guessing that the groaning woman has died and isn't feeling anything.

So far keeping Rose upright is working, as every woman in every row adjusts herself ever so slightly to keep the rows even. Keeping the rows even is important. The guards are maniacal about this, and it's one of the first things I learned since arriving here two weeks ago.

When I was issued the long, striped jacket and skirt of all the prisoners, I did not appreciate that the rough cotton would soften the sting of a whip against my legs. Now I know, and during *appelle*, I drag the skirt down as low as possible past my shins.

The siren goes and *appelle* is finally over. The line breathes and Rose leans against my shoulder. As we move to the day's work assignments, her sister, Marie, hurries forward, and together we half walk, half carry Rose to our barracks.

"Thank you, Irena." Marie's the older and stronger of the two Polish sisters, and it's through her sacrifices that Rose is still alive. She's been giving Rose her food rations, keeping her from the infirmary, where they're bound to kill her. Our blockova overseer calls Rose "the useless mouth."

When an SS officer caught Rose absently singing a song, a serious offense, he threw a cup full of hot coffee at her. Rose's broken nose and burns never healed properly. How could they? Since then, she's had dysentery and an incessant fever.

Inside the barracks, Gaby's waiting for us. The three of us get Rose onto the second bunk she shares with Marie. There we pile rags and clothes on top of her in the hope that she'll escape her work duty in the latrines today. On the bunk, her body barely makes a mound.

Gaby and I share the shadow of a smile. Yesterday, I found out that I'd been reassigned from the day shift to the night shift at Texled, the textile factory on the Ravensbrück grounds—seven p.m. to six a.m.—and then the long roll call after that. My heart sank, but when I heard that Gaby was also reassigned, I rallied.

A writer and illustrator for the French resistance paper *Combat*, Gaby was mistakenly given the red triangle badge for political prisoners, with a *P* in the center—like mine—because her father was Polish French, and she has a Polish last name. Between her bad Polish and my bad French, we've formed a friendship that's kept me alive these fourteen days. Betrayed by an uncle who works in the French police, she arrived with a convoy of French resisters last April, and has survived miraculously well. I learn from her example.

"I have a surprise for you," she says.

"And I have a surprise for you. You go first."

She opens a sheet of newspaper to show me a pile of charcoal pieces. "From the outdoor firepit. Look at this one—it's perfect. You take it."

"A perfect pencil. See what I found in the latrine this morning." I unwrap the book hidden in my headscarf. "Goethe's *Faust*. And look!" I flip through the book's fine paper to show her all the blank pages at the end of each scene. "Fifty scenes!"

We are beside ourselves. With charcoal and paper, we have everything we need for drawing. Since literature is useless to these dragons, we are expected to tear out pages from books to use in the latrines, which means a steady supply of drawing paper in the margins and covers of books, but nothing like this *Faust*.

I hand her the book. "Are you going to sleep before our night shift?"

"No. I have some designs I want to get on paper. And you?"

"I have an invitation I can't refuse."

"Oh, no."

Ever since the blockova told me that I'm next in line to be interrogated about my work in the AK, I've been convinced I'm going to be tortured. The Rising is over. The Germans have won. Their bombs decimated every inch of the Old Town, they killed tens of thousands of civilians, and captured thousands of AK soldiers. What possible reason could there be for interrogating the resisters except to punish them? I'm not sure what this Captain Wenders wants from me, but I have no choice in the matter.

THE BLOCKOVA KNOCKS on the door of his cabin, and when he opens it, I'm shoved inside.

"Five minutes late," he says in German, and slaps my face with his open palm.

The shock makes me flinch. But not the pain. In the *appelle*, a slap from one of the women guards can draw blood or break bones. This slap is sharp, but the sting doesn't last. I stare at him without blinking.

The officer sits down in a wheeled chair and puts his boots up on a desk, while I remain standing. He's a man I immediately mistrust. My instinct tells me that if I'm to get through this interrogation unscathed, I have to be able to read him, and yet even with my intelligence training, I find him mysteriously unreadable. Tall, with a thick head of dark hair and piercing blue eyes, he is handsome, with a voice unexpectedly high-pitched.

"Tell me exactly what you did in the Armia Krajowa."

So we're speaking Polish now. Interesting! "I was a major in the intelligence unit."

"I don't care what your rank was. What did you do? What was your job, and name all the people you worked with."

I tell him about guiding people through the sewers, and he slides his boots off the desk. "Go on. Who was in your cell?"

"Mati, Zofia, Fryderyk."

"These are code names?"

"Yes."

He pounds the desk with his fist. "I want real names."

"It was a security measure that we never knew each other's real names."

He gives me a half smile that sends a shiver up my spine. Zofia is likely dead, but Mati and Fryderyk might be in Sachsenhausen, the men's camp near us; I'm never going to tell him their real names.

"Was this Zofia as good as you at her job?"

What kind of question is that? Confused, I pause a moment, and he wheels his chair up to my feet, jumping up an inch away from me.

I stumble back. "In fact, she was much better at many things."

"Go on!" Hands on his hips, head jutting forward like a cannon.

I describe Zofia's dexterity in the tunnels, her fearlessness and her loyalty. His eyes take on a glint, and I steel myself for what's coming next.

"Does she look like you?"

Again, I'm taken aback. "No."

"Well?"

"She's small, two years younger."

"And? And?"

"Dark hair worn in a braid, dimples in each cheek. Dark eyes, round as marbles and full of light."

A sigh that's almost a sob escapes his lips before he shoves me hard in the chest.

"That's enough for today. Get out, filthy scum."

AT NIGHT, THE Texled factory is lit up like a lighthouse. Inside, the chugging locomotive clatter from the looms and sewing machines feels like a solid mass you could grab on to. Deafening as it is, it has the advantage of masking our talk, and Gaby and I are sewing side by side for once.

"Thought they were going to put you on the looms," she says, teasing me.

I roll my eyes. The looms that make the material for the camp clothing are terrifying because of the noise and their sheer size. "Luckily, the Russians objected."

We both grin. According to the manager of the factory, the Russian women are the strongest and best suited to the challenge of the looms.

Then again, at the whirring machine beside me is one of the best and fastest sewers.

"I sewed most of our clothes at home," Gaby tells me. "Even winter coats for my mother and little sister—A-line, with scalloped hems. I'll draw them for you."

She's smiling as she talks about her dream of being a Paris couturier, and I'm happy to pour out my dream of studying art in her city. For a blissful while, I'm flying like one of the crows, high in the night sky, above the Seine and Eiffel Tower. But while Gaby can sew and tell stories at the same time, I'm not so adept and waste material by sewing sleeves too tight, or shoulders askew.

On the day shift, these would be dangerous mistakes, but the night shift has fewer staff stalking the aisles and checking our work. As long as I get my quota of 180 SS uniforms in an eleven-hour shift, I should be okay, and Gaby always makes more than the quota. The price of failing to meet the quota is punishment for the whole factory. And that is too terrible to think about.

At the half-hour break, I tell Gaby about my strange interrogation by Captain Wenders. She tells me something that rattles me.

"He's the one who broke Rose's nose. What do you think he wants from you?"

I don't know how to answer, and, in any case, we're interrupted by two women who crowd us behind a loom.

"Either of you working with fur or buttons?"

I shake my head. But Gaby does buttons.

"Every third jacket, sew the buttons too far from the holes."

"What if we get the fur collars?" she asks.

"Take a scissors and cut into it partway. It looks fine, but it falls apart easily. Pass the plan along."

Gaby raises her eyebrows. "Well, Irena, it turns out your bad sewing is good for the cause."

SUNRISE LIVENS THE sky as we're marched back from the factory in time for *appelle*. Too tired and hungry for conversation, my mind, nevertheless, has been pondering Gaby's question about Captain Wenders. *What does he want from me?*

I sense it's not about sex; nor does he want something for the Reich, the Führer, or the camp. What is he looking for?

THERE COMES A point when you're so tired that you're no longer tired. During roll call, my senses are awake, my heart beating, lungs working, and even though my legs feel ready to give in, I'm able to stand erect between Marie and Gaby. I don't know how my body does this. I'm counting the crows again when I feel Marie's hand brushing mine. At first, I think she's trembling because of the cold, but at one point her little finger links mine. It comes to me with the chill wind that Rose is missing. Knowing how afraid the sisters are of the infirmary, it can only mean she's died in the night. Leaning against Gaby, I link my little finger with hers. Her squeeze tells me she knows. And like that the three of us cry a silent cry for Rose.

Thirty-Seven

Toronto, March 2011

I never know how to feel about a hot March day, because, lovely as it is, it so often guarantees snow in April or even May. On this sunny blue-sky morning, I've decided there's no point being superstitious. Taking our cue from the cardinal pair at the bird feeder, Irena and I are planning an alfresco lunch. Off to St. John's to visit Mati and Sophie, we've packed our sketchbooks, a folding chair, tea, and courtesy of Mon K Patisserie, ham and cheese croissants, followed by the entire point of it all—*pain au chocolat* for her and *pain aux raisin* for me.

Irena now has Mati's old wheelchair. So it wouldn't remind her of Mati's sickness, we painted the footrests and all the metal parts in colors of blue and silver. Irena put a few circles of orange and a splash of black against that and named it Mercury, "for the pleasure," she said. Today, Mercury's serving as both transportation and bearer of objects. Apart from our picnic, I've brought a blanket just in case March turns March-like.

Françoise's visit left Irena with a sort of peace—as though she'd had a little vacation from my anxiety and the lingering effects of her lengthy hospital stay. When she caught a cold at the end of February, I slid back down the panic chute. But with no resistance, she let me take her to her doctor, who declared this a simple cold that would take its course. Dr. Chan also suggested some antianxiety medication for me.

At St. John's, tree shadows stretch across the warming grass and gravestones. I asked the taxi driver to drop us near the main entrance, so I could wheel Irena down the avenue of giant sister maples. Still shorn of their leaf canopies, it's easy to admire their crusty trunks and branches, each tree, herself, a winter sculpture. On an almost spring day, we are not alone in this parkland of restructuring people. As we pass a bushy white cedar, a whole village of chiding, gossipy sparrows goes mute. Sparrow secrets.

Since Françoise left, the mundane essentials of my life have been protecting me all through the day—shopping, cooking, eating, cleaning, taking care of Irena, the bills, and Cheriblare leave little room for vengeance and remorse.

It's at night, alone in bed, that the events of Françoise's visit grip me. Sometimes I feel like I'm strangling in my own anger. Roland's deceit, Stefan's deceit—I want them to pay a price. Ever since meeting the women in the charcoals, I've been overwhelmed by a compulsion to remind people what happened in the Nazi camps, to punish those who want to forget.

I've been indulging a deep dive into the history of Ravensbrück concentration camp. Initially made for German women the Nazis deemed criminal, scandalous, or divergent—prostitutes, communists, lesbians, women who murdered their husbands—it became something else by the time Irena arrived: a hell reserved for women prisoners from the Nazi-occupied territories: France, Belgium, Holland, Russia. But by far, the greatest number of prisoners were Polish women—AK or communist insurgents, as well as civilians. In other words, the women Irena drew in those charcoals.

I can't get them out of my mind. I want to know who they are, and I want other people to know. Though once again, I'm scared to ask Irena directly. I don't want to risk another episode. These days, my grandmother's living in a vivid present, and maybe that's the best place for her to be.

Turning down a side path, we're coming up to Sophie's sculpture when we're surprised by a silver-haired man fondly gazing up at Sophie's metal spirals before running his hand over her name. We give him a moment before we take his place.

"Hello, Soph." We blow kisses and carry on to Mati's sculpture, where I set out my chair and unpack the tea and lunch.

Irena's nattering in Polish, and when I ask her what she and Mati are talking about, she waves her hand from side to side.

"It's a situation you will not understand."

"Try me," I say, smiling widely.

She shifts in the wheelchair. I pour the tea and wait.

"It's about Lotka."

My skin prickles.

She points her chin at Mati's sculpture. "He says I still love her."

"And do you?"

Her chest sinks in a sigh. "She was my sister." When she takes off her sunglasses, her eyes are wide, childlike. "But she said things that killed many people."

I set the mug of hot tea on the ground. This is it, then; it's all coming out now. I try to become still and small.

"I'm feeling sorry so many people died because of us."

"Not you and Mati." *So much for remaining silent*. "You two were heroes. Look how many people you saved."

She motions toward Mati's glass orb glowing in the sun.

"He is saying that is the case. But I disagree."

"You do?"

"Of course."

I let that percolate. Mati was a man who saw the good in everything, in everyone. But Irena's art tells a different side of the story. A cool breeze pricks up, and the twigs rattle against each other.

"Jo. Please give me my *pain au chocolat*."

"Before your ham sandwich?"

"Before."

Sophie's voice in my head: *Eighty-nine, Jo. Why are we saving the* pain au chocolat *for later?*

And with that, the war conversation is lost. I gaze up at the swaying branches above me. So Lotka said things that got people killed. I suppose that might be reason enough to erase her for decades. Yet, this fine March morning, my grandmother's conceding that she still loves her sister. I conclude that the vagaries of the heart elude my understanding—especially a heart that's been through all Irena has.

More than the usual number of runners and dog walkers, photographers, and family visitors are traveling the treed pathways of the old cemetery. But so far this morning, we are the only artists setting up camp.

Last night I had a brain wave. "Pencil or charcoal?" I say now, offering her both boxes.

She reaches for a blunt charcoal, and I lay the sketch pad on her lap.

Retreating to a spot under a nearby tree, I set up my chair across from her and gobble my lunch.

The idea for Irena's grave sculpture came to me early one February morning when I couldn't sleep. No tree bark kisses, no head knocks necessary, unless you count the metaphorical ones. Now, leafing through my drawings, I see immediately that a slight tilt to the angle will make the sculpture swing. My heart does a happy leap. This stage of a project is intoxicating. Almost ready to build the maquette. Better order the copper sheeting.

I look up from my sketches and see my grandmother snoozing in her wheelchair, chin on chest, the charcoal and half-eaten pastry in her lap. I get up to lay the blanket over her, and she slumps against the side of the wheelchair.

"Babcia," I say, shaking her knee. "Is it time to go home?"

She doesn't respond, and I hear my voice rising in a wail. Two young men come to my rescue. One of them calls 911, while the other asks if he can start CPR. I hear their voices in a fog, but I must be saying something because they lay Irena on the blanket on the path, and one of them begins pumping her chest, listening for breath. A small crowd gathers, and an older woman shoos them away before putting an arm around me. "The ambulance will be here soon."

I smile, and release myself from her arm. Irena's right boot is coming off, and she hates cold feet. I kneel on the path and wriggle the boot back onto her socked foot, noticing for the first time a small, deep scar on her left leg above her ankle. With her coat open, she's just a small woman lying on a blue blanket beneath the giant maples.

When the ambulance arrives, the attendants move quickly to get Irena into the back.

"Here." One of the young men hands me my knapsack.

"She dropped this," the woman says, giving me Irena's sketchbook.

"Thank you, thank you." I scramble into the ambulance, and we speed off, banshee siren howling, while everything inside me goes calm and still.

MY GRANDMOTHER DIED at the cemetery where I'll bury her. I knew that, sensed that, although the attendants kept up all their magnificent means and machinery along the way to St. Michael's Hospital.

When the paperwork was signed, I called Tahira, and she came to pick me up. We went back to St. John's and found the wheelchair and our picnic paraphernalia in a neat pile beside Mati's sculpture. All the while, a sad humming filled my chest, but talking and doing kept it low, like a beehive in a field on a summer day.

Back at the house, Tahira's making me coffee while Cheriblare gives my puffy face a lick. There are so many things I want to tell them, but all of them will make us cry again. Thank God for Tahira. "She's with Mati now, Jo," is what she says.

Stroking Cheri's velvet ears, I realize that I've got an iron grip on something in my other hand. I lift my arm and Irena's sketchbook dangles freely.

I lay it on the table and randomly open it to the last page.

Today, my grandmother made a charcoal sketch of me—curls in a messy bun, eyes wide, drawing pencil in my hand. My mouth stretched in a huge smile.

Thirty-Eight

Ravensbrück Concentration Camp, November 1944

Two in a small bunk is possible; three means one person gets no sleep. The night shift has turned out to be the best solution to a worsening horror. Every day, hundreds of women and children are transported here from the camps in the east. As the Russians advance westward, the Wehrmacht scrambles to cover its grisly tracks. Recent arrivals from Auschwitz-Birkenau report mass shootings, burnings, dismantling of the apparatus of the gas chambers—anything to hide the fact of what's been happening there for years.

Here at Ravensbrück, there is less food, but also less supervision; more typhus, but also more hope. In the factory, in the latrines, in the barracks, in many languages, you hear repeated, *If we could just hold on till the Allies get here.* Because there are fewer guards, there have been two escape attempts this November—one successful. As a warning, twenty prisoners were executed, but the guards were also punished.

At the end of the shift, our crew is being marched to the *Appellplatz* when Gaby's wooden clog gets stuck in the half-frozen mud. With one bare foot, she hops about while I bend to pull her shoe from the sucking ground. As the stream of prisoners marches by us, I hurriedly shake off one of my clogs to give her. When a guard catches sight of us, her dog strains at its leash, and then bounds toward us, scattering the women in line. Gaby is bitten on her calf and me on my ankle. It hurts terribly, but we must keep moving. To lie down or stop could mean the razor teeth at your throat.

The two of us hobble along, I in my thin sock and one clog, Gaby in one of my clogs and one of hers, both of us bleeding. We stand for hours during roll call as close to each other as we dare while we freeze. Staying alive has become an act of defiance, but I don't know how much longer I can defy the laws of nature. A body needs warmth, food, clean water, and sleep.

I stare at the crows ruffling their feathers on the roof of the crematorium. *I'm alive*, I tell myself. *I'm alive!*

IN OUR BLOCK, Marie dabs at Gaby's wound.

"It looks bad," she says. "Do you want to go to the infirmary?"

Gaby shakes her head vigorously. It was before my time here, but she remembers the horror of the *rabbits*—Polish women whose legs were cut open by a doctor in the infirmary for gruesome medical experiments.

The flesh above my ankle is pierced, but the dog didn't crunch my bone. For that I'm grateful.

"I don't like the look of these bites." Marie stands with her hands on her hips, but Gaby won't budge, and neither will I.

Our legs washed and bandaged with material torn from our uniforms, Gaby and I lie side by side on our bunk, trying to distract ourselves from the pain and the memory of the attack. I close my eyes and turn my thoughts to Mati—his smile, the curl of hair flopping over one eye. But it hurts too much to think of him. I keep him deep—a warming glow that never fades.

Beside me, Gaby stirs. "Imagine the two of us sharing a studio in Montparnasse. You making a big mess with your paints, me making a big mess with my sewing."

I smile. It's a like a storybook we open again and again—surviving Ravensbrück, making it to Paris, working together, reuniting with our families. She's told me about her mother and sister, her father who died fighting. I've told her about my father, who fell into a crevasse, my mother, and Mati.

"Irena. Promise me something."

Her voice pulls at me.

"In case we're separated, I want you to memorize my Paris address. I'll write you a note to give to my mother."

This touches me more than anything we've been through. Part of me doesn't believe my childhood fantasy of painting in Paris can ever come true. It's something that happens to famous men artists only. Knowing Gaby's address is in the fifth arrondissement near Marché Mouffetard makes it seem real. But something in her voice makes me worry that she's giving up hope.

THE YEAR'S COMING to a close with the infirmary overflowing with cases of typhus—even the pretense of treating patients is over. Bodies are piled like logs and the corpse crew can't keep up. The air is filled with sticky smoke as the crematorium works twenty-four hours a day. Prisoners on the crematorium shift dump the ash on the frozen lake and sprinkle it on the entrance road like sand.

Having said that, I'm now in a more fortunate position than most, and Captain Wenders is the reason. One morning when I arrived at his cabin right after *appelle*, he sat me at the desk with a pencil and paper and said, "Your blockova tells me you can draw. Draw me Zofia's face."

For the second time in this war, I drew Olenka in front of an SS officer. We never said her name, but by the end of that meeting, I understood that I was looking at Olenka's brother, and he was obsessed with hearing everything about her life in Warsaw.

Since then, while others freeze in the barracks, I spend hours near a woodstove at a desk, telling stories and drawing scenes of Olenka during the war. Today when I walked in, he threw a new set of colored pencils on the chair.

"Here you go, slut!"

Pig! I said in my mind and pounded my heel against the ground. It grates me, but I tolerate the name-calling and the slap he seems obliged to give me in front of the blockova because I get the paper, charcoal pencils, and pens that I ask for. At first, I had to keep everything in his cabin, but when I started hiding paper and charcoal in my pockets, he turned a blind eye. Even more important than the drawing materials is the medicine.

When he saw my festering dog bite, he got an infirmary nurse to come to the cabin to give me a tetanus shot and some special ointment. Gaby's wound turns out to be less deep than mine, but her dysentery is worse. I share the ointment and the extra food he throws my way with her—thick slices of bread; once, a raw potato and carrot; once, a piece of pork fat. I pick at the food, but my goal is to get Gaby well again, so it all goes with me back to the barracks.

In my block, Marie and I shave the edges of our wooden bunks with the sharp lid of a tin, and when we have enough pieces, we make a little fire with matches she stole from the kitchen, where she works. In the empty tin, we boil water with pieces of the potato and carrot and leftovers she gets from the officers' plates. Then we give the broth to Gaby and save the vegetables for the next meal, when we do it all over again.

SO FAR, CAPTAIN Wenders's favorite story is the one where Zofia saves me from being trapped in the rib cage in the sewer tunnel. I've had to tell it twice, which is how I got the idea of drawing scenes from the stories, so he could look at them again and again. Near the end of every visit, he asks me the same two questions:

"Is she still alive? When you last saw her, was she happy?"

I always say, "Yes." *Yes, of course.*

I've drawn Zofia with her braid flying, jumping across a wide canal to save a child, kicking away a platoon of rats to save a mother and her son—but today, I'm going much further. While he paces back and forth in the little cabin, I begin weaving my tale.

It's a clear day in the district of Wola, Warsaw. Zofia's in charge of a platoon of all women soldiers. They haven't eaten for days and the enemy has much bigger guns and much more ammunition. But under Zofia's command, the women draw courage. This day, their mission is to capture the Telephone Exchange, where the enemy has been holed up on the roof and the top floor, safely shooting at them and killing too many. But Zofia has an idea.

With flamethrowers made from garden hoses and petrol, they set the upper floors of the tall building on fire. That forces the men to jump off the roof or run down to the lower floors, where the women are waiting for them. Despite being vastly outnumbered, they capture the entire building. But that's not where the story ends.

I pause briefly at this point, and Captain Wenders shocks me by sitting cross-legged on the ground before me, his eyes glued to the drawings I hold up.

Inside the building, they find huge stores of food: hams and butter rolls with mustard and pickles. Sauerkraut and cucumber salad with cream and dill, and mounds of chocolate, strudel, and gingerbread. They bag the food and take it out to the starving people, and the whole district celebrates the victory of Zofia's platoon by raising her on their shoulders and parading her round the square, all the while shouting her name, "Ola! Ola! Ola!"

His eyes widen and fix on mine, and I wonder if he's going to kill me. I hear the cawing and clattering of crows on the roof of the cabin. He starts to cry—great shoulder-shaking sobs. I get to my feet and walk out, leaving the drawings behind.

Thirty-Nine

Toronto, May 2011

All I do is work these days. And even that reminds me of my grandmother.

In the doorway of my workshop, I peel off my gloves and raise my face shield, letting the night breeze cool my sweaty face. Today's been a test day to see how my new saw kit deals with the soft copper sheeting of Irena's sculpture.

Up in the city sky, I'm glad to see Sirius, the Dog Star, winking at me. It's not the worst way to spend Saturday night. Yet even this thought sends me back to my childhood.

On Saturday nights, when Sophie had better things to do, my grandparents and I huddled together on the living room couch, bowls of nuts and chips on our laps, martini glasses in our hands—vodka theirs, cranberry mine. Together we watched hours of black-and-white movies, each of us hoarding dialogue that we later sprung on each other like tricks.

A line that kept them giggling for hours: *Marriage is a beautiful mistake, which two people make together*, from *Trouble in Paradise.* It's only recently that I've come to appreciate that delicious joke. But we all adored Rosalind

Russell in *His Girl Friday* throwing herself into her manic, addictive work—partly to escape her impending, boring marriage.

Working on Irena's grave sculpture, there's been no escaping my grief. It mocks the sparkle of these May days. Part self-pity—I'm the last in my family now—more the physical ache of missing her and the rousing purpose she brought to my life. All the questions I never got to ask her: *What kept you going through all the hardship? Do you still believe in Europe—that quaint, tainted culture we so revere in the West?* Yet, if I ask myself how my grieving heart spends most of each day, the answer must be: in a rage that I haven't been able to get the charcoals back.

The sketches in my laptop have come to mean so much that is essential about my grandmother's life—her commitment to telling a truth about that war through her art.

Françoise reminds me that I do have one original charcoal, but that yellowed paper with its water-stained fingerprint is a Siren calling me from the place it was drawn. I can't help wondering who touched it, who saw it, and what it saw. It has a certain moldy smell, probably from the case it was stored in for so long. But beneath the moldiness is a strong smell of smoke. I get none of these sensations from the digital photos on my laptop.

From the corner of my eye, I catch sight of Cheri hunting in the dried leaves beneath the birch.

It occurs to me that some of those women in the charcoals might still be alive. Certainly, they'd have relatives still alive. So more important than me or my assessment of the charcoals is the fact of the women in them.

On the path to the house, Cheri cuts me off, dumps a mouse at my feet.

I wrestle her into my arms and the mouse scoots away.

In the kitchen, I give her extra, extra treats. "What do you think I should do, hmmm?"

I've sent Roland two extremely polite emails, two carefully crafted letters mailed to his addresses, all asking for Irena's sketches. I've left messages on his company and personal phones with nary a swear word—the most recent was embarrassingly groveling.

No answer.

It feels contemptuous.

ꟗ

CLOSE TO NINE, I get off the train in Oakville and head straight for the taxi ranks. I know where they live. As the light fades, and the trees grow dense, I have a moment of panic. But we arrive at a modern fortress ablaze with light overlooking pearly Lake Ontario. A convoy of cars is driving through the security gate, and my taxi follows. As nattily dressed people drift through the front doors, piano music drifts out. A party! This is perfect.

A wide hallway opens onto an indoor garden—a terra-cotta courtyard with a glass roof. Bordering the tile, sofas covered in botanical prints spread out under potted lemon, orange, and cedar trees, like a French *orangerie*. My feet pause to take in the view.

The courtyard's strung with white lights, and servers are circuiting the crowd. I catch sight of Cynthia in a long silvery gown and focus on her as she floats from group to group. It takes a while, but when she sees me, she frowns. A guest with an intricate hair weave takes her arm and leads her deeper into the house. I grab a drink from a passing tray.

As I anticipated, Roland materializes, trailing a smiling hulk of a man. Both make a beeline for me. *I've got this.*

"Roland!" I wave, my voice bright and loud. "I hear your father was an SS officer in a concentration camp." People stare. The two men back me toward the front door, but I swerve into an alcove, less crowded, but still full of people. "I understand your family stole from concentration camp victims. Isn't that true, Roland?"

People are exiting the alcove in a hurry.

I'm hustled through a door into a gym ringed with exercise machines and mirrors, the smell of chlorine pervading. "Stop touching me, Roland."

"Shut the fuck up," he hisses. He takes out his phone. "I'm calling the police."

"Go ahead," I say, folding my arms across my chest. "I'm not going without the charcoal sketches, and I don't think you'd like your customers knowing the Cegielski Landscaping Company was owned by an SS officer."

He doesn't make the call.

THE HULK MOVES closer to me, but Roland says, "It's okay, Jules." He rubs a hand over his jaw. "I don't know what you're after, but you've got to drop this charade. My father was in the Polish army. We had his official records sent to us. What do you want? Money?"

"I want my grandmother's sketches back. The ones she drew in 1944 when she was a prisoner at Ravensbrück concentration camp. Your father, Stefan Wenders, was her interrogating officer."

Hands on his hips now, he smirks. "How do you make this shit up?"

I raise my voice to a yell. "I know you have the sketches, Roland. I have photos."

At this point, a door opens at the back of the gym, and Cynthia hurries in. "You should get back out there. I'll talk to her. Jules can stay."

When Roland walks up to my face, I think he's going to spit on me, but he says, "If you try to bring my family down, after all our years of backbreaking work, I'll make sure you get what you deserve."

Cynthia has a quiet word with Jules and he moves as far away from us as possible.

"Have a seat, Jo." She points to a weight-lifting bench. "Please, just listen."

A laugh escapes me, and I plant my feet in the rough carpet.

She takes the bench, her face serious, her voice quiet. "I listened to the recording; I read the transcript. I know that was Stefan's voice. I believe you when you say he was in the German army. But he was also in the Polish army. His records are very clear and stamped with both the Polish and British seals. I can show them to you if you want, but that would be pointless."

An acid heat rises in my throat. "I'm not here to debate Stefan's role in the war. I saw that photo of him in a Polish uniform. I want my grandmother's sketches. The ones she drew in Ravensbrück, where your Nazi father-in-law—"

"They're gone. Roland burned them all after Françoise left."

My face collapses. Any exhilarating energy vanished with the word *burned*.

She looks at her phone. "Let's be honest here. Roland wants nothing to do with this stuff. He wasn't part of that war, he didn't have anything to do with it. Why should his life and his business that he's put his heart and soul into be tainted because of something his father did years ago?"

"He shouldn't have burned them."

"Well, he did. There's nothing we can do to bring them back, so stop threatening us, please. Security cameras are all over this property and you're on record as trespassing and causing a disturbance. Drop it, Jo."

An image of Irena's eyes, their brilliance and bite, crosses my mind. I lower my voice. "How could you look at those drawings and think they were worthless? Those women were resistance fighters who risked losing kids and families, women who Stefan and his Nazi colleagues tortured and starved to death."

She stands abruptly. "I think we're done here."

"What Roland destroyed are records of their imprisonment. Documents of what they went through at the hands of people like Stefan."

Her dress shimmers in the gym lights; she takes a few steps forward.

I block her path. "You don't have the guts to face the truth."

Brushing past me, she says, "I'll get Jules to walk you out."

When she opens the door, the sounds of music, laughter, clinking glasses trickle in.

Forty

Ravensbrück Concentration Camp, December 1944

Gaby's still alive. They have so many other bodies to choose from now that she only gets a few tepid whiplashes when she skirts her Texled shift.

Thanks to Captain Wenders, I work half a night shift, and then I report to his cabin. It's widely assumed that I'm his mistress, but that is not the case. Though I don't like to dwell on all the other parts I play for him—mother, sister, storyteller, fantasy maker, sometimes even sadistic father—in the last month, I've also become a feather in his cap.

Along with Gaby's drawings of dress designs and other prisoners' crafts—like the woven baskets the Russian women make—he displays my drawings in the officers' lounge. I'm not sure why, but I think this gives him some credit with his superiors. For visitors like the Red Cross, even for the job-seeking villagers from Fürstenberg and Ravensbrück, the SS is expert at creating the appearance that we are well-fed, well-housed, slightly spoiled prisoners of war. No doubt, that's why the blockovas' barracks closest to the camp entrance look like summer resort cabins.

I give him all the drawings I make of his sister's fabulist exploits. But he does not see, nor will he ever, the drawings I make for the women in my block. The majority of them are of Gaby and Marie. I hide them under our bunk, in between the pages of books I steal from the latrine, even rolled up and squeezed into knotholes in the walls. Yet it's not safe.

Against my better judgment, I drew a portrait of myself. I needed to know I was still a person, and not a number or a dog, as Wenders so often calls me. So I drew myself as I remember I used to be—with hair, all my teeth, the rounded face of a young, healthy woman. Now that portrait is missing.

I ask Marie and Gaby if they'd seen anyone searching our bunks, and Gaby says, "You know our dear blockova can't be trusted."

Marie shrugs. "She's Austrian. Even now they're still trying to impress the Germans."

We laugh, but it's not that funny. These days, whenever planes drone across the sky, we look for the shapes of British or American aircraft. I'm impatient for an Allied victory and our quick liberation from these dragon shackles, but impatience mingles with dread—will the SS rush to kill us all before that can happen? The idea that I've survived the invasion, the Siege of Warsaw, the Gestapo, the sewers, the Rising, that I have experienced the miracle of me and Mati, only to die in this camp, is almost enough to break me.

Gaby and Marie—we keep each other going. Between hurtings and humiliations, I spend a few hours in a drawing trance. Sketching women living out their lives here is strangely peaceful. What's more, I'm no longer ashamed of the increasingly fantastical tales I conjure for Wenders. Today, I'll continue unfolding my story of how he saved Ola and his mother from his vicious father, even though each chapter brings him to tears.

Yesterday, I left him hugging his knees and rocking back and forth, screeching, "Come back here, you slut, you whore. Finish the story."

I walked out with half a loaf of bread, a pencil, a pair of socks, a warm wool scarf.

THIS EVENING BEFORE the night shift starts, Marie brings news from the kitchen.

"Some special guests of the commandant are arriving from Berlin. You won't believe what the kitchen is cooking. No, I won't tell you. It could drive you mad."

"Give us a hint," I say.

She goes on to list the details of an elaborate meal that include a suckling pig.

Gaby shakes her head. "Anyone who's friends with Fritz Suhren has got to be a pig himself."

We spend the last hour before our shift sitting in a circle on the floor, picking lice from each other's heads and killing them between our thumbnails, while Gaby serenades us with her half-talking, half-singing version of "*Paris, je t'aime*"—technically not an offense. I go off to our shift happy that Gaby's got long socks, Marie has a scarf, and all of us have an extra slice of bread to share with one other woman.

Forty-One

Toronto, May 2011

The tequila shots with the sweet guy at the bar were not a great idea. Although making out in the back seat of his car was just what I needed. I had to let off the steam that's been building since my ejection from Roland's party. And yesterday was my birthday.

After the tumble in the Toyota, I took a cab to St. John's Cemetery, intending to visit my family, but I found myself in front of Stefan's shiny slab. One thing led to another, and the next thing I knew there was a large black swastika clinging to his gravestone—finely drawn, clean edges. Probably a criminal act, I thought. *Shit.* My fingers curled around the marker in the pocket of my leather jacket. *Guilty.*

I tried erasing the swastika with alcohol wipes—which seemed to work until I walked back up the incline and turned around. A silvery outline of the swastika was still visible, like a shiny trail left by a skinhead snail. I kept on walking.

This morning—actually, blinding afternoon—I'm on my third mug of coffee, fiddling on Facebook instead of getting to my workshop. Not exactly hungover, not exactly depressed, more exactly grieving—I snag a nail, weep fat raindrop tears, and have to settle for toilet paper because the Kleenex box is empty.

It's okay, Jo.

No, it's not okay, Sophie.

Sipping cold coffee, I scroll down my Facebook page. In black-and-white photos, I've been chronicling the progress of Irena's grave sculpture, and news of her death has initiated a spike in the number of comments—old fans of Irena's paintings, new converts discovering the bruising power of *Mokotów Angel*, visual artists curious about what I'm making for her. A new comment catches my attention: *To be reading about the death of your amazing grand-mother is very saddening. Please PM me. I think we might be family-related.*

Yeah, right. Shaking my head, I get up to microwave my coffee—but there's something weird about the syntax of the comment that draws me back to my seat. I read it again, search for the sender, and find a Leo Becken, Hamburg, Germany, currently online.

Germany.

My gut does a butterfly flutter. I forgo the coffee and pour myself a large glass of water. Need a clear head. And food.

Munching dry toast, I compose a brief message to this Leo. *Tell me more.*

Minutes pass while I try to imagine who he might be. Someone who knows of my *amazing* grandmother. A feeling of clouds gathering before a storm—the sudden pressure about to burst. I unlock the big window, struggle to lift it. A ping from my iPad calls me back to the table.

Leo's message: *My grandmother was Charlotte Maria Tarnberg. I believe she was the sister of your grandmother, Irena Marianowska, the Polish painter.*

You believe?

Yes, that is what she told us many times. I will send you a photo.

The picture has three people in it. Standing behind a seated old woman are a young man and a dark-haired, middle-aged woman, each with a hand on the shoulder of the old woman. She has plump pink cheeks, sparkling blue eyes, dyed-blond hair in a Thatcher-like "set," a demure smile on her lips, and, arrayed on her pillowy chest, a double string of pearls. She looks nothing like my grandmother, but she is unmistakably an older version of Lotka. I google the time difference between Toronto and Hamburg—nine thirty p.m. there now.

On impulse, I type: *Do you want to Skype?*

And this is how I discover my cousin Leo. Well, more like second cousin once removed—but still—a living relative!

Brown-haired like the middle-aged woman in the photo, he's wearing a black T-shirt with an image of Lou Reed, has a pierced left eyebrow, tattoos on both forearms.

"I use Staedtler, too," he laughs, pointing at the pencil holding up my top knot.

I'm suddenly conscious of my appearance. Baggy, slept-in Keith Haring T-shirt. I strike a distracting smile; Cheriblare helps by leaping onto the table for a close-up. I need these few seconds to construct a response—I don't know how much he knows about Lotka's role in the war. Or for that matter, what Irena and Mati did in that same debacle.

"So your grandmother talked about my grandmother?" I ask.

"Oh, yes, quite often. She followed her career from before I was born. There are several of her war paintings in Berlin, and we visited together the galleries. My mother, Astrid, in the photo, is not so keen on art, so I accompanied my grandmother by train. I have a married sister in Berlin. We stay always with her."

Chatty guy.

He raises a hand. "Hello, cat. Josephine, I understand you are also an artist. I was impressed to see a photo of your grave sculpture in *ArtNow*. How many have you made?"

"If all goes according to plan, Irena's sculpture will be unveiled in a few weeks. That will make six." I brush Cheri's tail out of the way. "So you read *ArtNow*?"

"Well, I am in art school, and the library has a subscription. But last year, I discovered I'm not an artist." He laughs. "At least, not like you and your grandmother. So now I've switched to documentary filmmaking. It's much more my style."

"Nice. You working on anything?"

"Actually, it's a short film about my grandmother—how she came to Germany during the last war, her life here. From a young age, I enjoyed her company, and I started filming her. I'm editing it now."

My eyebrows shoot up.

"Yes. It's quite a love story. If you like, I could send you a small excerpt with English subtitles that I finished editing."

A love story? I smile to hide my confusion. "I would love that."

"She bought me my first camera when I was sixteen, exactly ten years ago, in fact. I miss her quite a lot. She died in October, last year. I suppose you are missing your grandmother, too."

"I am. Every day. So you just turned twenty-six?"

"Yeah. My mates took me out this afternoon, so frankly, I'm a bit . . ." He raps his head with his knuckles.

I nod. "My birthday was yesterday."

"Amazing!"

"Crazy, huh?"

We have a staring smile fest—a bit embarrassed, a bit weirded out, a bit suspicious, happily surprised at our meeting.

OVER THE NEXT few days, Leo and I are frequently in touch—mostly messaging, some email, some Skype. And with much calamity in my heart, I learn about Charlotte-Lotka.

When Lotka died, his mother tried to contact Irena, but she never got a response. *Letter fragments in the ashtray, shards of a photograph*. How do I tell him that no one in my family ever mentioned his grandmother? That Lotka didn't exist for us; that I only discovered Irena had a sister a few months ago.

"Irena was quite a shy person," I say. "I don't know how much she knew about your side of the family."

"I was really hoping you could tell me more about the sisters. Do you think they were—do you say—estrangers because they chose different sides in the war?"

"Are you saying your grandmother was a . . . ?"

His blue eyes are earnest. "Yes. I believe she and my grandfather joined the Nazi Party."

I stare blankly. I was really asking if Lotka had been a traitor.

He twists the silver bracelet on his wrist. "I'm thinking, Jo, the best thing will be to hear it all from her mouth. My subtitles are almost finished. I'll send you the first little part tomorrow. Maybe you can help me with a good English title for my film."

When he asks to see my workshop, I take my iPad to the shed, show him the many layers of copper ready to be assembled for Irena's sculpture. He's super excited, but after we say goodbye, I feel deflated, disappointed. We have a connection that feels meant to be, normal in the way that people with mutual interests form a bond. But if Lotka was a Nazi and Irena fought against those ruthless occupiers, where does that leave us?

Yet Leo isn't Lotka and I'm not Irena. Why should I be afraid?

It's not rational, but I embark on a weird crusade. I send him articles about Irena's rescue work in the AK during the war, photos of her medals and commendations, which he hardly knows anything about, nor does he seem to know that the Warsaw Rising Museum website says that Lotka was abducted by the Gestapo.

"Could it be a mistake?" he asks.

I don't mention Irena's recent revelation that *Lotka said things that got people killed.* I want to hear what Lotka says in the film before I tell him anything more. The fact is, I don't know which version of his grandmother—Lotka's or Irena's story—will be the capital-T True one. And I like this new cousin of mine. I don't want to drive him away. I think of that line Sophie liked to quote: *Nothing is but what is not*, from *Macbeth*.

MIDMORNING, WHEN LEO'S film clip arrives in my inbox, I make myself wait until I've finished work for the day. In tribute to Irena.

Later, I settle in my grandmother's sitting room with a glass of wine, my laptop on my knees. To my surprise, the excerpt starts with the exact question I would have asked Lotka:

You grew up in Warsaw. How did you end up in Germany in the middle of the war?

Lotka's folded hands leave her lap and open in a grand gesture of surrender. "Love. Love brought me to this country. The doctor was the great love of my life, and when he was offered a senior position in a Berlin hospital, he asked me to go with him as his nurse, as his wife."

"And you said yes."

"I said yes. But it wasn't that simple." Her voice grows timorous. "Poland was at war with Germany, and my mother and sister would remain in Warsaw. I was afraid of what might happen to them if I left. You see, I was the one earning a good living, bringing food and comforts to the family, and, through the doctor, I also had contacts who were protecting them. I had no guarantee that when I left they'd be safe."

"But you still chose to leave."

"I made the only choice I could, and looking at my grandchildren [a tender smile for the cameraman], and now, my first great-grandchild, I am certain I made the right choice."

The film cuts to a framed photo on a side table. I'm expecting a photo of the great-grandchild, but it's a young blond woman seated at a piano, her hair in the waved fashion of the thirties, wearing a long evening dress.

"My mother was beautiful. She was a sensitive soul, and she did not survive the war. That was a great blow to me, but if I had brought her to Germany, she could have died here, too, just as many people did in the fighting and bombing."

Cut to a close-up of Lotka looking reflective, a shard of sunlight across her face.

"With my sister, Renka, it was different." The camera zooms in on a framed print of *River Dream* on the wall. "That is a picture of the Vistula River in Warsaw that my sister painted. I always knew she would become a famous painter. And she did survive the war in Poland—by luck and good fortune."

The excerpt ends. I jump up and start pacing, stamping down a cigarette craving. *Luck and good fortune?* That hardly describes Ravensbrück. My brain is burning with questions for Leo, but it's very late in Germany now.

I take a shower, watch a few episodes of *Breaking Bad* in bed on my laptop. I bet Leo would love this show.

Before I turn off the light, I click on Leo's film again. I can't quite reconcile Leo's soft, generous Charlotte, who lived with them after his parents' divorce and her husband's death—with the nurse Lotka, who was kidnapped by the Gestapo. Why doesn't she talk about being abducted? And what about her giving information to the Germans that got people killed?

Still, I have to remember Leo filmed her over a long period. This is just a short excerpt.

I stretch out my legs, and beside me, Cheri purrs in her sleep.

Carefully, I move backward and forward in the clip. Lotka's wearing the same set of pearls hanging almost to her waist, rings sunk into the fat of her fingers. She has a placid expression—the eyes, sometimes coy and sometimes guarded. Irena's *River Dream* on the wall to the right of her chair. I pause this section, try to go frame by frame. Zoom in—and my heart shrinks into itself.

Hanging on either side of *River Dream* are four framed charcoal sketches.

Forty-Two

Ravensbrück Concentration Camp, January 1945

Even with the striped cap I'm forced to wear, my ears are blocks of ice. Snow flies around us like icy needles and every step risks a slip or fall in these wooden clogs. Yet I'm still alive.

After just five and a half hours at the night shift, I join the women staggering out of the factory before roll call. Despite the changing fortunes of the Wehrmacht, the demands of the Texled company continue.

Last night, I brought bread for the other women in my sewing team. Yesterday, I managed paper and pencil for another woman. They look at me suspiciously, but applaud my efforts. Still, when they ask, I can't explain what I do for Captain Wenders. I don't really understand it myself.

These past few days, he's gotten slyer, more excited, demanding drawings of the kind I don't usually do. Last week I drew him holding his father in a headlock; this week it's vases with flowers, the lake in winter, trees in summer. It's been confusing, but I comply because it's easier to imagine these things than it is to fabricate the story of Captain Wenders saving his family from his father.

As we near the turnoff to the *Appellplatz*, a sleek black car comes into view.

A man and woman are standing beside it talking to Commandant Suhren. Murmurs ripple through our group. Suhren shakes hands with a tall, gray-haired man whose cape is billowing around him. When the woman offers him her hand, he bows low and kisses it. Who are they? This kind of fawning is usually reserved for SS higher-ups.

As we approach the group, all eyes slide toward them as if they were famous film stars. The woman's wearing a luxurious fur coat; her blond hair gleams in the winter sun. The driver opens the car door, and as she turns her head to lower herself inside, my stomach lurches. I retch into my hand and fling away my hard-won bread before the guards notice me. My feet march onward, even through the sensation of falling into endless darkness.

Forty-Three

Toronto, August 2011

This final morning, coppery light filters through the maples' low-hanging branches. The effect is a pink-gold stream shimmering across trunks, dappling stones and marble angels, even firing Mati's metal eyelid close by. The two sculptures look good together—Mati's on a horizontal plane, and Irena's upright.

For months, her sculpture plagued me. I started, but discarded, the old idea of a sword or cross. I made a series of copper cutout figures and put aside that idea. Neither of those concepts made sense anymore. Instead, I was struck by the negative spaces left in the copper sheets.

What finally emerged was the silhouette of a woman, arms swinging, striding through eighty-nine loosely spliced copper panels—one for each year of her life. I sprayed the copper at irregular intervals to keep some patches shiny, while others will age into verdigris. When I chanced upon the idea of fixing the panels at slightly different angles, her figure appeared to be moving, in a dogged way, out into the world. I'm pleased with the result. She always liked a glow in her paintings and the surprise of movement.

So much of Irena's life seemed important to commemorate that I couldn't find the right words to engrave on the granite plinth. Eventually, I settled on the ties that simultaneously bound and freed her: *Irena Marianowska, 1922–2011. Beloved daughter, wife, mother, grandmother, sister. Soldier & painter of the Second World War.*

On an overcast July day, we had the unveiling at St. John's. Françoise, Tahira, and Farzaad were there. Irena's old friend Leah came from Boston with her granddaughter, Melanie. Of course, Mati and Sophie were close by. I read Adam Zagajewski's poem "Try to Praise the Mutilated World."

What I remember of Leah is that when she called, Irena dropped whatever she was doing, and Mati would wink at me and say, "Old friends." Often, then, we'd smile at the rare, full-bodied laughter spilling from Irena's sitting room.

At the sculpture's unveiling, a frail Leah held my hands and said, "Exquisite sculpture! You are so much like her, you know."

No one's ever told me that before. It's a new way of understanding my symbiotic connection with my grandmother.

Before they left, Melanie, who teaches art history at MassArt, told me she would be bringing some of her students to Montreal for Irena's retrospective. I was grateful for their presence, which seemed to draw Irena's past and future together in this green living space.

I'm starting to swelter in my leather jacket—too warm for this August day—but I want to wear it on the plane tonight. For once, I packed early, packed light.

I run my fingers through my new puckish haircut. It seems like a long time ago, when Irena and I sat in this same green spot, that she told me, *I will make no more paintings.* Today, in front of my grandparents' graves, and a short walk from my mother's, I can say, *I will make no more grave sculptures.* I don't know when I'll be back.

Leo and I have planned a long trip together. First, I'll go to Hamburg to see his mother and visit Lotka's grave. Then we want to wander across Europe to Poland, to Irena's beloved Warsaw, where I'll kneel on the bank of the Vistula River and shake her remaining ashes into the water.

After that? A smile ripples across my face. Leo has artist friends in Berlin who've formed a collective. I might stay and join them, see what I can make. Leaning against the ribbed bark of the maple, I glance across at the two glinting sculptures, then over to my mother's spirals. Before I leave today, I have a final task to perform.

I press play on my iPad. Lotka's voice in the film clip is barely audible in the rustle of life around us, but that doesn't matter. Those who need to will hear it.

She begins: "The doctor and I were invited to Ravensbrück camp by the commandant near the end of the war. We operated on his young son, who had a cleft palate that terribly deformed his sweet face. The family had kept him hidden since he was born. We were doing a favor for a senior Reich officer who—I can say now—had been turning away from Hitler for some time. The operation took a long time, and we stayed several days to make sure the wounds were healing properly.

"Before that visit, I had never been to any of the camps, so I was deeply shocked by what we saw. My God! From that day, the faces of those women and children have stayed in my mind.

"On the second day, we were eating dinner in the officers' dining hall, and I saw a display of art and crafts done by the prisoners. I immediately recognized the work of my sister, Renka. She had done a self-portrait in charcoal. I was forced to grab on to the doctor's arm because I almost collapsed. I understood that my sister had been in this camp, or maybe she was still here. I didn't know there were thousands of women there. I asked to buy the portrait, and someone told us we should talk to the officer who had organized the display.

"We met him the next day, and he told us she was alive and well at the camp. I considered meeting her, but the doctor convinced me against it. So, I came to an arrangement with this officer to buy some of Irena's work at a very steep price in exchange for him protecting her until the end of the war. We corresponded over two months, and I sent him British pounds.

"In the beginning, he kept his word about protecting her, but when he discovered that I'd obtained Irena's release through the help of our high-ranking patron, he turned into a complete scoundrel. He threatened to kill her if I didn't secure his own escape from Germany. Believe me, that was complicated, involving all kinds of false papers. But in the end, it was worth it because my sister was freed from that terrible place, and she lived a long, happy life.

"Why did I do it? For love, of course. I loved my sister, and if I could have saved my mother, too, I would have done it. But what's important for you to understand is that the world was very different then. It was a heartless time with everybody taking one strong side or the other. Because of the doctor and our good work, I had the money and the position to save her. Without that, I could have begged, but it would have meant nothing."

I'VE WATCHED THE clip many times now, but it still sends seismic waves through me—this morning, both its cruelty and kindness enter my body and vibrate out into the trunk of the old maple, into her roots, seeding the ground and green air.

I turn off the iPad and stand in wonder at the voyage of these two lives: Irena and Lotka—sisters who both survived a terrifying war and its aftermath. They lived on separate islands in the same sea, sometimes drifting closer together, sometimes irreconcilably apart.

I crouch down to ruffle the frothy grass, and it comes to me as more than possibility, more than thinking—I'm in the circle that never ends, as I always have been, as I always will be.

Maybe this moment of knowing will shatter as I stand up, and I'll forget that in my full self, I carry a scar on my leg where Irena's scar was, or that Mati's and Sophie's cancers exist as opportunity in me. But in this instant, I'm holding it all without effort. As I go forward to meet my new family that's been there all along, there is no need to say goodbye.

These people I love, who love me, are all here in my strong bones.

Forty-Four

Paris, May 1945

Marie-Claude thinks my hair looks *très chique*. She's twelve and a little hooligan, and very like me at that age. Gazing in the bedroom mirror, I worry that my short hair makes me look like a boy, but the only important opinion will be Mati's. I've waited so long to know he's alive, you'd think a few hours more wouldn't matter.

When the Red Cross answered my letter and told me he was in Sweden, I wrote six letters in one day and would have written ten if I hadn't run out of paper and been afraid to ask for more. He replied to each one.

He's meeting me tonight on Quai Voltaire—two hours, twenty-five minutes, and six seconds from now. I don't know if I've ever felt so alive. At the kitchen table, slicing leeks for our celebration tonight, I'm clumsy with excitement, and I can tell Madame Fleury's becoming quite impatient with me. How can I blame her? Gaby's not with me.

Madame's magnificent daughter is the reason I'm here in this large, comfortable flat on Rue Buffon. Last February, after my surprising eviction from the squalor of my bunk, I arrived in Paris from Antwerp, looking like a broomstick with blue eyes, just the clothes on my back and the letter from

Gaby pinned inside the shoulder pad of my jacket. Madame took me in, as she'd done with so many resistance fighters.

With this thought, the snake in my stomach squirms, but I focus on slicing the thick leeks. Let Madame think my tears come from the stinging juice. Gaby's letter to her mother introduced me as an artist; it was fervent about our friendship, and made it clear that she felt a debt of gratitude to me for helping her when she was ill. But it also suggested that if I arrived without her, in all likelihood she'd not be making it out of Ravenbrück.

Late January, there'd been a sudden announcement in the camp that fifty women were going to be freed. The group seemed to be chosen at random, but all of them were Polish, except for Gaby. They were given back the clothes they arrived in, along with their bags and suitcases.

There were tearful goodbyes and promises to spread the truth about Ravensbrück camp. Marie and I were glad for Gaby, whose leg wound had healed well.

"When I get to Paris, I'll find us a studio," she said and kissed my cheeks. "This will be over soon. You still know the address?"

"I'll never forget." I let the tears fall and didn't care when they froze on my face.

The commandant made a sort of congratulatory speech, and the women guards saluted them before marching them out of the main entrance toward the waiting train. Even the crows on the crematorium roof flew off ahead of them in a fan-shaped farewell.

Not long after, we found out that they'd all been executed—shot. The guards were seen carrying the suitcases and bags back to the warehouses, where goods stolen from prisoners are sorted and stored.

Once she'd read Gaby's letter, I told Madame about this macabre play the camp staff had enacted. We wept, and after she blew her nose, she asked me the date it had happened. When I told her, she nodded.

"That whole day, I felt a pain in my heart. I knew something terrible had happened to my daughter." Then she thanked me for bringing her the news and went to tell Marie-Claude.

That evening, I gave Madame two drawings—one I'd made of Gaby, and one of Gaby's designs for a dress. She pinned them to a wall in her bedroom.

Since then, she's put me on a strict regimen: up every morning at seven, baguette and café noir, and then a walk to Galerie Mouffetard, where she's arranged for me to help clean and reassemble their collection, ransacked by the dragons. After supper, an hour and a half of painting or drawing in my room; work which she and Marie-Claude critique, outdoing each other in extravagant detail. It is a kind of heaven.

Alone at night in my room, I draw my mother's face from memory, trying to recover every proud, worried line. Then I sketch Mati, Olenka, Marysia, Fryderyk, and Mr. Godlewski. My gems.

Madame kneads the dough for the leek *tarte* she's making for Mati and me. I grow weepy again at her kindness—eggs, flour, milk, are all so expensive. She had to send our neighbor on his bicycle to the outskirts of Paris, where such things are much cheaper. Their generosity humbles me, and when I say I can never repay them, Madame says, "It's enough that you and Gabrielle were close friends."

When Mati and I settle somewhere in our own flat, I'll make space for a studio. I'll paint all the things my brain has been hiding from me throughout this sickening war.

Paris is helping me forget the sights of Ravensbrück. With that thought, my knife slips and I slice my finger. Sucking the cut, I gag on the mix of blood and leek juice. Marie-Claude hands me a glass of water to drink and a strip of newspaper to twirl around the cut.

No more pretending.

Living through the horrors of occupied Warsaw, I thought I'd seen everything. I was fool enough to imagine that if I were captured, I'd be able to resist. On the train snaking from Warsaw to Ravensbrück, I cried my goodbyes to Mama and Mati. Then I had no more time for drama. Nothing in my life, in history, or any fiction, prepared me for the concentration camp. And yet, in that immense theater of horror, starvation, degradation, and brutality, no experience cut me more than the sight of my sister getting into that car.

In the days after Mr. Godlewski told me about her, I ruthlessly interrogated myself—*Would I ever betray my mother or sister if it meant keeping Mati?* My heart went back and forth in its answer, but I knew I'd never speak my sister's name again.

Who I am now is not completely clear to me. What will Mati make of me? What will I make of him? It hasn't even been a year, but I'm afraid we won't recognize each other. In the camp, I used to torment myself with the thought that he'd met someone else—someone whole, someone healthy.

But that's not what his letters say. When I read the parts I can read aloud to Marie-Claude, trying my best to translate his outpouring of longing, she sighs. "I hope someday a boy will write a letter like that to me. Do you think it will happen?"

"Of course," I say, hoping she never has to experience what we have, but also hoping she finds a husband as magnificent as Mati.

My leek slicing complete, Madame hands me a section of lemon. "Scrub your hands. You don't want to smell like leeks when he kisses you."

That gets us all giggling.

I START TO make myself ready. Carefully, I wash and change into a white lace blouse I bartered for a drawing at the Marché aux Puces. Despite the Paris sun, it's a cool day, but I'm determined that this delicate blouse is what Mati will see me in. I have it all planned. After we meet, we'll walk along the banks of the Seine, where we can talk. Then, when we're ready, the two of us will ride my bicycle back to Rue Buffon, Mati on the seat, me on the handlebars, his bag in the basket.

"Oh, c'est magnifique," Marie-Claude squeals when I make my entrance into the kitchen. Madame kisses me on both cheeks, her eyes glistening.

———

IN THE BRAVE sunshine, I pedal down the crowded quay. How many of these men and women are hurrying to meet someone they haven't seen in years? Someone who's escaped.

I pause with my foot on the cobblestones, watching men remove wooden planks from the upper windows of the Louvre. Is da Vinci's *Woman's Head* still there, or his *Mona Lisa*?

When I resume my ride, a haunting question trails me like a ghost: *Why was I the one who got away and not Gaby, or not anyone else who risked her life to help others?* I grip the handles tighter.

On my bedside table is my drawing of Mati's beautiful face. I kiss him a hundred times before I fall asleep. Then I pray to Mary that I don't see Captain Wenders in my dreams, or hear his voice screeching and crying like a child for his mother. I hate him, yet he may have saved my life. That is my torture.

My bike rattles across the stones on Quai Voltaire. I get off at Pont Royal and lean the bike against the bridge. The blue Seine, splashed with twilight pink, smells like the Vistula River in my beloved Warsaw. People are crowding the bridge.

I search the faces for Mati.

Acknowledgments

Over the many years it's taken to write and publish *The Resistance Painter*, the novel has garnered a glorious, extended family of supporters.

My deepest thanks to Lisa Rivers—big-hearted friend and early editor, long-haul, never-say-die champion of this story in all its variations; your piercing questions, emotional intelligence, and frequent check-ins enabled me to complete a first draft. Lisa and I met in a playwriting class at the University of Toronto's School of Continuing Education, where we encountered Bianca Marais: friend, author, no-bullshit reader of many drafts, wise counselor, and hand-holder, co-podcaster of the inspired *The Shit No One Tells You About Writing,* and one-woman tornado of support for anyone brave enough to take on a writing life. There is nothing more powerful than having people who believe in you when you're not sure of yourself. These two are joined in my writing pantheon by my agent, Cassandra Rogers at 5 Otter Literary, who has stood by me from day one when she introduced herself at a University of Toronto awards ceremony where I was a finalist in a short story contest. Much gratitude to early mentors at U of T—Lee Gowan, Alissa York, and Catherine Graham—for generous portions of encouragement and time, and to Cass's fellow agents, Olga and Ali, for getting me to this point.

Sarah St. Pierre and Karen Silva, former editors at Simon & Schuster Canada, took a leap with this manuscript, saw potential, and suggested redrawing the boundaries of the story, challenging me to enter full-body into the hard places I was skirting. This novel is immeasurably better because of them. To Laurie Grassi, my editor for the final manuscript: I felt a kinship with you from my first, slightly bungled Zoom meeting. I could not have asked for a more humane, skillful, empathetic editor, who wholeheartedly embraced the characters in this story, along with their nervous author. You are a smooth operator, Ms. Grassi, and any finesse in this manuscript is owed to your gracious sensibility.

Adrienne Kerr, senior editor at Simon & Schuster Canada: you welcomed me and my novel with such warmth and zeal, skillfully propelling this debut author to final production. Much gratitude also to Jessica Lacy Boudreau for designing the exquisite cover of *The Resistance Painter* and to Cali Platek, Lisa Wray, and Paul Barker, stars on my terrific Simon & Schuster Canada team.

I've tugged at the sleeves of many friends and relatives for their expertise in everything from Second World War firearms to nursing and surgery, from social work and firefighting to sculpting and painting, and while I name them here, any errors are mine alone: Ed Dore, Barbara Jonathan, Amanda Bell, Harriet Eastman, John Ross, Neil Cox, Carolyn Megill, Suzanne Barnes, Anna Gruda, the sculptors at the Al Green Sculpting Studio, and Richard Jonathan's art and culture blog.

Sue Reynolds's Pyjama Writing Group got me up at seven a.m. for quiet Zoom writing, which carried me productively through the rest of the day. Jenna Kalinsky, neighbor and creator of the One Lit Place writing website, often paused on her walks to drop a detangling idea in my brain that saved me hours of work. The S. Walter Stewart branch of the magnificent Toronto Public Library system was a beautiful space to write my first draft. Jenny Prior was an insightful early reader, and the Toronto Area Women Authors group

(TAWA), led by Lydia Laceby, has been a joyful wave of laughter, solidarity, and education boosting me to shore.

As a member of my partner Mark's Polish family for more than thirty years, I've heard nailbiting stories of Second World War experiences recounted by "aunts" Bianka Kraszewski, Irma Zaleski, and Ala Gyzinski. But it was the story of my mother-in-law, Janina Zaborowska, and her resistance to the Nazi occupation of Poland that entered my imagination and quietly grew there, inspiring the novel I eventually came to write. I'm forever grateful to my sister-in-law, Eva, and her brother, Mark, for allowing me to fictionalize parts of their mother's experience. In my Author's Notes you can find more background on Janina's life and work.

To my sisters, Barbara, Christine, and Alice; sisters-in-law Carmela and Françoise, my brother, Richard; nephews Pierre and Nicolas and brother-in-law, Brendan; to Amanda, Josh, and Oliver—thank you all for recognizing how fervently I've always wanted to write and backing me every step of the way. To Mom and Dad, thank you for uprooting your lives and emigrating to Canada to begin a life of possibility for yourselves and your children.

Dear Mark: you, more than anyone, know what it means for me to bring this book into the world. When it didn't seem possible, you made it so through countless meals, house tidying, cat nursing, map reading, ego boosting, Polish translating, and sharing your beloved parents' life stories. My greatest gratitude to you. Hunkered in my study, there is nothing I love more than hearing you practicing guitar downstairs. You're home to me.

Author's Notes

For years, I had a story running in my head like a recurring dream: the protagonist was a young woman artist who created sculptures for gravesites based on the life stories of her dying clients. When I finally sat down to write it, something strange happened. Along with the story of Jo, the grave sculptor, I kept hearing the voice of an older woman—an artist named Irena, who turned out to be Jo's grandmother. I was rather miffed that this other voice kept intruding on my "real" story, and, truth be told, I was a little afraid of Irena. But the more I wrote, the more fluidly Irena's character came to me, while I struggled to get a grip on Jo! When I settled on a dual narrative—contemporary Jo and 1940s Irena—early readers said things like, "Irena's voice sounds like you're writing autobiography."

I never lived in Nazi-occupied Warsaw, never ferried people through the sewers or suffered through bombings and starvation, but Irena's story came pouring out of me. I thought I knew where this voice came from. My long time partner, Mark, is of Polish descent, and his mother, Janina Zaborowska, lived through all these nightmares—including being captured by the Nazis during the Warsaw Uprising and being interned as a military prisoner in Bergen-Belsen concentration camp. But she had also been an integral part of the main underground resistance group in Warsaw, the Armia Krajowa, rising from Girl Guide leader to the rank of second lieutenant as an official in charge of training liaison officers to leader of a counterintelligence group called the Brigade of the Anonymous. She has been written about in Polish history books, and a photo of her, along with fellow sewer Guides, hangs in the Warsaw Rising Museum in Warsaw. She was also awarded the *Virtuti Militari* Fifth Class and the Cross of Valour by the Polish government and was undeniably a hero.

Before the war, she had begun studying medicine in Warsaw, and, after she was liberated, she finished her medical studies at St. Andrew's University in Scotland, where she wrote lecture notes phonetically. Emigrating to Canada in the 1950s, she and her husband, Eugene, settled in Oakville, Ontario, where she was one of only two female family doctors. Later, she began taking painting lessons from artist Sybil Rampen.

By the time I met her in the 1990s, Janina had had a serious stroke. We communicated mainly through gestures—and smoking cigarettes. If you like old movies, you'll know how much can be conveyed by leaning in for a light or offering your last smoke.

From the start, I felt a great affinity for Janina, but I knew very little about the facts of her life, and it was only years later that I was introduced to her war experiences through autobiographical documents, translations of Polish biographies, and Janina's own paintings. Even then, when I began writing this novel, I did not feel I had the right to tell her story—nor did I want to write biography or history at all.

In the meantime, I also came to know several of the Polish "aunts," friends of my partner's parents who had also survived Nazi brutality and, as so often happens with migrants who've escaped conflict, had, in the absence of blood family, become family. One delightful aunt was *Ciocia* Ala, who lived in Montréal. On several occasions, she talked of her sister, Eva, whose name appears on the memorial wall of the Warsaw Rising Museum—and who was only nineteen when she was killed in 1944. It shocked me when Ala said sadly, "What a waste of life." Ala's response sounded so different from the usual one that glorified the sacrifice of people who'd given their lives fighting to free their country, and I understood her to mean that her sister should have lived a long, happy life instead of dying so young and needlessly. But then a question arose in my mind. Was capitulation the only alternative to fighting and killing? In such a bleak scenario as the Poles faced during the Nazi occupation of their country, were there other possibilities? Or was that a cowardly, traitorous question—or even worse, an evasion of moral choice?

It goes without saying that none of this was clear to me until I was well into my second draft. Clarity grew with the development of the characters Irena and Lotka—two sisters who seem to share the common goal of keeping their family and friends alive, yet whose approaches to violent occupation differ vastly.

Years of engagement with geopolitics, both academically and informally, have helped me understand something that may seem obvious: historical wars have repercussions that reverberate across the globe, far into the future. How could they not, since wars disrupt families for generations, and every leader, every soldier or policymaker, every child survivor, is born into some sort of family? In this context, it was important to me that the wars in *The Resistance Painter* not only ripple through several generations, but also reflect other, more recent wars.

If you're captured by Janina's real-life story, you can find her own words, along with photos, on my website, kathjonathanauthor.com. You'll also find links to some of the places, websites, and historical people who have colored the novel.

THIS SECOND WORLD War story touched me for another, perhaps more personal reason. I was born and grew up in apartheid-era South Africa, where I lived as an ethnically mixed person of East Indian, Black African, and European descent, until my family emigrated to Canada in 1967. Living under apartheid meant bearing witness to a different kind of war. It meant my parents couldn't vote or choose where to live or leave the country freely, and for me and my siblings, it meant we weren't allowed to go on the swings at the beach or sit on a bench at the park. It also meant I couldn't sleep at night for fear my parents might be taken by the secret police. Tactics used by the Nazis to eliminate the Polish intelligentsia, to unsuccessfully cow the Poles into submission, to commit genocide against the Jews, are familiar to me. And so are the stories of resisters—those who were murdered, and those, like my mother-in-law, Janina, who survived.

THE RESISTANCE PAINTER is a work of fiction based on historical fact. I've tried to be consistently factual with dates, names of political figures, and key places connected to the Second World War in Europe, but there are some things I've changed. I've included a map of Warsaw in the 1940s at the beginning of this book, but please don't go searching for Irena's routes (or even Jo's routes in 2010 Toronto). For the sake of the story, I've moved various streets, parks, churches, and monuments around. Likewise, while there are elements of my mother-in-law's real war experiences here, Janina was a different person from my character Irena.

Despite these diversions from life and geography, I would like to mention a few of the resources I found inspiring and helpful in my research: Caroline Moorehead's *A Train in Winter* and Sarah Helm's *Ravensbrück* gave me insight into the workings of that notorious women's concentration camp; Stefan Korbonski's *Fighting Warsaw* was an invaluable resource for its first-person accounts of resistance in occupied Warsaw; Norman Davies's *Rising '44* is a seminal, authoritative work of Polish history; *Irena's Children,* the story of social worker Irena Sendler, who worked tirelessly to smuggle children out of the Warsaw Jewish Ghetto, grounded me in hope; *For Your Freedom and Ours*, a book containing extraordinary photographs of the Polish Armed Forces in the Second World War, gave me needed visual context, as did the film *Kanal*, by Andrzej Wajda. You can find further resources listed on my website.

Finally, life intrudes on any working life, and in my case, I experienced two health crises in the course of writing this novel. I only mention them here to encourage anyone contemplating a writing life while living with health challenges. I've been lucky. I could not have accomplished the long, steady work of novel writing without the skill and compassion of concussion neurologist Dr. Carmela Tartaglia, nurse practitioner Artee Anjali Srivastava, and psychologist Dr. Lesley Ruttan at the University Health Network Concussion Clinic in Toronto. Much gratitude to godsent nurse Jodi-Ann Manhertz at Toronto's Princess Margaret Hospital, who picked up the phone, listened, and gave wise counsel whenever I had a torrent of questions after my surgery. Thank you also to Dr. Jodi Shapiro and Dr. Liat Hogen and their teams at Mount Sinai Hospital in Toronto. Immersion in imaginative writing continued to rule my days throughout these unexpected trials, and I was the better for it.

The Resistance Painter

Kath Jonathan

A Reading Group Guide

Offered here are some questions for any reader or book club members to consider and discuss.

1. How did your impressions of the two sisters, Irena and Lotka, change throughout the novel?
2. Did you have equal empathy for the differing ways Irena and Lotka responded to living under Nazi occupation?
3. How would you characterize the influence Mr. Godlewski has on Irena?
4. Was there one act in the novel that stood out for you as an act of bravery or cowardice?

5. How has old Irena living in Toronto changed from young Irena in Warsaw?
6. How do the secondary characters contribute to your understanding of Irena and Lotka? (Mati, Ola, Agata, Stefan, Marysia, Leah, Danuta, Elsa, Małgorzata, Elzbieta, Dr. Tarnowski)
7. Which of the main characters could you most easily imagine yourself as?
8. How would you describe the relationship between Jo and Irena?
9. Do you see the work Jo and Irena do as artists as being similar or different?
10. How has Jo's life been affected by her grandparents' war experiences?
11. What are your first impressions of Stefan, and do they change throughout the novel? If so, how?
12. How is Jo's relationship with her mother, Sophie, similar to Irena's relationship with Agata?
13. Jo asks the question—*Can you feel sorry for a Nazi?* How would you respond to this question?
14. How do you imagine Stefan has influenced his son, Roland's, life?
15. What role does St. John's Cemetery play in the novel?
16. By the end of the novel, Jo is clear that she won't make any more grave sculptures. Why do you think that is?
17. The novel plays with the idea that narrating your life story can be a transformative act. What instances in the novel seem to bear this out?
18. Are Roland and Cynthia justified in wanting to erase Stefan's Nazi past from their lives?
19. Are there revealed secrets in your family's past that have made an impact on you?
20. Censored, partial, or fabricated memories play a big role in the novel, especially as they relate to family. Is our memory ever a reliable way of understanding our past?

About the Author

KATH JONATHAN is a poetry, short story, and novel writer. Her work has been a finalist for the Marina Nemat Award and The Janice Colbert Poetry Award, and longlisted for the Puritan's Thomas Morton Memorial Prize for short story. Kath holds a Certificate in creative writing and an MA in English literature, both from the University of Toronto. She lives in Toronto. *The Resistance Painter* is her debut novel. Visit her at kathjonathanauthor.com.